The Works of W. M. Thackeray

General Editor: Peter L. Shillingsburg

———◇———

FLORE ET ZÉPHYR;

THE YELLOWPLUSH CORRESPONDENCE;

THE TREMENDOUS ADVENTURES OF

MAJOR GAHAGAN

GARLAND REFERENCE LIBRARY
OF THE HUMANITIES
(VOL. 1324)

The Thackeray Edition Project
General Editor: Peter L. Shillingsburg
Editorial Board
   Percy G. Adams
   Edgar F. Harden
   Gordon N. Ray
   Miriam J. Shillingsburg

1. *The History of Henry Esmond*
   edited by Edgar F. Harden
2. *Vanity Fair: A Novel*
   without a Hero
   edited by Peter L. Shillingsburg
3. *The History of Pendennis*
   edited by Peter L. Shillingsburg
4. *Flore et Zéphyr;*
   The Yellowplush Correspondence;
   The Tremendous Adventures of Major Gahagan
   edited by Peter L. Shillingsburg

WILLIAM MAKEPEACE THACKERAY

———◇———

FLORE ET ZÉPHYR;

THE YELLOWPLUSH CORRESPONDENCE;

THE TREMENDOUS ADVENTURES OF MAJOR GAHAGAN

———◇———

edited by

PETER L. SHILLINGSBURG

with commentary by

S. A. MURESIANU

AND

NICHOLAS PICKWOAD

GARLAND PUBLISHING, INC. • NEW YORK & LONDON
1991

© 1991 Garland Publishing, Inc.
All rights reserved

Support for research and production costs was provided by
the National Endowment for the Humanities, Division of Research Grants.

Library of Congress Cataloging-in-Publication Data

Thackeray, William Makepeace, 1811–1863.
Flore at Zéphyr : the Yellowplush correspondence, the Tremendous
adventures of Major Gahagan / William Makepeace Thackeray ; edited
by Peter L. Shillingsburg with a commentary by S.A. Muresianu and
Nicholas Pickwoad.
    p. cm. — (The works of W.M. Thackeray ; v. 4) (Garland
reference library of the humanities; vol. 1324)
    ISBN 0–8240–5097–5
    1. Shillingsburg, Peter L. II. Muresianu, S.A. (Selma Ann),
1954–   . III. Pickwoad, Nicholas. IV. Title. V. Series.
VI. Series: Thackeray, William Makepeace, 1811–1863. Works. 1990 ;
4.
PR5603.S55 1991
823'.8—dc20   90–25934
                                                        CIP

CENTER FOR
SCHOLARLY EDITIONS
AN APPROVED EDITION
MODERN LANGUAGE
ASSOCIATION OF AMERICA

Printed on acid-free, 250-year-life paper
Manufactured in the United States of America

For
Miriam

Note on the Text

This volume contains three separate works by Thackeray. Each is paginated separately and each is followed by critical and historical materials. The goals of this edition are three-fold: (1) to present a clear reading text free of matter not written or intended by the author, (2) to present a historical record of other versions of the text, first as the author shaped and changed it, and second as persons involved in production affected it substantively, and (3) to present a historical narrative of the circumstances attending the inception, composition, revision, and transmission of the text.

The General Textual Principles (included in the *Pendennis* volume) and the Editorial Procedures explain the practice followed in editing this volume. No note markers other than the author's appear in the text. The record of textual variants with a guide to how the author changed each work at various stages of its development and subsequent publications is given in the Introduction and Textual apparatus of the works.

Flore et Zéphyr was published once in book form as lithographs. It is photographically reproduced here and presents no textual complexities.

The Yellowplush Correspondence was published serially in *Fraser's Magazine*. Its next authorized appearance was in *Comic Tales*. This edition indicates the division into monthly installments.

The Tremendous Adventures of Major Gahagan was published serially in *The New Monthly Magazine*. Its next known appearance was in *Comic Tales*, where it received its overall title. This edition indicates the division into monthly installments. An addition to this work made in *Comic Tales* and the Preface to that book are given as appendices.

In the absence of any of the manuscript it is impossible to determine the authenticity of inconsistencies and archaisms characteristic to the narrators of these stories. Most have been left in the text; explanations for emendations and for some decisions not to emend are given in the list of emendations.

Notes elucidating topical, historical, and literary allusions and other matters that might prove puzzling will be found in separate annotations volumes compiled by Edgar F. Harden.

Acknowledgments

I acknowledge with pleasure the advice and encouragement on editorial matters given me by Professors Don Cook, Edgar Harden, Joseph Katz, Gordon Ray, Miriam Shillingsburg, G. Thomas Tanselle, and Mr. Bernard Stein. I thank Dr. Thomas McHaney for his advice resulting from his review of the volume for the Committee on Scholarly Editions.

For their cooperation in aiding the library research, I wish to thank Mrs. Martha Irby of the Mississippi State University Library, Miss Elizabeth James of the British Library, Dr. Theodore Grieder of the Bobst Library, New York University, Dr. David Kazer, and the staff of the Pennsylvania Historical Society, the New York Public Library, especially the Berg Collection and the Print Room, the Columbia University Library, the British Museum Print Room, and the Dartmouth College Library.

For faithful assistance over tedious ground I thank Dottie Blackledge, John Cloy, Margie Cloy, Gary Crawford, Carol Gassaway, Marian Gassaway, Becky Mulhearn, Mary Mullins, Janet Rosenthal, John Shillingsburg, and Norma Williamson. A special note of gratitude is owed to Mrs. Eleanor Dudley for her work with *Major Gahagan*.

For financial assistance, I am grateful to the Mississippi State University Office of Research and to the National Endowment for the Humanities, Division of Research Grants.

I thank S. A. Muresianu and Nicholas Pickwoad for their signed contributions to this volume.

CONTENTS

———◇———

FLORE ET ZÉPHYR

FLORE ET ZEPHYR

Ballet Mythologique

DEDIÉ

À

par *Théophile Wagstaff*

LONDON, PUBLISHED MARCH 1st 1836 BY J. MITCHELL, LIBRARY, 33. OLD BOND ST.

a Paris chez Rittner & Goupil, Boulevard Montmartre.

D'APRÈS PARROCEL   JEUX INNOCENS DE ZEPHYR ET FLORE   EDWARD MORTON

FLORE DEPLORE L'ABSENCE DE ZEPHYR

LONDON, PUBLISHED MARCH 1st 1836 BY /MITCHELL LIBRARY, 33 OLD BOND ST.

à Paris chez Rittner & Goupil, Boulevard Montmartre

Printed by Graf & Soret

DANS UN PAS-SEUL IL EXPRIME SON EXTRÊME DÉSESPOIR

THÉOPHILE WAGSTAFF   EDWARD MORTON

TRISTE ET ABATTU, LES SEDUCTIONS DES 3 NYMPHES LE TENTENT EN VAIN.

THEOPHILE WAGSTAFF. EDWARD MORTON.

RECONCILIATION DE FLORE & ZEPHYR.

LONDON, PUBLISHED MARCH 1ST 1836 BY J. MITCHELL, LIBRARY, 33 OLD BOND ST.

A Paris chez Rittner & Goupil, Boulevard Montmartre

Printed by Engl & Jones

LA RETRAITE DE FLORE

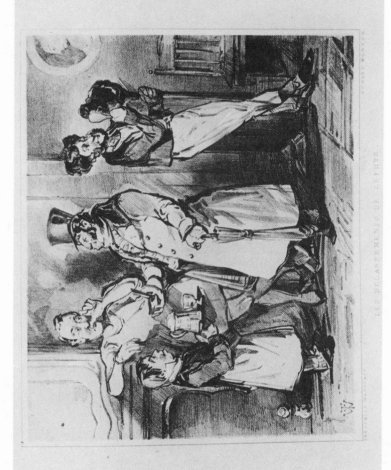

Translation of Captions

1. Title Page. *Flore and Zéphyr*, a mythological ballet, dedicated to Taglioni, by Theophile Wagstaff.[1]
2. The Dance makes its offerings at the altar of Harmony.
3. Innocent games of Flore and Zéphyr.
4. Flore laments Zéphyr's absence.
5. He expresses his extreme despair in a *pas-seul.*
6. Sad and dejected. The nymphs' charms fail to tempt him.
7. The reconciliation of Flore and Zéphyr.
8. Flore's retreat.
9. Zéphyr's relaxations.

---

1. Taglioni is the dedicatee of the piece, but this Thackeray shows only through the caricature.

Introduction to *Flore et Zéphyr*

Shortly after leaving Cambridge without taking a degree, Thackeray went to Paris to study art. Greatly impressed by the charms of the bohemian life he witnessed there, he came to believe that art was his true calling. "I think I can draw better than do anything else & certainly like it better than any other occupation why shouldn't I?" he informed his mother in 1833.[2] That the profession was not considered gentlemanly by contemporary standards disturbed but did not deter Thackeray, and he assured her, "An artist in this town is by far a more distinguished personage than a lawyer & a great deal more so than a clergyman . . . ."[3]

Although he dabbled in journalism for the next few years, Thackeray continued to draw, and practiced engraving in London with Cruikshank, as well as with others on the Continent. In 1836 he produced *Flore et Zéphyr*, a folio of nine lithographs satirizing the art of ballet. The book was issued by John Mitchell Publishers, Bond Street, London, together with Rittner & Goupil, Blvd. Montmartre, Paris. Its author was identified as "Theophile Wagstaff"—T. W. being of course Thackeray's initials in reverse, and Wagstaff, an early Thackeray pseudonym, probably intended as a humorous reworking of Shakespeare (Wag corresponding to Shake and staff to speare).

The young author realized, however, that whether he used a pseudonym or his real name made little difference, because he had not established himself in the literary world. Thackeray wrote to his friend William Jerdan, editor of *The Literary Gazette*, to ask "Will you give me a little puff for the accompanying caricatures?"[4] The following week Jerdan responded with a short review in which he insisted that *Flore et Zéphyr* was "hardly caricature"—rather highly developed "graphic humour," in which "our Wag (without the staff) has presented us with groups of the most

---

2. *The Letters and Private Papers of William Makepeace Thackeray*, Gordon Ray, ed. (Cambridge, Mass: Harvard University Press, 1945, 1946), Vol. I, p. 262. (This edition is referred to subsequently as *Letters*.)

3. *Letters*, I, p. 262.

4. *Letters*, I, p. 313.

grotesque drollery, though in attitude, expression and costume, perfectly in unison with the truth."[5] Yet *Flore et Zéphyr* attracted no other critical notice in Thackeray's lifetime and, despite Jerdan's praise, neither sold nor made Thackeray famous. It was not until 1847, when *Vanity Fair* began to appear in serial form, that the name Thackeray became a household word.

If *Flore et Zéphyr* is still overlooked by critics of Thackeray, this is because its accessibility prior to the present edition has been limited. A few copies may be found in rare book libraries, and it was reprinted, badly, in the 1899 *Biographical Edition* of Thackeray's works and in 1908 in the Oxford edition.[6] *Flore et Zéphyr*, however, is a work of no small consequence. Just as the deflationary jocularity of "Theophile Wagstaff" sets the pattern for most of the other pseudonyms Thackeray used throughout his career—"The Fat Contributor," "C. J. Yellowplush," and "Michael Angelo Titmarsh"—similarly *Flore et Zéphyr* establishes precedents and suggests patterns for most of Thackeray's later major works. In this sense it is a germ work, and especially worth the attention of anyone interested in the development of Thackeray's writing.

Flore et Zéphyr places Thackeray squarely in the tradition of illustration begun by Hogarth in the mid-eighteenth century. Even if we did not know from his essay in *English Humourists of the Eighteenth Century* and from his novels and art criticism how much he admired and tried to emulate Hogarth, the conscious didacticism of *Flore et Zéphyr*, as well as its anti-French and anti-theatrical bent, amply suggests that Thackeray was laboring under Hogarth's example. Not only was Hogarth francophobic, but many of his engravings exposed what he deemed to be the worthlessness and immorality of the theatre. *Flore et Zéphyr* introduces some themes recurrent in Thackeray's subsequent work—the glamour and tawdriness of the theatre and theatrical people, the nature of illusion, of deception, and of reality. All of these concepts relate to and emphasize the profound ambivalence Thackeray felt towards the world of the stage. On the one hand, he did admire the artistry of Marie Taglioni, the ballerina to whom the work is dedicated (she appears in the role of Flore on the title-page). But on the other hand, he shared the common nineteenth-century attitude towards dancers and the dance—that it was not a socially respectable profession, and its practitioners were of dubious character. Becky Sharp's mother, it will be recalled, "was by profession an

5. *The Literary Gazette*, Vol. XX, No. 1006 (30 April 1836), pp. 282–3.
6. Copies of *Flore et Zéphyr* are in the rare book collections of the following libraries: Huntington, Pierpont Morgan, New York Public, University of Illinois (Urbana), Stanford University, Syracuse University, Yale University, Harvard University (Houghton). It was also reprinted in the *Harvard Library Bulletin*, 27 (April 1979), pp. 225–233.

opera-girl,"[7] and in many ways Flore prefigures Becky's easy virtue. Cer-tainly the drawings of Flore emphasize her sexuality and frank willingness to play to a male audience, both onstage and behind the scenes. Beyond his dislike of the licentiousness, Thackeray also disapproved of the necessary deceptions of the theatre. Its beauty, he was quick to point out, was merely superficial. The theatre became for him a metaphor of duplicity. In as late a work as *The Adventures of Philip* he eagerly explained that his protagonist, "the simple young fellow, surveying the ballet from his stall at the opera, mistook carmine for blushes, pearl powder for na-tive snows, and cotton-wool for natural symmetry; and I dare say when he went into the world, he was not more clear-sighted about its rouged innocence, its padded pretension, and its painted candour."[8]

Thackeray's contradictory feelings about the theatre, as well as the theatre's contradictory nature, sustain the satire of *Flore et Zéphyr* and form the philosophical basis which at first glance is concealed by the light-hearted images. The humor of plate 5, "Dans un Pas-Seul Il Exprime Son Extrême Désespoir," is inescapable, for Zéphyr's sadness is communicated by a smirk and an acrobatic leap which places him several feet in the air, at right angles to his audience. Plate 4, in which "Flore Déplore l'Absence de Zéphyr," illustrates a similar discrepancy between the ideal and the real. The focus here is equally on Flore's *derrière*—she is seen from be-hind, standing on one foot, lifting her skirt with the other leg—and on her appreciative audience, a leering company of men. The crudely sketched-in faces of the men recall the besotted roués of Rowlandson, Gillray, and of course Hogarth; and as the reader traces Flore's course through the re-maining plates it becomes clear that the Hogarthian influence includes, in somewhat truncated form, the idea of the progress so integral to Hog-arth's vision of bourgeois society.

John Harvey has already shown that Thackeray adopted Hogarth's concept of the progress to his own fictional structures.[9] To argue that *Flore et Zéphyr* is in any conscious or profound way modeled on the progress would be something of an exaggeration, simply because its plot is minimal. One could say that the ballet has a plot that is resolved in the 7th plate with the reconciliation of Flore and Zéphyr (following the plot of the stage ballet). Thackeray then presents two concluding tableaux that take us into the off-stage life of the dancers and show us the con-trasting and on-going lives led in the diurnal world. In plate 8 we see Flore in her dressing room after the performance, still in costume, en-tertaining two fairly repulsive-looking men. Although an elderly female

7. *Vanity Fair* (London: Bradbury & Evans, 1848), p. 10.
8. *The Adventures of Philip* (London: Smith, Elder, 1862), Vol. I, p. 54.
9. *Victorian Novelists and their Illustrators* (London: Sidgwick & Jackson, 1970), pp. 97–100.

chaperone (Flore's mother, perhaps) sits quietly in the right foreground, her face is benign and she clearly presents no impediment to the suitors. They, while perhaps men of means, are obviously not well bred. One, with a receding chin and slicked-back hair, sits casually astride a chair in the presence of two women. The other, obese and somewhat older, stands familiarly close to Flore, hands stuffed deeply in his pockets. None of this seems to disturb Flore, who is intent on charming the young fop in the chair, perhaps with the hopes of marriage and respectability in mind.

The next and final plate gives us an offstage look at Zéphyr, who, un-wigged, taking snuff, and drinking beer, is even less glamorous than be-fore. After this, the tale ends. Both plot and characterization are abruptly terminated. Thackeray devotes seven plates to the spectacle on stage, and in the two remaining plates allows us to glimpse only briefly his per-formers after the curtain has fallen, where they become more human, if even less attractive than before. Because we are offered a beginning and a middle, we naturally expect an end where, presumably, the dancers' story will resolve in a comic fashion. And yet this conclusion is not forth-coming, perhaps because Thackeray thought that to imply rather than to illustrate was at this point subtler or less risqué. However, in the implicit moral of the story, and its plate-by-plate exposition, general resemblances can be seen between Thackeray's and Hogarth's approaches. It is not un-til Vanity Fair, however, that the presence of Hogarth is fully articulated in Thackeray's fiction. That novel is a nineteenth-century version of "The Harlot's Progress."

But whatever Thackeray's opinions on ballet in general, there is a spe-cific historical basis to Flore et Zéphyr. Marie Taglioni made famous a ballet of the same name (spelled differently, however—Flore et Zéphire) that had been choreographed by Didelot in 1796. Taglioni and her part-ner Albert (who is caricatured by Thackeray as Zéphyr) performed it in London during June 1830—when Thackeray may have seen it. It was not produced that year in Paris and there is no record of his having been in Paris during 1831, when it was last given there. He did see it in London in April 1833.

From the first he was quite taken with Taglioni's artistry. In 1829, when he saw La Fille Mal Gardée at the Opéra he exclaimed "They have a certain dancing damsel yclept Taglioni who hath the most superb pair of pins, & maketh the most superb use of them that ever I saw dancer do before."[10] But four years later, in April 1833, when he saw Flore et Zéphire in London and reviewed it in The National Standard, the ballet itself and Albert in particular were the objects of Thackeray's derision:

> What can be the possible end and signification of the ballet of Flore et Zéphyre, [sic] we are quite ignorant; and we never met with any

10. Letters, I, pp. 85–6.

one that could tell .... We should be glad to know what can be the pleasure of seeing persons of most unprepossessing physiognomies and unclassical figures tricked out in such extraordinary costumes ... ; it is a shame to shorten the days of a poor old man like M. Albert, by making him take such violent exercise, and wear such light clothing; particularly at a late hour of the night, when he ought to be in his own quiet home, with his grandchildren.[11]

He speaks, however, of the "privilege" of seeing Taglioni in "some of those divine *pas* which have enchanted Europe for the last three years." Furthermore, Ivor Guest notes that beginning with Fig. 2 the ballerina's features, if not her attitudes, seem to be in imitation of Pauline Duvernay, she also a dancer whom Thackeray followed with great interest.[12] And if Zéphyr's features match those of Albert, the poses in which Thackeray captures him are like those he had gleefully remarked in other dancers, for example, Paul, another of Taglioni's partners, who, Thackeray wrote, "will leap you quite off the perpendicular & on the horizontal & recover his feet with the greatest dexterity .... "[13] This information, recorded in a letter, was accompanied by a sketch crudely similar to Fig. 5, "Dans un Pas-Seul Il Exprime Son Extrême Désespoir."

Yet if the satire of *Flore et Zéphyr* is predicated on distaste or disapproval, it also, in spite of itself, displays compassion for the ridiculous dancers. Each plate is a forceful reminder of a humanity which cannot be suppressed or disguised. Whether this humanity is revealed through the grotesque posturing of Flore and Zéphyr, through their unchecked sexuality, or the *après* curtain refuge in banal comforts, its effect is to free the satire of bitterness and instill sympathy in the reader's heart. If Flore and Zéphyr have failed in their attempt to create high art, they have failed because their personalities were at odds with their rôles. The failure, however, may equally be blamed on the preposterous action of the ballet. Ultimately the dancers' personalities render them endearing to us because with certain inimitability they suggest that what separates men from mythic figures is a more relaxed and spontaneous approach to life's problems.

---

11. *The National Standard*, No. 18 (Saturday, 4 May 1833), pp. 286–7.

12. Ivor Guest, "Thackeray and the Ballet," *The Dancing Times*, LXII: 736 (January 1972), p. 190.

13. *Letters*, I, p. 86.

THE
YELLOWPLUSH
CORRESPONDENCE

THE YELLOWPLUSH CORRESPONDENCE

No. I.

———◇———

FASHNABLE FAX AND POLITE ANNYGOATS.

No. —, Grosvenor Square,
10th October.
(N.B. Hairy Bell.)

MY DEAR Y.—Your dellixy in sending me *My Book** does you honour;
for the subjick on which it treats cannot, like politix, metafizzix, or other
silly sciences, be criticized by the common writin creaturs who do your
and other Magazines at so much a yard. I am a chap of a different sort. I
have lived with some of the first families in Europe, and I say it, without
fear of contradistinction, that, since the death of George the IV., and Mr.
Simpson of Voxall Gardens, there doesn't, praps, live a more genlmnly
man than myself. As to figger, I beat Simpson all to shivers; and know
more of the world than the late George. He did things in a handsome
style enough, but he lived always in one set, and got narrow in his notions.
How could he be otherwise? Had he my opportunities, I say he would
have been a better dressed man, a better dined man (*poor angsy deer*, as
the French say), and a better furnitured man. These qualities an't got by
indolence, but by acute hobservation and foring travel, as I have had. But
a truce to heggotism, and let us proceed with bisniss.

Skelton's *Anatomy* (or Skeleton's, which, I presume, is his real name)
is a work which has been long wanted in the littery world. A reglar
slap-up, no-mistake, out-an'-out account of the manners and usitches of
genteel society, will be appreciated in every famly from Buckly Square to
Whitechapel Market. Ever since you sent me the volum, I have read it
to the gals in our hall, who are quite delighted of it, and every day grows
genteeler and genteeler. So is Jeames, coachman; so is Sam and George,
and little Halfred, the sugar-loafed page:—all 'xcept old Huffy, the fat
veezy porter, who sits all day in his hall-chair, and never reads a word of

---

* My Book; or, the Anatomy of Conduct. By John Henry Skelton. London, 1837. Simpkin and Marshall.

anythink but that ojus *Hage* newspaper. "Huffy," I often say to him, "why continue to read that blaggerd print? Want of decency, Huffy, becomes no man in your high situation: a genlman without morallity, is like a liv'ry-coat without a shoulder-knot." But the old-fashioned beast reads on, and don't care for a syllable of what I say. As for the *Sat'rist*, that's different: I read it myself, reg'lar; for it's of uncompromising Raddicle principils, and lashes the vices of the arristoxy. But again I am diverging from Skeleton.

What I like about him so pertiklerly is his moddisty. Before you come to the book, there is, first, a Deddication; then, a Preface; and nex', a Prolygomeny. The fust is about hisself; the second about hisself, too; and, cuss me! if the Prolygolygominy an't about hisself again, and his school-master, the Rev. John Finlay, late of Streatham Academy. I shall give a few extrax from them:

> Graceful manners are not intuitive,—so he, who through industry —or the smiles of fortune—*would emulate a polite carriage*,—must be *taught* not to outrage propriety. Many topics herein considered have been discussed more or less gravely or jocosely, according as the subject-matter admitted the varying treatment. I would that with propriety much might be expunged—but that I felt it is all required from the nature of the work. The public is the tribunal to which I appeal;—not friendship,—but public attestation must affix the signet to "My Book's" approval or condemnation. Sheridan, when manager of Drury, was known to say,—he had solicited and received the patronage of friends—but from the public only had he found support. So may it be with me!

There's a sentence for you, Mr. Yorke! We disputed about it, for three quarters of an hour, in the servant's-hall. Miss Simkins, my lady's *feel de chamber*, says it's complete ungramatticle, as so it is. "I would that," &c., "but that," and so forth: what can be the earthly meaning of it? "Graceful manners," says Skeleton, "is not intuitive." Nor more an't grammar, Skelton; sooner than make a fault in which, I'd knife my fish, or malt after my cheese.

As for "emulating a genteel carriage," not knowing what that might mean, we at once asked Jim Coachman; but neither he nor his helpers could help us. Jim thinks it was a baroosh; cook says, a brisky; Sam, the stable-boy (who, from living chiefly among the hosses and things, has got a sad low way of talking), said it was all dicky, and bid us drive on to the nex' page.

> For years, when I have observed any thing in false taste, I have remarked that when "My Book" makes its appearance, such an anomaly will be discontinued,—and, instead of an angry re-ply, it has ever been—what are *you* writing such a work? till at

length in several societies—"My Book" has been referred to whenever *une méprise* has taken place;—as thus,—" 'My Book' is indeed
wanted,"—or "if 'My Book' were here,"—or "we shall never be right
without 'My Book,' "—which led me to take minutes of the bar-
barisms I observed. I now give them to the world,—from a conviction that a rule of conduct should be studied, and impressed upon
the mind;—other studies come occasionally into play,—but the
conduct—the deportment—and the manner—are ever in view—
and should be a primary consideration,—and by no means left to
chance, (as at present,) "whether it be good, or whether it be evil."

Most books that have appeared on this vital subject, have generally been of a trashy nature,—intended, one would imagine, if you
took the trouble to read them, as advertisements to this trade,—or
for that man,—this draper,—or that dentist, instead of attempting
to form the mind,—and leaving the judgement to act.

To Lord Chesterfield other remarks apply;—but Dr. Johnson
has so truly and so wittily characterized in few words that heartless
libertine's advice to his son—that, without danger of corrupting the
mind, you cannot place his works in the hands of youth.

It should ever be kept in our recollection—that a graceful
carriage,—a noble bearing,—and a generous disposition,—to sit
with ease and grace, must be enthroned "in the mind's eye" on every virtuous sentiment.

There it is, the carriage again! But never mind that—to the nex' sentence it's nothink: "to sit with ease and grace must be enthroned 'in the
mind's eye' on every virtuous sentiment!" Heaven bless your bones, Mr.
Skeleton! where are you driving us? I say, this sentence would puzzle the
very Spinx himself! How *can* a man sit in his eye? If the late Mr. Finlay, of Streatham Academy, taught John Henry Anatomy Skeleton to do
this, he's a very wonderful pupil, and no mistake! as well as a finominy
in natural history, quite exceeding that of Miss Mackavoy. Sich *peculiar*
opportunities for hobservation must make his remarks really valuable.*

Well, he observes on every think that is at all observable, and can
make a gen'l'man fit for gen'l'manly society. His beayviour at dinner and

---

* I canot refrain from quattin, in a note, the following extract, from page 8.

To be done with propriety, every thing must be done quietly. When the cards are
dealt round, do not sort them in all possible haste, and having performed it in a most
hurried manner, clap your cards on the table, looking proudly round, conscious of
your own superiority. I speak to those in good society,—not to him who making
cards his trade has his motive for thus hurrying,—that he may remark the counte-
nances of those with whom he plays; that he may make observations in *his mind's
eye* from what passes around, and use those observations to *suit ulterior ends*.

This, now, is what I call a reg'lar parrylel passidge, and renders quite clear Mr. Skeltonses
notin of the situation of the mind's eye.—CHAS. YLPLSH.

brexfast, at bawls and swarries, at chuch, at vist, at skittles, at drivin' cabs, at gettin' in an' out of a carriage, at his death and burill—givin', on every one of these subjicks, a plenty of ex'lent maxums; as we shall very soon see. Let's begin about dinner—it's always a pleasant thing to hear talk of. Skeleton (who is a slap-up heppycure) says—

> Earn the reputation of being a good carver; it is a weakness to pretend superiority to an art in such constant requisition, and on which so much enjoyment depends. You must not crowd the plate, send only a moderate quantity, with fat and gravy; in short, whatever you may be carving, serve others as if you were helping yourself; this may be done with rapidity if the carver takes pleasure in his province, and endeavours to excel. It is cruel and disgusting to send a lump of meat to any one; if at the table of a friend, it is offensive; if at your own, unpardonable; no refined appetite can survive it—

Taken in general, I say this remark is admiral. I saw an instance, only last wick, at our table. There was, first, Sir James and my lady, in course, at the head of their own table; then there was Lord and Lady Smigsmag right and left of my lady; Capt. Flupp, of the huzzas (huzza he may be; but he looks, to my thinkin, much more like a bravo); and the Bishop of Biffeter, with his lady; Haldermin Snodgrass, and me,—that is, I waited.

Well, the haldermin, who was helpin the tuttle, puts on Biffeter's plate a wad of green fat, which might way a pound and three quarters. His ludship goes at it very hearty; but not likin to seprate it, tries to swallow the lump at one go. I recklect Lady Smigsmag saying gaily, "What, my lord, are you goin that whole hog at once?" The bishop looked at her, rowled his eyes, and tried to spick; but between the spickin and swallerin, and the green fat, the consquinsies were fatle! He sunk back on his chair, his spoon dropt, his face became of a blew colour, and down he fell as dead as a nit. He recovered, to be sure, nex day; but not till after a precious deal of bleedin and dosin, which Dr. Drencher described for him.

This would never have happened, had not the haldermin given him such a plate-full; and to Skeleton's maxim let me add mine.

Dinner was made for eatin, not for talkin: never pay compliments with your mouth full.

> The person carving must bear in mind that a knife is a saw, by which means it will never slip, and should it be blunt, or the meat be overdone, he will succeed neatly and expertly, while others are unequal to the task. For my part, I have been accustomed to think I could carve any meat, with any knife; but lately, in France, I have found my mistake, for the meat was so overdone, and the knives so blunt, that the little merit I thought I possessed completely failed

me. Such was never the case with any knife I ever met with in England.

Pity that there is not a greater reciprocity in the world! How much would France be benefited by the introduction of our cutlery and woollens; and we by much of its produce!

When the finger glass is placed before you, you must not drink the contents, or even rinse your mouth and spit it back;—although this has been done, by some inconsiderate persons.—Never, in short, do that of which, on reflection, you would be ashamed;—for instance, never help yourself to salt with your knife, a thing which is not unfrequently done in *la belle France* in the "perfumed chambers of the great."—We all have much to unlearn, ere we can learn much that we should.—My effort is "to gather up the tares—and bind them in bundles to destroy them," and then to "gather the wheat into the barn."

When the rose-water is carried round after dinner,—dip into it the corner of your napkin lightly, touch the tips of your fingers, and press the napkin on your lips.—Forbear plunging into the liquid, as into a bath.

This, to be sure, would be diffiklt, as well as ungenlmnly; and I have something to say on this head, too.

About them blue water bowls which are brought in after dinner, and in which the company makes such a bubblin and spirtin; people should be very careful in usin them, and mind how they hire short-sighted servants. Lady Smigsmag is a melancholy instance of this. Her ladyship wears two rows of false teeth (what the French call a *rattler*), and is, every body knows, one of the most absint of women. After dinner one day (at her own house), she whips out her teeth, and puts them into the blue bowl, as she always did, when the squirtin time came. Well, the conversation grew hanimated; and so much was Lady Smigsmag interested, that she clean forgot her teeth, and wen to bed without them.

Nex morning was a dreadful disturbance in the house; sumbady had stolen my lady's teeth out of her mouth! But this is a loss which a lady don't like positively to advertise; so the matter was hushed up, and my lady got a new set from Parkison's. But nobody ever knew who was the thief of the teeth.

A fortnight after, another dinner was given. Lady Smigsmag only kep a butler and one man, and this was a chap whom we used to call, professionally, Lazy Jim. He never did nothing but when he couldn't help it; he was as lazy as a dormus, and as blind as a howl. If the plate was dirty, Jim never touched it until the day it was wanted, and the same he did by the glas; you might go into his pantry, and see dozens on 'em with the water (he drenk up all the wind) which had been left in 'em since last dinner party. How such things could be allowed in a house, I don't know; it only shewed that Smigsmag was an easy master, and that Higgs, the butler, didn't know his bisniss.

Well, the day kem for the sek'nd party. Lazy Jim's plate was all as dutty as pos'bil, and his whole work to do; he cleaned up the plate, the glas, and every think else, as he thought, and set out the trays and things on the sideboard. "Law, Jim, you jackass," cried out the butler, at half-past seven, jist as the people was a comen down to dinner; "you've forgot the washand basins."

Jim spun down into his room,—for he'd forgotten 'em, sure enough; there they were, however, on his shelf, and full of water: so he brought 'em up, and said nothink; but gev 'em a polishin wipe with the tail of his coat.

Down kem the company to dinner, and set to it like good uns. The society was reg'lar *distangy* (as they say): there was the Duke of Halder-sgit, Lord and Lady Barbikin, Sir Gregory Jewin, and Lady Suky Smith-field, asides a lot of commontators. The dinner was removed, and the bubble and squeakers (as I call 'em) put down; and all the people be-gan a washin themselves, like any think. "Whrrrrr!" went Lady Smigs-mag; "Cloocloocloocloophizz!" says Lady Barbikin; "Goggleoggleoggle-blrrawaw!" says Jewin (a very fat g'n'l'm'n) "Blobblobgob!" began his grace of Haldersgit, who has got the widest mouth in all the peeridge, when all of a sudden he stopped, down went his washand-basin, and he gev such a piercing shrick! such a bust of agony as I never saw, excep when the prince sees the ghost in *Hamlick*: down went his basin, and up went his eyes; I really thought he was going to vomick!

I rushed up to his grace, squeeging him in the shoulders, and patting him on the back. Every body was in alarm; the duke as pale as hashes, grinding his teeth, frowning, and makin the most frightful extortions: the ladis were in astarrix; and I observed Lazy Jim leaning against the side-board, and looking as white as chock.

I looked into his grace's plate, and, on my honour as a gnlmn, among the amins and reasons, there was two rows of TEETH!

"Law!—Heavens!—what!—your grace!—is it possible," said Lady Smigsmag, puttin her hand into the duke's plate. "Dear Duke of Alders-gate! as I live, they are my lost teeth!"

Flesh and blud coodn't stand this, and I bust out laffin, till I thought I should split; a footman's a man, and as impregnable as hany other to the ridiklous. I bust, and every body bust after me—lords and ladies, duke and butler, and all—every body excep Lazy Jim.

Would you blieve it? *He hadn't cleaned out the glasses, and the company was a washin themselves in second-hand watèr, a fortnit old!*

I don't wish to insinuate that this kind of thing is general; only people had better take warnin by me and Mr. Skeleton, and wash theirselves at home. Lazy Jeames was turned off the nex morning, took to drinkin and evil habits, and is now, in consquints, a leftenant-general in the Axillary Legend. Let's now get on to what Skelton calls his "Derelictions"—here's some of 'em, and very funny one's they are too. What do you think of Number 1, by way of a dereliction?

1. A knocker on the door of a lone house in the country.

2. When on horseback—to be followed by a groom in a fine livery,—or when in your gig or cab—with a "tiger" so adorned by your side. George IV., whose taste was never excelled—if ever equalled—always,—excepting on state occasions, exhibited his retinue in plain liveries—a grey frock being the usual dress of his grooms.

4. To elbow people as you walk is rude; for such uncouth beings, perhaps a good thrashing would be the best monitor,—only, there might be disagreeables, attending the correction—in the shape of Legal functionaries.

9. When riding with a companion—be not two or three horse lengths before or behind.

10. When walking with one friend—and you encounter another—although you may stop and speak—never introduce the strangers—unless each expresses a wish to that effect.

13. Be careful to check vulgarities in children; for instance; —"Tom, did you get wet?"—"No,—Bob did, but I cut away." You should also affectionately rebuke an unbecoming tone and manner in children.

18. To pass a glass or any drinking vessel by the brim, or to offer a lady a bumper, are things equally in bad taste.

19. To look from the window to ascertain who has knocked— whilst the servant goes to the door—must not be done.

26. Humming—drumming—or whistling,—we must avoid,—as disrespectful to our company.

27. Never whisper in company—nor make confidants of mere acquaintance.

28. Vulgar abbreviations—such as Gent.,—for Gentleman;—or Buss—for Omnibus, &c.,—must be shunned.

29. Make no noise in eating—as, when you masticate with the lips unclosed—the action of the jaw is heard. It is equally bad in drinking—gulping loudly is abominable—it is but habit— unrestrained, no more;—but enough to disgust.

30. To do any thing that might be obnoxious to censure—or even bear animadversion from eccentricity, you must take care not to commit.

31. Be especially cautious not to drink—while your plate is sent to be replenished.

32. A bright light—in a dirty lamp*—is not to be endured.

33. The statue of the Achilles in Hyde Park is in bad taste;—to erect a statue in honour of a hero—in a defensive attitude—when his good sword has carved his renown—ha! ha! ha!

Ha, ha, ha! isn't that reg'lar ridiklous? Not the statute I mean, but the *dereliction*, as Skillyton calls it. Ha, ha, ha! indeed! *De*fensive hattitude! He may call that nasty naked figger *de*fensive—I say it's *hof*fensive, and no mistake. But read the whole bunch of remarx, Mr. YORKE; a'nt they *rich?*—a'nt they what you may call a perfect gallixy of derelictions?

Take, for instance, twenty-nine and thutty-one—gulpins, mastigatin, and the haction of the jaw! Why, sich things a'nt done, not by the knife-boy, and the skillery-made, who dine in the back kitchin after we've done! And nex appeal to thutty-one. *Why* shouldn't a man drink, when his plate's taken away? Is it unnatral? is it ungen'm'n'ly? is it unbecomin? If he'd said that a chap shouldn't drink when his *glass* is taken away, that would be a reason, and a good one. Now let's read "hayteen." Pass a glass *by the brim!* Put your thum and fingers, I spose. The very notin makes me all over uncomfrble; and, in all my experience of society, I never saw no not a coal-heaver do such a thing. Nex comes:

> The most barbarous modern introduction,—is the habit of wearing the hat in the "salon," as now practised even in the presence of the ladies.
>
> When in making a morning call, you give your card at the door—the servant should be instructed to do his duty—and not stand looking at the name on the card—while you speak to him.

There's two rules for you! Who *does* wear a hat in the salong? Nobody, as I ever saw. And as for Number 40, I can only say, on my own part individiwidiwally, and on the part of the perfession, that if ever Mr. Skelton comes to a house where I am the gen'l'm'n to open the door, and instrux me about doing my duty, I'll instruct him about the head, I will. No man should instruct other people's servants. No man should bully or talk loud to a gen'l'm'n who, from his wery situation, is hincapable of defense or reply. I've known this cistim to be carried on by low swaggerin fellars in clubbs and privit houses, but never by reel gen'l'm'n. And now for the last maxum, or dereliction:

> The custom of putting the knife in the mouth is so repulsive to our feelings as men, is so entirely at variance with the manners of

---

* If in the hall, or in your cab—this, if seen a second time—admits no excuse;—*turn away the man.*

gentlemen,—that I deem it unncessary to inveigh against it here. The very appearance of the act is

——"A monster of so odious mien—
That to be hated, needs but to be seen."

Oh, Heavens! the notion is overpowerin! I once see a gen'l'm'n cut his head off eatin peez that way. Knife in your mouth!—oh!—fawgh!—it makes me all over. Mrs. Cook, do have the kindniss to git me a basin!

*　　*　　*　　*　　*

In this abrupt way Mr. Yellowplush's article concludes. The notion conveyed in the last paragraph was too disgusting for his delicate spirit, and caused him emotions that are neither pleasant to experience nor to describe.

It may be objected to his communication, that it contains some orthographic eccentricities, and that his acuteness surpasses considerably his education. But a gentleman of his rank and talent was the exact person fitted to criticise the volume which forms the subject of his remarks. We at once saw that only Mr. Yellowplush was fit for Mr. Skelton, Mr. Skelton for Mr. Yellowplush. There is a luxury of fashionable observation, a fund of apt illustration, an intimacy with the first leaders of the ton, and a richness of authentic anecdote, which is not to be found in any other writer of any other periodical. He who looketh from a tower sees more of the battle than the knights and captains engaged in it; and, in like manner, he who stands behind a fashionable table knows more of society than the guests who sit at the board. It is from this source that our great novel-writers have drawn their experience, retailing the truths which they learned.

It is not impossible that Mr. Yellowplush may continue his communications, when we shall be able to present the reader with the only authentic picture of fashionable life which has been given to the world in our time. All the rest are stolen and disfigured copies of that original piece, of which we are proud to be in possession.

After our contributor's able critique, it is needless for us to extend our remarks upon Mr. Skelton's book. We have to thank that gentleman for some hours' extraordinary amusement; and shall be delighted at any further productions of his pen.

O. Y.

THE YELLOWPLUSH CORRESPONDENCE

No. II.

---◇---

MISS SHUM'S HUSBAND.

DEAR HOLLYVER Y.,—There was a pritty distubbance, as you may phancy, when your Magaseen arrived in our hall, and was read by all the men and gals there assambled. Fust there was coachmin: he takes his whig off when I comes into dinner, and boughing with a hair of mock gravity, drinks to "Mr. Charles, the littery man." Nex, Shalott, my lady's maid (a Frentch gal), says, "O Jew, Maseer Shawl, vous eight ung belispre." "Will you have some bile mutton, Yellowplush," cries cook; "it's the *leading Harticle* of our dinner to-day." Never, in fack, was such chaffin heard, the jockes and repparees flashin about like lightnin.

"I am," says I, in a neat spitch, "I am a littery man—there is no shame in it in the present instins; though, in genneral, it's a blaggerd employment enough. But it ain't my *trade*—it isn't for the looker of gain that I sitt penn to payper—it is in the saycred caws of nollitch. (*Hear, hear.*) The exolted class which *we* have the honour to serve," says I, "has been crooly misreparysented. Authors have profist to describe what they never see. Pepple in Russle Square, and that vulgar naybrood, bankers, slissitors, merchints' wives, and indeed snobs in general, are, in their ideer of *our* manners and customs, misguided, delooded, HUMBUGGED—for I can find no more ellygant espression—by the accounts which they receive of us from them authors. Does BULWER," says I, "for instans, know any think of fashnabble life? (*Snears, and hallygorical cries of "Hookey," "How's your mother?" &c.*) You jine with me in a pinion," says I, "and loudly hanser, No! Did SKELETON know any think more? (*Cries of "Hoff, hoff," from coachmin, "Fee dong," from my lady's maid.*) No, no more nor Bulwer. It is against these impostors that I harm myself; and you, my friends, will applod my resolution."

The drawing-room bell had been ringing all this time like mad, and I was here obliged to finish my spitch, in a pint of porter to the health of the cumpny. On entring the room, I only found miss smilin and readin a copy of your Magazine.

"Papa has been ringing this half hour, Chawls," says she, "and desires you will wait till he returns from the libry." And then Miss (Lucy her name is) simpered and stuttered, and looked down and looked up, and blushed, and seemed very od—bewtiful she always is. "Chawls," says she, a summonsing her curridge, "is this—that is—is that—I mean, is this article in *Fraser's Magazine* your composition?"

"It is, miss," says I, lookin at her most tendrilly, "an insignificant triffle from my pen."

"It is the best Magazine in Eurup," adds Miss Lucy.

"And no mistake."

"Your article is—really—very—amusing," says she, blushin as red as a piany.

"Do you, *do* you think so, miss?" says I: "miss, *dear* miss, if it gives you any pleasure, oh how amply it repays me!" I gev her, as I said this, one of my pecuniary loox—I never knew them loox fail with any woman at any hage. I was on my knees, as I said, quite appropo; for I had just been emptying coals from the skittle. I laid one of my hands on my left weskit, and said, "O Miss Lucy!" in a voice of such excrooshiating tenderness, that I saw at once it was all up with her. But "Hush!" cried she, all of a sudden; "get up, sir—here's papa."

And papa it was, sure enough. Sir Jeames came into the room very stately, and holdin a book in his hand. "Chawls," says he, "we have been readin your artickle in *Fraser's Magazine*, and very much amused we was. High life was never so well described, or so authenticly. Pray, sir," says he, "may I ask is this revew also yours?" and he holds up to me the *Quotly Revew* of October, on "Ettykitt." I saw at a glans that this was none of my doing.

"Sir," says I, "I never so much as see the thing."

"Well, sir," says he, "take it, and read it, and go about your bisniss; and, harky, hanser the bell when it's rung next time."

Cuss the aristoxy, say I, for a set of proud tyrants, who won't reckonise the highest order of merit, genus.

For the whole of that afternoon I shut myself in the pantry, and devoted myself to the perusial of that artickle. The author of it is particly proud, as I see, of the annygoats which he introjuices; and which are, though I say it, no more to my annygoats than wisky to milk and water. They are ingenus, they are pleasant (many of 'em being very old frens, and not the less welkim for that); but they are not the real thing—only a juke or a juke's footmin can do fashnabble life justice; and it is for that reason that I have determined to have another wack at magazine writin.

In this artickle the author quotes fifteen or sixteen boox about politeniss. Nonsins! only experunce can give authority on the subject—and experunce I have had.

I felt conwinced that, to describ fashnabble life, ONE OF US must do the thing, to do it well; and I determined to give you a few passidges from my own autobografy, in which I have passed through all grads of it, from a shopkeeper up to a duke, from a knife boy to the dignaty of a footman. Here is my fust tail: it aint about *wery* fashnabble society, but a man don't begin by being at once a leader of the ho tong—*my* fust survices was in a much more humble capasity.

CHAPTER I.

Well then, *poor commonsy*, as they say: I was born in the year one, of the present or Christian hera, and am in consquints, seven-and-thirty years old, and no mistake. My mamma called me Charles Edward Harrington Fitzroy Yellowplush, in compliment to several noble families, and to a sellybrated coachmin whom she knew, who wore a yellow livry, and drove the Lord Mayor of London.

Why she gev me this genlmn's name, is a diffiklty, or rayther the name of a part of his dress; however, it's stuck to me through life, in which I was, as it were, a footman by buth.

Praps he was my father—though on this subjict I can't speak suttinly, for my ma wrapped up my buth in a mistry. I may be illygitmit, I may have been changed at nuss; but I've always had genlmnly tastes through life, and have no doubt that I come of a genlmnly origum.

The less I say about my parint the better, for the dear old creature was very good to me, and, I fear, had very little other goodness in her. Why, I can't say; but I always passed as her nevyou. We led a strange life; sometimes ma was dressed in sattn and rooge, and sometimes in rags and dutt; sometimes I got kisses, and sometimes kix; sometimes gin, and sometimes shampang: law bless us! how she used to swear at me, and cuddle me; there we were, quarreling and making up, sober and tipsy, starving and guttling by turns, just as ma got money or spent it. But let me draw a vail over the seen, and speak of her no more—its 'sfishnt for the public to know, that her name was Miss Montmorency, and we lived in the New Cut.

My poor mother died one morning, Hev'n bless her! and I was left alone in this wide wicked wuld, without so much money as would buy me a penny roal for my brexfast. But there was some amongst our naybours (and let me tell you there's more kindness among them poor disreppytable creaturs than in half-a-dozen lords or barrynets) who took pity upon poor Sal's orfin (for they bust out laffin when I called her Miss Montmorency), and gev me bred and shelter. I'm afraid, in spite of their kindness, that my *morrils* wouldn't have improved if I'd stayed long among 'em. But a bennyviolent genlmn saw me, and put me to school. The acadmy which I went to was called the Free School of Saint Bartholomew's the Less—the young genlmn wore green baize coats, yellow leather whatsisnames, a tin plate on the left harm, and a cap about the size of a muffing. I stayed there sicks years, from sicks, that is to say, till my twelfth year, during three years of witch, I distinguished myself not a little in the musicle way, for I bloo the bellus of the church horgin, and very fine tunes we played too.

Well, it's not worth recounting my jewvenile follies (what trix we used to play the applewoman! and how we put snuf in the old clark's Prayer-book—my eye!); but one day, a genlmn entered the school-room—it was on the very day when I went to subtraxion—and asked the master for a young lad for a servant. They pitched upon me glad enough; and nex day found me sleeping in the skullery, close under the sink, at Mr. Bago's country-house, at Pentonwille.

Bago kep a shop in Smithfield market, and drov a taring good trade, in the hoil and Italian way. I've heard him say, that he cleared no less than fifty pounds every year, by letting his front room at hanging time. His winders looked right opsit Newgit, and many and many dozen chaps has he seen hangin there. Laws was laws in the year ten, and they screwed chaps' nex for nex to nothink. But my bisniss was at his country-house, where I made my first *ontray* into fashnabl life. I was knife, errint, and stable-boy then, and an't ashamed to own it; for my merrits have raised me to what I am—two livries, forty pound a year, malt-licker, washin, silk-stockins, and wax candles—not countin wails, which is somethink pretty considerable at *our* house, I can tell you.

I didn't stay long here, for a suckmstance happened which got me a very different situation. A handsome young genlmn, who kep a tilbury, and a ridin hoss at livry, wanted a tiger. I bid at once for the place; and, being a neat tidy-looking lad, he took me. Bago gave me a character, and he my first livry; proud enough I was of it, as you may fancy.

My new master had some business in the city, for he went in every morning at ten, got out of his tilbry at the Citty Road, and had it waiting for him at six; when, if it was summer, he spanked round into the Park, and drove one of the neatest turnouts there. Wery proud I was in a gold-laced hat, a drab coat, and a red weskit, to sit by his side, when he drove. I already began to ogle the gals, in the carridges, and to feel that longing for fashnabl life which I've had ever since. When he was at the oppera, or the play, down I went to skittles, or to White Condick Gardens; and Mr. Frederick Altamont's young man was somebody, I warrant; to be sure there is very few man-servants at Pentonwill, the poppylation being mostly gals of all work: and so, though only fourteen, I was as much a man down there as if I had been as old as Jerusalem.

But the most singlar thing was, that my master, who was such a gay chap, should live in such a hole. He had only a ground-floor in John

Street—a parlor and a bedroom. I slep over the way, and only came in with his boots and brexfast of a morning.

The house he lodged in belonged to Mr. and Mrs. Shum. They were a poor but proliffic couple, who had rented the place for many years; and they and their family were squeezed in it pretty tight, I can tell you.

Shum said he had been a hofficer, and so he had. He had been a sub-deputy, assistant, vice-commissary, or some such think; and, as I heerd afterwards, had been obliged to leave on account of his *nervousness*. He was such a coward, the fact is, that he was considered dangerous to the harmy, and sent home.

He had married a widow Buckmaster, who had been a Miss Slamcoe. She was a Bristol gal; and her father being a bankrup in the tallow-chandlering way, left, in course, a pretty little sum of money. A thousand pound was settled on her; and she was as high and mighty as if it had been a millium.

Buckmaster died, leaving nothink; nothink excep four ugly daughters by Miss Slamcoe: and her forty pound a year was rayther a narrow income for one of her appytite and pretensions. In an unlucky hour for Shum she met him. He was a widower with a little daughter of three years old, a little house at Pentonwill, and a little income about as big as her own. I believe she bullied the poor creature into marriage; and it was agreed that he should let his ground-floor at John Street, and so add somethink to their means.

They married; and the widow Buckmaster was the gray mare, I can tell you. She was always talking and blustering about her famly, the celebrity of the Buckmasters, and the antickety of the Slamcoes. They had a six-roomed house (not counting kitching and sculry), and now twelve daughters in all; whizz. 4 Miss Buckmasters: Miss Betsy, Miss Dosy, Miss Biddy, and Miss Winny; 1 Miss Shum, Mary by name, Shum's daughter, and seven others, who shall be nameless. Mrs. Shum was a fat, red-haired woman, at least a foot taller than S., who was but a yard and a half high, pale-faced, red-nosed, knock-kneed, bald-headed, his nose and shut-frill all brown with snuff.

Before the house was a little garden, where the washin of the famly was all ways hanging. There was so many of em that it was obliged to be done by relays. There was six rails and a stocking on each, and four small goosbry bushes, always covered with some bit of lining or other. The hall was a reglar puddle; wet dabs of dishclouts flapped in your face: soapy smoking bits of flanning went nigh to choke you; and while you were looking up to prevent hanging yourself with the ropes which were strung across and about, slap came the hedge of a pail against your shins, till one was like to be drove mad with hagony. The great slattnly doddling girls was always on the stairs, pokin about with nasty flower-pots, a-cooking something, or sprawling in the window seats with greasy curl papers, reading greasy novls. An infernal pianna was jingling from mornin till night—two eldest Miss Buckmasters "Battle of Prag"—six youngest Miss Shums, "In my cottage," till I knew every note in the "Battle of Prag," and cussed the day when "In my cottage" was rote. The younger girls, too, were always bouncing and thumping about the house, with torn pinnyfores, and dog's-eard grammars, and large pieces of bread and treacle. I never see such a house.

As for Mrs. Shum, she was such a fine lady, that she did nothing but lay on the drawing-room sophy, read novels, drink, scold, scream, and go into hystarrix. Little Shum kep reading an old newspaper from weeks' end to weeks' end, when he was not engaged in teachin the children, or goin for the beer, or cleanin the shoes, for they kep no servant. This house in John Street was in short a reglar Pandymony.

What could have brought Mr. Frederic Altamont to dwell in such a place? The reason is hobvius; he adoared the fust Miss Shum.

Chapter II.

And suttnly he did not shew a bad taste, for though the other daughters were as ugly as their hideous ma, Mary Shum was a pretty, little, pink, modest creatur, with glossy black hair and tender blue eyes, and a neck as white as plaster of Parish. She wore a dismal old black gownd, which had grown too short for her, and too tight; but it only served to shew her pretty angles and feet, and bewchus figger. Master, though he had looked rather low for the gal of his art, had certainly looked in the right place. Never was one more pretty or more hamiable. I gav her always the buttered toast left from our brexfast, and a cup of tea or chocklate as Altamont might fancy; and the poor thing was glad enough of it, I can vouch; for they had precious short commons up stairs, and she the least of all.

For it seemed as if which of the Shum famly should try to snub the poor thing most. There was the four Buckmaster gals always at her. It was, Mary, git the coal-skittle; Mary, run down to the public house for the beer; Mary, I intend to wear your clean stockens out walking, or your new bonnet to church. Only her poor father was kind to her; and he, poor old muff! his kindness was of no use. Mary bore all the scolding like an angel, as she was; no, not if she had a pair of wings and a goold trumpet, could she have been a greater angel.

I never shall forgit one seen that took place. It was when master was in the city; and so, having nothink earthly to do, I happened to be listening on the stairs. The old scolding was a-going on, and the old tune of that hojus "Battle of Prag." Old Shum made some remark; and Miss

Buckmaster cried out, "Law, pa! what a fool you are!" All the girls began laffin, and so did Mrs. Shum; all, that is, xcep Mary, who turned as red as flams, and going up to Miss Betsy Buckmaster, gave her two such wax on her great red ears, as made them tingle again.

Old Mrs. Shum screamed, and ran at her like a Bengal tiger. Her great arms went weeling about like a vinmill, as she cuffed and thumped poor Mary for taking her pa's part. Mary Shum, who was always a-crying before, didn't shed a tear now. I will do it again, she said, if Betsy insults my father. New thumps, new shreex! and the old horridan went on beatin the poor girl, till she was quite exosted, and fell down on the sophy, puffin like a poppus.

"For shame, Mary," began old Shum; "for shame, you naughty gal, you! for hurting the feelins of your dear mamma, and beating kind sister."

"Why, it was because she called you a —"

"If she did, you pert Miss," said Shum, looking mighty dignitified, "I could correct her, and not you."

"You correct me, indeed!" said Miss Betsy, turning up her nose, if possible, higher than before; "I should like to see you crect me! Imperence!" and they all began laffin again.

By this time Mrs. S. had recovered from the effex of her exsize, and she began to pour in *her* wolly. Fust, she called Mary names, then Shum. "O why," screeched she, "why did I ever leave a genteel famly, where I ad every ellygance and lucksry, to marry a creature like this? He is unfit to be called a man, he is unworthy to marry a gentlewoman; and as for that hussy, I disown her! Thank Heaven! she ant a Slamcoe; she is only fit to be a Shum!"

"That's true, mamma," said all the gals, for their mother had taught them this pretty piece of manners, and they despised their father heartily; indeed, I have always remarked that, in families where the wife is internally talking about the merits of her branch, the husband is invariably a spooney.

Well, when she was exosted again, down she fell on the sofy, at her old trix—more skreeching, more convulshuns—and she wouldn't stop, this time, till Shum had got her half a pint of her old remedy, from the Blue Lion, over the way. She grew more easy as she finished the gin; but Mary was sent out of the room, and told not to come back agin all day.

"Miss Mary," says I,—for my heart yurned to the poor gal, as she came sobbing and misrable down stairs,—"Miss Mary," says I, "If I might make so bold, here's master's room empty, and I know where the cold bif and pickles is." "O Charles!" said she, nodding her head sadly, "I'm too retched to have any happytite;" and she flung herself on a chair, and began to cry fit to bust.

At this moment, who should come in but my master. I had taken hold of Miss Mary's hand, somehow, and do believe I should have kist it, when,

Mr Altamonts Evening Party
Mr Yellowplush brings refreshments to the Ladies

Published by James Fraser 215 Regent Street

as I said, Haltamont made his appearance. "What's this?" cries he, lookin at me as black as thunder, or as Mr. Philips as Hickit, in the new tragedy of Mac Buff.

"It's only Miss Mary, sir," answered I.

"Get out, sir," says he, as fierce as posbil, and I felt something (I think it was the tip of his to) touching me behind, and found myself, nex minnit, sprawling among the wet flannings, and buckets and things.

The people from up stairs came to see what was the matter, as I was cussin and cryin out. "It's only Charles, ma," screamed out Miss Betsy.

"Where's Mary?" says Mrs. Shum, from the sofy.

"She's in master's room, miss," said I.

"She's in the lodger's room, ma," cries Miss Shum, heckoing me.

"Very good; tell her to stay there till he comes back." And then Miss Shum went bouncing up the stairs again, little knowing of Haltamont's return.

*　　*　　*　　*　　*

I'd long before observed that my master had an anchoring after Mary Shum; indeed, as I have said, it was purely for her sake that he took and kep his lodgings at Pentonvill. Excep for the sake of love, which is above being mersnary, fourteen shillings a wick was a *little* too strong for two such rat-holes as he lived in. I do blieve the family had nothing else but their lodger to live on: they brekfisted off his tea-leaves, they cut away pounds and pounds of meat from his jints (he always dined at home), and his baker's bill was at least enough for six. But that wasn't my business. I saw him grin, sometimes, when I laid down the cold bif of a morning, to see how little was left of yesterday's sirline; but he never said a syllabub;—for true love don't mind a pound of meat or so hextra.

At first, he was very kind an attentive to all the gals; Miss Betsy, in partickler, grew mighty fond of him; they sate, for whole evenings, playing cribbitch, he taking his pipe and glas, she her tea and muffing; but as it was improper for her to come alone, she brought one of her sisters, and this was genrally Mary,—for he made a pint of asking her, too,—and, one day, when one of the others came instead, he told her, very quitely, that he hadn't invited her; and Miss Buckmaster was too fond of muffings to try this game on again; besides, she was jealous of her three grown sisters, and considered Mary as only a child. Law bless us! how she used to ogle him, and quot bits of pottry, and play "Meet me by moonlike," on an old gitter;—she reglar flung herself at his head, but he wouldn't have it, been better ockypied elsewhere.

One night, as genteel as possible, he brought home tickets for Ashley's, and proposed to take the two young ladies—Miss Betsy and Miss Mary, in course. I recklect he called me aside that afternoon, and, assuming a solamon and misterus hare, "Charles," said he, "*are you up to snuff?*"

"Why, sir," said I, "I'm genraly considered tolelably downy."

"Well," says he, "I'll give you half a suffering if you can manage this bisniss for me; I've chose a rainy night on purpus. When the theatre is over, you must be waitin with two umbrellows; give me one, and hold the other over Miss Shum; and, hark ye, sir, *turn to the right* when you leave the theatre, and say the coach is ordered to stand a little way up the street, in order to get rid of the crowd."

We went (in a fly hired by Mr. H.), and never shall I forgit Cartliche's hacting on that memrable night. Talk of Kimble! talk of Magreedy! Ashley's for my money, with Cartlitch in the principle part. But this is nothink to the porpus. When the play was over, I was at the door with the umberelloes. It was raining cats and dogs, sure enough.

Mr. Altamont came out presently, Miss Mary under his arm, and Miss Betsy followin behind, rayther sulky. "This way, sir," cries I, pushin forward; and I threw a great cloak over Miss Betsy, fit to smother her. Mr. A. and Miss Mary skipped on, and was out of sight when Miss Betsy's cloak was settled, you may be sure.

"They're only gone to the fly, miss. It's a little way up the street, away from the crowd of carriages." And off we turned *to the right*, and no mistake.

After marchin a little through the plash and mud, "Has any body seen Cox's fly?" cries I, with the most innocent haxent in the world.

"Cox's fly!" hollows out one chap. "Is it the waggin you want?" says another. "I see the blackin wan pass," giggles out another genlmn; and there was such an interchange of complimints as you never heard. I pass them over, though, because some of 'em were not very genteel.

"Law, miss," said I, "what shall I do? My master will never forgive me; and I haven't a single sixpence to pay a coach." Miss Betsy was just going to call one when I said that, but the coachman wouldn't have it at that price, he said, and I knew very well that *she* hadn't four or five shillings to pay for a vehicle. So, in the midst of that tarin rain, at midnight, we had to walk four miles, from Westminster Bridge to Pentonvill; and, what was wuss, *I didn't happen to know the way*. A very nice walk it was, and no mistake.

At about half-past two, we got safe to John Street. My master was at the garden gate. Miss Mary flew into Miss Betsy's arms, while master began cussin and swearin at me for disobeying his orders, and *turning to the right instead of the left!* Law bless me! his acting of anger was very near as natral and as terrybil as Mr. Cartlitch's in the play.

They had waited half an hour, he said, in the fly, in the little street at the left of the theatre; they had drove up and down in the greatest fright possible; and at last came home, thinking it was in vain to wait any more. They gave her hot rum and water and roast oysters for supper, and this consoled her a little.

I hope nobody will cast an imputation on Miss Mary for *her* share in this adventer, for she was as honest a gal as ever lived, and I do believe is hignorant to this day of our little strattygim. Besides, all's fair in love; and, as my master could never get to see her alone, on account of her infernal eleven sisters and ma, he took this opportunity of expressin his attachmint to her.

If he was in love with her before, you may be sure she paid it him back agin now. Ever after the night at Ashley's, they were as tender as two tuttle-doves—witch fully accounts for the axdent what happened to me, in being kicked out of the room; and in course I bore no mallis.

I don't know whether Miss Betsy still fancied that my master was in love with her, but she loved muffings and tea, and kem down to his parlor as much as ever.

Now comes the sing'lar part of my history.

Chapter III.

But who was this genlmn with a fine name—Mr. Frederic Altamont? or what was he? The most mysterus genlmn that ever I knew. Once I said to him, on a very rainy day, "Sir, shall I bring the gig down to your office?" and he gave me one of his black looks, and one of his loudest hoaths, and told me to mind my own bizziniss, and attend to my orders. Another day,—it was on the day when Miss Mary slapped Miss Betsy's face,—Miss M., who adoared him, as I have said already, kep on asking him what was his buth, parentidg, and ediccation. "Dear Frederic," says she, "why this mistry about yourself and your hactions? why hide from your little Mary"—they were as tender as this, I can tell you—"your buth and your professin?"

I spose Mr. Frederic looked black, for I was *only* listening, and he said, in a voice agitated by a motion, "Mary," said he, "if you love me, ask me this no more; let it be sfishnt for you to know that I am a honest man, and that a secret, what it would be misery for you to larn, must hang over all my actions—that is, from ten o'clock till six."

They went on chaffin and talking in this melumcolly and misterus way, and I didn't lose a word of what they said, for them houses in Pentonwill have only walls made of pasteboard, and you hear rayther better outside the room than in. But, though he kep up his secret, he swore to her his affektion this day pint blank. Nothing should prevent him, he said, from leading her to the halter, from makin her his adoarable wife. After this was a slight silence. "Dearest Frederic," mummered out miss, speakin as if she was chokin, "I am yours—yours for ever." And then silence agen, and one or two smax, as if there was kissin going on. Here I thought it best to give a rattle at the door-lock; for, as I live, there was old Mrs. Shum a-walkin down the stairs!

It appears that one of the younger gals, a lookin out of the bed-rum window, had seen my master come in, and coming down to tea half an hour afterwards, said so in a cussary way. Old Mrs. Shum, who was a dragon of vertyou, cam bustling down the stairs, panting and frowning, as fat and as fierce as a old sow at feedin time.

"Where's the lodger, fellow?" says she to me.

I spoke loud enough to be heard down the street—"If you mean, ma'am, my master, Mr. Frederic Altamont, esquire, he's just stept in, and is puttin on clean shoes in his bed-room."

She said nothink in answer, but flumps past me, and opening the parlor-door, sees master lookin very queer, and Miss Mary a drooping down her head like a pale lily.

"Did you come into my family," says she, "to corrupt my daughters, and to destroy the hinnocence of that infamous gal? Did you come here, sir, as a seducer, or only as a lodger? Speak, sir, speak!"—and she folded her arms quite fierce, and looked like Mrs. Siddums in the Tragic Mews.

"I came here, Mrs. Shum," said he, "because I loved your daughter, or I never would have condescended to live in such a beggarly hole. I have treated her in every respeck like a genlmn, and she is as hinnocent now, mam, as she was when she was born. If she'll marry me, I am ready; if she'll leave you, she shall have a home where she shall be neither bullyd nor starved; no hangry frumps of sisters, no cross mother-in-law, only an affeckshnat husband, and all the pure pleasures of Hyming."

Mary flung herself into his arms.—"Dear, dear Frederic," says she, "I'll never leave you."

"Miss," says Mrs. Shum, "you ain't a Slamcoe nor yet a Buckmaster, thank God. You may marry this person if your pa thinks proper, and he may insult me—brave me—trample on my feelinx in my own house—and there's no-o-o-obody by to defend me."

I knew what she was going to be at: on came her histarrix agen, and she began screechin and roarin like mad. Down comes, of course, the eleven gals and old Shum. There was a pretty row. "Look here, sir," says she, "at the conduck of your precious trull of a daughter—alone with this man, kissin and dandling, and Lawd knows what besides."

"What, he?" cries Miss Betsy—"he in love with Mary! O, the wretch, the monster, the deceiver!"—and she falls down too, screeching away as loud as her mamma; for the silly creatur fancied still that Altamont had a fondness for her.

"*Silence these women*," shouts out Altamont, thundering loud. "I love your daughter, Mr. Shum. I will take her without a penny, and can afford to keep her. If you don't give her to me, she'll come of her own will. Is that enough?—may I have her?"

"We'll talk of this matter, sir," says Mr. Shum, looking as high and mighty as an alderman, "Gals, go up stairs with your dear mamma."—And they all trooped up again, and so the skrimmage ended.

You may be sure that old Shum was not very sorry to get a husband for his daughter Mary, for the old creatur loved her better than all the pack which had been brought him or born to him by Mrs. Buckmaster. But, strange to say, when he came to talk of settlements and so forth, not a word would my master answer. He said he made four hundred a-year reg'lar—he wouldn't tell how—but Mary, if she married him, must share all that he had, and ask no questions; only this he would say, as he'd said before, that he was a honest man.

They were married in a few days, and took a very genteel house at Islington; but still my master went away to business, and nobody knew where. Who could he be?

CHAPTER IV.

If ever a young kipple in the middlin classes began life with a chance of happiness, it was Mr. and Mrs. Frederick Altamont. There house at Cannon Row, Islington, was as comforable as house could be. Carpited from top to to; pore's rates small; furnitur elygant; and three dromestix, of which I, in course, was one. My life wasn't so easy as in Mr. A.'s bachelor days; but, what then? The three W's is my maxum: plenty of work, plenty of wittles, and plenty of wages. Altamont kep his gig no longer, but went to the city in an omlibuster.

One would have thought, I say, that Mrs. A., with such an effeckshnut husband, might have been as happy as her blessid majisty. Nothink of the sort. For the fust six months it was all very well; but then she grew gloomier and gloomier, though A. did every think in life to please her.

Old Shum used to come reglarly four times a wick to Cannon Row, where he lunched, and dined, and teed, and supd. The poor little man was a thought too fond of wind and spirits; and many and many's the night that I've had to support him home. And you may be sure that Miss Betsy did not now desert her sister; she was at our place mornink, noon, and night, not much to my master's liking, though he was too good natured to wex his wife in trifles.

But Betsy never had forgotten the recollection of old days, and hated Altamont like the foul feind. She put all kinds of bad things into the head of poor innocent missis; who, from being all gaiety and cheerfulness, grew to be quite melumcolly and pale, and retchid, just as if she had been the most misrable woman in the world.

In three months more, a baby comes, in course, and with it old Mrs. Shum, who stuck to Mrs. side as close as a wampire, and made her retchider and retchider. She used to bust into tears when Altamont came home; she used to sigh and wheep over the pore child, and say, "My child, my child, your father is false to me;" or, "your father deceives me;" or, "what will you do when your poor mother is no more;" or such like senti-mental stuff.

It all came from Mother Shum, and her old trix, as I soon found out. The fact is, when there is a mistry of this kind in the house, its a servant's *duty* to listen; and listen I did, one day when Mrs. was cryin as usual, and fat Mrs. Shum a sittin consolin her, as she called it, though, Heaven knows, she only grew wuss and wuss for the consolation.

Well, I listened; Mrs. Shum was a rockin the baby, and missis cryin as yousual.

"Pore dear innocint," says Mrs. S., heavin a great sigh, "you're the child of a unknown father, and a misrabble mother!"

"Don't speak ill of Frederic, mamma," says missis; "he is all kindness to me."

"All kindness, indeed! yes, he gives you a fine house, and a fine gownd, and a ride in a fly whenever you please; but *where does all his money come from?* Who is he—what is he? Who knows that he mayn't be a murdrer, or a housebreaker, or a utterer of forged notes? How can he make his money honestly, when he won't say where he gets it? Why does he leave you eight hours every blessid day, and won't say where he goes to? Oh, Mary, Mary, you are the most injured of women!"

And with this Mrs. Shum began sobbin; and Miss Betsy began yowling like a cat in a gitter; and pore missis cried, too—tears is so remarkable infeckshus.

"Perhaps, mamma," wimpered out she, "Fredric is a shopboy, and don't like me to know that he is not a gentleman."

"A shopboy," says Betsy; "he a shopboy! O no, no, no! more likely a wretched willain of a murderer, stabbin and robin all day, and feedin you with the fruits of his ill-gotten games!"

More cryin and screechin here took place, in which the baby joined; and made a very pretty consort, I can tell you.

"He can't be a robber," cries missis; "he's too good, too kind, for that; besides, murdering is done at night, and Frederic is always home at eight."

"But he can be a forger," says Betsy, "a wicked, wicked *forger.* Why does he go away every day? to forge notes, to be sure. Why does he go to the city? to be near the banks and places, and so do it more at his convenience."

"But he brings home a sum of money every day—about thirty shill-ings—sometimes fifty; and then he smiles, and says its a good day's work. This is not like a forger," said pore Mrs. A.

"I have it—I have it!" screams out Mrs. S. "The villain—the sneaking, double-faced Jonas! he's married to somebody else, he is, and that's why he leaves you, the base biggymist!"

At this, Mrs. Altamont, struck all of a heap, fainted clean away. A dreadful business it was—histarrix; then histarrix, in course, from Mrs. Shum; bells ringin, child squalin, suvvants tearin up and down stairs with hot water! If ever there is a noosance in the world, it's a house where faintin is always goin on. I wouldn't live in one,—no, not to be groom of the chambers, and git two hundred a-year.

It was eight o'clock in the evenin when this row took place; and such a row it was, that nobody but me heard master's knock. He came in, and heard the hooping, and screeching, and roaring. He seemed very much frightened at first, and said, "What is it?"

"Mrs. Shum's here," says I, "and Mrs. in astarrix."

Altamont looked as black as thunder, and growled out a word which I don't like to name,—let it suffice that it begins with a d and ends with a *nation*; and he tore up stairs like mad.

He bust open the bed-room door; missis lay quite pale and stony on the sofy; the babby was screechin from the craddle; Miss Betsy was sprawlin over missis; and Mrs. Shum half on the bed and half on the ground; all howlin and squeelin, like so many dogs at the moond.

When A. came in, the mother and daughter stopped all of a sudding. There had been one or two tiffs before between them, and they feared him as if he had been a hogre.

"What's this infernal screeching and crying about?" says he.

"Oh, Mr. Altamont," cries the old woman, "you know too well; it's about you that this darling child is misrabble!"

"And why about me, pray, maddam?"

"Why, sir, dare you ask why? Because you deceive her, sir; because you are a false, cowardly traitor, sir; because *you have a wife elsewhere, sir!*" And the old lady and Miss Betsy began to roar again as loud as ever.

Altamont pawsed for a minnit, and then flung the door wide open; nex he seized Miss Betsy as if his hand were a vice, and he world her out of the room; then up he goes to Mrs. S. "Get up," says he, thundering loud, "you lazy, trollopping, mischief-making, lying old fool! Get up, and get out of this house. You have been the cuss and bain of my happyniss since you entered it. With your d—d lies, and novvle reading, and histerrix, you have perwerted Mary, and made her almost as mad as yourself."

"My child! my child!" shriek out Mrs. Shum, and clings round missis. But Altamont ran between them, and griping the old lady by her arm dragged her to the door. "Follow your daughter, ma'am," says he, and down she went. *"Chawls, see those ladies to the door,"* he hollows out, "and never let them pass it again." We walked down together, and off they went; and master locked and double-locked the bed-room door after him, intendin, of course, to have a *tator tator* (as they say) with his wife. You may be sure that I followed up stairs again pretty quick, to hear the result of their confidence.

As they say at Saint Stevenses, it was rayther a stormy debate. "Mary," says master, "you're no longer the merry, grateful gal, I knew and loved at Pentonwill; there's some secret a pressin on you—there's no smilin welcom for me now, as there used formly to be! Your mother and sister-in-law have perwerted you, Mary; and that's why I've drove them from this house, which they shall not re-enter in my life."

"O, Frederic! it's *you* is the cause, and not I. Why do you have any mistry from me? Where do you spend your days? Why did you leave me, even on the day of your marridge, for eight hours, and continue to do so every day?"

"Because," says he, "I makes my livelihood by it. I leave you, and I don't tell you *how* I make it: for it would make you none the happier to know."

It was in this way the convysation ren on—more tears and questions on my missiseses part, more sturmness and silence on my master's: it ended, for the first time since their marridge, in a reglar quarrel. Wery difrent, I can tell you, from all the hammerous billing and kewing which had proceeded their nupshums.

Master went out, slamming the door in a fury; as well he might. Says he, "If I can't have a comforable life, I can have a jolly one;" and so he went off to the hed tavern, and came home that evening beesly intawsicated. When high words begin in a famly, drink genrally follows on the genlman's side; and then, fearwell to all conjubial happyniss! These two pipple, so fond and loving, were now sirly, silent, and full of il wil. Master went out earlier, and came home later; misses cried more, and looked even paler than before.

Well, things went on in this uncomforable way, master still in the mopes, missis tempted by the deamons of jellosy and curosity; until a singlar axident brought to light all the goings on of Mr. Altamont.

It was the tenth of Jennuary; I recklect the day, for old Shum gev me half-a-crownd (the fust and last of his money I ever see, by the way): he was dining along with master, and they were making merry together.

Master said, as he was mixing his fifth tumler of punch, and little Shum his twelfth, or so—master said, "I see you twice in the City to-day, Mr. Shum."

"Well, that's curous!" says Shum. "I *was* in the City. To-day's the day when the divvydins (God bless 'em!) is paid; and me and Mrs. S. went for our half-year's inkem. But we only got out of the coach, crossed the street to the Bank, took our money, and got in agen. How could you see me twice?"

Altamont stuttered, and stammered, and hemd, and hawd. "O!" says he, "I was passing—passing as you went in and out." And he instantly turned the conversation, and began talking about pollytix, or the weather, or some such stuf.

"Yes, my dear," said my missis; "but how could you see papa *twice?*" Master didn't answer, but talked pollytix more than ever. Still she would continy on. "Where was you, my dear, when you saw pa? What were you doing, my love, to see pa twice?" and so forth. Master looked angrier and angrier, and his wife only pressed him wuss and wuss.

This was, as I said, little Shum's twelfth tumler; and I knew pritty well that he could git very little further: for, as reglar as the thirteenth came, Shum was drunk. The thirteenth did come, and its consquinzies. I was obliged to leed him home to John Street, where I left him, in the hangry arms of Mrs. Shum.

"How the d—," sayd he all the way, "how the ddd—the deddy— deddy—devil—could he have seen me *twice?*"

CHAPTER V.

It was a sad slip on Altamont's part, for no sooner did he go out the nex morning than missis went out too. She tor down the street, and never stopped till she came to her pa's house at Pentonwill. She was closited for an hour with her ma, and when she left her she drove straight to the City. She walked before the Bank, and behind the Bank, and round the Bank: she came home disperryted, having learned nothink.

And it was now an extrornary thing, that from Shum's house, for the nex ten days, there was nothink but expyditions into the City. Mrs. S., tho her dropsiccle legs had never carred her half so fur before, was eternally on the *key veve*, as the French say. If she didn't go, Miss Betsy did, or missis did: they seemd to have an atrackshun to the Bank, and went there as natral as an omlibus.

At last, one day, old Mrs. Shum comes to our house—(she wasn't ad- mitted when master was there, but came still in his absints)—and she wore a hair of tryumf as she entered.

"Mary," says she, "where is the money your husbind brought to you yesterday?" My master used always to give it to missis when he returned.

"The money, ma!" says Mary. "Why, here!" And, pulling out her puss, she shewed a sovrin, a good heap of silver, and an odd-looking little coin.

"THAT'S IT! that's it!" cried Mrs. S. "A Queen Anne's sixpence, isn't it, dear—dated seventeen hunderd and three?"

It was so, sure enough: a Queen Ans sixpince of that very date.

"Now, my love," says she, "I have found him! Come with me to- morrow, and you shall KNOW ALL!"

And now comes the end of my story.

   *   *   *   *   *

The ladies nex morning set out for the City, and I walked behind, doing the genteel thing, with a nosegy and a goold stick. We walked down the New Road—we walked down the City Road—we walked to the Bank. We were crossing from that heddyfiz to the other side of Cornhill, when, all of a sudden, missis shreeked, and fainted spontaceously away.

I rushed forrard, and raised her to my arms; spiling thereby a new weskit, and a pair of crimson smalcloes. I rushed forrard, I say, wery nearly knocking down the old sweeper, who was hobling away as fast as possibil. We took her to Birch's; we provided her with a hackney-coach and every lucksury, and carried her home to Islington.

   *   *   *   *   *

That night master never came home. Nor the nex night, nor the nex. On the fourth day, an octioneer arrived; he took an infantry of the furnitur, and placed a bill in the window.

At the end of the wick, Altamont made his appearance. He was haggard, and pale; not so haggard, however, not so pale, as his misrable wife.

He looked at her very tendrilly. I may say, it's from him that I coppied my look to Miss ———. He looked at her very tendrilly, and held out his arms. She gev a suffycating shreek, and rusht into his umbraces.

"Mary," says he, "you know all now. I have sold my place; I have got three thousand pound for it, and saved two more. I've sold my house and furnitur, and that brings me another. We'll go abroad, and love each other, has formly."

   *   *   *   *   *

And now you ask me, Who he was? I shudder to relate.—Mr. Haltamont SWEP THE CROSSIN FROM THE BANK TO CORNHILL!!

Of cors, I left his servis. I met him, few years after, at Badden-Badden, where he and Mrs. A. were much respectid, and pass for pipple of propaty.

                   C. Y.

THE YELLOWPLUSH CORRESPONDENCE

No. III.

———◇———

DIMOND CUT DIMOND.

THE name of my nex master was, if posbil, still more ellygant and you-fonious than that of my fust. I now found myself boddy servant to the Honrabble Halgernon Percy Deuceace, youngest and fith son of the Earl of Crabs.

Halgernon was a barrystir—that is, he lived in Pump Court, Temple; a wulgar naybrood, witch praps my readers don't no. Suffiz to say, it's on the confines of the citty, and the choasen aboad of the lawyers of this metrappolish.

When I say that Mr. Deuceace was a barrystir, I don't mean that he went sesshums or surcoats (as they call 'em), but simply that he kep chambers, lived in Pump Court, and looked out for a commitionarship, or a revisinship, or any other place that the Wig guvvyment could give him. His father was a Wig pier (as the landriss told me), and had been a Toary pier. The fack is, his lordship was so poar, that he would be anythink, or nothink, to get previsions for his sons, and an inkum for him self.

I phansy that he aloud Halgernon two hunderd a-year; and it would have been a very comforable maintenants, only he knever paid him.

Owever, the young gnlmn was a gnlmn, and no mistake: he got his allowents of nothink a-year, and spent it in the most honrabble and fashnabble manner. He kep a kab—he went to Holmax and Crockfud's—he moved in the most xquizzit suckles—and trubbld the law-boox very little, I can tell you. Those fashnabble gents have ways of getten money, witch comman pipple doant understand.

Though he only had a therd floar in Pump Cort, he lived as if he had the welth of Cresas. The tenpun notes floo abowt as common as haypince—clarrit and shampang was at his house as vulgar as gin; and verry glad I was, to be sure, to be a valley to a zion of the nobillaty.

Deuceace had, in his sittin-room, a large pictur on a sheet of paper. The names of his family was wrote on it: it was wrote in the shape of a tree, a groin out of a man-in-armer's stomick, and the names were on little plates among the bows. The pictur said that the Deuceaces kem into

England in the year 1066, along with William Conqueruns. My master called it his podygree. I do bleev it was because he had this pictur, and because he was the *Honrabble* Deuceace, that he mannitched to live as he did. If he had been a common man, you'd have said he was no better than a swinler. It's only rank and buth that can warrant such singlarities as my master show'd. For it's no use disgysing it—the Honrabble Halgernon was a GAMBLER. For a man of wulgar Family, it's the wust trade that can be— for a man of common feelinx of honesty, this profession is quite imposbill; but for a real thorough-bread genlmn, it's the esiest and most prophetable line he can take.

It may, praps, appear curous that such a fashnabble man should live in the Temple; but it must be recklected, that its not only lawyers who live in what's called the Ins of Cort. Many batchylers, who have nothink to do with lor, have here their loginx; and many sham barrysters, who never put on a wig and gownd twise in their lives, kip apartments in the Temple, instead of Bon Street, Pickledilly, or other fashnabble places.

Frinstance, on our stairkis (so these houses are called), there was 8 sets of chamberses, and only 3 lawyers. These was, bottom floor, Screwson, Hewson, and Jewson, attorneys; fust floor, Mr. Sergeant Flabber—opsite, Mr. Counslor Bruffy; and secknd pair, Mr. Haggerstony, an Irish counslor, pracktising at the Old Baly, and lickwise what they call reporter to the *Morning Post* nyouspapper. Opsite him was wrote

Mr. RICHARD BLEWITT;

and on the thud floar, with my master, lived one Mr. Dawkins.

This young fellow was a new comer into the Temple, and unlucky it was for him too—he'd better have never been born; for its my firm apinion that the Temple ruined him—that is, with the help of my master and Mr. Dick Blewitt, as you shall hear.

Mr. Dawkins, as I was gave to understand by his young man, had jest left the Univerary of Oxford, and had a pretty little fortn of his own—six thousand pound, or so—in the stox. He was jest of age, an orfin who had lost his father and mother; and having distinkwished hisself at collitch, where he gained seffral prices, was come to town to push his fortn, and study the barryster's bisniss.

Not bein of a verry high fammly hisself—indeed, I've heard say his father was a chismonger, or somethink of that lo sort—Dawkins was glad to find his old Oxford frend, Mr. Blewitt, yonger son to rich Squire Blewitt of Listershire, and to take rooms so near him.

Now, tho' there was a considdrabble intimacy between me and Mr. Blewitt's gentleman, there was scarcely any betwixt our masters,—mine being too much of the aristoxy to associate with one of Mr. Blewitt's sort. Blewitt was what they call a bettin man: he went reglar to Tattlesall's, kep a pony, wore a white hat, a blue berd's-eye hankercher, and a cut- away coat. In his manners he was the very contrary of my master, who was a slim, ellygant man, as ever I see—he had very white hands, rayther a sallow face, with sharp dark is, and small wiskus neatly trimmed, and as black as Warren's jet—he spoke very low and soft—he seemed to be watchin the person with whom he was in convysation, and always flatterd every body. As for Blewitt, he was quite of another sort. He was always swearin, singin, and slappin people on the back, as hearty and as familiar as posbill. He seemed a merry, careless, honest cretur, whom one would trust with life and soul. So thought Dawkins, at least; who, though a quiet young man, fond of his boox, novvles, Byron's poems, floot-playing, and such like scientafic amusemints, grew hand in glove with honest Dick Blewitt, and soon after with my master, the Honrabble Halgernon. Poor Daw! he thought he was makin good connexions, and real frends—he had fallen in with a couple of the most etrocious swinlers that ever lived.

Before Mr. Dawkins's arrival in our house, Mr. Deuceace had barely condysended to speak to Mr. Blewitt: it was only about a month after that suckumstance that my master, all of a sudding, grew very friendly with him. The reason was pretty clear,—Deuceace *wanted him.* Dawkins had not been an hour in master's compny, before he knew that he had a pidgin to pluck.

Blewitt knew this too; and bein very fond of pidgin, intended to keep this one entirely to himself. It was amusin to see the Honrabble Halgernon manuvring to get this pore bird out of Blewitt's clause, who thought he had it safe. In fact, he'd brought Dawkins to these chambers for that very porpus, thinking to have him under his eye, and strip him at leisure.

My master very soon found out what was Mr. Blewitt's game. Gamblers know gamblers, if not by instink, at least by reputation; and though Mr. Blewitt moved in a much lower spear than Mr. Deuceace, they knew each other's dealins and caracters pufickly well.

"Charles, you scoundrel," says Deuceace to me one day (he always spoak in that kind way), "who is this person that has taken the opsit chambers, and plays the flute so industrusly?"

"It's Mr. Dawkins, a rich young gentleman from Oxford, and a great friend of Mr. Blewittses, sir," says I; "they seem to live in each other's rooms."

Master said nothink, but he *grin'd*—my eye, how he did grin! Not the fowl find himself could snear more satannickly.

I knew what he meant:

Imprimish. A man who plays the floot is a simpleton.

Secknly. Mr. Blewitt is a raskle.

Thirdmo. When a raskle and a simpleton is always together, and when the simpleton is *rich*, ones knows pretty well what will come of it.

I was but a lad in them days, but I knew what was what as well as my master; it's not gentlemen only that's up to snough. Law bless us! there was four of us on this stairkes, four as nice young men as you ever see; Mr.

Bruffy's young man, Mr. Dawkinses, Mr. Blewitt's, and me—and we knew what our masters was about as well as they did theirselfs. Frinstance, I can say this for *myself*, there wasn't a paper in Deuceace's desk or drawer, not a bill, a note, or miserandum, which I hadn't read as well as he: with Blewitt's it was the same—me and his young man used to read 'em all. There wasn't a bottle of wind that we didn't get a glas, nor a pound of sugar that we didn't have some lumps of it. We had keys to all the cubbards—we pipped into all the letters that kem and went—we pored over all the bill-files—we'd the best pickins out of the dinners, the livvers of the fowls, the force-mit balls out of the soup, the egs from the sallit. As for the coals and candles, we left them to the landrisses. You may call this robry—nonsince—it's only our rights—a suvvant's purquizzits is as sacred as the laws of Hengland.

Well, the long and short of it is this. Richard Blewitt, exquire, was sityouated as follows: He'd an inkum of three hundred a-year from his father. Out of this he had to pay one hundred and ninety for money borrowed by him at collidge, seventy for chambers, seventy more for his hoss, aty for his suvvant on bord wagis, and about three hunderd and fifty for a sepprat establishmint in the Regency Park; besides this, his pockit money, say a hunderd, his eatin, drinkin, and wine-marchant's bill, about two hunderd moar. So that you see he laid by a pretty handsome sum at the end of the year.

My master was diffrent; and being a more fashnabble man than Mr. B., in course he owed a deal more money. There was fust:

Account *contray*, at Crockford's	£3711 0 0
Bills of xchange and I.O.U's (but he didn't pay these in most cases)	4963 0 0
21 tailors' bills, in all	1306 11 9
3 hossdealers' do.......................	402 0 0
2 coachbilder	506 0 0
Bills contracted at Cambritch	2193 6 8
Sundries.............................	987 10 0
	£14069 8 5

I give this as a curosity—pipple doant know how in many cases fashnabble life is carried on; and to know even what a real gnlmn *owes* is somethink instructif and agreeable.

But to my tail. The very day after my master had made the inquiries concerning Mr. Dawkins, witch I have mentioned already, he met Mr. Blewitt on the stairs; and byoutiffle it was to see how this gnlman, who had before been almost cut by my master, was now received by him. One of the sweatest smiles I ever saw was now vizzable on Mr. Deuceace's countenence. He held out his hand, covered with a white kid glove, and said, in the most frenly tone of vice posbill, "What? Mr. Blewitt! It is an

age since we met. What a shame that such near naybors should see each
other so seldom!"

Mr. Blewitt, who was standing at his door, in a pe-green dressing gown,
smoakin a segar, and singing a hunting coarus, looked surprised, flattered,
and then sispicious.

"Why, yes," says he, "it is, Mr. Deuceace, a long time."

"Not, I think, since we dined at Sir George Hookey's. By the by, what
an evening that was—hay, Mr. Blewitt? what wine! what capital songs! I
recollect your 'May day in the morning'—cuss me, the best comick song
I ever heard. I was speaking to the Duke of Doncaster about it only yesterday. You know the duke, I think?"

Mr. Blewitt said, quite surly, "No, I don't."

"Not know him!" cries master; "why, hang it, Blewitt! he knows *you*,
as every sporting man in England does, I should think. Why, man, your
good things are in every body's mouth at Newmarket."

And so master went on chaffin Mr. Blewitt. That genlmn at fust answered him quite short and angry; but, after a little more flumery, he grew
as pleased as posbill, took in all Deuceace's flatry, and bleeved all his lies.
At last the door shut, and they both went in to Mr. Blewitt's chambers
togither.

Of course I can't say what past there; but in an hour master kem up
to his own room as yaller as mustard, and smellin sadly of backo smoke.
I never see any genlmn more sick than he was; *he'd been smoakin seagars*
along with Blewitt. I said nothink, in course, tho' I'd often heard him
xpress his horror of backo, and knew very well he would as soon swallow
pizon as smoke. But he wasn't a chap to do a thing without a reason: if
he'd been smoakin, I warrant he had smoked to some porpus.

I didn't hear the convysation between 'em; but Mr. Blewitt's man
did: it was,—"Well, Mr. Blewitt, what capital seagars! Have you one
for a friend to smoak?" (The old fox, it wasn't only the *seagars* he was a
smoakin!) "Walk in," says Mr. Blewitt; and then they began a chaffin together: master very ankshous about the young gintleman who had come
to live in our chambers, Mr. Dawkins, and always coming back to that
subject,—sayin that people on the same stairkis ot to be frenly; how glad
he'd be, for his part, to know Mr. Dick Blewitt, and *any friend of his*, and
so on. Mr. Dick, howsever, seamed quite aware of the trap laid for him.
"I really don't no this Dawkins," says he: "he's a chismonger's son, I hear;
and tho' I've exchanged visits with him, I doant intend to continyou the
acquaintance,—not wishin to assoshate with that kind of pipple." So
they went on, master fishin, and Mr. Blewitt not wishin to take the hook
at no price.

"Confound the vulgar thief!" muttard my master, as he was laying on
his sophy, after being so very ill; "I've poisoned myself with his infernal
tobacco, and he has foiled me. The cursed swindling boor! he thinks he'll
ruin this poor cheesemonger, does he? I'll step in, and *warn* him."

I thought I should bust a laffin, when he talked in this style. I knew very well what his "warning" meant,—lockin the stable-door, but stealin the hoss fust.

Nex day, his strattygam for becoming acquainted with Mr. Dawkins we exicuted, and very pritty it was.

Besides potry and the floot, Mr. Dawkins, I must tell you, had some other parshallities, wiz,—he was wery fond of good eatin and drinkin. After doddling over his music and boox all day, this young genlmn used to sally out of evenings, dine sumptiously at a tavern, drinkin all sots of wind along with his friend Mr. Blewitt. He was a quiet young fellow enough at fust; but it was Mr. B. who (for his own porpuses, no doubt) had got him into this kind of life. Well, I needn't say that he who eats a fine dinner, and drinks too much over night, wants a bottle of soda-water, and a gril praps, in the mornink. Such was Mr. Dawkinseses case; and reglar almost as twelve o'clock came, the waiter from Dix Coffy-House was to be seen on our stairkis, bringin up Mr. D's hot breakfast.

No man would have thought there was any think in such a trifling circkumstance; master did, though, and pounced upon it like a cock on a barlycorn.

He sent me out to Mr. Morell's, in Pickledilly, for wot's called a Strasbug-pie—in French, a *"patty defaw graw."* He takes a card, and nails it on the outside case (patty defaw graws come generally in a round wooden box, like a drumb); and what do you think he writes on it? why, as follos:—*"For the Honourable Algernon Percy Deuceace, &c. &c. &c. With Prince Talleyrand's compliments."*

Prince Tallyram's complimints, indeed! I laff when I think of it still, the old surpint! He *was* a surpint, that Deuceace, and no mistake.

Well, by a most extrornary piece of ill luck, the nex day, punctially as Mr. Dawkinses brexfas was coming *up* the stairs, Mr. Halgernon Percy Deuceace was going *down.* He was as gay as a lark, humming an Oppra tune, and twizzting round his head his hevy gold-headed cane. Down he went very fast, and by a most unlucky axdent struck his cane against the waiter's tray, and away went Mr. Dawkinses gril, kayann, kitchup, soda-water, and all! I can't think how my master should have choas such an exact time; to be sure, his windo looked upon the cort, and he could see every one who came into our door.

As soon as the axdent had took place, master was in such a rage as, to be sure, no man ever was in befor; he swoar at the waiter in the most dreddfle way; he threatened him with his stick; and it was only when he see that the waiter was rayther a bigger man than his self that he was in the least pazzyfied. He returned to his own chambres; and John, the waiter, went off for more grill to Dixes Coffy House.

"This is a most unlucky axdent, to be sure, Charles," says master to me, after a few minnits paws, during which he had been and wrote a note, put

it into an antelope, and sealed it with his bigg seal of arms. "But stay—
a thought strikes me—take this note to Mr. Dawkins, and that pye you
brought yesterday; and hearkye, you scoundrel, if you say where you got
it I will break every bone in your skin!"

These kind of prommises were among the few which I knew him to
keep; and as I loved boath my skinn and my boans, I carried the noat,
and, of cors, said nothink. Waiting in Mr. Dawkinses chambus for a few
minnits, I returned to my master with an anser. I may as well give both of
these documence, of which I happen to have taken coppies.

I.
"*The Hon.* A. P. DEUCEACE *to* T. S. DAWKINS, *Esq.*

"*Temple, Tuesday.*

"Mr. Deuceace presents his compliments to Mr. Dawkins, and
begs at the same time to offer his most sincere apologies and regrets
for the accident which has just taken place.

"May Mr. Deuceace be allowed to take a neighbour's privilege,
and to remedy the evil he has occasioned to the best of his power?
If Mr. Dawkins will do him the favour to partake of the contents
of the accompanying case (from Strasburg direct, and the gift of
a friend, on whose taste as a gourmand Mr. Dawkins may rely),
perhaps he will find that it is not a bad substitute for the *plat* which
Mr. Deuceace's awkwardness destroyed.

"It will, also, Mr. Deuceace is sure, be no small gratification to
the original donor of the *pâté*, when he learns that it has fallen into
the hands of so celebrated a *bon vivant* as Mr. Dawkins.

"*T. S. Dawkins, Esq., &c. &c. &c.*"

II.
"*From* T. S. DAWKINS, *Esq., to the Hon.* A. P.
DEUCEACE.

"Mr. Thomas Smith Dawkins presents his grateful compliments
to the Hon. Mr. Deuceace, and accepts with the greatest pleasure
Mr. Deuceace's generous proffer.

"It would be one of the *happiest moments* of Mr. Smith Dawkins's
life, if the Hon. Mr. Deuceace would *extend his generosity* still further, and condescend to partake of the repast which his *munificent
politeness* has furnished.

"*Temple, Tuesday.*"

Many and many a time, I say, have I grind over these letters, which
I had wrote from the orignal by Mr. Bruffy's copyin clark. Deuceace's
flam about Prince Tallyram was puffickly successful. I saw young Dawkins
blush with delite as he red the note; he toar up for or five sheets before

he composed the anser to it, which was as you read abuff, and roat in a hand quite trembling with pleasyer. If you could but have seen the look of triumth in Deuceace's wicked black eyes, when he read the noat! I never see a deamin yet, but I can phansy 1, a holding a writhing soal on his pitchfrock, and smilin like Deuceace. He dressed himself in his very best clothes, and in he went, after sending me over to say that he would xcept with pleasyour Mr. Dawkins's invite.

The pie was cut up, and a most frenly conversation begun betwixt the two genlmin. Deuceace was quite captivating. He spoke to Mr. Dawkins in the most respeckful and flatrin manner,—agread in every think he said,—prazed his taste, his furniter, his coat, his classick nolledge, and his playin' on the floot; you'd have thought, to hear him, that such a poly-gon of exlens as Dawkins did not breath,—that such a modist, sinsear, honrrable genlmn as Deuceace was to be seen no where xcept in Pump Cort. Pore Daw was complitly taken in. My master said he'd introduce him to the Duke of Doncaster, and Heaven knows how many nobs more, till Dawkins was quite intawsicated with pleasyour. I know as a fack (and it pretty well shews the young genlmn's carryter), that he went that very day, and ordered 2 new coats, on porpus to be introjuiced to the lords in.

But the best joak of all was at last. Singin, swagrin, and swarink—up stares came Mr. Dick Blewitt. He flung open Mr. Dawkins' door, shouting out, "Daw, my old buck, how are you?" when, all of a sudden, he sees Mr. Deuceace: his jor dropt, he turned chocky white, and then burnin red, and looked as if a stror would knock him down. "My dear Mr. Blewitt," says my master, smilin, and offring his hand, "how glad I am to see you. Mr. Dawkins and I were just talking about your pony! Pray sit down."

Blewitt did; and now was the question, who should sit the other out; but, law bless you! Mr. Blewitt was no match for my master; all the time he was fidgetty, silent, and sulky; on the contry, master was charmin. I never herd such a flo of conversatin, or so many wittacisms as he uttered. At last, completely beat, Mr. Blewitt took his leaf; that instant master followed him; and passin his arm through that of Mr. Dick, led him into our chambers, and began talkin to him in the most affabl and affeckshnat manner.

But Dick was too angry to listen; at last, when master was telling him some long stoary about the Duke of Doncaster, Blewitt bust out—

"A plague on the Duke of Doncaster! Come, come, Mr. Deuceace, don't you be running your rigs upon me; I an't the man to be bamboozl'd by long-winded stories about dukes and duchesses. You think I don't know you; every man knows you, and your line of country. Yes, you're after young Dawkins there, and think to pluck him; but you shan't,—no, by —— you shant." (The reader must recklect that the oaths which inters-pussd Mr. B's convysatin I hav lift out.) Well, after he'd fired a wolley of em, Mr. Deuceace spoke as cool and slow as posbill.

"Heark ye, Blewitt. I know you to be one of the most infernal thieves and scoundrels unhung. If you attempt to hector with me, I will cane you; if you want more, I'll shoot you; if you meddle between me and Dawkins, I will do both. I know your whole life, you miserable swindler and coward. I know you have already won two hundred pounds of this lad, and want all. I will have half, or you never shall have a penny." It's quite true that master knew things; but how was the wonder.

I couldn't see Mr. B.'s face during this dialogue, bein on the wrong side of the door; but there was a considdrabble paws after thuse complymints had passed between the two genlmn,—one walkin quickly up and down the room,—tother, angry and stupid, sittin down, and stampin with his foot.

"Now listen to this, Mr. Blewitt," continues master, at last; "if you're quiet, you shall have half this fellow's money: but venture to win a shilling from him in my absence, or without my consent, and you do it at your peril."

"Well, well, Mr. Deuceace," cries Dick, "it's very hard, and, I must say, not fair: the game was of my starting, and you've no right to interfere with my friend."

"Mr. Blewitt, you are a fool! You professed yesterday not to know this man, and I was obliged to find him out for myself. I should like to know by what law of honour I am bound to give him up to you?"

It was charmin to hear this pair of raskles talkin about *honour*. I declare I could have found it in my heart to warn young Dawkins of the precious way in which these chaps were going to serve him. But if *they* didn't know what honour was, *I* did; and never, never did I tell tails about my master when in their sarvice—*out*, in cors, the hobligation is no longer binding.

Well, the nex day there was a gran dinner at our chambers. White soop, turbit, and lobstir sos; saddil of Scoch muttn, grous, and M'Arony; winds, shampang, hock, maderia, a bottle of poart, and ever so many of clarrit. The compny presint was three; wiz., the Honrabble A. P. Deuceace, R. Blewitt, and Mr. Dawkins, Exquires. My i, how we genlmn in the kitchin did enjy it! Mr. Blewittes man eat so much grows (when it was brot out of the parlor), that I reely thought he would be sik; Mr. Dawkinses gnlmn (who was ony abowt 13 years of age) grew so il with M'Arony and plumb puddn, as to be obleeged to take sefral of Mr. D.'s pils, which $\frac{1}{2}$ kild him. But this is all promiscuous: I an't talkin of the survants now, but the masters.

Would you bleev it? After dinner (and praps 8 bottles of wind betwin the 3) the genlmn sat down to *écarty*. It's a game where only 2 plays, and where, in coarse, when there's ony 3, one looks on.

Fust, they playd crown pints, and a pound the bett. At this game they were wonderful equill; and about supper-time (when grilled am, more shampang, devld biskits, and other things, was brot in) the play stood thus: Mr. Dawkins had won 2 pounds; Mr. Blewitt, 30 shillings; the Honrabble Mr. Deuceace having lost 3*l*. 10*s*. After the devvle and the shampang the play was a little higher. Now it was pound pints, and five pound the bet. I thought, to be sure, after hearing the complments between Blewitt and master in the morning, that now pore Dawkins's time was come.

Not so: Dawkins won always, Mr. B. betting on his play, and giving him the very best of advice. At the end of the evening (which was abowt five o'clock the nex morning) they stopt. Master was counting up the skore on a card.

"Blewitt," says he, "I've been unlucky. I ow you—let me see—yes, five-and-forty pounds?"

"Five-and-forty," says Blewitt, "and no mistake!"

"I will give you a cheque," says the honrabble genlmn.

"Oh! don't mention it, my dear sir!" But master got a grate sheet of paper, and drew him a check on Messeers Pump, Algit, and Co., his bankers.

"Now," says master, "I've got to settle with you, my dear Mr. Dawkins. If you had backd your luck, I should have owed you a very handsome sum of money. *Voyons:* thirteen points, at a pound—it is easy to calculate;" and, drawin out his puss, he clinked over the table 13 goolden suverings, which shon till they made my eyes wink.

So did pore Dawkinses, as he put out his hand, all trembling, and drew them in.

"Let me say," added master, "let me say (and I've had some little experience), that you are the very best *écarté* player with whom I ever sat down."

Dawkinses eyes glissened as he put the money up, and said, "Law, Deuceace, you flatter me!"

Flatter him! I should think he did. It was the very thing which master ment.

"But mind you, Dawkins," continyoud he, "I must have my revenge; for I'm ruined—positively ruined—by your luck."

"Well, well," says Mr. Thomas Smith Dawkins, as pleased as if he had gained a millium, "shall it be to-morrow? Blewitt, what say you?"

Mr. Blewitt agread, in course. My master, after a little demurring, consented too. "We'll meet," says he, "at your chambers. But mind, my dear fello, not too much wind: I can't stand it at any time, especially when I have to play *écarté* with *you*."

Pore Dawkins left our rooms, as happy as a prins. "Here, Charles," says he, and flung me a sovring. Pore fellow! pore fellow! I knew what was a comin!

*   *   *   *   *

Mr Dismass taa ore with Mr I smiling in acc'dship is cts were

But the best of it was, that these 13 sovrings which Dawkins won, *master had borrowed them from Mr. Blewitt!* I brought 'em, with 7 more, from that young genlmn's chambers that very morning: for, since his interview with master, Blewitt had nothing to refuse him.

*   *   *   *   *

Well, shall I continue the tail? If Mr. Dawkins had been the least bit wiser, it would have taken him six months befoar he lost his money; as it was, he was such a confounded ninny, that it took him a very short time to part with it.

Nex day (it was Thusday, and master's acquaintance with Mr. Dawkins had only commenced on Tuesday), Mr. Dawkins, as I said, gev his party,—dinner at 7. Mr. Blewitt and the two Mr. D.'s as befoar. Play begins at 11. This time I knew the bisniss was pretty serious, for we suvvants was packed off to bed at 2 o'clock. On Friday, I went to chambers—no master—he kem in for 5 minutes at about 12, made a little toilit, ordered more devvles and soda-water, and back again he went to Mr. Dawkins's.

They had dinner there at 7 again, but nobody seamed to eat, for all the vittles came out to us genlmn: they had in more wind though, and must have drunk at least 2 dozen in the 36 hours.

*   *   *   *   *

At ten o'clock, however, on Friday night, back my master came to his chambers. I saw him as I never saw him before, namly, reglar drunk. He staggered about the room, he danced, he hickipd, he swoar, he flung me a heap of silver, and, finely, he sunk down exosted on his bed; I pullin off his boots and close, and makin him comfrabble.

When I had removed his garmints, I did what it's the duty of every servant to do—I emtied his pockits, and looked at his pockit-book and all his letters: a number of axdents have been prevented that way.

I found there, among a heap of things, the following pretty dockyment:

I. O. U.

£4700.

THOMAS SMITH DAWKINS.

Friday,

16th *January.*

There was another bit of paper, of the same kind—"I. O. U. four hundred pounds, Richard Blewitt:" but this, in cors, ment nothink.

*   *   *   *   *

Nex mornin, at nine, master was up, and as sober as a judg. He drest, and was off to Mr. Dawkins. At 10, he ordered a cab, and the two genlmn went together.

"Where shall he drive, sir?" says I.

"Oh, tell him to drive to THE BANK."

Pore Dawkins! his eyes red with remors and sleepliss drunkenniss, gave a shudder and a sob, as he sunk back in the wehicle; and they drove on.

That day he soald out every hapny he was worth, xcept five hundred pounds.

*   *   *   *   *

Abowt 12 master had returned, and Mr. Dick Blewitt came stridin up the stairs with a sollum and important hair.

"Is your master at home?" says he.

"Yes, sir," says I; and in he walks. I, in coars, with my ear to the keyhole, listning with all my mite.

"Well," says Blewitt, "we maid a pritty good night of it, Mr. Deuceace. You've settled, I see, with Dawkins."

"Settled!" says master. "Oh, yes—yes—I've settled with him."

"Four thousand seven hundred, I think?"

"About that—yes."

"That makes my share—let me see—two thousand three hundred and fifty; which I'll thank you to fork out."

"Upon my word—why—Mr. Blewitt," says my master, "I don't really understand what you mean."

"*You don't know what I mean!*" says Blewitt, in an axent such as I never before heard; "You don't know what I mean! Did you not promise me that we were to go shares? Didn't I lend you twenty sovereigns, the other night, to pay our losings to Dawkins? Didn't you swear, on your honour as a gentleman, to give me half of all that might be won in this affair?"

"Agreed, sir," says Deuceace; "agreed."

"Well, sir, and now what have you to say?"

"Why, *that I don't intend to keep my promise!* You infernal fool and ninny! do you suppose I was labouring for *you*? Do you fancy I was going to the expense of giving a dinner to that jackass yonder, that you should profit by it? Get away, sir! Leave the room, sir! Or, stop—here—I will give you four hundred pounds—your own note of hand, sir, for that sum, if you will consent to forget all that has passed between us, and that you have never known Mr. Algernon Deuceace."

I've sean pipple angery before now, but never any like Blewitt. He stormed, groned, belloed, swoar! At last, he fairly began blubbring; now cussing and nashing his teeth, now praying dear Mr. Deuceace to grant him mercy.

At last, master flung open the door (Heavn bless us! it's well I didn't tumble, hed over eels, into the room!), and said, "Charles, shew the gentleman down stairs!" My master looked at him quite steddy. Blewitt slunk down, as misrabble as any man I ever see. As for Dawkins, Heaven knows where he was!

*   *   *   *   *

"Charles," says my master to me, about an hour afterwards, "I am going to Paris; you may come, too, if you please."

C. Yellowplush.

THE YELLOWPLUSH CORRESPONDENCE

No. IV.

———◇———

SKIMMINGS
FROM
"THE DAIRY OF GEORGE IV."

Charles Yellowplush, Esq. to Oliver Yorke, Esq.

DEAR WHY,—Takin advantage of the Crismiss holydays, Sir John and me (who is a member of parlyment) had gone down to our place in York-shire for six wicks, to shoot grows and woodcox, and enjoy old English hospatalaty. This ugly Canady bisniss unluckaly put an end to our sports in the country, and brot us up to Buckly Square as fast as four posterses could gallip. When there I found your parsel, containing the two vol-lums of a new book, witch, as I have been away from the littery world, and emplied soly in athlatic exorcises, have been laying neglected in my pantry, among my knife-cloaths, and dekanters, and blacking-bottles, and bed-room candles, and things.

This will, I'm sure, account for my delay in notussing the work. I see sefral of the papers and magazeens have been befoarhand with me, and have given their apinions concerning it; specially the *Quotly Revew,* which has most mussilessly cut to peases the author of this *Dairy of the Times of George IV.* *

That it's a woman who wrote it is evydent from the style of the writ-ing, as well as from certain proofs in the book itself. Most suttnly a femail wrote this *Dairy;* but who this *Dairy-maid* may be, I, in coarse, cant con-jecter: and, indeed, commin galliantry forbids me to ask. I can only judge of the book itself, which, it appears to me, is clearly trenching upon my ground and favrite subjicks, viz. fashnabble life, as igsibited in the houses of the nobility, gentry, and rile fammly.

---

* Diary illustrative of the Times of George the Fourth, interspersed with original Letters from the late Queen Caroline, and from various other distinguished Persons.

"Tôt ou tard, tout se sçait."—MAINTENON.

In 2 vols. London, 1838. Henry Colburn.

But I bare no mallis—infamation is infamation, and it doesn't matter where the infamy comes from; and whether the *Dairy* be from that distinguished pen to witch it is ornarily attributed—whether, I say, it comes from a lady of honor to the late quean, or a scullion to that diffunct majisty, no matter; all we ask is nollidge, never mind how we have it. Nollidge, as our cook says, is like trikel-possit—its always good, though you was to drink it out of an old shoo.

Well, then, although this *Dairy* is likely searusly to injer my pussonal intrests, by fourstalling a deal of what I had to say in my private memoars—though many, many guineas, is taken from my pockit, by cuttin short the tail of my narratif—though much that I had to say in souperior languidge, greased with all the ellygance of my orytory, the benefick of my classicle reading, the chawms of my agreble wit, is thus abruply brot before the world by an inferor genus, neither knowing nor writing English, yet I say, that nevertheless I must say, what I am puffickly prepaired to say, to gainsay which no man can say a word—yet I say, that I say I consider this publication welkom. Far from viewing it with enfy, I greet it with applaws; because it increases that most exlent specious of nollidge, I mean "FASHNABBLE NOLLIDGE;" compayred to witch all other nollidge is nonsince—a bag of goold to a pare of snuffers.

Could Lord Broom, on the Canady question, say moar? or say what he had to say better? We are marters, both of us, to prinsple; and every body who knows eather knows we would sacrafice any think rather than that. Fashion is the goddiss I adoar. This delightful work is an offring on her srine; and as sich all her wushippers are bound to hail it. Here is not a question of trumpry lords and honrabbles, generals and barronites, but the crown itself, and the king and queen's actions; witch may be considered as the crown jewels. Here's princes, and grand-dukes, and airs-aparent, and Heaven knows what; all with blood-royal in their veins, and their names mentioned in the very fust page of the peeridge. In this book you become so intmate with the Prince of Wales, that you may follow him, if you please, to his marridge-bed; or, if you prefer the Princiss Charlotte, you may have with her an hour's tator-tator.*

Now, though most of the remarkable extrax from this book have been given already (the cream of the *Dairy*, as I wittily say), I shall trouble you, nevertheless, with a few; partly because they can't be repeated too often, and because the toan of obsyvation with witch they have been genrally received by the press, is not igsackly such as I think they merit. How, indeed, can these common magaseen and newspaper pipple know anythink of fashnabble life, let alone ryal?

Conseaving, then, that the publication of the *Dairy*, has done reel good on this scoar, and may probly do a deal moor, I shall look through it, for

---

* Our estimable correspondent means, we presume, *tête-à-tête.*—O.Y.

the porpus of selecting the most ellygant passidges, and which I think may be peculiarly adapted to the reader's benefick.

For you see, my dear Mr. Yorke, that, in the fust place, that this is no commin catchpny book, like that of most authors and authoresses who write for the base looker of gain. Heaven bless you! the Dairy-maid is above any thing musnary. She is a woman of rank, and no mistake; and is as much above doin a common or vulgar action as I am supearor to taking beer after dinner with my cheese. She proves that most satisfackarily, as we see in the following passidge:

> Her royal highness "came to me, and having spoken a few phrases on different subjects, produced all the papers she wishes to have published:—her whole correspondence with the Prince relative to Lady J——'s dismissal; his subsequent neglect of the Princess; and, finally, the acquittal of her supposed guilt, signed by the Duke of Portland, &c., at the time of the secret inquiry,—when, if proof could have been brought against her, it certainly would have been done; and which acquittal, to the disgrace of all parties concerned, as well as to the justice of the nation in general, was not made public at the time. A common criminal is publicly condemned or acquitted. Her Royal Highness commanded me to have these letters published forthwith, saying, 'You may sell them for a great sum.' At first, (for she had spoken to me before, concerning this business,) I thought of availing myself of the opportunity; but, upon second thoughts, I turned from this idea with detestation; for, if I do wrong by obeying her wishes and endeavouring to serve her, I will do so at least from good and disinterested motives, not from any sordid views. The Princess commands me, and I will obey her, whatever may be the issue, but not for fare or fee. I own, I tremble, not so much for myself as for the idea that she is not taking the best and most dignified way of having these papers published.—Why make a secret of it all? If wrong it should not be done; if right, it should be done openly and in the face of her enemies. In her Royal Highness's case, as in that of wronged princes in general, why do they shrink from straight-forward dealings, and rather have recourse to crooked policy? I wish in this particular instance I could make her Royal Highness feel thus; but she is naturally indignant at being falsely accused, and will not condescend to an avowed explanation."

Can any thing be more just and honrabble than this? The Dairy-lady is quite fair and abovebored. A clear stage, says she, and no faviour! "I won't do behind my back what I am ashamed of before my face: not I!" No more she does: for you see that, though she was offered this manyscrip by the princess *for nothink*, though she knew that she could actially get for it a large sum of money, she was above it, like an honest, noble, grateful, fashnabble woman, as she was. She aboars secrecy, and never will have recors to disguise or crookid polacy. This ought to be an ansure to them *Raddicle sneerers*, who pretend that they are the equals of fashnabble pepple; whereas it's a well-known fact, that the vulgar roagues have no notion of honour.

And, after this positif declaration, which reflex honor on her ladyship (long life to her! I've often waited behind her chair!)—after this positif declaration, that, even for the porpus of *defending* her missis, she was so hi-mindid as to refuse anythink like a peculiary consideration, it is actially asserted in the public prints by a booxeller, that he has given her *a thousand pound* for the *Dairy*. A thousand pound! nonsince!—it's a phigment! a base lible! This woman take a thousand pound, in a matter where her dear mistriss, frend, and benyfactriss was concerned! Never! A thousand baggonits would be more prefrabble to a woman of her xquizzit feelins and fashion.

But, to proceed. It's been objected to me, when I wrote some of my expearunces in fashnabble life, that my languidge was occasionally vulgar, and not such as is genrally used in those exquizzit famlies which I frequent. Now, I'll lay a wager that there is in this book, wrote, as all the world knows, by a rele lady, and speakin of kings and queens as if they were as common as sand-boys—there is in this book more wulgarity than ever I displayed, more nastiniss than ever I would dare *to think on*, and more bad grammar than ever I wrote since I was a boy at school. As for authografy, evry genlmn has his own: never mind spellin, I say, so long as the sence is right.

Let me here quot a letter from a corryspondent of this charming lady of honour; and a very nice corryspondent he is, too, without any mistake:

"Lady O——, poor Lady O——! knows the rules of prudence, I fear me, as imperfectly as she doth those of the Greek and Latin grammars; or she hath let her brother, who is a sad swine, become master of her secrets, and then contrived to quarrel with him. You would see the outline of the mélange in the newspapers, but not the report that Mr. S—— is about to publish a pamphlet, as an addition to the Harleian Tracts, setting forth the amatory adventures of his sister. We shall break our necks in haste to buy it, of course crying 'Shameful' all the while; and it is said that Lady O—— is to be cut, which I cannot entirely believe. Let her tell two or three old women about town that they are young and handsome, and give some well-timed parties, and she may still keep the society which she hath been used to. The times are not so hard as they once were, when a woman could not construe Magna Charta with any thing like impunity. People were full as gallant many years ago. But the days are gone by wherein my Lord-Protector of the Commonwealth of England was wont to go a love-making to Mrs. Fleetwood, with the bible under his arm.

"And so Miss Jacky Gordon is really clothed with a husband at last, and Miss Laura Manners left without a mate! She and Lord Stair should marry and have children, in mere revenge. As to Miss Gordon, she's a Venus well suited to such a Vulcan,—whom nothing but money and a title could have rendered tolerable, even to a kitchen wench. It is said that the matrimonial correspondence between this couple is to be published—full of sad scandalous relations, of which you may be sure scarcely a word is true. In former times the Duchess of St. A——'s made use of these elegant epistles in order to intimidate Lady Johnstone; but that ruse would not avail, so, in spite, they are to be printed. What a cargo of amiable creatures!—Yet will some people scarcely believe in the existence of Pandemonium!

"Tuesday morning.—You are perfectly right respecting the hot rooms here, which we all cry out against, and all find very comfortable—much more so than the cold sands and bleak neighborhood of the sea; which looks vastly well in one of Vander Velde's pictures hung upon crimson damask, but hideous and shocking in reality. H—— and his 'Elle' (talking of parties) were last night at Cholmondeley House, but seem not to ripen in their love. He is certainly good-humoured, and, I believe, good-hearted, so deserves a good wife; but his *cara* seems a genuine London miss, made up of many affectations. Will she form a comfortable helpmate? For me I like not her origin, and deem many strange things to run in blood, besides madness and the Hanoverian evil.

"Thursday.—I verily do believe that I never shall get to the end of this small sheet of paper, so many unheard of interruptions have I had; and now I have been to Vauxhall and caught the tooth-ache. I was of Lady E. B——m and H——'s party—very dull—the lady giving us all a supper after our promenade—

'Much ado was there, God wot,
She would love, but he would not.'

He ate a great deal of ice, although he did not seem to require it; and she 'faisoit les yeux doux,' enough not only to have melted all the ice which he swallowed, but his own hard heart into the bargain. The thing will not do. In the mean time Miss Long hath become quite cruel to Wellesley Pole, and divides her favour equally between Lords Killeen and Kilworth, two as simple Irishmen as ever gave birth to a bull. I wish to Hymen that she were fairly married, for all this pother gives one a disgusting picture of human nature."

A disgusting pictur of human nature, indeed—and isn't he who mo-rilises about it, and she to whom he writes, a couple of pretty heads in the same piece? Which, Mr. Yorke, is the wust, the scandle or the scandle-mongers? See what it is to be a moral man of fashn. Fust, he scrapes togither all the bad stoaries about all the people of his acquentance—he goes to a ball, and laffs or snears at every body there—he is asked to a dinner, and brings away, along with meat and wind to his heart's content, a sour stomick, filled with nasty stories of all the people present there. He has such a squeamish appytite, that all the world seems to *disagree* with him. And what has he got to say to his dellicate female frend? Why, that—

Fust. Mr. S. is going to publish indesent stoaries about Lady O——, his sister, which every body's goin to by.

Nex. That Miss Gordon is going to be cloathed with an usband; and that all their matramonial corryspondins is to be published too.

3. That Lord H. is goin to be married; but there's something rong in his wife's blood.

4. Miss Long has cut Mr. Wellesley, and is gone after two Irish lords.

Wooden you phancy, now, that the author of such a letter, instead of writin about pipple of tip-top qualaty, was describin Vinegar Yard? Would you beleave that the lady he was a ritin to was a chased, modist lady of honour, and mother of a famly? O *trumpery, O morris!* as Homer says, this is a higeous pictur of manners, such as I weap to think of, as every morl man must weap.

The above is one pritty pictur of mearly fashnabble life: what follows is about famlies even higher situated than the most fashnabble. Here we have the princess-regint, her daughter the Princess Sharlot, her grand-mamma the old quean, and her madjisty daughters the two princesses. If this is not high life, I don't know where it is to be found: and it's pleasing to see what affeckshn and harmny rains in such an exolted spear.

> "Sunday, 24th.—Yesterday, the princess went to meet the Prin-
> cess Charlotte at Kensington. Lady —— told me that when the
> latter arrived she rushed up to her mother, and said, 'for God's sake,
> be civil to her'—meaning the Duchess of Leeds, who followed her.
> Lady —— said she felt sorry for the latter, but when the Princess
> of Wales talked to her, she soon became so free and easy that one
> could not have any *feeling* about her *feelings*. Princess Charlotte, I
> was told, was looking handsome, very pale, but her head more be-
> comingly dressed, that is to say, less dressed than usual. Her figure
> is of that full round shape which is now in its prime; but she disfig-
> ures herself by wearing her boddice so short, that she literally has
> no waist. Her feet are very pretty, and so are her hands and arms,
> and her ear and the shape of her head. Her countenance is expres-
> sive, when she allows her passions to play upon it; and I never saw

any face with so little shade express so many powerful and varied emotions. Lady —— told me that the Princess Charlotte talked to her about her situation, and said, in a very quiet, but determined way, she *would not bear it*, and that as soon as Parliament met, she intended to come to Warwick House, and remain there; that she was also determined not to consider the Duchess of Leeds as her *governess*, but only as her *first lady*. She made many observations on other persons and subjects, and appears to be very quick, very penetrating, but imperious, and wilful. There is a tone of romance, too, in her character, which will only serve to mislead her.

"She told her mother, that there had been a great battle at Windsor, between the Queen and the Prince; the former refusing to give up Miss Knight from her own person, to attend on Princess Charlotte as sub-governess; but the Prince-Regent had gone to Windsor himself and insisted on her doing so, and the 'Old Beguin' was forced to submit, but has been ill ever since; and Sir Henry Halford declared it was a complete breaking up of her constitution,— (to the great delight of the two Princesses, who were talking about this affair.) Miss Knight was the very person they wished to have: they think they can do as they like with her. It had been ordered that the Princess Charlotte should not see her mother alone for a single moment; but the latter went into her room, stuffed a pair of large shoes full of papers, and, having given them to her daughter, she went home. Lady —— told me every thing was written down, and sent to Mr. Brougham *next day*."

See what dishcord will creap even into the best reglated famlies. Here are six of 'em, viz. the quean and her two daughters, her son, and his wife and daughter; and the manner in which they hate one another is a compleat puzzle.

$$\text{The Prince hates} \cdots \cdots \left\{ \begin{array}{l} \text{his mother.} \\ \text{his wife.} \\ \text{his daughter.} \end{array} \right.$$

Princess Charlotte hates her father.

Princess of Wales hates her husband.

The old quean, by their squobbles, is on the pint of death; and her two jewtiful daughters are delighted at the news. What a happy, fashnabble, Christian famly! O Mr. Yorke, Mr. Yorke, if this is the way in the drawin rooms, I'm quite content to live below, in pease and charaty with all men; writin, as I am now, in my pantry, or els havin a quite game at cards in the servants-all. With *us* there's no bitter, wicked, quarling of this sort. *We* don't hate our children, or bully our mothers, or wish em ded when they're sick, as this Dairy-woman says kings and queans do. When we're writing to our friends or sweethearts, *we* don't fill our letters with nasty stoaries, takin away the carrickter of our fellow-servants, as this maid of honour's amusin, moral, frend does. But, in coarse, it's not for us to judge of our betters;—these great people are a supearur race, and we can't comprehend their ways.

Do you recklect—it's twenty years ago now—how a bewtiffle princess died in givin buth to a poar baby, and how the whole nation of Hengland wep, as though it was one man, over that sweet woman and child, in which were sentered the hopes of every one of us, and of which each was as proud as of his own wife or infnt? Do you recklect how pore fellows spent their last shillin to buy a black crape for their hats, and clergymen cried in the pulpit, and the whole country through was no better than a great dismal funeral? Do you recklect, Mr. Yorke, who was the person that we all took on so about? We called her the Princiss Sharlot of Wales; and we valyoud a single drop of her blood more than the whole heartless body of her father. Well, we looked up to her as a kind of saint or angle, and blest God (such foolish loyal English pipple as we ware in those days) who had sent this sweet lady to rule over us. But, Heaven bless you! it was only souperstition. She was no better than she should be, as it turns out—or at least the Dairy-maid says so—no better?—if my daughters or yours was ½ so bad, we'd as leaf be dead ourselves, and they hanged. But listen to this pritty charritabble storry, and a truce to reflexshuns.

"Sunday, January 9th, 1814.—Yesterday, according to appointment, I went to Princess Charlotte. Found at Warwick House the harp-player Dizzi; was asked to remain and listen to his performance, but was talked to during the whole time, which completely prevented all possibility of listening to the music. The Duchess of Leeds and her daughter were in the room, but left it soon. Next arrived Miss Knight, who remained all the time I was there. Princess Charlotte was very gracious—shewed me all her *bonny dyes*, as B—— would have called them—pictures, and cases, and jewels, &c. She talked in a very desultory way, and it would be difficult to say of what. She observed her mother was in very low spirits. I asked her how she supposed she could be otherwise.— This *questioning* answer saves a great deal of trouble, and serves two purposes—*i.e.* avoids committing oneself, or giving offence by silence. There was hung in the apartment one portrait, amongst others, that very much resembled the Duke of D——. I asked Miss Knight whom it represented; she said that was not known; it had been supposed a likeness of the Pretender when young. This answer suited my thoughts so comically, I could have laughed, if one ever did at courts anything but the contrary of what one was inclined to do.

"Princess Charlotte has a very great variety of expression in her countenance—a play of features, and a force of muscle, rarely seen in connection with such soft and shadeless colouring. Her hands and arms are beautiful, but I think her figure is already gone, and will soon be precisely like her mother's: in short, it is the very picture of her, and *not in miniature*. I could not help analysing my own sensations during the time I was with her, and thought more of them than I did of her. Why was I at all flattered, at all more amused, at all more supple to this young Princess, than to her who is only the same sort of person, set in the shade of circumstances and of years? It is that youth, and the approach of power, and the latent views of self interest, sway the heart, and dazzle the understanding. If this is so with a heart not, I trust, corrupt, and a head not particularly formed for interested calculations, what effect must not the same causes produce on the generality of mankind?

"In the course of the conversation, the Princess Charlotte contrived to edge in a good deal of *tum-de-dy*, and would, if I had entered into the thing, have gone on with it, while looking at a little picture of herself, which had about thirty or forty different dresses to put over it, done on *isinglass*, and which allowed the general colouring of the picture to be seen through its transparency. It was, I thought, a pretty enough conceit, though rather like dressing up a doll. 'Ah!' said Miss Knight, 'I am not content though, madam— for I yet should have liked one more dress—that of the favourite Sultana.'

" 'No, no!' said the Princess, 'I never was a favourite, and never can be one,'—looking at a picture which she said was her father's, but which I do not believe was done for the Regent any more than for me, but represented a young man in a hussar's dress—probably a former favourite.

"The Princess Charlotte seemed much hurt at the little notice that was taken of her birthday. After keeping me for two hours and a half, she dismissed me, and I am sure I could not say what she said, except that it was an *olio* of *décousus* and heterogenous things, partaking of the characteristics of her mother, grafted on a younger scion. I dined *tête-à-tête* with my dear old aunt: hers is always a sweet and soothing society to me."

There's a pleasing, lady-like, moral extrack for you! An innocent young thing of fifteen has pictures of *two* lovers in her room, and expex a good number more. This dellygate young creature *edges in* a good deal of *tumdedy* (I can't find it in Johnson's Dixonary), and would have *gone on with the thing* (ellygance of languidge), if the dairy-lady would have let her.

Now, to tell you the truth, Mr. Yorke, I doant beleave a single syllible of this story. This lady of honner says, in the fust place, that the princess would have talked a good deal of *tumdedy;* which means, I suppose, indeasnsy, if she, the lady of honner, *would have let her.* This *is* a good one! Why, she lets every body else talk tumdedy to their hearts' content; she lets her friends *write* tumdedy, and, after keeping it for a quarter of a sentry, she *prints* it. Why, then, be so squeamish about *hearing* a little? And, then, there's the stoary of the two portricks. This woman has the honner to be received in the frendlyest manner by a British princess; and what does the grateful, loyal creature do? 2 pictures of the princess's relations are hanging in her room, and the dairy-woman swears away the poor young princess's carrickter, by swearing they are pictures of her *lovers.* For shame, oh, for shame! you slanderin, backbitin, dairy-woman you! If you told all them things to your "dear old aunt," on going to dine with her, you must have had very "sweet and soothing society," indeed.

I had marked out many moar extrax, witch I intended to write about; but I think I have said enough about this Dairy: in fack, the butler, and the gals in the servants' hall, are not well pleased that I should go on readin this naughty book; so we'll have no more of it, only one passidge about Pollytics, witch is sertnly quite new.

"No one was so likely to be able to defeat Bonaparte, as the Crown Prince, from the intimate knowledge he possessed of his character. Bernadotte was also instigated against Bonaparte by one who not only owed him a personal hatred, but who possessed a mind equal to his, and who gave the Crown Prince both information and advice how to act. This was no less a person than Madame de Stael. It was not, as some have asserted, *that she was in love with Bernadotte;* for, at the time of their intimacy, *Madame de Stael was in love with Rocca.* But she used her influence (which was not small) with the Crown Prince, to make him fight against Bonaparte; and to her wisdom may be attributed much of the success which accompanied his attack upon him. Bernadotte has raised the flame of liberty, which seems fortunately to blaze all around. May it liberate Europe; and from the ashes of the laurel, may olive branches spring up, and overshadow the earth!"

There's a discuvery! that the overthrow of Boneypart is owing *to* *Madame de Stael!* What nonsince for Colonel Southey, or Doctor Napier, to write histories of the war with that Capsican hupstart and murderer, when here we have the whole affair explained by the lady of honour!

"Sunday, April 10th, 1814.—The incidents which take place every hour are miraculous. Bonaparte is deposed, but alive;— subdued, but allowed to choose his place of residence. The island of Elba is the spot he has selected for his ignominious retreat. France is holding forth repentant arms to her banished sovereign. The Poissardes who dragged Louis the Sixteenth to the scaffold are presenting flowers to the Emperor of Russia, the restorer of their legitimate king! What a stupendous field for philosophy to expatiate in! What an endless material for thought! What humiliation to the pride of mere human greatness! How are the mighty fallen! Of all that was great in Napoleon, what remains? Despoiled of his usurped power, he sinks to insignificance. There was no moral greatness in the man. The meteor dazzled, scorched, is put out,—utterly, and for ever. But the power which rests in those who have delivered the nations from bondage, is a power that is delegated to them from Heaven; and the manner in which they have used it is a guarantee for its continuance. The Duke of Wellington has gained laurels unstained by any useless flow of blood. He has done more than conquer others—he has conquered himself; and in the midst of the blaze and flush of victory, surrounded by the homage of nations, he has not been betrayed into the commission of any act of cruelty, or wanton offence. He was as cool and self-possessed under the blaze and dazzle of fame, as a common man would be under the shade of his garden-tree, or by the hearth of his home. But the tyrant who kept Europe in awe, is now a pitiable object for scorn to point the finger of derision at; and humanity shudders as it remembers the scourge with which this man's ambition was permitted to devastate every home tie, and every hearfelt joy."

And now, after this sublime passidge, as full of awfle reflections and pious sentyments as those of Mrs. Cole in the play, I shall only quot one little extrack more.

"All goes gloomily with the poor Princess. Lady Charlotte Campbell told me, she regrets not seeing all these curious personages; but, she said, the more the Princess is forsaken, the more happy she is at having offered to attend her at this time. *This is very amiable in her,* and cannot fail to be gratifying to the Princess."

So it is,—wery amiable, wery kind and considdrate in her, indeed. Poor princess! how lucky you was to find a frend who loved you for your own sake, and when all the rest of the wuld turned its back kep steady to you. As for beleaving that Lady Sharlot had any hand in this book,* Heaven forbid! she is all gratitude, pure gratitude, depend upon it. *She* would not go for to blacken her old frend and patron's carrickter, after having been so outragusly faithful to her; *she* wouldn't do it, at no price, depend upon it. How sorry she must be that others a'nt quite so squeamish, and show up in this indesent way the follies of her kind, genrus, foolish bennyfactriss!

---

* The "authorised" announcement, in the *John Bull* newspaper, sets this question at rest. It is declared that her ladyship is not the writer of the *Diary.*— O.Y.

THE YELLOWPLUSH CORRESPONDENCE

No. V.

———◇———

FORING PARTS.

IT WAS a singlar proof of my master's modesty, that though he had won this handsome sum of Mr. Dawkins, and was inclined to be as extravygant and osntatious as any man I ever seed, yet, wen he determined on going to Paris, he didn't let a single frend know of all them winnings of his, didn't acquaint my Lord Crabs, his father, that he was about to leave his natiff shoars—neigh, didn't even so much as call together his tradesmin, and pay off their little bills befor his departure.

On the contry, "Chawles," said he to me, "stick a piece of paper on my door," which is the way that lawyers do, "and write 'Back at seven' upon it." Back at seven I wrote, and stuck it on our outer oak. And so mistearus was Deuceace about his continental tour (to all excep me), that when the landriss brought him her acount for the last month (amountain, at the very least, to 2l. 10s.), master told her to leave it till Monday mornin, when it should be proply settled. It's extrodny how ickonomical a man becomes, when he's got five thousand lbs. in his pockit.

Back at 7 indeed! At 7 we were a roalin on the Dover Road, in the Reglator Coach—master inside, me out. A strange company of people there was, too, in that vehicle,—3 sailors; an Italyin, with his music-box and munky; a missionary, goin to convert the hethens in France; 2 oppra girls (they call 'em figure-aunts), and the figure-aunts' mothers inside; 4 Frenchmin, with gingybread caps, and mustashes, singin, chatterin, and jesticklating in the most vonderful vay. Such compliments as passed between them and the figure-aunts! such a munchin of biskits and sippin of brandy! such *O mong Jews*, and *O sacrrrés*, and *kill fay frwaws!* I didn't understand their languidge at that time, so of course can't igsplain much of their conwersation; but it pleased me, nevertherless, for now I felt that I was reely going into foring parts, which, ever sins I had had any edication at all, was always my fondest wish. Heaven bless us! thought I, if these are specimeens of all Frenchmen, what a set they must be. The pore Italyin's monky, sittin mopin and meluncolly on his box, was not half so ugly, and seamed quite as reasonabble.

Well, we arrived at Dover—Ship Hotel—weal cutlets half a ginny, glas of ale a shilling, glas of neagush half-a-crownd, a hap'ny-worth of wax-lites four shillings, and so on. But master paid without grumling; as long as it was for himself, he never minded the expens: and nex day we embarked in the packit for Balong sir mare—which means, in French, the town of Balong sityouated on the sea. I, who had heard of foring wonders, expected this to be the fust and greatest: phansy, then, my disapintment, when we got there, to find this Balong, not sityouated on the sea, but on the *shoar.*

But, oh! the gettin there was the bisniss. How I did wish for Pump Court agin, as we were tawsing abowt in the Channel! Gentle reader, av you ever been on the otion?—"The sea, the sea, the hopen sea!" as Barry Cromwell says. As soon as we entered our little wessel, and I'd looked to master's luggitch and mine (mine was rapt up in a very small hankercher), as soon, I say, as we entered our little wessel, as soon as I saw the waivs, black and frothy, like fresh-drawn porter, a dashin against the ribbs of our galliant bark, the keal, like a wedge, splittin the billoes in two, the sales a flaffin in the hair, the standard of Hengland floating at the mask-head, the steward a gettin ready the basins and things, the capting proudly tredding the deck and givin orders to the salers, the white rox of Albany and the bathin-masheens disappearing in the distans—then, then I felt, for the first time, the mite, the madgisty of existence. "Yellowplush, my boy," said I, in a dialog with myself, "your life is now about to commens—your carear, as a man, dates from your entrans on board this packit. Be wise, be manly, be cautious—forgit the follies of your youth. You are no longer a boy now, but a FOOTMAN. Throw down your tops, your marbles, your boyish games—throw off your childish habbits with your inky clerk's jackit—throw up your——"

*   *   *   *   *

Here, I recklect, I was obleeged to stopp. A fealin, in the fust place singlar, in the nex place painful, and at last compleatly overpowering, had come upon me while I was making the abuff speach, and I now found myself in a sityouation which Dellixy for Bids me to discribe. Suffis to say, that now I dixcovered what basins was made for—that for many, many hours, I lay in a hagony of exostion, dead to all intence and porpuses, the rain pattering in my face, the salers a tramplink over my body—the panes of purgertory going on inside. When we'd been about four hours in this sityouation (it seam'd to me four ears), the steward comes to that part of the deck where we servants were all huddled up together, and calls out, "Charles."

"Well," says I, gurgling out a faint "yes," "what's the matter?"

"You're wanted."

The Calais Packet
Mr Tillotson's emotions on first going to sea

Published by James Fraser, 216 Regent Street London.

"Where?"

"Your master's wery ill," says he, with a grin.

"Master be hanged!" says I, turning round more miserable than ever. I woodn't have moved that day for twenty thousand masters—no, not for the Empror of Russia or the Pop of Room.

Well, to cut this sad subjick short, many and many a voyitch have I sins had upon what Shakespur calls "the wasty dip," but never such a retched one as that from Dover to Balong, in the year Anna Domino 1818. Steamers were scarce in those days; and our journey was made in a smack. At last, when I was in such a stage of despare and exostion as reely to phansy myself at Death's doar, we got to the end of our journy. Late in the evening we hailed the Gaelic shoars, and hankered in the arbour of Balong sir Mare.

It was the entrans of Parrowdice to me and master; and as we entered the calm water, and saw the comfrable lights gleaming in the houses, and felt the roal of the vessel degreasing, never was two mortials gladder, I warrant, than we were. At length our capting drew up at the key, and our journey was down. But such a bustle and clatter, such jabbering, such shrieking and swearing, such wollies of oafs and axicrations as saluted us on landing, I never knew! We were boarded, in the fust place, by custom-house officers in cock-hats, who seased our luggitch, and called for our passpots: then a crowd of inn-waiters came, tumbling and screaming, on deck—"Dis way, sare," cries one; "Hotel Meurice," says another; "Hotel de Bang," screeches another chap—the tower of Bayble was nothink to it. The fust thing that struck me on landing was a big fellow with earrings, who very nigh knock me down, in wrenching master's carpet-bag out of my hand, as I was carrying it to the hotell. But we got to it safe at last; and, for the fust time in my life, I slep in a foring country.

I shan't describe this town of Balong, which, as it has been visited by not less (on an avaridge) than two milliuns of English since I fust saw it twenty years ago, is tolrabbly well known already. It's a dingy, melumcolly place, to my mind: the only thing moving in the streets is the gutter which runs down 'em. As for wooden shoes, I saw few of 'em; and for frogs, upon my honour, I never see a single Frenchman swallow one, which I had been led to beleave was their reglar, though beastly, custom. One thing which amazed me was the singlar name which they give to this town of Balong. It's divided, as every boddy knows, into an upper town (sityouate on a mounting, and surrounded by a wall, or *bullyvar*), and a lower town, which is on the level of the sea. Well, will it be believed that they call the upper town the *Hot Veal*, and the other the *Base Veal*, which is, on the contry, genrally good in France, though the beaf, it must be confest, is exscrabble.

It was in the Base Veal that Deuceace took his lodgian, at the Hotel de Bang, in a very crooked street called the Rue del Ascew; and if he'd been the Archbishop of Devonshire, or the Duke of Canterbury, he could not have given himself greater hairs, I can tell you. Nothink was too fine for us now; we had a sweet of rooms on the first floor, which belonged to the prime minister of France (at least, the landlord said they were the *premier's*); and the Hon. Algernon Percy Deuceace, who had not paid his landriss, and came to Dover in a coach, seamed now to think that goold was too vulgar for him, and a carridge and six would break down with a man of his weight. Shampang flew about like ginger-pop, besides bordo, clarit, burgundy, burgong, and other winds, and all the delixes of the Balong kitchins. We stopped a fortnit at this dull place, and did nothing from morning to night, excep walk on the beach, and watch the ships going in and out of arber; with one of them long, sliding, opera-glasses, which they call, I don't know why, tallow-scoops. Our amusemens for the fortnit we stopt here were boath numerous and daliteful; nothink, in fact, could be more *pickong*, as they say. In the morning before breakfast, we boath walked on the Peer; master in a blue mareen jackit, and me in a slap-up new livry; both provided with long sliding opra-glasses, called as I said (I don't know Y, but I spose it's a scientafick term) tallow-scoops. With these we igsamined, very attentively, the otion, the sea-weed, the pebbils, the dead cats, the fishwimin, and the waives (like little children playing at leap-frog), which came tumbling over 1 and other on to the shoar. It seemed to me as if they were scrambling to get there, as well they might, being sick of the sea, and anxious for the blessid, peaceable *terry-firmy*.

After brexfast, down we went again (that is, master on his beat, and me on mine,—for my place in this foring town was a complete *shinycure*), and puttin our tally-scoops again in our eyes, we egsamined a little more the otion, pebbils, dead cats, and so on; and this lasted till dinner, and dinner lasted till bed-time, and bed-time lasted till nex day, when came brexfast, and dinner, and tally-scooping, as befoar. This is the way with all people of this town, of which, as I've heard say, there is ten thousand happy English, who lead this plesnt life from year's end to year's end.

Besides this, there's billiards and gambling for the gentlemen, a little dancing for the gals, and scandle for the dowygers. In none of these amusements did we partake. We were *a little* too good to play crown pints at cards, and never get paid when we won; or to go dangling after the portionless gals, or amuse ourselves with slops and penny-wist along with the old ladies. No, no, my master was a man of fortun now, and behayved himself as sich. If ever he condysended to go into the public room of the Hotel de Bang—the French (doubtliss for reasons best known to themselves) call this a sallymanjy—he swoar more and lowder than any one there; he abyoused the waiters, the wittles, the winds. With his glas in his i, he staired at every body. He took always the place before the fire.

He talked about "My carridge," "My currier," "My servant;" and he did wright. I've always found through life, that if you wish to be respected by English people, you must be insalent to them, especially if you're a sprig of nobillaty. We *like* being insulted by noablemen,—it shows they're familiar with us. Law bless us! I've known many and many a genlmn about town who'd rather be kicked by a lord than not be noticed by him; they've even had an aw of *me*, because I was a lord's footman. While my master was hectoring in the parlor, at Balong, pretious airs I gave myself in the kitch-ing, I can tell you; and the consequints was, that we were better served, and moar liked, than many pipple with twice our merrit.

Deuceace had some particklar plans, no doubt, which kep him so long at Balong; and it clearly was his wish to act the man of fortune there for a little time before he tried the character at Paris. He purchased a carridge, he hired a currier, he rigged me in a fine new livry blazin with lace, and he past through the Balong bank a thousand pound of the money he had won from Dawkins, to his credit at a Paris house; showing the Balong bankers, at the same time, that he'd plenty moar in his potfolio. This was killin two birds with one stone; the bankers' clarks spread the nuse over the town, and in a day after master had paid the money every old dowyger in Balong had looked out the Crab's family podigree in the Peeridge, and was quite intimate with the Deuceace name and estates. If Sattn himself were a Lord, I do beleave there's many vurtuous English mothers would be glad to have him for a son-in-law.

Now, though my master had thought fitt to leave town without ex-communicating with his father on the subject of his intended continental tripe, as soon as he was settled at Balong he roat my lord Crabbs a letter, of which I happen to have a copy. It run thus

"Boulogne, January 25.

"My dear Father,—I have long, in the course of my legal studies, found the necessity of a thorough knowledge of French, in which language all the early history of our profession is written, and have determined to take a little relaxation from chamber reading, which has seriously injured my health. If my modest finances can bear a two months' journey, and a residence at Paris, I propose to remain there that period.

"Will you have the kindness to send me a letter of introduction to Lord Bobtail, our ambassador? My name, and your old friendship with him, I know would secure me a reception at his house; but a pressing letter from yourself would at once be more courteous, and more effectual.

"May I also ask you for my last quarter's salary? I am not an expensive man, my dear father, as you know; but we are no chameleons, and fifty pounds (with my little earnings in my profession) would vastly add to the *agrémens* of my continental excursion.

"Present my love to all my brothers and sisters. Ah! how I wish the hard portion of a younger son had not been mine, and that I could live without the dire necessity for labour, happy among the rural scenes of my childhood, and in the society of my dear sisters and you! Heaven bless you, dearest father, and all those beloved ones now dwelling under the dear old roof at Sizes.

"Ever your affectionate son,
"ALGERNON.

"The Right Hon. the Earl of Crabs, &c.
"Sizes Court, Bucks."

To this affeckshnat letter his lordship replied, by return of poast, as follos:

"My dear Algernon,—Your letter came safe to hand, and I enclose you the letter for Lord Bobtail as you desire. He is a kind man, and has one of the best cooks in Europe.

"We were all charmed with your warm remembrances of us, not having seen you for seven years. We cannot but be pleased at the family affection which, in spite of time and absence, still clings so fondly to home. It is a sad, selfish world, and very few who have entered it can afford to keep those fresh feelings which you have, my dear son.

"May you long retain them, is a fond father's earnest prayer. Be sure, dear Algernon, that they will be through life your greatest comfort, as well as your best worldly ally; consoling you in misfortune, cheering you in depression, aiding and inspiring you to exertion and success.

"I am sorry, truly sorry, that my account at Coutts's is so low, just now, as to render a payment of your allowance for the present impossible. I see by my book that I owe you now nine quarters, or 450*l*. Depend on it, my dear boy, that they shall be faithfully paid over to you on the first opportunity.

"By the way, I have enclosed some extracts from the newspapers, which may interest you; and have received a very strange letter from a Mr. Blewitt, about a play transaction, which, I suppose, is the case alluded to in these prints. He says you won 4700*l*. from one Dawkins; that the lad paid it; that he, Blewitt, was to go what he calls 'snacks' in the winning; but that you refused to share the booty. How can you, my dear boy, quarrel with these vulgar people, or lay yourself in any way open to their attacks? I have played myself a good deal, and there is no man living who can accuse me of a

doubtful act. You should either have shot this Blewitt or paid him.
Now, as the matter stands, it is too late to do the former; and,
perhaps, it would be Quixotic to perform the latter. My dearest
boy! recollect through life that *you never can afford to be dishonest
with a rogue.* Two thousand four hundred pounds was a great *coup*
to be won.

"As you are now in such high feather, can you, dearest Algernon!
lend me five hundred pounds? Upon my soul and honour, I will
repay you. Your brothers and sisters send you their love. I need not
add, that you have always the blessings of your affectionate father,

"CRABS.

"P.S.—Make it 550, and I will give you my note of hand for a
thousand."

*   *   *   *   *

I neadnt say, that this did not *quite* enter into Deuceace's eyedears.
Lend his father 500 pound, indeed! He'd as soon have lent him a box
on the year! In the fust place, he hadn seen old Crabs for seven years,
as that nobleman remarked in his epistol; in the secknd, he hated him,
and they hated each other; and nex, if master had loved his father ever
so much, he loved somebody else better—his father's son, namely: and,
sooner than deprive that exlent young man of a penny, he'd have sean all
the fathers in the world hangin at Newgat, and all the "beloved ones," as
he called his sisters, the Lady Deuceacisses, so many convix at Bottomy
Bay.

The newspaper parrowgrafs shewed that, however secret *we* wished to
keep the play transaction, the public knew it now full well. Blewitt, as I
found after, was the author of the libles which appeared, right and left,—

"GAMBLING IN HIGH LIFE: the *Honourable* Mr. De—c—ce again!
—This celebrated whist-player has turned his accomplishments
to some profit. On Friday, the 16th January, he won five thousand pounds from a *very* young gentleman, Th—m—s Sm—th
D—wk—ns, Esq., and lost two thousand five hundred to R. Bl—
w—tt, Esq., of the T—mple. Mr. D. very honourably paid the sum
lost by him to the honourable whist-player, but we have not heard
that, *before his sudden trip to Paris,* Mr. D—uc—ce paid *his* losings
to Mr. Bl—w—tt."

Nex came a "Notice to Corryspondents:"

"Fair Play asks us, if we know of the gambling doings of the notorious Deuceace? We answer, WE DO; and, in our very next Number,
propose to make some of them public."

*   *   *   *   *

They didn't appear, however; but, on the contry, the very same newspepper, which had been before so abusiff of Deuceace, was now loud in his praise. It said:

> "A paragraph was inadvertently admitted into our paper of last week, most unjustly assailing the character of a gentleman of high birth and talents, the son of the exemplary E—rl of Cr—bs. We repel, with scorn and indignation, the dastardly falsehoods of the malignant slanderer who vilified Mr. De—ce—ce, and beg to offer that gentleman the only reparation in our power for having thus tampered with his unsullied name. We disbelieve the *ruffian* and *his story*, and most sincerely regret that such a tale, or *such a writer*, should ever have been brought forward to the readers of this paper."

This was satisfactory, and no mistake; and much pleased we were at the denial of this conshentious editor. So much pleased, that master sent him a ten-pound noat, and his complymints. He'd sent another to the same address, *before* this parrowgraff was printed; why, I can't think: for I woodnt suppose any thing musnary in a littery man.

Well, after this bisniss was concluded, the currier hired, the carridge smartened a little, and me set up in my new livries, we bade ajew to Bulong in the grandest state posbill. What a figger we cut! and, my i, what a figger the postillion cut! A cock-hat, a jackit made out of a cow's skin (it was in cold whether), a pig-tale about 3 fit in lenth, and a pare of boots! Oh, sich a pare! A bishop might almost have preached out of one, or a modrat-sized famly slep in it. Me and Mr. Schwigschnaps, the currier, sate behind in the rumbill; master aloan in the inside, as grand as a Turk, and rapt up in his fine fir-cloak. Off we sett, bowing gracefly to the crowd; the harniss-bells jinglin, the great white hosses snortin, kickin, and squeelin, and the postillium cracking his wip, as loud as if he'd been drivin her majesty the quean.

*   *   *   *   *

Well, I shant describe our voyitch. We passed sefral sitties, willitches, and metrappolishes; sleeping the fust night at Amiens, witch, as every boddy knows, is famous ever since the year 1802 for what's called the Pease of Amiens. We had some, very good, done with sugar and brown sos, in the Amiens way. But, after all the boasting about them, I think I like our marrowphats better.

Speaking of wedgytables, another singler axdent happened here concarning them. Master, who was brexfasting before going away, told me to go and get him his fur travling-shoes. I went and toald the waiter of the inn, who stared, grinned (as these chaps always do), said *"Bong"* (which means, very well), and presently came back.

I'm blest, if he didn't bring master a plate of cabbitch! Would you bleave it, that now, in the nineteenth sentry, when they say there's schoolmasters abroad, these stewpid French jackasses are so extonishingly ignorant as to call a *cabbidge* a *shoo!* Never, never let it be said, after this, that these benighted, souperstitious, misrabble *savidges,* are equill, in any respex, to the great Brittish people! The moor I travvle, the moor I see the world, and other natiums, I am proud of my own, and despise and deplore the retchid ignorance of the rest of Yourup.

*　　*　　*　　*　　*

My remark on Parris you shall have by an early opportunity. Me and Deuceace played some curious pranx there, I can tell you.

C. Y.

THE YELLOWPLUSH CORRESPONDENCE

Nos. VI–VIII.

———◇———

MR. DEUCEACE AT PARIS.

CHAP. I.—THE TWO BUNDLES OF HAY.

LEFTENANT-GENERAL SIR GEORGE GRIFFIN, K.C.B., was about seventy-five years old when he left this life, and the East Ingine army, of which he was a distinguisht ornyment. Sir George's fust appearance in Injar was in the character of a cabbing-boy to a vessel; from which he rose to be clerk to the owners at Calcutta, from which he became all of a sudden a capting in the Company's service; and so rose and rose, until he rose to be a leftenant-general, when he stopped rising all togther—hopping the twigg of this life, as drummers, generals, dustmen, and emprors, must do.

Sir George did not leave any male hair to perpatuate the name of Griffin. A widow of about twenty-seven, and a daughter avaritching twenty-three, was left behind to deplor his loss, and share his proppaty. On old Sir George's deth, his intresting widdo and orfan, who had both been with him in Injer, returned home—tried London for a few months, did not like it, and resolved on a trip to Paris, where very small London people become very great ones, if they've money, as these Griffinses had. The intelligent reader kneed not be told that Miss Griffin was not the daughter of Lady Griffin; for though marritches are made tolrabbly early in Injer, people are not quite so precoashoos as all that: the fact is, Lady G. was Sir George's second wife. I need scarcely add, that Miss Matilda Griffin was the offspring of his fust marritch.

Miss Leonora Kicksey, a hansum, lively Islington gal, taken out to Calcutta, and, amongst his other goods, very comforably disposed of by her uncle, Capting Kicksey, was one-and-twenty when she married Sir George at seventy-one; and the 13 Miss Kickseys, nine of whom kep a school at Islington (the other 4 being married variously in the city), were not a little envius of my lady's luck, and not a little proud of their relatiunship to her. One of 'em, Miss Jemima Kicksey, the oldest, and by no means the least ugly of the sett, was staying with her ladyship, and gev me all the parteklars. Of the rest of the famly, being of a lo sort, I in course no nothink; *my* acquaintance, thank my stars, don't lie among them, or the likes of them.

Well, this Miss Jemima lived with her younger and more fortnat sister, in the qualaty of companion, or toddy. Poar thing! I'd a soon be a gally slave, as lead the life she did! Every body in the house dispised her; her ladyship insulted her; the very kitching gals scorned and flouted her. She roat the notes, she kep the bills, she made the tea, she whipped the chocklate, she cleaned the Canary birds, and gev out the linning for the wash. She was my lady's walking pocket, or rittycule; and fetched and carried her handkercher, or her smell-bottle, like a well-bred spaniel. All night, at her ladyship's swarries, she thumped kidrills (nobody ever thought of asking *her* to dance!); when Miss Griffin sung, she played the piano, and was scolded because the singer was out of tune; abommanating dogs, she never drove out without her ladyship's puddle in her lap; and, reglarly unwell in a carriage, she never got any thing but the back seat. Poar Jemima! I can see her now in my lady's *secknd-best* old clothes (the ladies'-maids always got the prime leavings): a liloc sattn gown, crumpled, blotched, and greasy; a pair of white sattn shoos, of the colour of Inger rubber; a faded yellow velvet hat, with a wreath of hartifishl flowers run to sead, and a bird of Parrowdice perched on the top of it, melumcolly and moulting, with only a couple of feathers left in its unfortunate tail.

Besides this ornyment to their saloon, Lady and Miss Griffin kep a number of other servants in the kitching; 2 ladies'-maids; 2 footmin, six feet high each, crimson coats, goold knots, and white cassymear pantyloons; a coachmin to match; a page; and a Shassure, a kind of servant only known among forriners, and who looks more like a major-general than any other mortial, wearing a cock-hat, a unicorn covered with silver lace, mustashos, eplets, and a sword by his side. All these to wait upon two ladies; not counting a host of the fair six, such as cooks, scullion, housekeepers, and so forth.

My Lady Griffin's lodging was at forty pound a-week, in a grand sweet of rooms in the Plas Vandome at Paris. And, having thus described their house, and their servants' hall, I may give a few words of description concerning the ladies themselves.

In the fust place, and in coarse, they hated each other. My lady was twenty-seven—a widdo of two years—fat, fair, and rosy. A slow, quiet, cold-looking woman, as those fair-haired gals genrally are, it seemed difficult to rouse her either into likes or dislikes; to the former, at least. She never loved any body but *one*, and that was herself. She hated, in her calm, quiet way, almost every one else who came near her—every one, from her neighbour the duke, who had slighted her at dinner, down to John the footman, who had torn a hole in her train. I think this woman's heart was like one of them lithograffic stones, you *can't rub out any thing* when once it's drawn or wrote on it; nor could you out of her ladyship's stone—heart, I mean—in the shape of an affront, a slight, or a real or phansied injury. She boar an exlent, irreprotchable character, against which the tongue of scandle never wagged. She was allowed to be the best wife posbill—and so she was; but she killed her old husband in two years, as dead as ever Mr. Thurtell killed Mr. William Weare. She never got into a passion, not she—she never said a rude word; but she'd a genius—a genius which many women have—of making *a hell* of a house, and tort'ring the poor creatures of her family, until they were wellnigh drove mad.

Miss Matilda Griffin was a good deal uglier, and about as amiable as her mother-in-law. She was crooked, and squinted: my lady, to do her justas, was straight, and looked the same way with her i's. She was dark, and my lady was fair—sentimental, as her ladyship was cold. My lady was never in a passion—Miss Matilda always; and awfle were the scenes which used to pass between these 2 women, and the wickid, wickid quarls which took place. Why did they live together? There was the mistry. Not related, and hating each other like pison, it would surely have been easier to remain seprat, and so have detested each other at a distans.

As for the fortune which old Sir George had left, that, it was clear, was very considrabble—300 thowsnd lb. at the least, as I have heard say. But nobody knew how it was disposed of. Some said that her ladyship was sole mistriss of it, others that it was divided, others that she had only a life inkum, and that the money was all to go (as was natral) to Miss Matilda. These are subjix which are not, praps, very interesting to the British public; but were mighty important to my master, the Honrabble Algernon Percy Deuceace, esquire, barrister-at-law, etsettler, etsettler.

For I've forgot to inform you that my master was very intimat in this house; and that we were now comfortably settled at the Hotel Mirabew (pronounced Marobô in French), in the Rew delly Pay, at Paris. We had our cab, and two riding horses; our banker's book, and a thousand pound for a balants at Lafitt's; our club at the corner of the Rew Gramong; our share of a box at the oppras; our apartments, spacious and elygant; our swarries at court; our dinners at his exlensy Lord Bobtail's, and elsewhere. Thanks to poar Dawkins's five thousand pound, we were as complete a gentleman as any in Paris.

Now my master, like a wise man as he was, seaing himself at the head of a smart sum of money, and in a country were his debts could not bother him, determined to give up for the presnt every think like gambling—at least, high play; as for losing or winning a ralow of Napoleums at whist or ecarty, it did not matter: it looks like money to do such things, and gives a kind of respectabillaty. "But as for play, he wouldn't—O no! not for worlds!—do such a thing." "He *had* played, like other young men of fashn, and won and lost [old fox! he didn't say he had *paid*]; but he had given up the amusement, and was now determined, he said, to live on his inkum." The fact is, my master was doing his very best to act the respectable man: and a very good game it is, too; but it requires a precious great roag to play it.

He made his appearans reglar at church—me carrying a handsome large black marocky Prayer-book and Bible, with the psalms and lessons marked out with red ribbings; and you'd have thought, as I graivly laid the volloms down before him, and as he berried his head in his nicely brushed hat, before survice began, that such a pious, proper, morl, young nobleman was not to be found in the whole of the peeridge. It was a comfort to look at him. Efry old tabby and dowyger at my Lord Bobtail's turned up the wights of their i's when they spoke of him, and vowd they had never seen such a dear, daliteful, exlent young man. What a good son he must be, they said; and, oh, what a good son-in-law! He had the pick of all the English gals at Paris before we had been there 3 months. But, unfortnatly, most of them were poar; and love and a cottidge was not quite in master's way of thinking.

Well, about this time my Lady Griffin and Miss G. maid their appearants at Parris, and master, who was up to snough, very soon changed his noat. He sate near them at chapple, and sung hims with my lady; he danced with 'em at the embassy balls; he road with them in the Boy de Balong and the Shandeleasies (which is the French High Park); he roat potry in Miss Griffin's halbim, and sang jewets along with her and Lady Griffin; he brought sweatmeats for the puddle-dog; he gave money to the footmin, kissis and gloves to the sniggering ladies'-maids; he was sivvle even to poar Miss Kicksey: there wasn't a single soal at the Griffinses that didn't adoar this good young man.

The ladies, if they hated befoar, you may be sure detested each other now wuss than ever. There had been always a jallowsy between them; miss jellows of her mother-in-law's bewty; madam of miss's espree; miss taunting my lady about the school at Islington, and my lady snearing at miss for her squint and her crookid back. And now came a stronger caws. They both fell in love with Mr. Deuceace—my lady, that is to say, as much as she could, with her cold selfish temper. She liked Deuceace, who amused her, and made her laff. She liked his manners, his riding, and his good loox; and, being a *pervinew* herself, had a dubble respect for real aristocratick flesh and blood. Miss's love, on the contry, was all flams and fury. She'd always been at this work from the time she had been at school, where she very nigh run away with a Frentch master; next with a footman (which I may say, in confidence, is by no means unnatral nor unusyouall, as I *could shew if I liked*); and so had been going on sins fifteen. She reglarly flung herself at Deuceace's head—such sighing, crying, and ogling, I never see. Often was I ready to bust out laffin, as I brought master skoars of rose-coloured *billydoos*, folded up like cock-hats, and smellin like barber's shops, which this very tender young lady used to address to him. Now, though master was a scoundrill, and no mistake, he was a gentlemin, and a man of good breading; and miss *came a little too strong* (pardon the wulgarity of the xpression) with her hardor and attachmint, for one of his taste. Besides, she had a crookid spine, and a squint; so that (supposing their fortns tolrabbly equal) Deuceace reely preferred the mother-in-law.

Now, then, it was his bisniss to find out which had the most money. With an English famly, this would have been easy: a look at a will at Doctor Commons'es would settle the matter at once. But this India naybob's will was at Calcutty, or some outlandish place; and there was no getting sight of a coppy of it. I will do Mr. Algernon Deuceace the justas to say, that he was so little musnary in his love for Lady Griffin, that he would have married her gladly, even if she had ten thousand pound less than Miss Matilda. In the mean time, his plan was to keep 'em both in play, until he could strike the best fish of the two—not a difficult matter for a man of his genus; besides, Miss was hooked for certain.

CHAP. II.—"HONOUR THY FATHER."

I said that my master was adoared by every person in my Lady Griffin's extablishmint. I should have said by every person excep one,— a young French gnlmn, that is, who, before our appearants, had been mighty particklar with my lady, ockupying by her side exackly the same pasition which the Honrabble Mr. Deuceace now held. It was bewtiffle and headifying to see how coolly that young nobleman kicked the poar Shevalliay de L'Orge out of his shoes, and how gracefully he himself stept into 'em. Munseer de L'Orge was a smart young French jentleman, of about my master's age and good looks, but not possesst of $\frac{1}{2}$ my master's impidince. Not that that quallaty is uncommon in France; but few, very few, had it to such a degree as my exlent employer, Mr. Deuceace. Besides, De L'Orge was reglarly and reely in love with Lady Griffin, and master only pretending: he had, of coars, an advantitch, which the poar Frentchman never could git. He was all smiles and gaty, while Delorge was ockward and melumcolly. My master had said twenty pretty things to Lady Griffin, befor the shevalier had finished smoothing his hat, staring at her, and sighing fit to bust his weskit. O luv, luv! *This* isn't the way to win a woman, or my name's not Fitzroy Yellowplush! Myself, when I begun my carear among the fair six, I was always sighing and moping, like this poar Frenchman. What was the consquints? The foar fust women I adoared lafft at me, and left me for somethink more lively. With the rest I have edopted a diffrent game, and with tolrabble suxess, I can tell you. But this is eggatism, which I aboar.

Well, the long and short of it is, that Munseer Ferdinand Hyppolite Xavier Stanislas, Shevallier de L'Orge, was reglar cut out by Munseer Algernon Percy Deuceace, Exquire. Poar Ferdinand did not leave the house—he hadn't the heart to do that—nor had my lady the desire to dismiss him. He was usefle in a thousand diffrent ways,—gitting oppra boxes, and invitations to Frentch swarries, bying gloves and O de Co-long, writing French noats, and such like. Always let me recommend an English famly, going to Paris, to have at least one young man of the sort about them. Never mind how old your ladyship is, he will make love to you; never mind what errints you send him upon, he'll trot off and do them. Besides, he's always quite and well-drest, and never drinx moar than a pint of wind at dinner, which (as I say) is a pint to consider. Such a conveniants of a man was Munseer de L'Orge—the greatest use and com-fort to my lady posbill; if it was but to laff at his bad pronounciatium of English, it was somethink amusink: the fun was to pit him against poar Miss Kicksey, she speakin French, and he our naytif British tong.

My master, to do him justace, was perfickly sivvle to this poar young Frenchman; and, having kicked him out of the place which he occupied, sertingly treated his fallen anymy with every rispect and consideration. Poar modist down-hearted little Ferdinand adoared my lady as a goddice; and so he was very polite, likewise, to my master—never ventring once to be jellows of him, or to question my Lady Griffin's right to change her lover, if she choase to do so.

Thus, then, matters stood; master had two strinx to his bo, and might take either the widdo or the orfn, as he preferred: *com bong lwee somblay*, as the Frentch say. His only pint was to discover how the money was dis-posed off, which evidently belonged to one or other, or boath. At any rate, he was sure of one; as sure as any mortial man can be in this sublimary spear, where nothink is suttn excep unsertnty.

*   *   *   *   *

A very unixpected insdint here took place, which in a good deal changed my master's calkylations.

One night, after conducting the two ladies to the oppra, after suppink of white soop, sammy-de-perdrow, and shampang glassy (which means, eyced), at their house in the Plas Vandom, me and master droav hoam in the cab, as happy as posbill.

"Chawls, you d—d scoundrel," says he to me (for he was in an exlent humer), "when I'm marrid, I'll dubbil your wagis."

This he might do, to be sure, without injaring himself, seeing that he had as yet never paid me any. But, what then? Law bless us! things would be at a pretty pass if we suvvants only lived on our *wagis*: our puckwisits is the thing, and no mistake.

I ixprest my gratatude as best I could; swoar that it wasnt for wagis I served him—that I would as leaf weight upon him for nothink; and that never, never, so long as I livd, would I, of my own acord, part from such an exlent master. By the time these two spitches had been made—my spitch and his—we arrived at the Hôtel Mirabeu; which, as every body knows, aint very distant from the Plas Vandome. Up we marched to our apartmince, me carrying the light and the cloax, master hummink a hair out of the oppra, as merry as a lark.

I opened the doar of our salong. There was lights already in the room; an empty shampang bottle roaling on the floar, another on the table; near which the sofy was drawn, and on it lay a stout old genlmn, smoaking seagars as if he'd bean in an inn tap-room.

Deuceace (who abommanates seagars, as I've already shewn) bust into a furious raige against the genlmn, whom he could hardly see for the smoak; and, with a number of oaves quite unnecessary to repeat, asked him what bisniss he'd there.

The smoakin chap rose, and, laying down his seagar, began a ror of laffin, and said, "What, Algy! my boy! don't you know me?"

The reader may, praps, recklect a very affecting letter which was published in the last Number of these memoars; in which the writer requested a loan of five hundred pound from Mr. Algernon Deuceace, and which boar the respected signatur of the Earl of Crabs, Mr. Deuceace's own father. It was that distinguished arastycrat who now was smokin and laffin in our room.

My Lord Crabs was, as I preshumed, about 60 years old. A stowt, burly, red-faced, bald-headed nobleman, whose nose seemed blushing at what his mouth was continually swallowing; whose hand, praps, trembled a little; and whose thy and legg was not quite so full or as steddy as they had been in former days. But he was a respecktabble, fine-looking, old nobleman; and though, it must be confest, ½ drunk when we fust made our appearance in the salong, yet by no means moor so than a reel noblemin ought to be.

"What, Algy! my boy!" shouts out his lordship, advancing and seasing master by the hand, "doan't you know your own father?"

Master seemed anythink but overhappy. "My lord," says he, looking very pail, and speakin rayther slow, "I didn't—I confess—the unexpected pleasure—of seeing you in Paris. The fact is, sir," said he, recovering himself a little; "the fact is, there was such a confounded smoke of tobacco in the room, that I really could not see who the stranger was who had paid me such an unexpected visit."

"A bad habit, Algernon; a bad habit," said my lord, lighting another segar: "a disgusting and filthy practice, which you, my dear child, will do very well to avoid. It is at best, dear Algernon, but a nasty, idle pastime,

unfitting a man as well for mental exertion as for respectable society; sac-
rificing, at once, the vigour of the intellect and the graces of the person.
By the by, what infernal bad tobacco they have, too, in this hotel. Could
not you send your servant to get me a few segars at the Café de Paris?
Give him a five-franc piece, and let him go at once, that's a good fellow."

Here his lordship hiccupt, and drank off a fresh tumbler of shampang.
Very sulkily, master drew out the coin, and sent me on the errint.

Knowing the Café de Paris to be shut at that hour, I didn't say a word,
but quietly establisht myself in the anteroom; where, as it happend by a
singler coinstdints, I could hear every word of the conversation between
this exlent pair of relatifs.

"Help yourself, and get another bottle," says my lord, after a sollum
paws. My poar master, the king of all other compnies in which he moved,
seamed here but to play secknd fiddill, and went to the cubbard, from
which his father had already igstracted two bottils of his prime Sillary.

He put it down before his father, coft, spit, opened the windows, stirred
the fire, yawned, clapt his hand to his forehead, and suttnly seamed as
uneezy as a genlmn could be. But it was of no use; the old one would not
budg. "Help yourself," says he again, "and pass me the bottil."

"You are very good, father," says master; "but, really, I neither drink
nor smoke."

"Right, my boy; quite right. Talk about a good conscience in this life—
a good *stomack* is everythink. No bad nights, no headachs—eh? Quite
cool and collected for your law-studies in the morning—eh?" And the old
nobleman here grinned, in a manner which would have done creddit to
Mr. Grimoldi.

Master sate pale and wincing, as I've seen a pore soldier under the cat.
He didn't anser a word. His exlent pa went on, warming as he continued
to speak, and drinking a fresh glas at evry full stop.

"How you must improve, with such talents and such principles! Why,
Algernon, all London talks of your industry and perseverance! You're not
merely a philosopher, man; hang it! you've got the philospher's stone.
Fine rooms, fine horses, champagne, and all for 200 a-year!"

"I presume, sir," says my master, "that you mean the two hundred a-
year which *you* pay me?"

"The very sum, my boy; the very sum!" cries my lord, laffin as if he
would die. "Why, that's the wonder! I never pay the two hundred a-
year, and you keep all this state up upon nothing. Give me your secret,
O you young Trismegistus! Tell your old father how such wonders can be
worked, and I will—yes, then, upon my word, I will—pay you your two
hundred a-year!"

"*Enfin*, my lord," says Mr. Deuceace, starting up, and losing all patience, "will you have the goodness to tell me what this visit means? You

leave me to starve, for all you care; and you grow mighty facetious because I earn my bread. You find me in prosperity, and——"

"Precisely, my boy; precisely. Keep your temper, and pass that bottle. I find you in prosperity; and a young gentleman of your genius and acquirements asks me why I seek his society? Oh, Algernon! Algernon! this is not worthy of such a profound philosopher. Why do I seek you? Why, because you *are* in prosperity, O my son! else, why the devil should I bother myself about you? Did I, your poor mother, or your family, ever get from you a single affectionate feeling? Did we, or any other of your friends or intimates, ever know you to be guilty of a single honest or generous action? Did we ever pretend any love for you, or you for us? Algernon Deuceace, you don't want a father to tell you that you are a swindler and a spendthrift! I have paid thousands for the debts of yourself and your brothers; and, if you pay nobody else, I am determined you shall repay me. You would not do it by fair means, when I wrote to you and asked you for a loan of money. I knew you would not. Had I written again to warn you of my coming, you would have given me the slip; and so I came, uninvited, to *force* you to repay me. *That's* why I am here, Mr. Algernon; and so, help yourself and pass the bottle."

After this speach, the old genlmn sunk down on the sofa, and puffed as much smoke out of his mouth as if he'd been the chimley of a steam-injian. I was pleasd, I confess, with the sean, and liked to see this venrabble and virtuous old man a nocking his son about the hed; just as Deuceace had done with Mr. Richard Blewitt, as I've before shewn. Master's face was, fust, red-hot; next, chawk-white; and then, sky-blew. He looked, for all the world, like Mr. Tippy Cooke in the tragady of *Frankinstang*. At last, he mannidged to speek.

"My lord," says he, "I expected when I saw you that some such scheme was on foot. Swindler and spendthrift as I am, at least it is but a family failing; and I am indebted for my virtues to my father's precious example. Your lordship has, I perceive, added drunkenness to the list of your accomplishments; and, I suppose, under the influence of that gentlemanly excitement, have come to make these preposterous propositions to me. When you are sober, you will, perhaps, be wise enough to know, that, fool as I may be, I am not such a fool as you think me; and that if I have got money, I intend to keep it—every farthing of it, though you were to be ten times as drunk, and ten times as threatening, as you are now."

"Well, well, my boy," said Lord Crabs, who seemed to have been half-asleep during his son's oratium, and received all his smears and surcasms with the most complete good-humour; "well, well, if you will resist—*tant pis pour toi*—I've no desire to ruin you, recollect, and am not in the slightest degree angry; but I must and will have a thousand pounds. You had better give me the money at once; it will cost you more if you don't."

"Sir," says Mr. Deuceace, "I will be equally candid. I would not give you a farthing to save you from——"

Here I thought proper to open the doar, and, touching my hat, said, "I have been to the Café de Paris, my lord, but the house is shut."

"*Bon:* there's a good lad; you may keep the five francs. And now, get me a candle and shew me down stairs."

But my master seized the wax taper. "Pardon me, my lord," says he. "What! a servant do it, when your son is in the room? Ah, *par exemple*, my dear father," said he, laughing, "you think there is no politeness left among us." And he led the way out.

"Good night, my dear boy," said Lord Crabs.

"God bless you, sir," says he. "Are you wrapped warm? Mind the step!" And so this affeckshnate pair parted.

CHAP. III.—MINEWVRING.

Master rose the nex morning with a dismal countinants—he seamed to think that his pa's visit boded him no good. I heard him muttering at his brexfast, and fumbling among his hundred pound notes; once he had laid a parsle of them aside (I knew what he meant), to send 'em to his father. "But, no," says he, at last, clutching them all up together again, and throwing them into his escritaw; "what harm can he do me? If he is a knave, I know another who's full as sharp. Let's see if we cannot beat him at his own weapons." With that, Mr. Deuceace drest hisself in his best clothes, and marched off to the Plas Vandom, to pay his cort to the fair widdo and the intresting orfn.

It was abowt ten o'clock, and he proposed to the ladies, on seeing them, a number of planns for the day's rackryation. Riding in the Body Balong, going to the Twillaries to see King Looy Disweet (who was then the raining sufferin of the French crownd), go to Chapple, and, finely, a dinner at 5 o'clock at the Caffy de Parry; whents they were all to ajourn, to see a new peace at the theatre of the Pot St. Martin, called *Susannar and the Elders.*

The gals agread to every think, exsep the two last prepositiums. "We have an engagement, my dear Mr. Algernon," said my lady. "Look—a very kind letter from Lady Bobtail." And she handed over a pafewmd noat from that exolted lady. It ran thus:

"*Fbg. St. Honoré, Thursday,*
Feb. 15, 1817.

"My dear Lady Griffin,—It is an age since we met. Harassing public duties occupy so much myself and Lord Bobtail, that we have scarce time to see our private friends; among whom, I hope, my dear Lady Griffin will allow me to rank her. Will you excuse so very unceremonious an invitation, and dine with us at the Embassy to-day? We shall be *en petit comité*, and shall have the pleasure of hearing, I hope, some of your charming daughter's singing in the evening. I ought, perhaps, to have addressed a separate note to dear Miss Griffin; but I hope she will pardon a poor *diplomate*, who has so many letters to write, you know.

"Farewell till seven, when I *positively must* see you both. Ever, dearest Lady Griffin, your affectionate

"ELIZA BOBTAIL."

Such a letter from the ambassdriss, brot by the ambasdor's Shassure, and sealed with his seal of arms, would affect any body in the middling ranx of life. It droav Lady Griffin mad with delight; and, long before my master's arrivle, she'd sent Mortimer and Fitzclarence, her two footmin, along with a polite reply in the affummatif.

Master read the noat with no such fealinx of joy. He felt that there was somethink a-going on behind the seans, and, though he could not tell how, was sure that some danger was near him. That old fox of a father of his had begun his M'Inations pretty early!

Deuceace handed back the letter; sneared, and poohd, and hinted that such an invatation was an insult at best (what he called a *pees ally*); and, the ladies might depend upon it, was only sent because Lady Bob-tail wanted to fill up two spare places at her table. But Lady Griffin and miss would not have his insinwations; they knew too fu lords ever to refuse an invitatium from any one of them. Go they would; and poor Deuceace must dine alone. After they had been on their ride, and had had their other amusemince, master came back with them, chatted, and laft; mighty sarkastix with my lady; tender and sentrymentle with miss; and left them both in high sperrits to perform their twollet, before dinner.

As I came to the door (for I was as famillyer as a servnt of the house), as I came into the drawing-room to announts his cab, I saw master very qui-etly taking his pocket-book (or *pot-fool*, as the French call it) and thrusting it under one of the cushinx of the sofa. What game is this? thinx I.

Why, this was the game. In abowt two hours, when he knew the ladies were gon, he pretends to be vastly anxious abowt the loss of his potfolio; and back he goes to Lady Griffinses, to seek for it there.

"Pray," says he, on going in, "ask Miss Kicksey if I may see her for a single moment." And down comes Miss Kicksey, quite smiling, and happy to see him.

"Law, Mr. Deuceace!" says she, trying to blush as hard as ever she could, "you quite surprise me! I don't know whether I ought, really, being alone, to admit a gentleman."

"Nay, don't say so, dear Miss Kicksey! for, do you know, I came here for a double purpose—to ask about a pocket-book which I have lost, and

Jennie Grant welcomes the Ladies his parting benediction

Published by James Fraser 215 Regent Street London

may, perhaps, have left here; and then, to ask if you will have the great
goodness to pity a solitary bachelor, and give him a cup of your nice tea?"

Nice tea! I thot I should have split; for, I'm blest if master had eaten a
morsle of dinner!

Never mind: down to tea they sate. "Do you take cream and sugar,
dear sir?" says poar Kicksey, with a voice as tender as a tuttle-duff.

"Both, dearest Miss Kicksey!" answers master; and stowed in a power
of sashong and muffinx, which would have done honour to a washa-
woman.

I sha'n't describe the conversation that took place betwigst master and
this young lady. The reader, praps, knows y Deuceace took the trouble to
talk to her for an hour, and to swallow all her tea. He wanted to find out
from her all she knew about the famly money matters, and settle at once
which of the two Griffinses he should marry.

The poar thing, of cors, was no match for such a man as my master. In a
quarter of an hour, he had, if I may use the igspression, "turned her inside
out." He knew every thing that she knew, and that, poar creature, was
very little. There was nine thousand a-year, she had heard say, in money,
in houses, in banks in Injar, and what not. Boath the ladies signed papers for selling or buying, and the money seemed equilly divided betwigst
them.

Nine thousand a-year! Deuceace went away, his cheex tingling, his art
beating. He, without a penny, could nex morning, if he liked, be master
of five thousand per hannum!

Yes. But how? Which had the money, the mother or the daughter? All
the tea-drinking had not taught him this piece of nollidge; and Deuceace
thought it a pity that he could not marry both.

*   *   *   *   *

The ladies came back at night, mightaly pleased with their reseption
at the ambasdor's; and, stepping out of their carriage, bid coachmin drive
on with a gentleman who had handed them out,—a stout old gentleman,
who shook hands most tenderly at parting, and promised to call often
upon my Lady Griffin. He was so polite, that he wanted to mount the
stairs with her ladyship; but no, she would not suffer it. "Edward," says
she to coachmin, quite loud, and pleased that all the people in the hotel
should hear her, "you will take the carriage, and drive *his lordship* home."
Now, can you gess who his lordship was? The Right Hon. Earl of Crabs,
to be sure; the very old gnlmn whom I had seen on such charming terms
with his son the day before. Master knew this the nex day, and began to
think he had been a fool to deny his pa the thousand pound.

Now, though the suckmstansies of the dinner at the ambasdor's only
came to my years some time after, I may as well relate 'em here, word for

word, as they was told me by the very genlmn who waited behind Lord Crabseses chair.

There was only a *"petty comity"* at dinner, as Lady Bobtail said; and my Lord Crabs was placed betwigst the two Griffinses, being mighty ellygant and palite to both. "Allow me," says he to Lady G. (between the soop and the fish), "my dear madam, to thank you—fervently thank you, for your goodness to my poor boy. Your ladyship is too young to experience, but, I am sure, far too tender not to understand the gratitude which must fill a fond parent's heart, for kindness shewn to his child. Believe me," says my lord, looking her full and tenderly in the face, "that the favours you have done to another have been done equally to myself, and awaken in my bosom the same grateful and affectionate feelings with which you have already inspired my son Algernon."

Lady Griffin blusht, and droopt her head till her ringlets fell into her fish-plate; and she swallowed Lord Crabs's flumry just as she would so many musharuins. My lord (whose powers of slack-jaw was notoarious) nex addrasst another spitch to Miss Griffin. He said he'd heard how Deuceace was *situated.* Miss blusht—what a happy dog he was—Miss blusht crimson, and then he sighed deeply, and began eating his turbat and lobster sos. Master was a good 'un at flumry; but, law bless you! he was no moar equill to the old man than a molehill is to a mounting. Before the night was over, he had made as much progress as another man would in a ear. One almost forgot his red nose, and his big stomick, and his wicked leering i's, in his gentle, insiniwating woice, his fund of annygoats, and, above all, the bewtifle, morl, religious, and honrabble toan of his genral conversation. Praps you will say that these ladies were, for such rich pipple, mightily esaly captivated; but recklect, my dear sir, that they were fresh from Injar,—that they'd not sean many lords,—that they adoard the peeridge, as every honest woman does in England who has proper feelinx, and has read the fashnabble novvles,—and that here at Paris was their very fust step into fashnabble sosiaty.

Well, after dinner, while Miss Matilda was singing *"Die tantie,"* or *"Dip your chair,"* or some of them sellabrated Italyin hairs (when she began, this gall, hang me if she'd ever stop), my lord gets hold of Lady Griffin again, and gradgaly begins to talk to her in a very diffrent strane.

"What a blessing it is for us all," says he, "that Algernon has found a friend so respectable as your ladyship."

"Indeed, my lord; and why? I suppose I am not the only respectable friend that Mr. Deuceace has?"

"No, surely; not the only one he *has had*: his birth, and, permit me to say, his relationship to myself, have procured him many. But—" (here my lord heaved a very affecting and large sigh.)

"But what?" says my lady, laffing at the igspression of his dismal face. "You don't mean that Mr. Deuceace has lost them, or is unworthy of them?"

"I trust not, my dear madam, I trust not; but he is wild, thoughtless, extravagant, and embarrassed; and you know a man under these circumstances is not very particular as to his associates."

"Embarrassed? Good heavens! He says he has two thousand a-year left him by a godmother; and he does not seem even to spend his income—a very handsome independence, too, for a bachelor."

My lord nodded his head sadly, and said,—"Will your ladyship give me your word of honour to be secret? My son has but a thousand a-year, which I allow him, and is heavily in debt. He has played, madam, I fear; and for this reason I am so glad to hear that he is in a respectable domestic circle, where he may learn, in the presence of far greater and purer attractions, to forget the dice-box, and the low company which has been his bane."

My Lady Griffin looked very grave indeed. Was it true? Was Deuceace sincere in his professions of love, or was he only a sharper wooing her for her money? Could she doubt her informer? his own father, and, what's more, a real flesh and blood pear of parlyment? She determined she would try him. Praps she did not know she had liked Deuceace so much, until she kem to feel how much she should *hate* him, if she found he'd been playing her false.

The evening was over, and back they came, as we've seen,—my lord driving home in my lady's carridge, her ladyship and Miss walking up stairs to their own apartmince.

Here, for a wonder, was poar Miss Kicksy quite happy and smiling, and evidently full of a secret,—something mighty pleasant, to judge from her loox. She did not long keep it. As she was making tea for the ladies (for in that house they took a cup reglar before bedtime), "Well, my lady," says she, "who do you think has been to drink tea with me?" Poar thing, a frendly face was an event in her life—a tea-party quite a hera!

"Why, perhaps, Lenoir, my maid," says my lady, looking grave. "I wish, Miss Kicksy, you would not demean yourself by mixing with my domestics. Recollect, madam, that you are sister to Lady Griffin."

"No, my lady, it was not Lenoir; it was a gentleman, and a handsome gentleman, too."

"Oh, it was Monsieur de l'Orge, then," says miss; "he promised to bring me some guitar strings."

"No, nor yet M. de l'Orge. He came, but was not so polite as to ask for me. What do you think of your own beau, the honorable Mr. Algernon Deuceace;" and, so saying, poar Kicksy clapped her hands together, and looked as joyfle as if she'd come into a fortin.

"Mr. Deuceace here; and why, pray?" says my lady, who recklected all that his exlent pa had been saying to her.

"Why, in the first place, he had left his pocket-book, and in the second he wanted, he said, a dish of my nice tea, which he took, and staid with me an hour, or moar."

"And pray, Miss Kicksy," said Miss Matilda, quite contempshusly, "what may have been the subject of your conversation with Mr. Algernon? Did you talk politics, or music, or fine arts, or metaphysics?" Miss M. being what was called a *blue* (as most hump-backed women in sosiaty are), always made a pint to speak on these grand subjects.

"No, indeed; he talked of no such awful matters. If he had, you know, Matilda, I should never have understood him. First we talked about the weather, next about muffins and crumpets. Crumpets, he said, he liked best; and then we talked (here Miss Kicksy's voice fell) about poor dear Sir George in heaven! what a good husband he was, and——"

"And what a good fortune he left,—eh, Miss Kicksy?" says my lady, with a hard, snearing voice, and a diabollicle grin.

"Yes, dear Leonora, he spoke so respectfully of your blessed husband, and seemed so anxious about you and Matilda, it was quite charming to hear him, dear man!"

"And pray, Miss Kicksy, what did you tell him?"

"Oh, I told him that you and Leonora had nine thousand a-year, and ——"

"What then?"

"Why nothing; that is all I know. I am sure, I wish I had ninety," says poor Kicksy, her eyes turning to heaven.

"Ninety fiddlesticks! Did not Mr. Deuceace ask how the money was left, and to which of us?"

"Yes; but I could not tell him."

"I knew it!" says my lady, slapping down her teacup,—"I knew it!"

"Well!" says Miss Matilda, "and why not, Lady Griffin? There is no reason you should break your teacup, because Algernon asks a harmless question. *He* is not mercenary; he is all candour, innocence, generosity! He is himself blest with a sufficient portion of the world's goods to be content; and often and often has he told me, he hoped the woman of his choice might come to him without a penny, that he might shew the purity of his affection."

"I've no doubt," says my lady. "Perhaps the lady of his choice is Miss Matilda Griffin!" and she flung out of the room, slamming the door, and leaving Miss Matilda to bust into tears, as was her reglar custom, and pour her loves and woas into the buzzom of Miss Kicksy.

CHAP. IV.—"HITTING THE NALE ON THE HEDD."

The nex morning, down came me and master to Lady Griffinses,—I amusing myself with the gals in the antyroom, he paying his devours to the ladies in the salong. Miss was thrumming on her gitter; my lady was before a great box of papers, busy with accounts, bankers' books, lawyers' letters, and what not. Law bless us! it's a kind of bisniss I should like well enuff, especially when my hannual account was seven or eight thousand on the right side, like my lady's. My lady in this house kep all these matters to herself. Miss was a vast deal too sentrimentle to mind business.

Miss Matilda's eyes sparkled as master came in; she pinted gracefully to a place on the sofy beside her, which Deuceace took. My lady only looked up for a moment, smiled very kindly, and down went her head among the papers agen, as busy as a B.

"Lady Griffin has had letters from London," says miss, "from nasty lawyers and people. Come here and sit by me, you naughty man, you!"

And down sat master. "Willingly," says he, "my dear Miss Griffin; why, I declare it is quite a *tête-à-tête!*"

"Well," says miss (after the prillimnary flumries, in coarse), "we met a friend of yours at the embassy, Mr. Deuceace."

"My father, doubtless; he is a great friend of the ambassador, and surprised me myself by a visit the night before last."

"What a dear, delightful old man! how he loves you, Mr. Deuceace!"

"Oh, amazingly!" says master, throwing his i's to heaven.

"He spoke of nothing but you, and such praises of you!"

Master breathed more freely. "He is very good, my dear father; but blind, as all fathers are, he is so partial and attached to me."

"He spoke of your being his favourite child, and regretted that you were not his eldest son. 'I can but leave him the small portion of a younger brother,' he said; 'but, never mind, he has talents, a noble name, and an independence of his own.'"

"An independence? yes, oh yes! I am quite independent of my father."

"Two thousand pounds a year left you by your godmother; the very same you told us, you know."

"Neither more nor less," says master, bobbing his head; "a sufficiency, my dear Miss Griffin,—to a man of my moderate habits an ample provision."

"By the by," cries out Lady Griffin, interrupting the conversation, "you who are talking about money matters there, I wish you would come to the aid of poor *me!* Come, naughty boy, and help me out with this long, long sum."

Didn't he go—that's all! My i, how his i's shone, as he skipt across the room, and seated himself by my lady!

"Look!" said she, "my agents write me over that they have received a remittance of 7200 ruppees, at 2s. 9d. a rupee. Do tell me what the sum is, in pounds and shillings;" which master did with great gravity.

"Nine hundred and ninety pounds. Good; I dare say you are right. I'm sure I can't go through the fatigue to see. And now comes another question. Whose money is this, mine or Matilda's? You see it is the interest of a sum in India, which we have not had occasion to touch; and, according to the terms of poor Sir George's will, I really don't know how to dispose of the money, except to spend it. Matilda, what shall we do with it?"

"La, ma'am, I wish you would arrange the business yourself."

"Well, then, Algernon, *you* tell me;" and she laid her hand on his, and looked him most pathetickly in the face.

"Why," says he, "I don't know how Sir George left his money; you must let me see his will, first."

"Oh, willingly."

Master's chair seemed suddenly to have got springs in the cushns; he was obliged to *hold himself down.*

"Look here, I have only a copy, taken by my hand from Sir George's own manuscript. Soldiers, you know, do not employ lawyers much, and this was written on the night before going into action." And she read, " 'I, George Griffin,' &c. &c.—you know how these things begin—'being now of sane mind'—um, um, um—'leave to my friends, Thomas Abraham Hicks, a colonel in the H. E. I. Company's Service, and to John Monro Mackirkincroft (of the house of Huffle, Mackirkincroft and Dobbs, at Calcutta), the whole of my property, to be realised as speedily as they may (consistently with the interests of the property), in trust for my wife, Leonora Emilia Griffin (born L. E. Kicksy), and my only legitimate child, Matilda Griffin. The interest resulting from such property to be paid to them, share and share alike; the principal to remain untouched, in the names of the said T. A. Hicks and J. M. Mackirkincroft, until the death of my wife, Leonora Emilia Griffin, when it shall be paid to my daughter, Matilda Griffin, her heirs, executors, or assigns.' "

"There," said my lady, "we won't read any more; all the rest is stuff. But, now you know the whole business, tell us what is to be done with the money?"

"Why, the money, unquestionably, should be divided between you."

"*Tant mieux*, say I, I really thought it had been all Matilda's."

*   *   *   *   *

There was a paws for a minit or two after the will had been read. Master left the desk at which he had been seated with her ladyship, paced up and down the room for a while, and then came round to the place where Miss Matilda was seated. At last he said, in a low, trembling voice,

"I am almost sorry, my dear Lady Griffin, that you have read that will to me; for an attachment such as I feel must seem, I fear, mercenary, when the object of it is so greatly favoured by worldly fortune. Miss Griffin— Matilda! I know I may say the word; your dear eyes grant me the permission. I need not tell you, or you, dear mother-in-law, how long, how fondly, I have adored you. My tender, my beautiful Matilda, I will not affect to say I have not read your heart ere this, and that I have not known the preference with which you have honoured me. *Speak it,* dear girl! from your own sweet lips, in the presence of an affectionate parent, utter the sentence which is to seal my happiness for life. Matilda, dearest Matilda! say, oh say, that you love me!"

Miss M. shivered, turned pail, rowled her eyes about, and fell on master's neck, wispering hoddibly, "*I do!*"

My lady looked at the pair for a moment with her teeth grinding, her i's glaring, her busm throbbing, and her face chock white, for all the world like Madam Pasty, in the oppra of *Mydear* (when she's goin to mudder her childring, you recklect), and out she flounced from the room, without a word, knocking down poar me, who happened to be very near the dor, and leaving my master along with his crook-back mistress.

I've repotted the speech he made to her pretty well. The fact is, I got it in a ruff copy, which, if any boddy likes, they may see at Mr. Frazierses, only on the copy it's wrote, "*Lady Griffin, Leonora!*" instead of "*Miss Griffin, Matilda,*" as in the abuff, and so on.

Master had hit the right nail on the head this time, he thought; but his adventors an't over yet.

CHAP. V.—THE GRIFFIN'S CLAWS.

Well; master had hit the right nail on the head this time: thanx to luck—the crooked one, to be sure, but then it had the *goold nobb,* which was the part Deuceace most valued, as well he should; being a connyshure as to the rellatif valyou of pretious metals, and much preferring virging goold like this to poor old battered iron like my Lady Griffin.

And so, in spite of his father (at which old noblemin Mr. Deuceace now snapt his fingers), in spite of his detts (which, to do him Justas, had never stood much in his way), and in spite of his povatty, idleness, extravygans, swindling, and debotcheries of all kinds (which an't *generally* very favorabble to a young man who has to make his way in the world); in spite of all, there he was, I say, at the topp of the trea, the fewcher master of a perfect fortun, the defianced husband of a fool of a wife. What can mortial man want more? Vishns of ambishn now occoupied his soal. Shooting boxes, oppra boxes, money boxes always full; hunters at Melton; a seat in the House of Commins, Heaven knows what! and not a poar footman, who only describes what he's seen, and can't, in cors, pennytrate into the idears and the busms of men.

You may be shore that the three-cornerd noats came pretty thick now from the Griffinses. Miss was always a writing them befoar; and now, nite, noon, and mornink, breakfast, dinner, and sopper, in they came, till my pantry (for master never read 'em, and I carried 'em out) was puffickly intolrabble from the oder of musk, ambygrease, bargymot, and other sense with which they were impregniated. Here's the contense of three on 'em, which I've kept in my dex these twenty years as skewriosities. Faw! I can smel 'em at this very minit, as I am copying them down.

Billy Doo. No. I.

"Monday morning, 2 o'clock.

" 'Tis the witching hour of night. Luna illumines my chamber, and falls upon my sleepless pillow. By her light I am inditing these words to thee, my Algernon. My brave and beautiful, my soul's lord! when shall the time come when the tedious night shall not separate us, nor the blessed day? Twelve! one! two! I have heard the bells chime, and the quarters, and never cease to think of my husband. My adored Percy, pardon the girlish confession,—I have kissed the letter at this place. Will thy lips press it too, and remain for a moment on the spot which has been equally saluted by your Matilda?"

This was the *fust* letter, and was brot to our house by one of the poar footmin, Fitzclarence, at sicks o'clock in the morning. I thot it was for life and death, and woak master at that extrornary hour, and gave it to him. I shall never forgit him, when he red it; he cramped it up, and he cust and swoar, applying to the lady who roat, the genlmn that brought it, and me who introjuiced it to his notice, such a collection of epitafs as I seldom hered, excep at Billinxgit. The fact is thiss, for a fust letter, miss's noat was *rather* too strong, and sentymentle. But that was her way; she was always reading melancholy stoary books—Thaduse of Wawsaw, the Sorrows of Mac Whirter, and such like.

After about 6 of them, master never yoused to read them; but handid them over to me, to see if there was any think in them which must be answered, in order to kip up appearuntses. The nex letter is

No. II.

"Beloved! to what strange madnesses will passion lead one! Lady Griffin, since your avowal yesterday, has not spoken a word to your poor Matilda; has declared that she will admit no one (heigho! not even you, my Algernon); and has locked herself into her own dressing-room. I do believe that she is *jealous*, and fancies that you were in love with *her!* Ha, ha! I could have told her *another tale—* n'est-ce pas? Adieu, adieu, adieu! A thousand, thousand, million kisses! M. G.

"*Monday afternoon, 2 o'clock.*"

There was another letter kem before bedtime; for though me and master called at the Griffinses, we wairnt aloud to enter at no price. Mortimer and Fitzclarence grind at me, as much as to say we were going to be relations; but I dont spose master was very sorry when he was obleachd to come back without seeing the fare objict of his affeckshns.

Well, on Chewsdy there was the same game; ditto on Wensday; only, when we called there, who should we see but our father, Lord Crabs, who was waiving his hand to Miss Kicksey, and saying *he should be back to dinner at 7,* just as me and master came up the stares. There was no admittns for us though. "Bah! bah! never mind," says my lord, taking his son affeckshnatly by the hand. "What, two strings to your bow; ay, Algernon? The dowager a little jealous, miss a little lovesick. But my lady's fit of anger will vanish, and I promise you, my boy, that you shall see your fair one to-morrow."

And, so saying, my lord walked master down stares, looking at him as tender and affeckshnat, and speaking to him as sweet as posbill. Master did not know what to think of it. He never new what game his old father was at; only he somehow felt that he had got his head in a net, in spite of his suxess on Sunday. I knew it—I knew it quite well, as soon as I saw the old genlmn igsammin him, by a kind of smile which came over his old face, and was somethink betwigst the angellic and the direbollicle.

But master's dowts were cleared up nex day, and every thing was bright again. At brexfast, in comes a note with inclosier, boath of witch I here copy.

No. IX.

"*Thursday morning.*

"Victoria, Victoria! Mamma has yielded at last; not her consent to our union, but her consent to receive you as before; and has promised to forget the past. Silly woman, how could she ever think of you as any thing but the lover of your Matilda? I am in a whirl of delicious joy and passionate excitement. I have been awake all this long night, thinking of thee, my Algernon, and longing for the blissful hour of meeting.

"Come! M. G."

This is the inclosier from my lady.

"I will not tell you that your behaviour on Sunday did not deeply shock me. I had been foolish enough to think of other plans, and to fancy your heart (if you had any) was fixed elsewhere than on one at whose foibles you have often laughed with me, and whose person at least cannot have charmed you.

"My step-daughter will not, I presume, marry without at least going through the ceremony of asking my consent; I cannot, as yet, give it. Have I not reason to doubt whether she will be happy in trusting herself to you?

"But she is of age, and has the right to receive in her own house all those who may be agreeable to her,—certainly you, who are likely to be one day so nearly connected with her. If I have honest reason to believe that your love for Miss Griffin is sincere; if I find in a few months that you yourself are still desirous to marry her, I can, of course, place no further obstacles in your way.

"You are welcome, then, to return to our hotel. I cannot promise to receive you as I did of old; you would despise me if I did. I can promise, however, to think no more of all that has passed between us, and yield up my own happiness for that of the daughter of my dear husband.   L. E. G."

Well, now, an't this a manly, straitforard letter enough, and natral from a woman whom we had, to confess the truth, treated most scuvvily? Master thought so, and went and made a tender, respeckful speach to Lady Griffin (a little flumry costs nothink). Grave and sorrofle he kist her hand, and, speakin in a very low adgitayted voice, calld Hevn to witness how he deplord that his conduct should ever have given rise to such an unfortnt ideer; but if he might offer her esteem, respect, the warmest and tenderest admiration, he trusted she would accept the same, and a deal moar flumry of the kind, with dark, sollum, glansis of the eyes, and plenty of white pockit hankercher.

He thought he'd made all safe. Poar fool! he was in a net—sich a net as I never yet see set to ketch a roag in.

CHAP. VI.—THE JEWEL.

The Shevalier de l'Orge, the young Frenchmin whom I wrote of in my last, who had been rather shy of his visits while master was coming it so very strong, now came back to his old place by the side of Lady Griffin; there was no love now, though, betwigst him and master, although the shevallier had got his lady back agin, Deuceace being compleatly devoted to his crookid Veanus.

The shevalier was a little, pale, moddist, insinifishnt creature; and I shoodn't have thought, from his appearants, would have the heart to do harm to a fli, much less to stand befor such a tremendious tiger and fire-eater as my master. But I see putty well, after a week, from his manner of going on—of speakin at master, and lookin at him, and holding his lips tight when Deuceace came into the room, and glaring at him with his i's, that he hated the Honrabble Algernon Percy.

Shall I tell you why? Because my lady Griffin hated him; hated him wuss than pison, or the devvle, or even wuss than her daughter-in-law. Praps you phansy that the letter you have juss red was honest; praps you amadgin that the sean of the reading of the wil came on by mere chans, and in the reglar cors of suckmstansies: it was all a *game*, I tell you—a reglar trap; and that extrodnar clever young man, my master, as neatly put his foot into it, as ever a pocher did in fesnt preserve.

The shevalier had his q from Lady Griffin. When Deuceace went off the feald, back came De l'Orge to her feet, not a witt less tender than befor. Por fellow, por fellow! he really loved this woman. He might as well have foln in love with a bore-constructor! He was so blindid and beat by the power which she had got over him, that if she told him black was white, he'd beleave it, or if she ordered him to commit murder, he'd do it—she wanted something very like it, I can tell you.

I've already said how, in the fust part of their acquaintance, master used to laff at De l'Orge's bad Inglish, and funny ways. The little creature had a thowsnd of these; and being small, and a Frenchman, master, in cors, looked on him with that good-humoured kind of contemp which a good Brittn ot always to show. He rayther treated him like an intelligent munky than a man, and ordered him about as if he'd bean my lady's footman.

All this munseer took in very good part, until after the quarl betwigst Master and Lady Griffin; when that lady took care to turn the tables. Whenever master and miss were not present (as I've heard the servants say), she used to laff at the shevalliay for his obeajance and sivillaty to master. "For her part, she wondered how a man of his birth could act a servnt; how any man could submit to such contemsheous behaviour from another; and then she told him how Deuceace was always snearing at him behind his back; how, in fact, he ought to hate him corjaly, and how it was suttnly time to shew his sperrit."

Well, the poar little man beleavd all this from his hart, and was angry or pleased, gentle or quarlsum, igsactly as my lady liked. There got to be frequint rows betwigst him and master; sharp words flung at each other across the dinner-table; dispewts about handing ladies their smeling-botls, or seeing them to their carridge; or going in and out of a room fust, or any such nonsince.

"For Hevn's sake," I heerd my lady, in the midl of one of these tiffs, say, pail, and the tears trembling in her i's, "do, do be calm, Mr. Deuceace. Monsieur de l'Orge, I beseech you to forgive him. You are, both of you, so esteemed, lov'd by members of this family, that for its peace as well as your own, you should forbear to quarrel."

It was on the way to the Sally Mangy that this brangling had begun, and it ended jest as they were seating themselves. I shall never forgit poar little De l'Orge's eyes, when my lady said "*both* of you." He stair'd at my lady for a momint, turned pail, red, look'd wild, and then, going round to master, shook his hand as if he would have wrung it off. Mr. Deuceace only bowd and grind, and turned away quite stately; miss heaved a loud O from her busm, and lookd up in his face with an igspreshn, jest as if she could have eat him up with love; and the little shevalliay sate down to his soop-plate, and wus so happy, that I'm blest if he wasn't crying! He thought the widdow had made her declyration, and would have him; and so thought Deuceace, who lookd at her for some time mighty bitter and contempshus, and then fell a talking with miss.

Now, though master didn't choose to marry for Lady Griffin, as he might have done, he yet thought fit to be very angry at the notion of her marrying any body else; and so, consquintly, was in a fewry at this confision which she had made regarding her parshaleaty for the French shevaleer.

And this I've perseaved in the cors of my expearants through life, that when you vex him, a roag's no longer a roag; you find him out at onst when he's in a passion, for he shows, as it ware, his cloven foot the very instnt you tread on it. At least, this is what *young* roags do; it requires very cool blood and long practis to get over this pint, and not to show your pashn when you feel it, and snarl when you are angry. Old Crabs wouldn't do it; being like another noblemin, of whom I heard the Duke of Wellington say, while waiting behind his gracis chair, that if you were kicking him from behind, no one standing before him wuld know it, from the bewtiflle smiling igspreshn of his face. Young master hadn't got so far in the thiefs' grammer, and, when he was angry, showd it. And its also to be remarked (a very profownd observatin for a footmin, but we have i's though we *do* wear plush britchis), it's to be remarked, I say, that one of these chaps is much sooner maid angry than another, because honest men yield to other people, roags never do; honest men love other people, roags only themselves; and the slightest thing which comes in the way of thir beloved object sets them fewrious. Master hadn't led a life of gambling, swindling, and every kind of debotch to be good tempered at the end of it, I prommis you.

He was in a pashun, and when he *was* in a pashn, a more insalent, insuffrable, overbearing broot, didn't live.

This was the very pint to which my lady wished to bring him; for I must tell you, that though she had been trying all her might to set master and the shevalliay by the years, she had suxcaded only so far as to make them hate each profowndly; but, somehow or other, the 2 cox woodnt *fight*.

I doan't think Deuceace ever suspected any game on the part of her ladyship, for she carried it on so admirally, that the quarls which daily

took place betwigst him and the Frenchman, never seemed to come from
her; on the contry, she acted as the reglar pease-maker between them,
as I've just shown in the tiff which took place at the door of the Sally
Mangy. Besides, the 2 young men, thoagh reddy enough to snarl, were
natrally unwilling to cum to bloes. I'll tell you why: being friends, and
idle, they spent their mornins as young fashabbles genrally do, at billiads,
fensing, riding, pistle-shooting, or some such improoving study. In billiads,
master beat the Frenchmn hollow (and had won a pretious sight of money
from him, but that's neither here nor there, or, as the French say, *ontry
noo*); at pistle shooting, master could knock down eight immidges out of
ten, and De l'Orge seven; and in fensing, the Frenchman could pink the
Honrabble Algernon down evry one of his weskit buttns. They'd each
of them been out more than onst, for every Frenchman will fight, and
master had been obleag'd to do so in the cors of his bisniss; and knowing
each other's curridg, as well as the fact that either could put a hundrid
bolls running into a hat at 30 yards, they wairn't *very* willing to try such
exparrymence upon their own hats with their own heads in them. So you
see they kep quiet, and only grould at each other.

But to-day, Deuceace was in one of his thundering black humers; and
when in this way he woodnt stop for man or devvle. I said that he walked
away from the shevalliay, who had given him his hand in his sudden bust
of joyfle good-humour, and who, I do bleave, would have hugd a she-bear,
so very happy was he. Master walked away from him pale and hotty, and,
taking his seat at table, no moor mindid the brandishments of Miss Griffin,
but only replied to them with a pshaw, or a dam at one of us servnts, or
abuse of the soop, or the wind; cussing and swearing like a trooper, and
not like a wel-bred son of a noble Brittish peer.

"Will your ladyship," says he, slivering off the wing of a *pully ally bashy-
mall,* "allow me to help you?"

"I thank you! no; but I will trouble Monsieur de l'Orge." And towards
that gnlmn she turned, with a most tender and fasnatng smile.

"Your ladyship has taken a very sudden admiration for Mr. de l'Orge's
carving. You used to like mine once."

"You are very skilful; but to-day, if you will allow me, I will partake of
something a little simpler."

The Frenchmn helped; and, being so happy, in cors, spilt the gravy.
A great blob of brown sos spurted on to master's chick, and myandrewd
down his shert collar, and virging-white weskit.

"Confound you!" says he; "M. de l'Orge, you have done this on purpose." And down went his knife and fork, over went his tumbler of wind,
a deal of it into poar Miss Griffinses lap, who looked fritened and ready
to cry.

My lady bust into a fit of laffin, peel upon peel, as if it was the best joak
in the world. De l'Orge giggled and grind too. *"Pardong,"* says he; *"meal*

*pardong, mong share munseer."** And he looked as if he would have done it again for a penny.

The little Frenchman was quite in exstsis: he found himself all of a suddn at the very top of the trea; and the laff for onst turned against his rivle, he actialy had the ordassaty to propose to my lady in English to take a glass of wind.

"Veal you," says he, in his jargin, "take a glas of Madére viz me, mi ladi?" And he looked round, as if he'd igsackly hit the English manner and pronunciation.

"With the greatest pleasure," says Lady G. most graciously nodding at him, and gazing at him as she drenk up the wind. She'd refused master befor, and *this* didn't increase his good humer.

Well, they went on, master snarling, snapping, and swearing, making himself, I must confess, as much of a blaggard as any I ever see; and my lady employing her time betwigst him and the shevalliay, doing every think to irratate master, and flatter the Frenchmn. Desert came; and, by this time, miss was stock-still with fright, the chevaleer half tipsy with pleasure and gratafied vannaty. My lady puffickly raygent with smiles, and master bloo with rage.

"Mr. Deuceace," says my lady, in a most winning voice, after a little chaffing (in which she only worked him up moar and moar), "may I trouble you for a few of those grapes? they look delicious."

For answer, master seas'd hold of the grayp dish, and sent it sliding down the table to De l'Orge; upsetting, in his way, fruit-plates, glasses, dickanters, and Heaven knows what.

"Monsieur de l'Orge," says he, shouting out at the top of his voice, "have the goodness to help Lady Griffin. She wanted *my* grapes long ago, and has found out they are sour!"

*   *   *   *   *

There was a dead paws of a moment or so.

*   *   *   *   *

"Ah!" says my lady, "*vous osez m'insulter, devant mes gens, dans ma propre maison—c'est par trop fort, monsieur.*" And up she got, and flung out of the room. Miss followed her, screeching out, "Mamma—for God's sake—Lady Griffin!" and here the door slammed on the pair.

Her ladyship did very well to speak French. *De l'Orge would not have understood her else;* as it was, he heard quite enough; and as the door clikt too, in the presents of me, and Messeers Mortimer and Fitzclarence, the family footmen, he walks round to my master, and hits him a slap on the

---

* In the long dialogues, we have generally ventured to change the peculiar spelling of our friend, Mr. Yellowplush.

face, and says, "*Prends ça, menteur et láche!*" Which means, "Take that, you liar and coward!"—rayther strong igspreshns for one genlmn to use to another.

Master staggered back, and looked bewildered; and then he gave a kind of a scream, and then he made a run at the Frenchman, and then me and Mortimer flung ourselves upon him, whilst Fitzclarence imbraced the shevalliay.

"*A demain!*" says he, clinching his little fist, and walking away, not very sorry to git off.

When he was fairly down stares, we let go of master; who swallowed a goblit of water, and then pawsing a little, and pulling out his pus, he presented to Messeers Mortimer and Fitzclarence, a luydor each. "I will give you five more to-morrow," says he, "if you will promise to keep this secrit."

And then he walked into the ladies. "If you knew," says he, going up to Lady Griffin, and speaking very slow (in cors we were all at the kea-hole), "the pain I have endured in the last minute, in consequence of the rudeness and insolence of which I have been guilty to your ladyship, you would think my own remorse was punishment sufficient, and would grant me pardon."

My lady bowed, and said she didn't wish for explanations. Mr. Deuceace was her daughter's guest, and not hers; but she certainly would never demean herself by sitting again at table with him. And so saying, out she boltid again.

"Oh! Algernon! Algernon!" says miss, in teers, "what is this dreadful mystery—these fearful, shocking quarrels? Tell me, has any thing happened? Where, where is the chevalier?"

Master smiled, and said, "Be under no alarm, my sweetest Matilda. De l'Orge did not understand a word of the dispute; he was too much in love for that. He is but gone away for half an hour, I believe; and will return to coffee."

I knew what master's game was, for if miss had got a hinkling of the quarrel betwigst him and the Frenchman, we should have had her screeming at the Hôtel Mirabeu, and the juice and all to pay. He only stopt for a few minuits, and cumfitted her, and then drove off to his friend, Captain Bullseye, of the Rifles; with whom, I spose, he talked over this unplesnt bisniss. We fownd, at our hotel, a note from De l'Orge, saying where his secknd was to be seen.

Two mornings after there was a parrowgraf in *Gallynanny's Messinger*, which I hear beg leaf to transcribe:

"*Fearful Duel.*—Yesterday morning, at six o'clock, a meeting took place, in the Bois de Boulogne, between the Hon. A. P. D—ce—ce, a younger son of the Earl of Cr—bs, and the Chevalier de l'O——. The chevalier was attended by Major de M——, of the Royal Guard, and the Hon. Mr. D—— by Captain B—lls—ye, of the British Rifle Corps. As far as we have been able to learn the particulars of this deplorable affair, the dispute originated in the house of a lovely lady (one of the most brilliant ornaments of our embassy), and the duel took place on the morning ensuing.

"The chevalier (the challenged party, and the most accomplished amateur swordsman in Paris) waived his right of choosing the weapons, and the combat took place with pistols.

"The combatants were placed at forty paces, with directions to advance to a barrier which separated them only eight paces. Each was furnished with two pistols. Monsieur de l'O—— fired almost immediately, and the ball took effect in the left wrist of his antagonist, who dropped the pistol which he held in that hand. He fired, however, directly with his right, and the chevalier fell to the ground, we fear mortally wounded. A ball has entered above his hip-joint, and there is very little hope that he can recover.

"We have heard that the cause of this desperate duel was a *blow*, which the chevalier ventured to give to the Hon. Mr. D. If so, there is some reason for the unusual and determined manner in which the duel was fought.

"Mr. Deu—a—e returned to his hotel; whither his excellent father, the Right Hon. Earl of Cr—bs, immediately hastened on hearing of the sad news, and is now bestowing on his son the most affectionate parental attention. The news only reached his lordship yesterday at noon, while at breakfast with his excellency, Lord Bobtail, our ambassador. The noble earl fainted on receiving the intelligence; but, in spite of the shock to his own nerves and health, persisted in passing last night by the couch of his son."

And so he did. "This is a sad business, Charles," says my lord to me, after seeing his son, and settling himself down in our salong. "Have you any segars in the house? And, hark ye, send me up a bottle of wine and some luncheon. I can certainly not leave the neighbourhood of my dear boy."

CHAP. VII.—THE CONSQUINSIES.

The shevalliay did not die, for the ball came out of it's own accord, in the midst of a violent fever and inflammayshn which was brot on by the wound. He was kep in bed for 6 weeks though, and did not recover for a long time after.

As for master, his lott, I'm sorry to say, was wuss than that of his advisary. Inflammation came on too; and, to make an ugly story short, they were obliged to take off his hand at the rist.

He bore it, in cors, like a Trojin, and in a month he too was well, and his wound heel'd; but I never sea a man look so like a devvle as he used sometimes, when he looked down at the stump!

To be sure, in Miss Griffinses eyes, this only indeerd him the mor. She sent twenty noats a-day to ask for him, calling him her beloved, her unfortnat, her hero, her wictim, and I dono what. I've kep some of the noats as I tell you, and curiously sentimentle they are, beating the sorrows of Mac Whirter all to nothink.

Old Crabs used to come offen, and consumed a power of wind and seagars at our house. I bleave he was at Paris because there was an exycution in his own house in England; and his son was a sure find (as they say) during his illness, and couldn't deny himself to the old genlmn. His eveninx my lord spent reglar at Lady Griffin's, where, as master was ill, I didn't go any more now, and where the chevalier wasn't there to disturb him.

"You see how that woman hates you, Deuceace," says my lord, one day, in a fit of cander, after they had been talking about Lady Griffin: "*she has not done with you yet,* I tell you fairly."

"Curse her," says master, in a fury, lifting up his maim'd arm—"curse her, but I will be even with her one day. I am sure of Matilda: I took care to put that beyond the reach of a failure. The girl must marry me for her own sake."

"*For her own sake!* O ho! Good, good!" My lord lifted his i's, and said, gravely, "I understand, my dear boy: it is an excellent plan."

"Well," says master, grinning fearcely and knowingly at his exlent old father, "as the girl is safe, what harm can I fear from the fiend of a stepmother?"

My lord only gev a long whizzle, and, soon after, taking up his hat, walked off. I saw him sawnter down the Plas Vandome, and go in quite calmly to the old door of Lady Griffinses hotel. Bless his old face! such a puffickly good-natured, kind-hearted, merry, selfish old scoundrill, I never shall see again.

His lordship was quite right in saying to master that "Lady Griffin hadn't done with him." No moar she had. But she never would have thought of the nex game she was going to play, *if somebody hadn't put her up to it.* Who did? If you red the above passidge, and saw how a venrabble old genlmn took his hat, and sauntered down the Plas Vandome (looking hard and kind at all the nussary-maids—*buns* they call them in France—in the way), I leave you to guess who was the auther of the nex skeam: a woman, suttnly, never would have pitcht on it.

In the fust payper which I wrote concerning Mr. Deuceace's adventers, and his kind behayviour to Messeers Dawkins and Blewitt, I had the honor of laying befor the public a skidewl of my master's detts, in witch was the following itim:

"Bills of xchange and I.O.U.'s, 4963*l.* 0s. 0d."

The I.O.U.se were trifling, say a thowsnd pound. The bills amountid to four thowsnd moar.

Now, the lor is in France, that if a genlmn gives these in England, and a French genlmn gits them in any way, he can pursew the Englishman who has drawn them, even though he should be in France. Master did not know this fact—laboring under a very common misteak, that, when onst out of England, he might wissle at all the debts he left behind him.

My Lady Griffin sent over to her slissators in London, who made arrangemints with the persons who possest the fine collection of ortografs on stampt paper which master had left behind him; and they were glad enuff to take any oppertunity of getting back their money.

One fine morning, as I was looking about in the court-yard of our hotel, talking to the servant gals, as was my reglar custom, in order to improve myself in the French languidge, one of them comes up to me and says, "Tenez, Monsieur Charles, down below in the office there is a bailiff, with a couple of gend'armes, who is asking for your master—*a-t'-il des dettes par hasard?*"

I was struck all of a heap—the truth flasht on my mind's hi. "Toinette," says I, for such was the gal's name—"Toinette," says I, giving her a kiss, "keep them for two minnits, as you valyou my affeckshn;" and then I gave her another kiss, and ran up stares to our chambers. Master had now pretty well recovered of his wound, and was aloud to drive abowt; it was lucky for him that he had the strenth to move. "Sir, sir," says I, "the bailiffs are after you, and you must run for your life."

"Bailiffs," says he: "nonsense! I don't, thank Heaven, owe a shilling to any man."

"Stuff, sir," says I, forgetting my respeck; "don't you owe money in England? I tell you the bailiffs are here, and will be on you in a moment."

As I spoke, cling cling, ling ling, goes the bell of the anty-shamber, and there they were sure enough!

What was to be done? Quick as litening, I throws off my livry coat, claps my goold lace hat on master's head, and makes him put on my livry. Then I wraps myself up in his dressing-gown, and lolling down on the sofa, bids him open the dor.

There they were—the bailiff—two jondarms with him—Toinette, and an old waiter. When Toinette sees master, she smiles, and says: "Dis donc, Charles! où est, donc, ton maitre? Chez lui, n'est-ce pas? C'est le jeune homme à monsieur," says she, curtsying to the bailiff.

The old waiter was just a going to blurt out, "Mais ce n'est pas!" when Toinette stops him, and says, "Laissez donc passer ces messieurs, vieux bête;" and in they walk, the 2 jon d'arms taking their post in the hall.

Master throws open the salong doar very gravely, and, touching *my* hat, says, "Have you any orders about the cab, sir?"

"Why, no, Chawls," says I; "I shan't drive out to-day."

The old bailiff grinned, for he understood English (having had plenty of English customers), and says, in French, as master goes out, "I think, sir, you had better let your servant get a coach, for I am under the painful necessity of arresting you, *au nom de la loi,* for the sum of ninety-eight thousand seven hundred francs, owed by you to the Sieur Jacques François Lebrun, of Paris;" and he pulls out a number of bills, with master's acceptances on them sure enough.

"Take a chair, sir," says I; and down he sits: and I began to chaff him, as well as I could, about the weather, my illness, my sad axdent, having lost one of my hands, which was stuck into my busm, and so on.

At last, after a minnit or two, I could contane no longer, and bust out in a horse laff.

The old fellow turned quite pail, and began to suspect somethink. "Hola!" says he; "gendarmes! à moi! à moi! Je suis floué, volé!" which means, in English, that he was reglar sold.

The jondarmes jumpt into the room, and so did Toinette and the waiter. Grasefly rising from my arm-chare, I took my hand from my dressing-gownd, and, flinging it open, stuck up on the chair one of the neatest legs ever seen.

I then pinted myjestickly—to what do you think?—to my PLUSH TITES! those sellabrated inigspressables which have rendered me faymous in Yourope.

Taking the hint, the jondarmes and the servnts rord out laffing; and so did Charles Yellowplush, Exquire, I can tell you. Old Grippard, the bailiff, looked as if he would faint in his chare.

I heard a kab galloping like mad out of the hotel-gate, and knew then that my master was safe.

CHAP. VIII.—LIMBO.

MY tail is droring rabidly to a close: my suvvice with Mr. Deuceace didn't continyou very long after the last chapter, in which I discribed my admiral strattyjam, and my singlar self-devocean. There's very few servnts, I can tell you, who'd have thought of such a contrivnce, and very few moar would have eggsycuted it when thought of.

But, after all, beyond the trifling advantich to myself in selling master's roab de sham, which you, gentle reader, may remember I woar, and in dixcovering a fipun note in one of the pockits,—beyond this, I say, there was to poar master very little advantitch in what had been done. It's true he had escaped. Very good. But Frans is not like Great Brittn; a man in a livry coat, with 1 arm, is pretty easily known, and caught, too, as I can tell you.

Such was the case with master. He coodn leave Paris, moarover, if he would. What was to become, in that case, of his bride—his unchbacked hairis? He knew that young lady's *temprimong* (as the Parishers say) too well to let her long out of his site. She had nine thousnd a-yer. She'd been in love a duzn times befor, and mite be agin. The Honrabble Algernon Deuceace was a little too wide awake to trust much to the constnsy of so very inflammable a young creacher. Heavn bless us, it was a marrycle she wasn't earlier married! I do bleave (from suttn seans that past betwigst us) that she'd have married me, if she hadn't been sejuiced by the supearor rank and indianuity of the genlmn in whose survace I was.

Well, to use a commin igspreshn, the beaks were after him. How was he to manitch? He coodn get away from his debts, and he wooden quit the fare objict of his affeckshns. He was ableejd, then, as the French say, to lie perdew,—going out at night, like a howl out of a hivy-bush, and returning in the daytime to his roast. For its a maxum in France (and I wood it were followed in Ingland), that after dark no man is lible for his detts; and in any of the royal gardens—the Twillaries, the Pally Roil, or the Lucksimbug, for example—a man may wander from sunrise to evening, and hear nothing of the ojus dunns: they an't admitted into these places of public enjyment and rondyvoo any more than dogs; the centuries at the garden gate having orders to shuit all such.

Master, then, was in this uncomfrable situation—neither liking to go nor to stay; peeping out at nights to have an intervew with his miss; ableagd to shuffle off her repeated questions as to the reason of all this disguise, and to talk of his two thowsnd a-year, jest as if he had it, and didn't owe a shilling in the world.

Of course, now, he began to grow mighty eager for the marritch.

He roat as many noats as she had done befor; swoar aginst delay and cerymony; talked of the pleasures of Hyming, the ardship that the ardor of two arts should be allowed to igspire, the folly of waiting for the consent of Lady Griffin. She was but a stepmother, and an unkind one. Miss was (he said) a major, might marry whom she liked; and suttnly had paid Lady G. quite as much attention as she ought, by paying her the compliment to ask her at all.

And so they went on. The curious thing was, that when master was pressed about his cause for not coming out till nighttime, he was misterus; and Miss Griffin, when asked why she wooden marry, igsprest, or rather *didn't* igspress, a simlar secrasy. Wasn't it hard? the cup seemed to be at the lip of both of 'em, and yet, somehow, they could not manitch to take a drink.

But one moring, in reply to a most desprat epistol wrote by my master over night, Deuceace, delighted, gits an answer from his soal's beluffd, which ran thus:—

"MISS GRIFFIN *to the Hon.* A. P. DEUCEACE.

"Dearest,—You say you would share a cottage with me; there is no need, luckily, for that! You plead the sad sinking of your spirits at our delayed union. Beloved, do you think *my* heart rejoices at our separation? You bid me disregard the refusal of Lady Griffin, and tell me that I owe her no further duty.

"Adored Algernon! I can refuse you no more. I was willing not to lose a single chance of reconciliation with this unnatural stepmother. Respect for the memory of my sainted father bid me do all in my power to gain her consent to my union with you; nay, shall I own it, prudence dictated the measure; for to whom should she leave the share of money accorded to her by my father's will but to my father's child?

"But there are bounds beyond which no forbearance can go; and, thank Heaven, we have no need of looking to Lady Griffin for sordid wealth: we have a competency without her. Is it not so, dearest Algernon?

"Be it as you wish, then, dearest, bravest, and best. Your poor Matilda has yielded to you her heart long ago; she has no longer need to keep back her name. Name the hour, and I will delay no more; but seek for refuge in your arms from the contumely and insult which meet me ever here.

"MATILDA.

"P.S. O, Algernon! if you did but know what a noble part your dear father has acted throughout, in doing his best endeavours to further our plans, and to soften Lady Griffin! It is not *his* fault that she is inexorable as she is. I send you a note sent by her to Lord Crabs; we will laugh at it soon, *n'est ce pas?*"

II.

"My lord,—In reply to your demand for Miss Griffin's hand, in favour of your son, Mr. Algernon Deuceace, I can only repeat what I before have been under the necessity of stating to you,—that I do not believe a union with a person of Mr. Deuceace's character would conduce to my stepdaughter's happiness, and therefore *refuse my consent.* I will beg you to communicate the contents of this note to Mr. Deuceace; and implore you no more to touch upon a subject which you must be aware is deeply painful to me.

"I remain your lordship's most humble servant,

"L. E. GRIFFIN.

"The Right Hon. the Earl of Crabs."

"Hang her ladyship!" says my master, "what care I for it?" As for the old lord who'd bean so afishous in his kindniss and advice, master recknsiled that pretty well, with thinking that his lordship knew he was going to marry ten thousnd a-year, and igspected to get some share of it; for he roat back the following letter to his father, as well as a flaming one to miss:

> "Thank you, my dear father, for your kindness in that awkward business. You know how painfully I am situated just now, and can pretty well guess *both the causes* of my disquiet. A marriage with my beloved Matilda will make me the happiest of men. The dear girl consents, and laughs at the foolish pretensions of her mother-in-law. To tell you the truth, I wonder she yielded to them so long. Carry your kindness a step further, and find for us a parson, a license, and make us two into one. We are both major, you know; so that the ceremony of a guardian's consent is unnecessary.
>
> "Your affectionate
"ALGERNON DEUCEACE.
>
> "How I regret that difference between us some time back! Matters are changed now, and shall be more still *after the marriage.*"

I knew what my master meant,—that he would give the old lord the money after he was married; and as it was probble that Miss would see the letter he roat, he made it such as not to let her see two clearly in to his presnt uncomfrable situation.

I took this letter along with the tender one for Miss, reading both of 'em, in course, by the way. Miss, on getting hers, gave an inegspressable look with the white of her is, kist the letter, and prest it to her busm. Lord Crabs read his quite calm, and then they fell a talking together; and told me to wait awhile, and I should git an anser.

After a deal of counseltation, my lord brought out a card, and there was simply written on it,

To-morrow, at the Ambassador's,

at Twelve.

"Carry that back to your master, Chawls," says he, "and bid him not to fail."

You may be sure I stept back to him pretty quick, and gave him the card and the messinge. Master looked sattasfied with both; but suttnly not over happy: no man is the day before his marridge; much more his marridge with a humpback, Harriss though she be.

Well, as he was a going to depart this bachelor life, he did what every man in such suckmstansies ought to do; he made his will,—that is, he made a dispasition of his property, and wrote letters to his creditors, telling them of his lucky chance; and that after his marriage he would sutnly pay them every stiver. *Before*, they must know his povvaty well enough to be sure that paymint was out of the question.

To do him justas, he seam'd to be inclined to do the thing that was right, now that it didn't put him to any inkinveniants to do so.

"Chawls," says he, handing me over a tenpun note, "Here's your wagis, and thank you for getting me out of the scrape with the bailiffs: when you are married, you shall be my valet out of liv'ry, and I'll treble your salary."

His vallit! praps his butler! Yes, thought I, here's a chance—a vallit to ten thousand a-year. Nothing to do but to shave him, and read his notes, and let my wiskkrs grow; to dress in spick and span black, and a clean shut per day; muffings every night in the housekeeper's room; the pick of the gals in the servnts' hall; a chap to clean my boots for me, and my master's oppera bone reglar once a-week. I knew what a vallit was as well as any genlmn in service; and this I can tell you, he's generally a happier, idler, hundsomer, more genlmnly man than his master. He has more money to spend, for genlm *will* leave their silver in their weskit pockets; more suxess among the gals; as good dinners, and as good wind—that is, if he's friends with the butler, and friends in cors they will be if they know which way their interest lies.

But these are only cassels in the air, what the French call *shutter dEspang*. It wasn't roat in the book of fate that I was to be Mr. Deuceace's vallit.

Days will pass at last—even days before a wedding, (the longist and unplesntist day in the whole of a man's life, I can tell you, excep, may be, the day before his hanging); and at length Aroarer dawned on the suspicious morning which was to unite in the bonds of Hyming the Honrabble Algernon Percy Deuceace, Exquire, and Miss Matilda Griffin. My master's wardrobe wasn't so rich as it had been; for he'd left the whole of his nicknax and trumpry of dressing-cases, and rob dy shams, his bewtifle museum of varnished boots, his curous colleckshn of Stulz and Staub coats, when he had been ableaged to quit so sudnly our pore, dear lodginx at the Hotel Mirabew; and, being incog at a friend's house, had contentid himself with ordring a couple of shoots of cloves from a common tailor, with a suffishnt quantaty of linning.

Well, he put on the best of his coats—a blue; and I thought it my duty to ask him whether he'd want his frock again; and he was good-natured, and said, "Take it, and be hanged to you." And half-past eleven o'clock came, and I was sent to look out at the door, if there were any sispicious charicters (a precious good nose I have to find a bailiff out, I can tell you, and an i which will almost see one round a corner); and presnly a very modist green glass-coach droav up, and in master stept. I didn't, in cors, appear on the box; because, being known, my appearints might have compromised master. But I took a short cut, and walked as quick as possbill down to the Rue de Fobug St. Honoré, where his exlnsy the English ambasdor lives, and where marridges are always performed betwigst English folk at Paris.

*　　*　　*　　*　　*

There is, almost nex door to the ambasdor's hotel, another hotel, of that lo kind which the French call cabbyrays, or wine-houses; and jest as master's green glass-coach pulled up, another coach drove off, out of which came two ladies, whom I knew pretty well,—suffiz, that one had a humpback, and the ingenious reader well knew why *she* came there; the other was poor Miss Kicksey, who came to see her turned off.

Well, master's glass-coach droav up jest as I got within a few yards of the door; our carriage, I say, drove up, and stopt. Down gits coachmin to open the door, and up comes I to give Mr. Deuceace an arm, when—out of the cabaray shoot four fellows, and draw up betwigst the coach and the embassy-doar; two other chaps go to the other doar of the carriage, and, opening it, one says—"*Rendez vous, M. Deuceace! Je vous arrête au nom de la Loi*" (which means, "Get out of that, Mr. D.; you are nabbed, and no mistake)." Master turned gashly pail, and sprung to the other side of the coach, as if a serpint had stung him. He flung open the door, and was for making off that way; but he saw the four chaps standing betwigst libbarty and him. He slams down the front window, and screams out, "*Fouettez, cocher!*" (which means, "Go it, coachmin!") in a despert loud voice; but coachmin wooden go it, and, besides, was off his box.

The long and short of the matter was, that jest as I came up to the door two of the bums jumped into the carriage. I saw all; I knew my duty, and so very mornfly I got up behind.

"*Tiens,*" says one of the chaps in the street; "*c'est ce drôle qui nous a joué l'autre jour.*" I knew 'em, but was too melumcolly to smile.

"*Où irons-nous donc?*" says coachmin to the genlmn who had got inside.

A deep woice from the intearor shouted out, in reply to the coachmin, "À SAINTE PÉLAGIE!"

*　　*　　*　　*　　*

And now, praps, I ot to dixcribe to you the humours of the prizn of Sainte Pelagie, which is the French for Fleat, or Queen's Bentch; but on this subject I'm rather shy of writing, partly because the admiral Boz has, in the history of Mr. Pickwick, made such a dixcripshn of a prizn, that mine wooden read very amyousingly afterwids; and, also, because, to tell you the truth, I did'n stay long in it, being not in a humer to waist my igsistance by passing away the ears of my youth in such a dull place.

My fust errint now was, as you may phansy, to carry a noat from Master to his destined bride. The poar thing was sadly taken aback, as I can tell you, when she found, after remaining two hours at the Embassy, that her husband didn't make his appearance. And so, after staying on and on, and yet seeing no husband, she was forsed at last to trudge dishconslit home, where I was already waiting for her with a letter from my master.

There was no use now denying the fact of his arrest, and so he confest it at onst; but he made a cock-and-bull story of treachery of a friend, infimous fodgery, and Heaven knows what. However, it didn't matter much; if he had told her that he had been betrayed by the man in the moon, she would have bleavd him.

Lady Griffin never used to appear now at any of my visits. She kep one drawing-room, and Miss dined and lived alone in another; they quarld so much that praps it was best they should live apart: only my Lord Crabs used to see both, comforting each with that winning and innsnt way he had. He came in as Miss, in tears, was lisning to my account of master's seazure, and hopin that the prisn wasn't a horrid place, with a nasty horrid dunjeon, and a dreadfle jailer, and nasty horrid bread and water. Law bless us! she had borrod her ideers from the novvles she had been reading!

"O my lord, my lord," says she, "have you heard this fatal story?"

"Dearest Matilda, what? For Heaven's sake, you alarm me! What—yes—no—is it—no, it can't be! Speak!" says my lord, seizing me by the choler of my coat, "what has happened to my boy?"

"Please you, my lord," says I, "he's at this moment in prisn, no wuss,—having been incarserated about two hours ago."

"In prison? Algernon in prison! 'tis impossible! Imprisoned, for what sum? Mention it, and I will pay to the utmost farthing in my power."

"I'm sure your lordship is very kind," says I (recklecting the sean betwigst him and master, whom he wanted to diddil out of a thowsnd lb.); "and you'll be happy to hear he's only in for a trifle. Five thousand pound is, I think, pretty near the mark."

"Five thousand pounds!—confusion!" says my lord, clasping his hands, and looking up to heaven, "and I have not five hundred! Dearest Matilda, how shall we help him?"

"Alas, my lord, I have but three guineas, and you know how Lady Griffin has the——"

"Yes, my sweet child, I know what you would say: but be of good cheer—Algernon, you know, has ample funds of his own."

Thinking my lord meant Dawkins's five thousnd, of which, to be sure, a good lump was left, I held my tung; but I cooden help wondering at Lord Crabs's igstream compashn for his son, and miss, with her 10,000*l.* a-year, having only 3 guineas in her pockit.

I took home (bless us, what a home!) a long and very inflamble letter from miss, in which she dixscribed her own sorror at the disappintment;

swoar she lov'd him only the moar for his misfortns; made light of them; as a pusson for a paltry sum of five thousnd pound ought never to be cast down, 'specially as he had a certain independence in view; and vowd that nothing, nothing, should ever injuice her to part from him, etsettler, etsettler.

I told master of the conversation which had past betwigst me and my lord, and of his handsome offers, and his horrow at hearing of his son's being taken: and likewise mentioned how strange it was that miss should only have 3 guineas, and with such a fortn: bless us, I should have thot that she would always have carried a hundred thowsnd lb. in her pockit!

At this master only said, Pshaw! But the rest of the story about his father seemed to dixquiet him a good deal, and he made me repeat it over agin.

He walked up and down the room agytated, and it seam'd as if a new lite was breaking in upon him.

"Chawls," says he, "did you observe—did miss—did my father seem *particularly intimate* with Miss Griffin?"

"How do you mean, sir?" says I.

"Did Lord Crabs appear very fond of Miss Griffin?"

"He was suttnly very kind to her."

"Come, sir, speak at once; did Miss Griffin seem very fond of his lordship?"

"Why, to tell the truth, sir, I must say she seemed *very* fond of him."

"What did he call her?"

"He called her his dearest gal."

"Did he take her hand?"

"Yes, and he——"

"And he what?"

"He kist her, and told her not to be so wery down-hearted about the misfortn which had hapnd to you."

"I have it now!" says he, clinching his fist, and growing gashly pail—"I have it now—the infernal old hoary scoundrel! the wicked, unnatural wretch! He would take her from me!" And he poured out a volly of oaves which are imposbill to be repeatid here.

I thot as much long ago: and when my lord kem with his vizits so pretious affeckshnt at my Lady Griffinses, I expected some such game was in the wind. Indeed, I'd heard a somethink of it from the Griffinses servnts, that my lord was mighty tender with the ladies.

One thing, however, was evident to a man of his intleckshal capassaties; he must either marry the gal at onst, or he stood very small chance of having her. He must git out of limbo immediantly, or his respectid father might be stepping into his vaykint shoes. Oh! he saw it all now—the fust attempt at arest, the marridge fixt at 12 o'clock, and the bayliffs fixt

to come and intarup the marridge!—the jewel, praps, betwigst him and
De l'Orge: but, no, it was the *woman* who did that—a *man* don't deal such
fowl blows, igspecially a father to his son: a woman may, poar thing!—
she's no other means of reventch, and is used to fight with under-hand
wepns all her life through.

Well, whatever the pint might be, this Deuceace saw pretty clear, that
he'd bean beat by his father at his own game—a trapp set for him onst,
which had been defitted by my presnts of mind—another trap set afterwids, in which my lord had been suxesfle. Now, my lord, roag as he was,
was much too good-naterd to do an unkind ackshn, mearly for the sake
of doing it. He'd got to that pich that he didn't mind injaries—they were
all fair play to him—he gave 'em, and reseav'd them, without a thought
of mallis. If he wanted to injer his son, it was to benefick himself. And
how was this to be done? By getting the hairiss to himself, to be sure. The
Honrabble Mr. D. didn't *say so*, but I knew his feelinx well enough—he
regretted that he had not given the old genlmn the money he askt for.

Poar fello! he thought he had hit it, but he was wide of the mark after
all.

Well, but what was to be done? It was clear that he must marry the gal
at any rate—*cootky coot*, as the French say; that is, marry her, and hang
the igspence.

To do so he must fust git out of prisn—to git out of prisn, he must
pay his debts—and, to pay his debts, he must give every shilling he was
worth. Never mind, four thousnd pound is a small stake to a reglar gambler, igspecially when he must play it, or rot for life in prisn, and when, if
he plays it well, it will give him ten thousnd a-year.

So, seeing there was no help for it, he maid up his mind, and accordingly wrote the follying letter to Miss Griffin:

"My adored Matilda,—Your letter has indeed been a comfort to
a poor fellow, who had hoped that this night would have been the
most blessed in his life, and now finds himself condemned to spend
it within a prison wall! You know the accursed conspiracy which
has brought these liabilities upon me, and the foolish friendship
which has cost me so much. But what matters? We have, as you
say, enough, even though I must pay this shameful demand upon
me; and five thousand pounds are as nothing, compared to the happiness which I lose in being separated a night from thee! Courage,
however! If I make a sacrifice, it is for you; and I were heartless
indeed, if I allowed my own losses to balance for a moment against
your happiness.

"Is it not so, beloved one? *Is* not your happiness bound up with
mine, in a union with me? I am proud to think so—proud, too, to

offer such a humble proof as this of the depth and the purity of my
affection.

"Tell me that you will still be mine; tell me that you will be mine
to-morrow; and to-morrow these vile chains shall be removed, and
I will be free once more—or if bound, only bound to you! My
adorable Matilda! my betrothed bride! write to me ere the evening
closes, for I shall never be able to shut my eyes in slumber upon my
prison-couch, until they have been first blest by the sight of a few
words from thee! Write to me, love! write to me! I languish for the
reply which is to make or mar me for ever.

"Your affectionate,
"A. P. D."

Having polisht off this epistol, master intrustid it to me to carry, and
bade me, at the same time, to try and give it into Miss Griffin's hand alone.
I ran with it to Lady Griffinses. I found miss, as I desired, in a sollatary
condition; and I presented her with master's pafewmed Billy.

She read it, and the number of size to which she gave vint, and the
tears which she shed, beggar digscription. She wep and sighed until I
thought she would bust. She claspt my hand even in her's, and said, "O,
Charles! is he very, very miserable?"

"He is, ma'am," says I; "very miserable indeed—nobody, upon my honour, could be miserablerer."

On hearing this pethetic remark, her mind was made up at onst: and
sitting down to her eskrewtaw, she immediantly ableaged master with an
anser. Here it is in black and white:

"My prisoned bird shall pine no more, but fly home to its nest in
these arms! Adored Algernon, I will meet thee to-morrow, at the
same place, at the same hour. Then, then, it will be impossible for
aught but death to divide us.

"M. G."

This kind of flumry stile comes, you see, of reading novvles, and cul-
tivating littery purshuits in a small way. How much better is it to be
puffickly ignorant of the hart of writing, and to trust to the writing of
the heart. This is my style; artyfiz I dispise, and trust compleatly to natur:
but revnong a no mootong, as our continental frends remark, to that nice
white sheep, Algernon Percy Deuceace, Exquire; that wenrabble old ram,
my Lord Crabs, his father; and that tender and dellygit young lamb, Miss
Matlida Griffin.

She had just foalded up into its proper trianglar shape the noat tran-
scribed abuff, and I was jest on the point of saying, according to my master's orders, "Miss, if you please, the Honrabble Mr. Deuceace would be
very much ableaged to you to keep the seminary which is to take place

to-morrow a profound se——," when my master's father entered, and I fell back to the door. Miss, without a word, rusht into his arms, bust into teers agin, as was her reglar way (it must be confest she was of a very mist constitution), and shewing to him his son's note, cried, "Look, my dear lord, how nobly your Algernon, *our* Algernon, writes to me. Who can doubt after this of the purity of his matchless affection?"

My lord took the letter, read it, seamed a good deal amyoused, and returning it to its owner, said, very much to my surprise, "My dear Miss Griffin, he certainly does seem in earnest; and if you choose to make this match without the consent of your mother-in-law, you know the consequence, and are of course your own mistress."

"Consequences!—for shame, my lord! A little money, more or less, what matters it to two hearts like ours?"

"Hearts are very pretty things, my sweet young lady; but three per cents are better."

"Nay, have we not an ample income of our own, without the aid of Lady Griffin?"

My lord shrugged his shoulders. "Be it so, my love," says he. "I'm sure I can have no other reason to prevent a union which is founded upon such disinterested affection."

And here the conversation dropt. Miss retired, clasping her hands, and making play with the whites of her i's. My lord began trotting up and down the room, with his fat hands stuck in his britches pockits, his countnince lighted up with igstream joy, and singing, to my inordnit igstonishment:

> "See the conquering hero comes!
> Tiddy diddy doll—tiddydoll, doll, doll."

He began singing this song, and tearing up and down the room like mad. I stood amaizd—a new light broke in upon me. He wasn't going, then, to make love to Miss Griffin! Master might marry her! Had she not got the for—?

I say, I was just standing stock still, my eyes fixt, my hands puppindicklar, my mouf wide open, and these igstrordinary thoughts passing in my mind, when my lord, having got to the last "doll" of his song, just as I came to the sillible "for" of my ventriloquism, or inward speech—we had eatch jest reached the pint digscribed, when the meditations of both were sudnly stopt, by my lord, in the midst of his singin and trottin match, coming bolt up aginst poar me, sending me up aginst one end of the room, himself flying back to the other; and it was only after considrabble agitation that we were at lenth restord to any thing like a liquilibrium.

"What, *you* here, you infernal rascal?" says my lord.

"Your lordship's very kind to notus me," says I; "I am here;" and I gave him a look.

He saw I knew the whole game.

And after whisling a bit, as was his habit when puzzled (I bleave he'd have only whisled if he had been told he was to be hanged in five minnits), after whisling a bit, he stops sudnly, and coming up to me, says:

"Hearkye, Charles, this marriage must take place to-morrow."

"Must it, sir," says I; "now, for my part, I don't think——"

"Stop, my good fellow; if it does not take place, what do you gain?"

This stagger'd me. If it didn't take place, I only lost a situation, for master had but just enough money to pay his detts; and it wooden soot my book to serve him in prison or starving.

"Well," says my lord, "you see the force of my argument. Now, look here," and he lugs out a crisp, fluttering, snowy HUNDER PUN NOTE! "if my son and Miss Griffin are married to-morrow, you shall have this; and I will, moreover, take you into my service, and give you double your present wages."

Flesh and blood cooden bear it. "My lord," says I, laying my hand upon my busm, "only give me securaty, and I'm yours for ever."

The old noblemin grind, and pattid me on the shoulder. "Right, my lad," says he, "right—you're a nice promising youth. Here is the best security," and he pulls out his pockit-book, returns the hundred pun bill, and takes out one for fifty—"here is half to-day; to-morrow you shall have the remainder."

My fingers trembled a little as I took the pretty fluttering bit of paper, about five times as big as any sum of money I had ever had in my life. I cast my i upon the amount: it was a fifty, sure enough—a bank poss-bill, made payable to *Leonora Emilia Griffin,* and indorsed by her. The cat was out of the bag. Now, gentle reader, I spose you begin to see the game.

"Recollect, from this day, you are in my service."

"My lord, you overpoar me with your faviours."

"Go to the devil, sir," says he; "do your duty, and hold your tongue."

And thus I went from the service of the Honorable Algernon Deuce-ace to that of his exlnsy the Right Honorabble Earl of Crabs.

*   *   *   *   *

On going back to prisn, I found Deuceace locked up in that oajus place to which his igstravygansies had deservedly led him, and felt for him, I must say, a great deal of contemp. A raskle such as he—a swin-ler, who had robbed poar Dawkins of the means of igsistance, who had cheated his fellow-roag, Mr. Richard Blewitt, and who was making a mus-nary marridge with a disgusting creacher like Miss Griffin, didn merit any compashn on my purt; and I determined quite to keep secret the suckm-stansies of my privit interview with his exlnsy my presnt master.

I gev him Miss Griffinses trianglar, which he read with a satasfied air. Then, turning to me, says he: "You gave this to Miss Griffin alone?"

"Yes, sir."

"You gave her my message?"

"Yes, sir."

"And you are quite sure Lord Crabs was not there when you gave either the message or the note?"

"Not there, upon my honour," says I.

"Hang your honour, sir! Brush my hat and coat, and go *call a coach*, do you hear?"

* * * * *

I did as I was ordered; and on coming back found master in what's called, I think, the *greffe* of the prisn. The officer in waiting had out a great register, and was talking to master in the French tongue, in coarse: a number of poar prisners were looking eagerly on.

"Let us see, my lor," says he; "the debt is 98,700 francs; there are capture expenses, interest, so much: and the whole sum amounts to a hundred thousand francs, *moins* 13."

Deuceace, in a very myjestic way, takes out of his pocket-book four thowsnd pun notes. "This is not French money, but I presume that you know it, M. Greffier," says he.

The greffier turned round to old Solomon, a money-changer, who had one or two clients in the prisn, and hapnd luckily to be there. "Les billets sont bons," says he, "je les prendrai pour cent mille douze cent francs, et j'éspere, my lor, de vous revoir."

"Good," says the greffier; "I know them to be good, and I will give my lor the difference, and make out his release."

Which was done. The poar debtors gave a feeble cheer, as the great dubble iron gates swung open, and clangd to again, and Deuceace stept out, and me after him, to breathe the fresh hair.

He had been in the place but six hours, and was now free again—free, and to be married to ten thousnd a-year nex day. But, for all that, he lookt very faint and pale. He *had* put down his great stake; and, when he came out of Saint Pelagie, he had but fifty pounds left in the world!

Never mind—when onst the money's down, make your mind easy; and so Deuceace did. He drove back to the Hotel Mirabew, where he ordered apartmince infinatly more splendid than befor; and I pretty soon told Toinette, and the rest of the suvvants, how nobly he behayvd, and how he valyoud four thousand pound no more than ditch water. And such was the consquincies of my praises, and the poplarity I got for us boath, that the delighted landlady immediantly charged him dubble what she would have done, if it hadn been for my stoaries.

He ordered splendid apartmince, then, for the nex week, a carriage and four for Fontainebleau to-morrow at 12 presizely; and having settled all these things, went quietly to the Roshy de Cancale, where he dined, as well he might, for it was now eight o'clock. I didn't spare the shampang neither that night, I can tell you; for when I carried the note he gave me for Miss Griffin in the evening, informing her of his freedom, that young lady remarked my hagitated manner of walking and speaking, and said, "Honest Charles! he is flusht with the events of the day. Here, Charles, is a napoleon; take it, and drink to your mistress."

I pockitid it, but I must say I didn't like the money—it went aginst my stomick to take it.

CHAP. IX.—THE MARRIAGE.

Well, the nex day came; at 12 the carridge and four was waiting at the ambasdor's doar; and Miss Griffin and the faithfle Kicksy were punctial to the apintment.

I don't wish to digscribe the marridge seminary—how the embasy chapling jined the hands of this loving young couple—how one of the embasy footmin was called in to witniss the marridge—how miss wep and faintid, as usial—and how Deuceace carried her, fainting, to the brisky, and drove off to Fontingblo, where they were to pass the fust weak of the honey-moon. They took no servnts, because they wisht, they said, to be privit. And so, when I had shut up the steps, and bid the postillion drive on, I bid ajew to the Honrabble Algernon, and went off strait to his exlent father.

"Is it all over, Chawls?" says he.

"I saw them turned off at igsackly a quarter past 12, my lord," says I.

"Did you give Miss Griffin the paper, as I told you, before her marriage?"

"I did, my lord, in the presnts of Mr. Brown, Lord Bobtail's man, who can swear to her having had it."

I must tell you that my lord had made me read a paper which Lady Griffin had written, and which I was commishnd to give in the manner menshnd abuff. It ran to this effect:

> "According to the authority given me by the will of my late dear husband, I forbid the marriage of Miss Griffin with the Honorable Algernon Percy Deuceace. If Miss Griffin persists in the union, I warn her that she must abide by the consequences of her act.
>
> "LEONORA EMILIA GRIFFIN.
>
> "*Rue de Rivoli, May 8, 1818.*"

When I gave this to miss, as she entered the cort-yard, a minnit before my master's arrivle, she only read it contemptiously, and said, "I laugh at the threats of Lady Griffin;" and she toar the paper in two, and walked on, leaning on the arm of the faithful and obleaging Miss Kicksey.

I picked up the paper, for fear of axdents, and brot it to my lord. Not that there was any necessaty, for he'd kep a copy, and made me and another witniss (my Lady Griffin's solissator) read them both, before he sent either away.

"Good!" says he; and he projuiced from his potfolio the fello of that bewchus fifty-pun note, which he'd given me yesterday. "I keep my promise, you see, Charles," says he. "You are now in Lady Griffin's service, in the place of Mr. Fitzclarence, who retires. Go to Frojé's, and get a livery."

"But, my lord," says I, "I was not to go into Lady Griffinses service, according to the bargain, but into——"

"It's all the same thing," says he; and he walked off.

I went to Mr. Frojé's, and ordered a new livry; and found, lickwise, that our coachmin, and Munseer Mortimer, had been there too. My lady's livery was changed, and was now of the same color as my old coat, at Mr. Deuceace's; and I'm blest if there wasn't a tremenjious great earl's corronit on the butns, instid of the Griffin rampint, which was worn befoar.

I asked no questions, however; but had myself measured; and slep, that night, at the Plas Vandôme. I didn't go out with the carridge for a day or two, though; my lady only taking one footmin, she said, until *her new carridge* was turned out.

I think you can guess what's in the wind *now!*

I bot myself a dressing-case, a box of Ody colong, a few duzen lawn sherts and neckcloths, and other things which were necessary for a genlmn in my rank. Silk stockings was provided by the rules of the house. And I complete the bisniss by writing the follying ginteel letter to my late master:—

"CHARLES YELLOWPLUSH, *Esquire, to the*
Honourable A. P. DEUCEACE.

"Sur,—Suckmstansies have acurd sins I last had the honner of wating on you, which render it imposbill that I should remane any longer in your suvvice, I'll thank you to leave out my thinx, when they come home on Sattady from the wash.

"Your obeajnt servnt,
"CHARLES YELLOWPLUSH.

"Plas Vendome."

The athografy of the abuv noat, I confess, is atrocious; but, *ke voolyvoo?* I was only eighteen, and hadn then the expearance in writing which I've enjide sins.

Having thus done my jewty in evry way, I shall prosead, in the nex chapter, to say what hapnd in my new place.

CHAP. X.—THE HONEY-MOON.

THE weak at Fontingblow past quickly away; and, at the end of it, our son and daughter-in-law—a pare of nice young tuttle-duvs—returned to their nest, at the Hotel Mirabew. I suspeck that the *cock* turtle-dove was preshos sick of his barging.

When they arriv'd, the fust thing they found on their table was a large parsle wrapt up in silver paper, and a newspaper, and a couple of cards, tied up with a peace of white ribbing. In the parsle, was a hansume piece of plum-cake, with a deal of sugar. On the cards was wrote, in Goffick characters,

𝕰𝖆𝖗𝖑 𝖔𝖋 𝕮𝖗𝖆𝖇𝖘.

And, in very small Italian,

Countess of Crabs.

And in the paper was the follying parrowgraff:—

"MARRIAGE IN HIGH LIFE.—Yesterday, at the British embassy, the Right Honorable John Augustus Altamont Plantagenet, Earl of Crabs, to Leonora Emilia, widow of the late Lieutenant-general Sir George Griffin, K.C.B. An elegant *dejeuné* was given to the happy couple, by his excellency Lord Bobtail, who gave away the bride. The *élite* of the foreign diplomacy, the Prince of Talleyrand, and the Marshal Duke of Dalmatia, on behalf H.M. the King of France, honoured the banquet and the marriage ceremony. Lord and Lady Crabs intend passing a few weeks at Saint Cloud."

The above dockyments, along with my own triffling billy, of which I have also givn a copy, greated Mr. and Mrs. Deuceace on their arrivle from Fontingblo. Not being presnt, I can't say what Deuceace said, but I can fansy how he *lookt,* and how poor Mrs. Deuceace lookt. They weren't much inclined to rest after the fiteeg of the junny, for, in ½ an hour after their arrivle at Paris, the hosses were put to the carridge agen, and down they came thundering to our country-house, at Saint Cloud (pronounst by those absud Frenchmin, Sing Kloo), to interrup our chaste loves, and delishs marridge injyments.

My lord was sittn in a crimsn satan dress, lolling on a sofa at an open windy, smoaking seagars, as ushle; her ladyship, who, to do him justice, didn mind the smell, occupied another end of the room, and was working, in wusted, a pare of slippers, or an umbrellore case, or a coal skittle, or some such nonsints. You would have thought, to have sean 'em, that they had been married a sentry, at least. Well, I bust in upon this conjugal *tatortator*, and said, very much alarmed, "My lord, here's your son and daughter-in-law."

"Well," says my lord, quite calm, "and what then?"

"Mr. Deuceace!" says my lady, starting up, and looking fritened.

"Yes, my love, my son; but you need not be alarmed. Pray, Charles, say that Lady Crabs and I will be very happy to see Mr. and Mrs. Deuceace; and that they must excuse us receiving them *en famille*. Sit still, my blessing—take things coolly. Have you got the box with the papers?"

My lady pointed to a great green box—the same from which she had taken the papers, when Deuceace fust saw them,—and handed over to my lord a fine gold key. I went out, met Deuceace and his wife on the stepps, gave my messinge, and bowd them palitely in.

My lord didn't rise, but smoak'd away as usual (praps a little quicker, but I can't say); my lady sate upright, looking handsum and strong. Deuceace walked in, his left arm tied to his breast, his wife and hat on the other. He looked very pale and frightened; his wife, poar thing! had her head berried in her handkerchief, and sobd fit to break her heart.

Miss Kicksy, who was in the room (but I didn mention her, she was less than nothink in our house), went up to Mrs. Deuceace at onst, and held out her arms—she had a heart, that old Kicksey, and I respect her for it. The poor hunchback flung herself into Miss's arms, with a kind of whooping screech, and kep there for some time, sobbing in quite a historical manner. I saw there was going to be a sean, and so, in cors, left the door ajar.

"Welcome to Saint Cloud, Algy, my boy!" says my lord, in a loud, hearty voice. "You thought you would give us the slip, eh, you rogue? But we knew it, my dear fellow; we knew the whole affair—did we not, my soul? And, you see, kept our secret better than you did yours."

"I must confess, sir," says Deuceace, bowing, "that I had no idea of the happiness which awaited me, in the shape of a mother-in-law."

"No, you dog; no, no," says my lord, giggling; "old birds, you know, not to be caught with chaff, like young ones. But, here we are, all spliced and happy, at last. Sit down, Algernon; let us smoke a segar, and talk over the perils and adventures of the last month. My love," says my lord, turning to his lady, "you have no malice against poor Algernon, I trust? Pray shake *his* hand." (A grin.)

But my lady rose, and said, "I have told Mr. Deuceace, that I never wished to see him, or speak to him, more. I see no reason, now, to change my opinion." And, herewith, she sailed out of the room, by the door through which Kicksey had carried poor Mrs. Deuceace.

"Well, well," says my lord, as Lady Crabs swept by, "I was in hopes she had forgiven you; but I know the whole story, and, I must confess, you used her cruelly ill. Two strings to your bow!—that was your game, was it,you rogue?"

"Do you mean, my lord, that you know all that past between me and Lady Grif—Lady Crabs, before our quarrel?"

"Perfectly—you made love to her, and she was almost in love with you; you jilted her for money, she got a man to shoot your hand off in revenge: no more dice-boxes, now, Deuceace; no more *sauter la coupe*. I can't think how the deuce you will manage to live without them."

"Your lordship is very kind, but I have given up play altogether," says Deuceace, looking mighty black and uneasy.

"Oh, indeed! Benedick has turned a moral man, has he? This is better and better. Are you thinking of going into the church, Deuceace?"

"My lord, may I ask you to be a little more serious."

"Serious! *à quoi bon?* I am serious—serious in my surprise that, when you might have had either of these women, you should have preferred that hideous wife of yours."

"May I ask you, in turn, how you came to be so little squeamish about a wife, as to choose a woman who had just been making love to your own son?" says Deuceace, growing fierce.

"How can you ask such a question? I owe forty thousand pounds— there is an execution at Size's Hall—every acre I have is in the hands of my creditors; and that's why I married her. Do you think there was any love? Lady Crabs is a dev'lish fine woman, but she's not a fool—she married me for my coronet, and I married her for her money."

"Well, my lord, you need not ask me, I think, why I married the daughter-in-law."

"Yes, but I *do,* my dear boy. How the deuce are you to live? Dawkins's five thousand pounds won't last for ever; and afterwards?"

"You don't mean, my lord—you don't—I mean, you can't. D—!" says he, starting up, and losing all patience, "you don't dare to say that Miss Griffin had not a fortune of ten thousand a year?"

My lord was rolling up, and wetting betwigst his lips, another segar; he lookt up, after he'd lighted it, and said, quietly,—

"Certainly, Miss Griffin had a fortune of ten thousand a year."

"Well, sir, and has she not got it now? Has she spent it in a week?"

"She has not got a sixpence now: she married without her mother's consent!"

Deuceace sunk down in a chair; and I never see sich a dreadful pictur of despair as there was in the face of that retchid man!—he writhed, and nasht his teeth, he tore open his coat, and wriggled madly the stump of his left hand, until, fairly beat, he threw it over his livid pale face, and, sinking backwards, fairly wept alowd.

Bah! it's a dreddfle thing to hear a man crying! his pashn torn up from the very roots of his heart, as it must be before it can git such a vent. My lord, meanwhile, rolled his segar, lighted it, and went on.

"My dear boy, the girl has not a shilling. I wished to have left you alone in peace, with your four thousand pounds: you might have lived decently upon it in Germany, where money is at 5 per cent, where your duns would not find you, and a couple of hundred a year would have kept you and your wife in comfort. But, you see, Lady Crabs would not listen to it. You had injured her, and, after she had tried to kill you, and failed, she determined to ruin you, and succeeded. I must own to you that I directed the arresting business, and put her up to buying your protested bills; she got them for a trifle, and, as you have paid them, has made a good two thousand pounds by her bargain. It was a painful thing, to be sure, for a father to get his son arrested; but, *que voulez-vous?* I did not appear in the transaction; she would have you ruined; and it was absolutely necessary that *you* should marry before I could, so I pleaded your cause with Miss Griffin, and made you the happy man you are. You rogue, you rogue! you thought to match your old father, did you? But, never mind; lunch will be ready soon. In the mean time, have a segar, and drink a glass of Saûterne."

Deuceace, who had been listening to this speech, sprung up wildly.

"I'll not believe it," he said; "it's a lie, an infernal lie! forged by you, you hoary villain, and by the murderess and strumpet you have married. I'll not believe it; shew me the will. Matilda! Matilda!" shouted he, screaming hoarsely, and flinging open the door by which she had gone out.

"Keep your temper, my boy. You *are* vexed, and I feel for you; but don't use such bad language: it is quite needless, believe me."

"Matilda!" shouted out Deuceace, again; and the poor crookid thing came trembling in, followed by Miss Kicksey.

"Is this true, woman?" says he, clutching hold of her hand.

"What, dear Algernon?" says she.

"What?" screams out Deuceace, "What? Why, that you are a beggar, for marrying without your mother's consent; that you basely lied to me, in order to bring about this match; that you are a swindler, in conspiracy with that old fiend yonder, and the she-devil, his wife?"

"It is true," sobbed the poar woman, "that I have nothing, but——"

"Nothing but what? Why don't you speak, you drivelling fool?"

"I have nothing!—but you, dearest, have two thousand a year. Is that not enough for us? You love me for myself, don't you, Algernon? You have told me so a thousand times—say so again, dear husband; and do not, do not be so unkind." And here she sank on her knees, and clung to him, and tried to catch his hand, and kiss it.

"How much did you say?" says my lord.

"Two thousand a year, sir; he has told us so a thousand times."

"*Two thousand!* Two thou—ho, ho, ho,—haw! haw! haw!" roars my lord. "That is, I vow, the best thing I ever heard in my life. My dear creature, he has not a shilling—not a single maravedi, by all the gods and goddesses." And this exlent noblemin began laffin louder than ever; a very kind and feeling genlmn he was, as all must confess.

There was a paws; and Mrs. Deuceace didn begin cussing and swearing at her husband, as he had done at her: she only said, "O, Algernon! is this true?" and got up, and went to a chair, and wep in quiet.

My lord opened the great box. "If you or your lawyers would like to examine Sir George's will, it is quite at your service; you will see here the proviso which I mentioned, that gives the entire fortune to Lady Griffin— Lady Crabs that is: and here, my dear boy, you see the danger of hasty conclusions. Her ladyship only shewed you the *first page of the will;* of course, she wanted to try you. You thought you made a great stroke in at once proposing to Miss Griffin—do not mind it, my love, he really loves you now very sincerely!—when, in fact, you would have done much better to have read the rest of the will. You were completely bitten, my boy—humbugged, bamboozled—ay, and by your old father, you dog. I told you I would, you know, when you refused to lend me a portion of your Dawkins's money. I told you I would; and I *did.* I had you the very next day. Let this be a lesson to you, Percy, my boy; don't try your luck again against such old hands; look deuced well before you leap; *audi alteram partem,* my lad, which means, read both sides of a will. I think lunch is ready; but I see you don't smoke. Shall we go in?"

"Stop, my lord," says Mr. Deuceace, very humble; "I shall not share your hospitality—but—but—you know my condition; I am penniless— you know the manner in which my wife has been brought up——"

"The Honorable Mrs. Deuceace, sir, shall always find a home here, as if nothing had occurred to interrupt the friendship between her dear mother and herself."

"And for me, sir," says Deuceace, speaking faint, and very slow, "I hope—I trust—I think, my lord, you will not forget me?"

"Forget you, sir; certainly not."

"And that you will make some provision?"

"Algernon Deuceace," says my lord, getting up from the sophy, and looking at him with sich a jolly malignaty, as I never see, "I declare, before Heaven, that I will not give you a penny!"

Hereupon, my lord held out his hand to Mrs. Deuceace, and said, "My dear, will you join your mother and me? We shall always, as I said, have a home for you."

"My lord," said the poar thing, dropping a curtsy, "my home is with *him!*"

*   *   *   *   *
  *   *   *   *
*   *   *   *   *

About three months after, when the season was beginning at Paris, and the autum leafs was on the ground, my lord, my lady, me, and Mortimer,

The last Stroke of Fortune

were taking a stroal in the Boddy Balong, the carridge driving on slowly a head, and us as happy as posbill, admiring the plesnt woods, and the gooldn sunset.

My lord was expayshating to my lady upon the egsquizit beauty of the sean, and pouring forth a host of butifle and virtuous sentaments sootable to the hour. It was dalitefle to hear him. "Ah!" said he, "black must be the heart, my love, which does not feel the influence of a scene like this; gathering, as it were, from those sunlit skies, a portion of their celestial gold, and gaining somewhat of heaven with each pure draught of this delicious air!"

Lady Crabs did not speak, but prest his arm and looked upwards. Mortimer and I, too, felt some of the infliwents of the sean, and lent on our goold sticks in silence. The carriage drew up close to us, and my lord and my lady sauntered slowly tords it.

Jest at the place was a bench, and on the bench sate a poorly drest woman, and by her, leaning against a tree, was a man whom I thought I'd sean befor. He was drest in a shabby blew coat, with white seems and copper buttons; a torn hat was on his head, and great quantaties of matted hair and whiskers disfiggared his countnints. He was not shaved, and as pale as stone.

My lord and lady didn tak the slightest notice of him, but past on to the carriage. Me and Mortimer lickwise took *our* places. As we past, the man had got a grip of the woman's shoulder, who was holding down her head, sobbing bitterly.

No sooner were my lord and lady seated, than they both, with igstreme dellixy and good natur, bust into a ror of lafter, peal upon peal, whooping and screaching, enough to frighten the evening silents.

DEUCEACE turned round. I saw his face now—the face of a devvle of hell! Fust, he lookt towards the carridge, and pinted to it with his maimed arm; then he raised the other, *and struck the woman by his side.* She fell, screaming.

Poor thing! Poor thing!

CHARLES YELLOWPLUSH.

THE YELLOWPLUSH CORRESPONDENCE

No. VII.

———◇———

MR. YELLOWPLUSH'S AJEW.

THE end of Mr. Deuceace's history is going to be the end of my cor-rispondince. I wish the public was as sory to part with me as I am with the public; becaws I fansy reely that we've become frends, and feal for my part a becoming greaf at saying ajew.

It's imposbill for me to continyow, however, a writin, as I have done— violetting the rules of authography, and trampling upon the fust prin-cepills of English grammar. When I began, I new no better: when I'd carrid on these papers a little further, and grew accustmd to writin, I be-gan to smel out somethink quear in my style. Within the last sex weaks I have been learning to spell: and when all the world was rejoicing at the festivvaties of our youthful quean—when all i's were fixt upon her long sweet of ambasdors and princes, following the splendid carridge of Marshle the Duke of Damlatiar, and blinking at the pearls and dimince of Prince Oystereasy—Yellowplush was in his loanly pantry—*his* eyes were fixt upon the spelling-book—his heart was bent upon mastring the dif-fickleties of the littery professhn. I have been, in fact, *convertid.*

You shall here how. Ours, you know, is a Wig house; and ever sins his 3d son has got a place in the Treasury, his secknd a captingsy in the Guards, his fust the secretary of embasy at Pekin, with a prospick of being appinted ambasdor at Loo Choo—ever sins master's sons have reseavd these attentions, and master himself has had the promis of a pearitch, he has been the most reglar, consistnt, honrabble Libbaral, in or out of the House of Commins.

Well, being a Whig, it's the fashn, as you know, to reseave littery pipple; and accodingly, at dinner tother day, whose name do you think I had to hollar out on the fust landing-place about a wick ago? After sevral dukes and markises had been enounced, a very gentell fly drives up to our doar, and out steps two gentlemen. One was pail, and wor spektickles, a wig, and a white neckcloth. The other was slim, with a hook nose, a pail fase, a small waist, a pare of falling shoulders, a tight coat, and a catarack of black satting tumbling out of his busm, and falling into a gilt velvet weskit. The little genlmn settled his wigg, and pulled out his ribbinns; the younger one fluffed the dust off his shoos, looked at his wiskers in a little pockit-glas, settled his crevatt; and they both mountid up stairs.

"What name, sir?" says I, to the old genlmn.

"Name!—a! now, you thief o' the wurrrld," says he, "do you pretind nat to know *me?* Say it's the Cabinet Cyclopa—no, I mane the Litherary Chran—psha!—bluthanowns!—say it's DOCTHOR DIOCLESIAN LARNER—I think he'll know me now—ay, Nid?" But the genlmn called Nid was at the botm of the stare, and pretended to be very busy with his shoo-string. So the little genlmn went up stares alone.

"DOCTOR DIOCLESIUS LARNER!" says I.

"DOCTOR ATHANASIUS LARNDER!" says Greville Fitz-Roy, our secknd footman, on the fust landing-place.

"**Doctor Ignatius Loyola!**" says the groom of the chumbers, who pretends to be a schollar; and in the little genlmn went. When safely housed, the other chap came; and when I asked him his name, said, in a thick, gobbling kind of voice:

"Sawedwadgeorgeearllittnbulwig."

"Sir what?" says I, quite agast at the name.

"Sawedwad—no, I mean *Mistaw*edwadLyttnBulwig."

My neas trembled under me, my i's fild with tiers, my voice shook, as I past up the venrabble name to the other footman, and saw this fust of English writers go up to the drawing-room!

It's needless to mention the names of the rest of the compny, or to dixcribe the suckmstansies of the dinner. Suffiz to say that the two littery genlm behaved very well, and seamed to have good appytights; igspecially the little Irishman in the Whig, who et, drunk, and talked as much as ½ a duzn. He told how he'd been presented at cort by his friend, Mr. Bulwig, and how the quean had received 'em both with a dignaty undigscribable, and how her blessid majisty asked what was the bony fidy sale of the Cabinit Cyclopædy, and how he (Doctor Larner) told her that, on his honner, it was under ten thowsnd.

You may gess that the Doctor, when he made this speach, was pretty far gone. The fact is, that whether it was the cornation, or the goodness of the wind (cappile it is in our house, I can tell you), or the natral propensaties of the gests assembled, which made them so igspecially jolly, I don't know, but they had kep up the meating pretty late, and our poar butler was quite tired with the perpechual baskits of clarrit which he'd been called upon to bring up. So that, about 11 o'clock, if I were to say they were merry, I should use a mild term; if I wer to say they were intawsicated, I should use an igspresshn more near to the truth, but less rispeckful in one of my situashn.

The cumpny reseaved this annountsmint with mute extonishment.

"Pray, Doctor Larnder," says a spiteful genlmn, willing to keep up the littery conversation, "what is the Cabinet Cyclopædia?"

"It's the littherary wontherr of the wurrld," says he; "and sure your lordship must have seen it, the latther numbers ispicially—cheap as durrt, bound in gleezed calico, six shillings a vollum. The illusthrious neems of Walther Scott, Thomas Moore, Doctor Southey, Sir James Mackintosh, Docther Donovan, and meself, are to be found in the list of conthributors. It's the Phaynix of Cyclopajies—a litherary Bacon."

"A what?" says the genlmn nex to him.

"A Bacon, shining in the darkness of our age; fild wid the pure and lambent flame of science, burning with the gorrgeous scintillations of divine litherature—a *monumintum*, in fact, *are perinnius*, bound in pink calico, six shillings a vollum."

"This wigmawole," said Mr. Bulwig (who seemed rather disgusted that his frend should take up so much of the convasation), "this wigmawole is all vewy well; but it's cuwious that you don't wemember, in chawactewising the litewawy mewits of the vawious magazines, cwonicles, weviews, and encyclopædias, the existence of a cwitical weview and litewawy chwonicle, which, though the æwa of its appeawance is dated only at a vewy few months pwevious to the pwesent pewiod, is, nevertheless, so wemarkable for its intwinsic mewits, as to be wead, not in the metwopolis alone, but in the countwy—not in Fwance merely, but in the west of Euwope—whewever our pure Wenglish is spoken, it stwetches its peaceful sceptre—pewused in Amewica, fwom New York to Niagawa—wepwinted in Canada, fwom Montweal to Towonto—and, as I am gwatified to hear fwom my fwend the governor of Cape Coast Castle, wegularly weceived in Afwica, and twanslated into the Mandingo language by the missionawies and the bushwangers. I need not say, gentlemen—sir—that is, Mr. Speaker—I mean, Sir John—that I allude to the Litewawy Chwonicle, of which I have the honour to be the pwincipal contwibutor."

"Very true, my dear Mr. Bullwig," says my master; "you and I being Whigs must, of course, stand by our own friends; and I will agree, without a moment's hesitation, that the Literary what-d'ye-callem is the prince of periodicals."

"The Pwince of pewiodicals?" says Bullwig; "my dear Sir John, it's the empewow of the pwess."

"*Soit*,—let it be the emperor of the press, as you poetically call it; but, between ourselves, confess it,—Do not the Tory writers beat your Whigs hollow? You talk about magazines. Look at——"

"Look at hwat?" shouts out Larder. "There's none, Sir Jan, compared to ourrs."

"Pardon me, I think that——"

"Is it Bentley's Mislany you mane?" says Ignatius, as sharp as a niddle.

"Why no; but——"

"O, thin, it's Co'burn, sure; and that divvle Thayodor—a pretty paper, sir, but light—thrashy, milk-and-wathery—not sthrong, like the Litherary Chran—good luck to it."

"Why, Doctor Lander, I was going to tell at once the name of the periodical,—it is FRASER'S MAGAZINE."

"FRESER!" says the Doctor. "O thunder and turf!"

"FWASER!" says Bullwig. "O—ah—hum—haw—yes—no—why,— that is, weally—no, weally, upon my weputation, I never before heard the name of the pewiodical. By the by, Sir John, what wemarkable good clawet this is; is it Lawose or Laff——?"

Laff, indeed! he cooden git beyond laff; and I'm blest if I could kip it neither,—for hearing him pretend ignurnts, and being behind the skreend, settlin sumthink for the genlmn, I bust into such a raw of laffing as never was igseeded.

"Hullo!" says Bullwig, turning red. "Have I said any thing impwobable, aw widiculous? for, weally, I never befaw wecollect to have heard in society such a twemendous peal of cachinnation,—that which the twagic bard who fought at Mawathon has called an *anēwithmon gelasma*."

"Why, be the holy piper," says Larder, "I think you are dthrawing a little on your imagination. Not read *Fraser*! Don't believe him, my lord duke; he reads every word of it, the rogue! The boys about that magazine baste him as if he was a sack of oatmale. My reason for crying out, Sir Jan, was because you mintioned *Fraser* at all. Bullwig has every syllable of it be heart—from the pallitix down to the 'Yellowplush Correspondence.' "

"Ha, ha!" says Bullwig, affecting to laff (you may be sure my years prickt up when I heard the name of the "Yellowplush Correspondence"). "Ha, ha! why, to tell twuth, I *have* wead the cowespondence to which you allude; it's a gweat favowite at court. I was talking with Spwing Wice and John Wussell about it the other day."

"Well, and what do you think of it?" says Sir John, looking mity waggish,—for he knew it was me who roat it.

"Why, weally and twuly, there's considewable cleverness about the cweature; but it's low, disgustingly low: it violates pwobability, and the orthogwaphy is so carefully inaccuwate, that it requires a positive study to compwehend it."

"Yes, faith," says Larner, "the arthagraphy is detistible; it's as bad for a man to write bad spillin as it is for 'em to speak wid a brrogue. Iducation furst, and ganius aftherwards. Your health, my lord, and good luck to you."

"Yaw wemark," says Bullwig, "is vewy appwopwiate. You will wecollect, Sir John, in Hewodotus (as for you, Doctor, you know more wabout Iwish than about Gweek),—you will wecollect, without doubt, a stowy nawwated by that cwedulous though fascinating chwonicler, of a certain kind of sheep which is known only in a certain distwict of Awabia, and of which the tail is so enormous, that it either dwaggles on the gwound, or is bound up by the shepherds of the country into a small wheelbaw-wow, or cart, which makes the chwonicler sneewingly wemark, that thus 'the sheep of Awabia have their own chawiots.' I have often thought, sir (this clawet is weally nectaweous)—I have often, I say, thought that the wace of man may be compawed to these Awabian sheep—genius is our tail, education our wheelbawwow. Without art and education to pwop it, this genius dwops on the gwound, and is polluted by the mud, or injured by the wocks upon the way: with the wheelbawwow it is stwengthened, incweased, supported—a pwide to the owner, a blessing to mankind."

"A very appropriate simile," says Sir John; "and I am afraid that the genius of our friend Yellowplush has need of some such support."

"Apropos," said Bullwig; "who is Yellowplush? I was given to under-stand that the name was only a fictitious one, and that the papers were written by the author of the Diary of a Physician: if so, the man has won-derfully improved in style, and there is some hope of him."

"Bah!" says the Duke of Doublejowl; "every body knows it's Barnard, the celebrated author of 'Sam Slick.' "

"Pardon, my dear duke," says Lord Bagwig; "it's the authoress of High Life, Almacks, and other fashionable novels."

"Fiddlestick's end!" says Doctor Larner; "don't be blushing, and pretinding to ask questions: don't we know you, Bullwig? It's you yourself, you thief of the world; we smoked you from the very beginning."

Bullwig was about indignantly to reply, when Sir John interrupted them, and said,—"I must correct you all, gentlemen; Mr. Yellowplush is no other than Mr. Yellowplush: he gave you, my dear Bullwig, your last glass of champagne at dinner, and is now an inmate of my house, and an ornament of my kitchen!"

"Gad!" says Doublejowl, "let's have him up."

"Hear, hear!" says Bagwig.

"Ah, now," says Larner, "your grace is not going to call up and talk to a footman, sure? is it gintale?"

"To say the least of it," says Bullwig, "the pwactice is iwwegular, and indecowous; and I weally don't see how the interview can be in any way pwofitable."

But the vices of the company went against the two littery men, and ev-ery body excep them was for having up poor me. The bell was wrung; but-ler came. "Send up Charles," says master; and Charles, who was standing behind the skreand, was persnly abliged to come in.

"Charles," says master, "I have been telling these gentlemen who is the author of the 'Yellowplush Correspondence,' in Fraser's Magazine."

"It's the best magazine in Europe," says the duke.

"And no mistake," says my lord.

"Hwhat!" says Larner; "and where's the Litherary Chran.?"

I said myself nothink, but made a bough, and blusht like pickle cab-bitch.

"Mr. Yellowplush," says his grace, "will you, in the first place, drink a glass of wine?"

I boughd agin.

"And what wine do you prefer, sir? humble port or imperial burgundy?"

"Why, your grace," says I, "I know my place, and aint above kitchin winds. I will take a glass of port, and drink it to the health of this honrab-ble compny."

When I'd swiggd off the bumper, which his grace himself did me the honor to pour out for me, there was a silints for a minnit; when my master said:

"Charles Yellowplush, I have perused your memoirs in *Fraser's Maga-zine* with so much curiosity, and have so high an opinion of your talents as a writer, that I really cannot keep you as a footman any longer, or allow you to discharge duties for which you are now quite unfit. With all my ad-miration for your talents, Mr. Yellowplush, I still am confident that many of your friends in the servants' hall will clean my boots a great deal better than a gentleman of your genius can ever be expected to do—it is for this purpose that I employ footmen, and not that they may be writing articles in magazines. But—you need not look so red, my good fellow, and had better take another glass of port—I don't wish to throw you upon the wide world without means of a livelihood, and have made interest for a little place which you will have under government, and which will give you an income of eighty pounds per annum, which you can double, I presume, by your literary labours."

"Sir," says I, clasping my hands, and busting into tears, "do not—for Heaven's sake, do not!—think of any such think, or drive me from your suvvice, because I have been fool enough to write in magaseens. Glans but one moment at your honor's plate—every spoon is as bright as a mir-ror; condysend to igsamine your shoes—your honour may see reflected in them the fases of every one in the compny. I blacked them shoes, Icleaned that there plate. If occasionally Ive forgot the footman in the littery man, and committed to paper my remindicencies of fashnabble life, it was from a sincere desire to do good, and promote nollitch; and I appeal to your honour,—I lay my hand on my busm, and in the fase of this noble company beg you to say, When you rung your bell, who came to you fust? When you stopt out at Brookes's till morning, who sate up for you? When you was ill, who forgot the natral dignaties of his station, and answered the two-pair bell? O, sir," says I, "I know what's what; don't send me away.

I know them littery chaps, and, bleave me, I'd rather be a footman. The work's not so hard—the pay is better; the vittels incompyrably supearor. I have but to clean my things, and run my errints, and you put cloves on my back, and meat in my mouth. Sir! Mr. Bullwig! an't I right; shall I quit *my* station, and sink—that is to say, rise—to *yours?*"

Bulwig was violently affected; a tear stood in his glistening i. "Yellow-plush," says he, seizing my hand, "you *are* right. Quit not your present occupation; black boots, clean knives, wear plush, all your life, but don't turn literary man. Look at me. I am the first novelist in Europe. I have ranged with eagle wing over the wide regions of literature, and perched on every eminence in its turn. I have gazed with eagle eye on the sun of philosophy, and fathomed the mysterious depths of the human mind. All languages are familiar to me, all thoughts are known to me, all men un-derstood by me. I have gathered wisdom from the honeyed lips of Plato, as we wandered in the gardens of Acadames—wisdom, too, from the mouth of Job Johnson, as we smoked our 'backy in Seven Dials. Such must be the studies, and such is the mission, in this world, of the Poet-Philosopher. But the knowledge is only emptiness; the initiation is but misery; the ini-tiated, a man shunned and bann'd by his fellows. O," said Bullwig, clasp-ing his hands, and throwing his fine i's up to the chandelier, "the curse of Pwometheus descends upon his wace. Wath and punishment pursue them from genewation to genewation! Wo to genius, the heaven-scaler, the fire-stealer! Wo and thrice bitter desolation! Earth is the wock on which Zeus, wemorseless, stwetches his withing victim—men, the vul-tures that feed and fatten on him. Ai, Ai! it is agony eternal—gwoaning, and solitawy despair! And you, Yellowplush, would penetwate these mys-tewies; you would waise the awful veil, and stand in the Twemendous Presence. Beware; as you value your peace, beware! Withdwaw, wash Neophyte! For heaven's sake—O, for heaven's sake!"—here he looked round with agony—"give me a glass of bwandy and water, for this clawet is beginning to disagwee with me."

Bullwig having concluded this spitch, very much to his own sattasfack-shn, looked round to the compny for aplaws, and then swigged off the glass of brandy and water, giving a sollum sigh as he took the last gulph; and then Doctor Ignatius, who longed for a chans, and, in order to shew his independnce, began flatly contradicting his friend, and addressed me, and the rest of the genlmn present, in the following manner:—

"Hark ye," says he, "my gossoon, doant be led asthray by the nonsince of that divl of a Bullwig. He's jillous of ye, my bhoy; that's the rale, un-doubted thruth; and it's only to keep you out of litherary life that he's palavering you in this way. I'll tell ye what—Plush, ye blackguard,—my honarable frind, the mimber there, has told me a hunder times by the smallest computation of his intinse admiration for your talents, and the wontherful sthir they were making in the worlld. He can't bear a rival. He's mad with envy, hathred, oncharatableness. Look at him, Plush, and look at me. My father was not a juke exackly, nor aven a markis, and see, nevertheliss, to what a pitch I am come. I spare no ixpinse; I'm the iditor of a cople of pariodicals; I dthrive about in me carridge; I dine wid the lords of the land; and why—in the name of the piper that pleed before Mosus, hwy? Because I'm a litherary man. Because I know how to play me cards. Because I'm Docther Larner, in fact, and mimber of every society in and out of Europe. I might have remained all my life in Thrinity Colledge, and never made such an incom as that offered you by Sir Jan; but I came to London—to London, my boy, and now, see! Look again at me friend, Bullwig. He *is* a gentleman, to be sure, and bad luck to 'im," say I; and what has been the result of his litherary labor? I'll tell you what, and I'll tell this gintale society, by the shade of Saint Pathrick, they're going to make him A BARINET."

"A BARNET, Doctor!" says I; "you don't mean to say they're going to make him a barnet?"

"As sure as I've made meself a docthor," says Larner.

"What, a baronet, like Sir John?"

"The divle a bit else."

"And pray what for?"

"What faw!" says Bullwig. "Ask the histowy of litewatuwe what faw? Ask Colburn, ask Bentley, ask Saunders and Otley, ask the gweat Bwitish nation, what faw? The blood in my veins comes puwified thwough ten thousand years of chivalwous ancestwy; but that is neither here nor there: my political principles—the equal wights which I have advocated—the gweat cause of fweedom that I have celebwated, are known to all. But this, I confess, has nothing to do with the question. No, the question is this—on the thwone of litewatuwe I stand, unwivalled, pwe-eminent; and the Bwitish government, honowing genius in me, compliments the Bwitish nation by lifting into the bosom of the heweditawy nobility, the most gifted member of the democwacy." (The honrabble genlm here sunk down amidst repeated chairs.)

"Sir John," says I, "and my lord duke, the words of my revrint frend, Ignatius, and the remarks of the honrabble genlmn who has just sate down, have made me change the detumminaton which I had the honor of igspressing just now.

"I igsept the eighty pound a-year; knowing that I shall have plenty of time for pursuing my littery cereer, and hoping some day to set on that same bentch of barranites, which is deckarated by the presnts of my honrabble friend.

"Why shooden I? It's trew I aint done any think as *yet* to deserve such an honor; and it's very probable that I never shall. But what then?— *qwaw dong*, as our friends say. I'd much rayther have a coat of arms than a coat of livry. I'd much rayther have my blud-red hand sprawlink in the middle of a shield, than underneath a tea-tray. A barranit I will be, and, in consquints, must cease to be a footmin.

"As to my politticle princepills, these, I confess, aint settled: they are, I know, nessary; but they aint nessary *until askt for;* besides, I reglar read the *Sattarist* newspaper, and so iginirince on this pint would be inigscusable.

"But if one man can git to be a doctor, and another a barranit, and another a capting in the navy, and another a countess, and another the wife of a governor of the Cape of Good Hope, I begin to perseave that the littery trade aint such a very bad un; igspecially if you're up to snough, and know what's o'clock. I'll learn to make myself usefle, in the fust place; then I'll larn to spell; and, I trust, by reading the novvles of the honrabble member, and the scientafick treatiseses of the revrend doctor, I may find the secrit of suxess, and git a litell for my own share. I've sevral frends in the press, having paid for many of those chaps' drink, and given them other treets; and so I think I've got all the emilents of suxess; therefore, I am detummind, as I said, to igsept your kind offer, and beg to withdraw the wuds which I made yous of when I refyoused your hoxpatable offer. I must, however——"

"I wish you'd withdraw yourself," said Sir John, busting into a most igstrorinary rage, "and not interrup the company with your infernal talk! Go down, and get us coffee; and, heark ye! hold your impertinent tongue, or I'll break every bone in your body. You shall have the place, as I said; and while you're in my service, you shall be my servant; but you don't stay in my service after to-morrow. Go down stairs, sir; and don't stand staring here!"

*   *   *   *   *

In this abrupt way, my evening ended: it's with a melancholy regret that I think what came of it. I don't wear plush any more. I am an altered, a wiser, and, I trust, a better man.

I'm about a novvle (having made great progriss in spelling), in the style of my friend Bullwig; and preparing for publigation, in the Doctor's Cyclopedear, The Lives of Eminent Brittish and Foring Washerwomen.

CHARLES YELLOWPLUSH.

THE YELLOWPLUSH CORRESPONDENCE

No. VIII.

———◇———

EPISTLES TO THE LITERATI. NO. XIII.

CH-S Y-LL-WPL-SH, ESQ. TO SIR EDWARD LYTTON BULWER, BART.

JOHN THOMAS SMITH, ESQ. TO C—S Y—H, ESQ.

NOTUS.

THE suckmstansies of the folloing harticle are as follos:—Me and my friend, the sellabrated Mr. Smith, reckonised each other in the Haymarket Theatre, during the paformints of the new play. I was settn in the gallery, and sung out to him (he was in the pit), to jine us after the play, over a glass of bear and a cold hoyster, in my pantry, the famly being out.

Smith came as appinted. We descorsed on the subjick of the comady; and, after sefral glases, we each of us agread to write a letter to the other, giving our notiums of the pease. Paper was brought that momint; and Smith writing his harticle across the knife-bord, I dasht off mine on the dresser.

Our agreemint was, that I (being remarkabble for my style of riting) should cretasize the languidge, whilst he should take up with the plot, of the play; and the candied reader will parding me for having holtered the original address of my letter, and directed it to Sir Edward himself; and for having incopperated Smith's remarks in the midst of my own.

Mayfair, Nov. 30, 1839. Midnite.

Honrabble Barnet!—Retired from the littery world a year or moar, I didn't think anythink would injuice me to come forrards again; for I was content with my share of reputation, and propoas'd to add nothink to those immortial wux which have rendered this Magaseen so sallybrated.

Shall I tell you the reazn of my re-appearants?—a desire for the benefick of my fellow-creatures? Fiddlestick! A mighty truth with which my busm laboured, and which I must bring forth or die? Nonsince— stuff: money's the secret, my dear Barnet,—money—*l'argong, gelt, spicunia.* Here's quarter-day coming, and I'm blest if I can pay my landlud, unless I can ad hartificially to my inkum.

This is, however, betwigst you and me. There's no need to blacard the streets with it, or to tell the British public that Fitzroy Y-ll-wpl-sh is short of money, or that the sallybrated hauthor of the Y—— Papers is in peskewniary diffichklties, or is fiteagued by his shuperhuman littery labors, or by his famly suckmstansies, or by any other pusnal matter: my maxim, dear B, is on these pints to be as quiet as posbile. What the juice does the public care for you or me? Why must we always, in prefizzes and what not, be a talking about ourselves, and our igstrodnary merrats, woas, and injaries? It is on this subjick that I porpies, my dear Barnet, to speak to you in a frendly way; and praps you'll find my advise tolrabbly holesum.

Well, then,—if you care about the apinions, fur good or evil, of us poor suvvants, I tell you, in the most candied way, I like you, Barnet. I've had my fling at you in my day (for, *entry nou*, that last stoary I roat about you and Larnder was as big a bownsir as ever was),—I've had my fling at you; but I like you. One may objeck to an immence deal of your writings, which, betwigst you and me, contain more sham scentiment, sham morallaty, sham poatry, than you'd like to own; but, in spite of this, there's the *stuf* in you: you've a kind and loyal heart in you, Barnet— a trifle deboshed, perhaps; a kean i, igspecially for what's comic (as for your tradgady, it's mighty flatchulent), and a ready plesnt pen. The man who says you are an As is an As himself. Don't believe him, Barnet; not that I suppose you wil,—for, if I've formd a correck apinion of you from your wucks, you think your small-beear as good as most men's: every man does,—and why not? We brew, and we love our own tap—amen; but the pint betwigst us, is this stewpid, absudd way of crying out, because the public don't like it too. Why shood they, my dear Barnet? You may vow that they are fools; or that the critix are your enemies; or that the wuld should judge your poams by your critticle rules, and not their own: you may beat your breast, and vow you are a marter, and you won't mend the matter. Take heart, man! you're not so misrabble after all; your spirits need not be so *very* cast down; you are not so *very* badly paid. I'd lay a wager that you make, with one thing or another—plays, novvles, pamphlicks, and little odd jobbs here and there—your three thowsnd a-year. There's many a man, dear Bullwig, that works for less, and lives content. Why shouldn't you? Three thowsnd a-year is no such bad thing,—let alone the barnetcy: it must be a great comfort to have that bloody hand in your skitching.

But don't you sea, that in a wuld naturally envius, wickid, and fond of a joak, this very barnetcy, these very cumplaints,—this ceaseless groning, and moning, and wining of yours, is igsackly the thing which makes people laff and snear more? If you were ever at a great school, you must recklect who was the boy most bullid, and buffitid, and purshewd—he who minded it most. He who could take a basting got but few; he who rord and wep because the knotty boys called him nicknames, was nicknamed wuss and wuss. I recklect there was at our school, in Smithfield, a chap of this milksop, spoony sort, who appeared among the romping, ragged fellers in a fine flanning dressing-gownd, that his mama had given him. That pore boy was beaten in a way that his dear ma and aunts didn't know him: his fine flanning dressing-gownd was torn all to ribbings, and he got no pease in the school ever after; but was abliged to be taken to some other saminary, where, I make no doubt, he was paid off igsackly in the same way.

Do you take the halligory, my dear Barnet? *Mutayto nominy*—you know what I mean. You are the boy, and your barnetcy is the dressing-gownd. You dress yourself out finer than other chaps, and they all begin to sault and hustle you; it's human nature, Barnet. You shew weakness, think of your dear ma, mayhap, and begin to cry: it's all over with you; the whole school is at you—upper boys and under, big and little; the dirt-iest little fag in the place will pipe out blaggerd names at you, and take his pewny tug at your tail.

The only way to avoid such consperracies is to put a pair of stowt shoalders forrards, and bust through the crowd of raggymuffins. A good bold fellow dubls his fistt, and cries, "Wha dares meddle wi' me?" When Scott got *his* barnetcy, for instans, did any one of us cry out? No, by the laws, he was our master; and wo betide the chap that said neigh to him! But there's barnets and barnets. Do you recklect that fine chapter in *Squintin Durward*, about the two fellos and the cups, at the siege of the bishop's castle? One of them was a brave warrier, and kep *his* cup; they strangled the other chap—strangled him, and laffd at him too.

With respeck, then, to the barnetcy pint, this is my advise: brazen it out. Us littery men I take to be like a pack of schoolboys—childish, greedy, envius, holding by our friends, and always ready to fight. What must be a man's conduck among such? He must either take no notis, and pass on myjastick, or else turn round and pummle soundly—one, two, right and left, ding dong over the face and eyes; above all, never acknowledge that he is hurt. Years ago, for instans (we've no ill blood, but only mention this by way of igsample), you began a sparring with this Magaseen. Law bless you! such a ridicklus gaym I never see: a man so belaybord, beflusterd, bewolloped, was never known; it was the laff of the whole town. Your intelackshal natur, respected Barnet, is not fizzickly adapted, so to speak, for encounters of this sort. You must not indulge in combats with us course bullies of the press; you have not the *staminy* for a reglar set-to. What, then, is your plan? In the midst of the mob to pass as quiet as you can; you won't be undistubbed. Who is? Some stray kix and buffits will fall to you—mortial man is subjick to such; but if you begin to wins and cry out, and set up for a marter, wo betide you!

These remarks, pusnal as I confess them to be, are yet, I assure you, written in perfick good-natur, and have been inspired by your play of the

Sea-Capting, and prefiz to it; which latter is on matters intirely pusnall, and will, therefore, I trust, igscuse this kind of *ad hominam* (as they say) diskcushion. I propose, honrabble Barnit, to cumsider calmly this play and prephiz, and to speak of both with that honisty which, in the pantry or studdy, I've been always phamous for. Let us, in the first place, listen to the opening of the "Preface to the Fourth Edition:"

> "No one can be more sensible than I am of the many faults and deficiencies to be found in this play; but, perhaps, when it is considered how very rarely it has happened in the history of our dramatic literature that good *acting* plays have been produced, except by those who have either been actors themselves, or formed their habits of literature, almost of life, behind the scenes, I might have looked for a criticism more generous, and less exacting and rigorous, than that with which the attempts of an author accustomed to another class of composition have been received by a large proportion of the periodical press.
>
> "It is scarcely possible, indeed, that this play should not contain faults of two kinds: first, the faults of one who has necessarily much to learn in the mechanism of his art; and, secondly, of one who, having written largely in the narrative style of fiction, may not unfrequently mistake the effects of a novel for the effects of a drama. I may add to these, perhaps, the deficiencies that arise from uncertain health and broken spirits, which render the author more susceptible than he might have been some years since to that spirit of depreciation and hostility which it has been his misfortune to excite amongst the general contributors to the periodical press: for the consciousness that every endeavour will be made to cavil, to distort, to misrepresent, and, in fine, if possible, to *run down*, will occasionally haunt even the hours of composition, to check the inspiration and damp the ardour.
>
> "Having confessed thus much frankly and fairly, and with a hope that I may ultimately do better, should I continue to write for the stage, (which nothing but an assurance that, with all my defects, I may yet bring some little aid to the drama, at a time when any aid, however humble, ought to be welcome to the lovers of the art, could induce me to do,) may I be permitted to say a few words as to some of the objections which have been made against this play?"

Now, my dear sir, look what a pretty number of please you put forrards here, why your play shouldn't be good.

First. Good plays are almost always written by actors.

Secknd. You are a novice to the style of composition.

Third. You *may* be mistaken in your effects, being a novelist by trade, and not a play-writer.

Fourthly. Your in such bad helth and sperrits.

Fifthly. Your so afraid of the critix, that they damp your arder.

For shame, for shame, man! What confeshns is these,—what painful pewling and piping! Your not a babby. I take you to be some seven or eight and thutty years old—"in the morning of youth," as the flosofer says. Don't let any such nonsince take your reazn prisoner. What you, an old hand amongst us,—an old soljer of our sovring quean the press,— you, who have had the best pay, have held the topmost rank (ay, and *deserved* them too!—I gif you leaf to quot me in sasiaty, and say, "I *am* a man of genius; Y-ll-wpl-sh says so"),—you to lose heart, and cry pickavy, and begin to howl, because little boys fling stones at you! Fie, man! take courage; and, bearing the terrows of your blood-red hand, as the poet says, punish us, if we've ofended you, punish us like a man, or bear your own punishment like a man. Don't try to come off with such misrabble lodgic as that above.

What do you? You give four satisfackary reazns that the play is bad (the secknd is naught,—for your no such chicking at play-writing, this being the forth). You shew that the play must be bad, and *then* begin to deal with the critix for finding folt!

Was there ever wuss generalship? The play *is* bad,—your right,—a wuss I never see or read. But why kneed *you* say so? If it was so *very* bad, why publish it? *Because you wish to serve the drama!* O fie! don't lay that flattering function to your sole, as Milton observes. *Do* you believe that this *Sea-Capting* can serve the drama? Did you never intend that it should serve any thing, or any body *else?* Of cors you did! You wrote it for money,—money from the maniger, money from the bookseller,— for the same reason that I write this. Sir, Shakspeare wrote for the very same reasons, and I never heard that he bragged about serving the drama. Away with this canting about great motifs! Let us not be too prowd, my dear Barnet, and fansy ourselves marters of the truth, marters or apostels. We are but tradesmen, working for bread, and not for righteousness' sake. Let's try and work honestly; but don't lets be prayting pompisly about our "sacred calling." The taylor who makes your coats (and very well they are made, too, with the best of velvit collars)—I say Stulze, or Nugee, might cry out that *their* motifs were but to assert the eturnle truth of tayloring, with just as much reazn; and who would believe them?

Well; after this acknollitchmint that the play is bad, come sefral pages of attack on the critix, and the folt those gentry have found with it. With these I shan't middle for the presnt. You defend all the characters 1 by 1, and conclude your remarks as follows:—

"I must be pardoned for this disquisition on my own designs. When every means is employed to misrepresent, it becomes, perhaps, allowable to explain. And if I do not think that my faults as a dramatic author are to be found in the study and delineation of character, it is precisely because *that* is the point on which all my previous pursuits in literature and actual life would be most likely to preserve me from the errors I own elsewhere, whether of misjudgment or inexperience.

"I have now only to add my thanks to the actors for the zeal and talent with which they have embodied the characters intrusted to them. The sweetness and grace with which Miss Faucit embellished the part of Violet, which, though only a sketch, is most necessary to the colouring and harmony of the play, were perhaps the more pleasing to the audience from the generosity, rare with actors, which induced her to take a part so far inferior to her powers. The applause which attends the performance of Mrs. Warner and Mr. Strickland attests their success in characters of unusual difficulty; while the singular beauty and nobleness, whether of conception or execution, with which the greatest of living actors has elevated the part of Norman (so totally different from his ordinary range of character) is a new proof of his versatility and accomplishment in all that belongs to his art. It would be scarcely gracious to conclude these remarks without expressing my acknowledgment of that generous and indulgent sense of justice which, forgetting all political differences in a literary arena, has enabled me to appeal to approving audiences—from hostile critics. And it is this which alone encourages me to the hope that, sooner or later, I may add to the dramatic literature of my country something that may find perhaps almost as many friends in the next age as it has been the fate of the author to find enemies in this."

See, now, what a good comfrabble vanaty is! Pepple have quarld with the dramatic characters of your play. "No," says you; "if I *am* remarkabble for anythink, it's for my study and delineation of character; *that* is presizely the pint to which my littery purshuits have led me." Have you read Jil Blaw, my dear sir? Have you pirouzed that exlent tragady, the *Critic?* There's something so like this in Sir Fretful Plaguy, and the Archbishop of Granadiers, that I'm blest if I can't laff till my sides ake. Think of the critix fixing on the very pint for which you are famus!—the roags! And spose they had said the plot was absudd, or the languitch absudder, still, don't you think you would have had a word in defens of them too—you who hope to find frends for your dramatic wux in the nex age? Poo! I tell thee, Barnet, that the nex age will be wiser and better than this; and do you think that it will imply itself a reading of your trajadies? This is misantrofy, Barnet—reglar Byronism; and you ot to have a better apinion of human natur.

Your apinion about the actors I shan't here middle with. They all acted exlently as far as my humbile judgement goes, and your write in giving them all possbile prays. But let's consider the last sentence of the prefiz, my dear Barnet, and see what a pretty set of apiniuns you lay down.

1. The critix are your inymies in this age.

2. In the nex, however, you hope to find newmrous frends.

3. And it's a satisfackshn to think that, in spite of politticle diffrances, you have found frendly aujences here.

Now, my dear Barnet, for a man who begins so humbly with what my friend Father Prout calls an *argamantum ad misericorjam*, who ignoledges that his play is bad, that his pore dear helth is bad, that those cussid critix have played the juice with him—I say, for a man who beginns in such a humbill toan, it's rayther *rich* to see how you end.

My dear Barnet, *do* you suppose that *politticle diffrances* prejudice pepple against *you*? What *are* your politix? Wig, I presume—so are mine, *ontry noo*. And what if they *are* Wig, or Raddicle, or Cumsuvvative? Does any mortial man in England care a phig for your politix? Do you think yourself such a mity man in parlymint, that critix are to be angry with you, and aujences to be cumsidered magnanamous because they treat you fairly? There, now, was Sherridn, he who roat the *Rifles* and *School for Scandle* (I saw the *Rifles* after your play, and, O Barnet, if you *knew* what a relief it was!)—there, I say, was Sherridn—he *was* a politticle character, if you please—he *could* make a spitch or two—do you spose that Pitt, Purseyvall, Castlerag, old George the Third himself, wooden go to see the *Rivles*—ay, and clap hands too, and laff and ror, for all Sherry's Wiggery? Do you spose the critix wouldn't applaud too? For shame, Barnet! what ninnis, what hartless raskles, you must beleave them to be,—in the fust plase, to fancy that you *are* a politticle genius; in the secknd, to let your politix interfear with their notiums about your littery merrits!

"Put that nonsince out of your head," as Fox said to Bonnypart. Wasn't it that great genus, Dennis, that wrote in Swiff and Poop's time, who fansid that the French king wooden make pease unless Dennis was delivered up to him? Upon my wud, I doant think he carrid his diddlusion much futher than a serting honrabble barnet of my acquentance.

And, then, for the nex age. Respected sir, this is another diddlusion; a grose misteak on your part, or my name is not Y—sh. These plays immortial? Ah, *parrysample*, as the French say, this *is* too strong—the small-beer of the *Sea-Capting*, or of any suxessor of the *Sea-Capting*, to keep sweet for sentries and sentries! Barnet, Barnet! do you know the natur of bear? Six weeks is not past, and here your last casque is sour—the public won't even now drink it; and I lay a wager that, betwigst this day (the thuttieth

November) and the end of the year, the barl will be off the stox altogether, never, never to return.

I've notted down a few frazes here and there, which you will do well to igsamin:—

NORMAN.
        "The eternal Flora
Wooes to her odorous haunts the western wind;
While, circling round and upward from the boughs,
Golden with fruits that lure the joyous birds,
Melody, like a happy soul released,
Hangs in the air, and from invisible plumes
Shakes sweetness down!"

NORMAN.
        "And these the lips
Where, till this hour, the sad and holy kiss
Of parting linger'd—as the fragrance left
By *angels* when they touch the earth and vanish."

NORMAN.
"Hark! she has bless'd her son! I bid ye witness,
Ye listening Heavens—thou circumambient air:
The ocean sighs it back—and with the murmur
Rustle the happy leaves. All Nature breathes
Aloud—aloft—to the Great Parent's ear,
The blessing of the mother on her child."

NORMAN.
"I dream of love, enduring faith, a heart
Mingled with mine—a deathless heritage,
Which I can take unsullied to the *stars,*
When the Great Father calls his children home."

NORMAN.
"The blue air breathless in the *starry* peace,
After long silence, hush'd as heaven, but fill'd
With happy thoughts as heaven with *angels.*"

NORMAN.
"Till one calm night, when over earth and wave
Heaven look'd its love from all its numberless *stars.*"
NORMAN.
"Those eyes the guiding *stars* by which I steer'd."

NORMAN.
        "That great mother

(The only parent I have known), whose face
Is bright with gazing ever on the *stars*—
The Mother Sea."

NORMAN.
   "My bark shall be our home;
The *stars* that light the *angel* palaces
Of air, our lamps."

NORMAN.
"A name that glitters, like *a star*, amidst
The galaxy of England's loftiest born."

LADY ARUNDEL.
"And see him princeliest of the lion tribe
Whose swords and coronals gleam around the throne,
The guardian *stars* of the Imperial Isle."

The fust spissymen has been going the round of all the papers, as real, reglar poatry. Those wickid critix! they must have been laffing in their sleafs when they quoted it. Malody, suckling round and uppards from the bows, like a happy soul released, hangs in the air, and from inviz-able plumes shakes sweetness down. Mighty fine, truly! but let mortial man tell the meanink of the passidge. Is it *musickle* sweetniss that Mal-ody shakes down from its plumes—its wings, that is, or tail—or some pekewliar scent that proceeds from happy souls released, and which they shake down from the trees when they are suckling round and uppards? Is this poatry, Barnet? Lay your hand on your busm, and speak out boldly: Is it poatry, or sheer windy humbugg, that sounds a little melojous, and won't bear the commanest test of comman sence?

In passidge number 2, the same bisniss is going on, though in a more comprehensable way: the air, the leaves, the otion, are fild with emocean at Capting Norman's happiness. Pore Nature is dragged in to partisap-ate in his joys, just as she has been befor. Once in a poem, this uni-versle simfithy is very well; but once is enuff, my dear Barnet: and that once should be in some great suckmstans, surely,—such as the meeting of Adam and Eve, in *Pardice Lost*, or Jewpeter and Jewno, in Hoamer, where there seems, as it were, a reasn for it. But sea-captings should not be eternly spowting and invoking gods, hevns, starrs, angels, and other silestial influences. We can all do it, Barnet; nothing in life is esier. I can compare my livry buttons to the stars, or the clouds of my backopipe to the dark vollums that ishew from Mount Hetna; or I can say that angels are looking down from them, and the tobacco silf, like a happy sole re-leased is circling round and upwards, and shaking sweetness down. All this is as ezy as drink; but it's not poatry, Barnet, nor natural. People, when their mothers reckonise them, don't howl about the suckumambint air, and paws to think of the happy leaves a rustling—at least, one mistrusts them if they do. Take another instans out of your own play. Capting Norman (with his eternll *slack-jaw!*) meets the gal of his art:—

> "Look up, look up, my Violet—weeping? fie!
> And trembling too—yet leaning on my breast.
> In truth thou art too soft for such rude shelter.
> Look up! I come to woo thee to the seas,
> My sailor's bride! Hast thou no voice but blushes?
> Nay—from those roses let me, like the bee,
> Drag forth the secret sweetness!"

> VIOLET.
> "Oh, what thoughts
> Were kept for *speech* when we once more should meet,
> Now blotted from the *page*—and all I feel
> Is—*Thou* art with me!"

Very right, Miss Violet—the scentiment is natral, affeckshnit, pleasing, simple (it might have been in more grammaticle languidge, and no harm done): but never mind, the feeling is pritty; and I can fancy, my dear Barnet, a pritty, smiling, weeping lass, looking up in a man's face and saying it. But the capting!—O this capting!—this windy, spouting capting, with his prittinesses, and conseated apollogies for the hardness of his busm, and his old, stale, vapid similies, and his wishes to be a bee! Pish! Men don't make love in this finniking way. It's the part of a sentymentle, poeticle taylor, not a galliant gentleman, in command of one of her madjisty's vessels of war.

Look at the remaining extrac, honored Barnet, and acknollidge that Capting Norman is eturnly repeating himself, with his endless jabber about stars and angels. Look at the neat grammaticle twist of Lady Arundel's spitch, too, who, in the cors of three lines, has made her son a prince, a lion, with a sword and coronal, and a star. Why jumble and sheak up matafors in this way? Barnet, one simily is quite enuff in the best of sentenses (and, I preshume, I kneedn't tell you that it's as well to have it *like*, when you are about it). Take my advise, honrabble sir—listen to a humble footmin: it's genrally best in poatry to understand puffickly what you mean yourself, and to igspress your meaning clearly afterwoods—in the simpler words the better, praps. You may, for instans, call a coronet a coronal (an "ancestral coronal," p. 74) if you like, as you might call a hat a "swart sombrero," "a glossy four-and-nine," "a silken helm, to storm impermeable, and lightsome as the breezy gossamer;" but, in the long run, it's as well to call it a hat. It *is* a hat; and that name is quite as poetticle as another. I think it's Playto, or els Harrystottle, who observes that what

we call a rose by any other name would smell as sweet. Confess, now, dear
Barnet, don't you long to call it a Polyanthus?

I never see a play more carelessly written. In such a hurry you seam to
have bean, that you have actially in some sentenses forgot to put in the
sence. What is this, for instance?—

> "This thrice-precious one
> Smiled to my eyes—drew being from my breast—
> Slept in my arms;—the very tears I shed
> Above my treasure were to men and angels
> Alike such holy sweetness!"

In the name of all the angels that ever you invoked—Raphael, Gabriel,
Uriel, Zadkiel, Azrael—what does this "holy sweetness" mean? We're not
spinxes to read such durk conandrums. If you knew my state sins I came
upon this passidg—I've neither slep nor eton; I've neglected my pantry;
I've been wandring from house to house with this ridl in my hand, and
nobody can understand it. All Mr. Frazier's men are wild, looking gloomy
at one another, and asking what this may be. All the cumtributors have
been spoak to. The Docter, who knows every languitch, has tried and
giv'n up; we've sent to Docter Pettigruel, who reads horyglifics a deal
ezier than my way of spellin'—no anser. Quick! quick with a fifth edition,
honored Barnet, and set us at rest! While your about it, please, too, to
igsplain the two last lines:—

"His merry bark with England's flag to crown her."

See what dellexy of igspreshn, "a flag to crown her!"

> "His merry bark with England's flag to crown her,
> Fame for my hopes, and woman in my cares."

Likewise the following:—

> "Girl, beware
> THE LOVE THAT TRIFLES ROUND THE CHARMS IT GILDS,
> OFT RUINS WHILE IT SHINES."

Igsplane this, men and angels! I've tried every way; backards, forards,
and in all sorts of trancepositions, as thus:—

> The love that ruins round the charms it shines,
> Gilds while it trifles oft;

Or,

> The charm that gilds around the love it ruins,
> Oft trifles while it shines;

Or,

> The ruins that love gilds and shines around,
> Oft trifles while it charms;

Or,

> Love, while it charms, shines round, and ruins oft
> The trifles that it gilds;

Or,

> The love that trifles, gilds and ruins oft,
> While round the charms it shines.

All which are as sensable as the fust passidge.

And with this I'll alow my friend Smith, who has been silent all this time, to say a few words. He has not ritten near so much as me (being an infearor genus, betwigst ourselves), but he says he never had such mortial difficklty with any thing as with the dixcripshn of the plott of your pease. Here his letter.

To Ch-rl-s F-tzr-y Pl-nt-g-n-t Y-ll-wpl-sh,
Esq., *&c. &c.*

30th Nov. 1839.

My dear and honoured Sir,—I have the pleasure of laying before you the following description of the plot, and a few remarks upon the style of the piece called *The Sea-Captain.*

Five-and-twenty years back, a certain Lord Arundel had a daughter, heiress of his estates and property; a poor cousin, Sir Maurice Beevor (being next in succession); and a page, Arthur Le Mesnil by name.

The daughter took a fancy for the page, and the young persons were married unknown to his lordship.

Three days before her confinement (thinking, no doubt, that period favourable for travelling), the young couple had agreed to run away together, and had reached a chapel near on the sea-coast, from which they were to embark, when Lord Arundel abruptly put a stop to their proceedings by causing one Gaussen, a pirate, to murder the page.

His daughter was carried back to Arundel House, and, in three days, gave birth to a son. Whether his lordship knew of this birth I cannot say; the infant, however, was never acknowledged, but carried by Sir Maurice Beevor to a priest, Onslow by name, who educated the lad and kept him for twelve years in profound ignorance of his birth. The boy went by the name of Norman.

Lady Arundel meanwhile married again, again became a widow, but had a second son, who was the acknowledged heir, and called Lord Ashdale. Old Lord Arundel died, and her ladyship became countess in her own right.

When Norman was about twelve years of age, his mother, who wished to *"waft* young Arthur to a distant land," had him sent on board ship. Who should the captain of the ship be but Gaussen, who received a smart bribe from Sir Maurice Beevor to kill the lad. Accordingly, Gaussen tied him to a plank, and pitched him overboard.

*   *   *   *   *

About thirteen years after these circumstances, Violet, an orphan niece of Lady Arundel's second husband, came to pass a few weeks with her ladyship. She had just come from a sea-voyage, and had been saved from a wicked Algerine by an English sea-captain. This sea-captain was no other than Norman, who had been picked up off his plank, and fell in love with, and was loved by, Miss Violet.

A short time after Violet's arrival at her aunt's, the captain came to pay her a visit, his ship anchoring off the coast near Lady Arundel's residence. By a singular coincidence, that rogue Gaussen's ship anchored in the harbour too. Gaussen at once knew his man, for he had "tracked" him (after drowning him), and he informed Sir Maurice Beevor that young Norman was alive.

Sir Maurice Beevor informed her ladyship. How should she get rid of him? In this wise. He was in love with Violet, let him marry her and be off; for Lord Ashdale was in love with his cousin too; and, of course, could not marry a young woman in her station of life. "You have a chaplain on board," says her ladyship to Captain Norman; "let him attend to-night in the ruined chapel, marry Violet, and away with you to sea." By this means she hoped to be quit of him for ever.

But, unfortunately, the conversation had been overheard by Beevor, and reported to Ashdale. Ashdale determined to be at the chapel and carry off Violet; as for Beevor, he sent Gaussen to the chapel to kill both Ashdale and Norman, thus there would only be Lady Arundel between him and the title.

Norman, in the meanwhile, who had been walking near the chapel, had just seen his worthy old friend, the priest, most barbarously murdered there. Sir Maurice Beevor had set Gaussen upon him; his reverence was coming with the papers concerning Norman's birth, which Beevor wanted in order to extort money from the countess. Gaussen was, however, obliged to run before he got the papers; and the clergyman had time, before he died, to tell Norman the story, and give him the documents, with which Norman sped off to the castle to have an interview with his mother.

He lays his white cloak and hat on the table, and begs to be left alone with her ladyship. Lord Ashdale, who is in the room, surlily quits it; but, going out cunningly, puts on Norman's cloak. "It will be dark," says he, "down at the chapel; Violet won't know me; and, egad! I'll run off with her!"

Norman has his interview. Her ladyship acknowledges him, for she cannot help it; but will not embrace him, love him, or have any thing to do with him.

Away he goes to the chapel. His chaplain was there waiting to marry him to Violet, his boat was there to carry him on board his ship, and Violet was there, too.

"Norman," says she in the dark, "dear Norman, I knew you by your white cloak; here I am," and she and the man in the cloak go off to the inner chapel to be married.

There waits Master Gaussen, he has seized the chaplain and the boat's crew, and is just about to murder the man in the cloak, when

Norman rushes in and cuts him down, much to the surprise of Miss, for she never suspected it was sly Ashdale who had come, as we have seen, disguised, and very nearly paid for his masquerading.

Ashdale is very grateful; but, when Norman persists in marrying Violet, he says—no, he shan't. He shall fight; he is a coward if he doesn't fight. Norman flings down his sword, and says he *won't* fight; and

Lady Arundel, who has been at prayers all this time, rushes in—says, "Hold! this is your brother, Percy—your elder brother!" Here is some restiveness on Ashdale's part, but he finishes by embracing his brother.

Norman burns all the papers; vows he will never peach; reconciles himself with his mother; says he will go loser; but, having ordered his ship to "veer" round to the chapel, orders it to veer back again, for he will pass the honeymoon at Arundel Castle.

As you have been pleased to ask my opinion, it strikes me that there are one or two very good notions in this plot. But the author does not fail, as he would modestly have us believe, from ignorance of stage-business; he seems to know too much, rather than too little, about the stage, to be too anxious to cram in effects, incidents, perplexities. There is the perplexity concerning Ashdale's murder, and Norman's murder, and the priest's murder, and the page's murder, and Gaussen's murder. There is the perplexity about the papers, and that about the hat and cloak (a silly, foolish obstacle), which only tantalize the spectator, and retard the march of the drama's action; it is as if the author had said, "I must have a new incident in every act, I must keep tickling the spectator perpetually, and never let him off until the fall of the curtain."

The same disagreeable bustle and petty complication of intrigue you may remark in the author's drama of *Richelieu*. *The Lady of Lyons* was a much simpler and better-wrought plot. The incidents following each other either not too swiftly or startlingly. In *Richelieu*, it always seemed to me as if one heard doors perpetually clapping and banging; one was puzzled to follow the train of conversation, in the midst of the perpetual small noises that distracted one right and left.

Nor is the list of characters of *The Sea-Captain* to be despised. The outlines of all of them are good. A mother, for whom one feels a proper tragic mixture of hatred and pity; a gallant single-hearted son, whom she disdains, and who conquers her at last by his noble conduct; a dashing, haughty Tybalt of a brother; a wicked, poor cousin, a pretty maid, and a fierce bucanier. These people might pass three hours very well on the stage, and interest the audience hugely; but the author fails in filling up the outlines. His language is absurdly stilted, frequently careless; the reader or spectator hears a number of loud speeches, but scarce a dozen lines that seem to belong of nature to the speakers.

Nothing can be more fulsome or loathsome to my mind than the continual sham-religious clap-traps which the author has put into the mouth of his hero; nothing more unsailor-like than his namby-pamby starlit descriptions, which my ingenious colleague has, I see, alluded to. "Thy faith my anchor, and thine eyes my haven," cries the gallant captain to his lady. See how loosely the sentence is constructed, like a thousand others in the book. The captain is to cast anchor with the girl's faith in her own eyes; either image might pass by itself, but together, like the quadrupeds of Kilkenny, they devour each other. The captain tells his lieutenant *to bid his bark veer round* to a point in the harbour. Was ever such language? My lady gives Sir Maurice a thousand pounds to *waft* him (her son) to some distant shore. Nonsense, sheer nonsense; and, what is worse, affected nonsense!

Look at the comedy of the poor cousin. "There is a great deal of game on the estate—partridges, hares, wild geese, snipes, and plovers (*smacking his lips*)—besides a magnificent preserve of sparrows, which I can sell *to the little blackguards* in the streets at a penny a hundred. But I am very poor—a very poor old knight."

Is this wit, or nature? It is a kind of sham wit; it reads as if it were wit, but it is not. What poor, poor stuff, about the little blackguard boys! what flimsy ecstasies and silly "smacking of lips" about the "plovers!" Is this the man who writes for the next age? O fie! Here is another joke:—

"*Sir Maurice.* Mice!—Zounds, how can I
Keep mice?—I can't afford it! They were starved
To death an age ago. The last was found,
Come Christmas three years, stretched beside a bone

In that same larder—so consumed and worn
By pious fast—'twas awful to behold it!
I canonized its corpse in spirits of wine,
And set it in the porch—a solemn warning
To thieves and beggars!"

Is not this rare wit? "Zounds! how can I keep mice?" is well enough
for a miser; not too new, or brilliant either; but this miserable dilution of
a thin joke, this wretched hunting down of the poor mouse! It is humil-
iating to think of a man of *esprit* harping so long on such a mean, pitiful
string. A man who aspires to immortality, too! I doubt whether it is to be
gained thus; whether our author's words are not too loosely built to make
"starry pointing pyramids of." Horace clipped and squared his blocks
more carefully before he laid the monument which, *imber edax,* or *Aquila
impotens,* or *fuga temporum,* might assail in vain. Even old Ovid, when he
raised his stately, shining, heathen temple, had placed some columns in
it, and hewn out a statue or two which deserved the immortality that he
prophesied (somewhat arrogantly) for himself. But let us not all be looking forward to a future, and fancying that, *"incerti spatium dum finiat avi,"*
our books are to be immortal. Alas! the way to immortality is not so easy,
nor will our *Sea-Captain* be permitted such an unconscionable cruise. If
all the immortalities were really to have their wish, what a work would
our descendants have to study them all!

Not yet, in my humble opinion, has the honourable baronet achieved
this deathless consummation. There will come a day (may it be long distant!) when the very best of his novels will be forgotten; and it is reasonable to suppose that his dramas will pass out of existence, some time
or other, in the lapse of the *secula seculorum.* In the meantime, my dear
Plush, if you ask me what the great obstacle is towards the dramatic fame
and merit of our friend, I would say that it does not lie so much in hostile
critics or feeble health, as in a careless habit of writing, and a peevish vanity which causes him to shut his eyes to his faults. The question of original capacity I will not moot; one may think very highly of the honourable
baronet's talent, without rating it quite so high as he seems disposed to
do.

And to conclude: as he has chosen to combat the critics in person,
the critics are surely justified in being allowed to address him directly.

> With best compliments to Mrs. Yellowplush,
> I have the honour to be, dear Sir,
> Your most faithful and obliged
> humble servant,
> JOHN THOMAS SMITH.

And now, Smith having finisht his letter, I think I can't do better than clothes mine lickwise; for though I should never be tired of talking, praps the public may of hearing, and therefore it's best to shet up shopp.

What I've said, respected Barnit, I hoap you woan't take unkind. A play, you see, is public property for every one to say his say on; and I think, if you read your prefez over agin, you'll see that it ax as a direct incouridgemint to us critix to come forrard and notice you. But don't fansy, I besitch you, that we are actiated by hostillaty; fust write a good play, and you'll see we'll prays it fast enuff. Waiting which, *Agray, Munseer le Chevaleer, l'ashurance de ma hot cumsideratun.*

Voter distangy,
Y.

Editorial Apparatus

for *The Yellowplush Correspondence*

Composition and Publication

◇

The Yellowplush Correspondence, or *Papers by Mr. Yellowplush*, or *Memoirs of Mr. Charles J. Yellowplush*, as the work has variously been titled, was published in ten installments in *Fraser's Magazine* in November 1837, January through August 1838, and January 1840. No manuscripts or proofs for the work are known to survive.

From October 1837 to July 1838, when Thackeray was writing the bulk of the Yellowplush papers, he was a very busy, happy man "writing for his life," as Carlyle later remarked. His ill-starred proprietorship of *The Constitution*, the radical newspaper in which his step-father invested so large a portion of his fortune, had ended in July with the demise of the paper; so Thackeray was seeking as many outlets as possible for his free-lance writing. During this period he illustrated, among other things, Charles G. Addison's *Journey to Damascus and Palmyra* (London: Bentley, 1838); he wrote a long tale, "The Professor," for *Bentley's Magazine* and contributed fairly regularly to *The Times*, *The New Monthly Magazine*, *Galignani's Messenger* and perhaps to one or two other periodicals hinted at but unidentified in his account book for 1838 (*Letters*, I, 513). His contributions to *Fraser's* at that time include reviews and occasional essays in addition to *Yellowplush*—the whole amounting to about 25 to 30 magazine pages each month. And, in *The New Monthly*, two installments of "Major Gahagan's Historical Reminiscences" appeared in February and March, 1838, though the bulk of that story did not appear until November and December and the following February. In short, as Gordon Ray's biography makes clear, Thackeray was really just beginning to struggle his way forward in what at best was a disreputable profession (Ray, *Uses*, 194–99).[1] His successes depended in part on the good recommendations of his friends but also on the favorable reception given to *Yellowplush*. By

---

1. Harold Strong Gulliver's *Thackeray's Literary Apprenticeship* (Valdosta, Ga., 1929), concentrating on the doubtful attributions, nevertheless continues to be a valuable discussion of Thackeray's relations with *Fraser's Magazine* and other periodicals. Miriam Thrall's *Rebellious Fraser's* (New York: Columbia University Press, 1929), is also useful, but its attributions have in many cases been questioned by subsequent scholarship.

March, 1838, Thackeray was able to write to the publishers: "Bad as he is, Mr. Yellowplush is the most popular contributor to your magazine ... " (*Letters*, I, 351).

When Thackeray submitted the first Yellowplush paper, "Fashnable Fax and Polite Annygoats," to James Fraser for *Fraser's Magazine* in October, 1837, his letter hinted at further plans:

> Here is a paper on Skelton—I expect you will pay handsomely for it; for it is good fun.
>
> If you don't like it, or can't put it in this month, please send it me back: I can place it advantageously elsewhere.
>
> I think I could make half a dozen stories by the same author, if you incline.— [*Letters*, I, 348-49]

The Yellowplush review of John Skelton's *My Book; or, The Anatomy of Conduct* (London: Simpkins and Marshall, 1837) appeared in the November issue of *Fraser's*, and though the next Yellowplush paper did not appear until January of the next year, it is clear that the publisher did "incline," for eventually ten installments of the writings of Charles Edward (later changed to Charles James) Harrington Fitzroy Yellowplush were printed.

In March, 1838, following the publication of the fourth Yellowplush paper, Thackeray struck for higher wages: "... I intend to make some fresh conditions about Yellowplush. I shall write no more of that gentleman's remarks except at the rate of twelve guineas a sheet. ... " He was already being paid ten pounds a sheet (sixteen magazine pages) while some writers received as little as six or eight. But the publisher clearly agreed with the author about the importance and popularity of Yellowplush, for the series continued with Thackeray getting the twelve guineas plus two guineas apiece for the drawings (*Letters*, I, 351; Ray, *Uses*, 198). In April Thackeray turned in the bulk of "Mr. Deuceace at Paris," the whole of which he felt should be printed as one long installment; for it would, he wrote, "be spoiled by being split into 3." It was so split, nonetheless, when it appeared in May, June, and July. In his request that "Deuceace" appear in one issue of the magazine rather than three, Thackeray may have been influenced as much by the hope of getting fifty pounds for the story in one month as by a regard for its aesthetic integrity (*Letters*, I, 364). In the present edition, nevertheless, his wish is honored by the suppression of the two divisions.

In July Thackeray's attention to *Yellowplush* was being replaced by the preparation of *Stubbs's Calendar* for Cruikshank's *Comic Almanack* for 1839 (*Letters*, I, 367). The August number, "Mr. Yellowplush's Ajew," written the previous month, effectively closed the Yellowplush series; but it also gave a lingering life to the ostensible author who, having lost his place as footman because of his "littery" activities, is thrown back upon them for a livelihood. As he announces at the end of his "Ajew," he is "about a novvle (having made great progriss in spelling), in the style of my friend Bullwig; and preparing for publgation, in the Doctor's Cyclo-pedear, The Lives of Eminent Brittish and Foring Washerwomen."

A little over a year later, when Yellowplush next broke into print, Thackeray had apparently forgotten that Yellowplush was now imitating Bulwer; or, perhaps, Yellowplush had repented of that move. In December, 1839, after having been "to the play where I was very much bored by Bulwer's new piece," Thackeray "turned off a thundering article against Bulwer" in the style and language of Yellowplush (Letters, I, 394–95). Titled "Epistles to the Literati," it appeared in January, 1840, a year and five months after "Ajew."

To aid in his recollection of the play, The Sea-Captain; or The Birthright, Thackeray had recourse to a copy of the fourth edition (London: Saunders and Otley, 1839), to the preface of which he addressed a good many of his remarks. The quotations from the play are extensive and for the most part accurate enough; but there are over 40 alterations which include the usual minor punctuation changes, the dropping of two lines without ellipses, changes in capitalization, and the italicization of words which the 'reviewer' wished to emphasize. Perhaps the most interesting are the "quotations" which are not in the play at all. In the part ostensibly by John Thomas Smith, who was to discuss the plot, there are four short invented quotations in the plot summary which contrast satirically with the actual language of the play. For example, Smith's summary has it that Norman "lays his white cloak and hat on the table, and begs to be left alone with her ladyship. Lord Ashdale, who is in the room, surlily quits it; but, going out cunningly, puts on Norman's cloak. 'It will be dark,' says he, 'down at the chapel; Violet won't know me; and, egad! I'll run off with her!' " In the play itself he said, as he exchanged the cloak and hat, "Ho! / The signal plume—a fair exchange,—so please you, / The cloak too. Tarry now as long as lists you; / I'll be your likeness elsewhere." A moment later when Ashdale in Norman's cloak meets Violet in the dark, Smith's summary has it that she says, "Norman, dear Norman, I knew you by your white cloak; here I am." But in the play she says in the dark, "Speak! The silence and the darkness chill me." To which Ashdale says, "Dearest, No cause for fear!" And Violet responds, "Thy voice sounds sharp and strange. Ah, my heart fails me!" And a few moments later she adds, "Mine ear mocks me; / But terror plays sad tricks with the senses! Norman, / My frame may tremble, but my heart is brave— / For that can never doubt thee." The gist is there, but the "misquotations" add their part to the criticism of the high-flown tone of the play.

Evolving as it did from a tentative idea, the Yellowplush correspondence is not particularly unified. Not only was the second installment delayed two months in appearing, but the first paper seems, both from its opening letter to Oliver Yorke—the mythical editor of Fraser's—and from the postscript signed "O. Y.," to be a trial piece run to test public reaction to Yellowplush. Also it is slightly different in form from the ensuing installments in being, ostensibly, a book review, while the remainder purports to be largely autobiography, though "Skimmings from 'The Dairy of George IV.' " and "Epistles to the Literati, No. XIII" can also be called reviews. Furthermore, when the series was reprinted in *Comic Tales and Sketches* (1841), "Fashnable Fax" was omitted. On the other hand, the series title, "The Yellowplush Correspondence," was provided with the first installment, "Fashnable Fax," and accompanied all others save the last. In addition, Thackeray's initial letter to James Fraser shows an inclination to write a series. The footman's view of the upper classes from his particularly intimate relation to them is an aspect that unifies all of Yellowplush's papers. Moreover, the omission of this first installment from *Comic Tales* (and, thence, from all subsequent editions) may have been influenced less by its lack of uniformity with the other numbers than by the fact that it rested alone near the end of volume sixteen of *Fraser's Magazine* and may merely have been overlooked in 1841. There are, however, direct references to the first installment in the letter introducing the second number, "Miss Shum's Husband," which would have reminded an editor of the existence of "Fashnable Fax"; and so it may have been consciously rejected, rather than simply ignored, perhaps because of the sense of gastronomic repulsiveness which it alone contains. The letter introducing "Miss Shum's Husband" was also omitted in 1841.

The series poses another problem of unity. The last installment, "Epistles to the Literati," not only appeared over a year after the ninth installment, "Mr. Yellowplush's Ajew," but it is not under the usual Yellowplush banner title. It appeared as number XIII in an occasional *Fraser's* series called "Epistles to the Literati" which were written by a number of people, most notably William Maginn and Thomas Carlyle. And finally, it too is in a rather different form, being a quasi-review, quasi-letter to the author, addressed to "Sir Edward Lytton Bulwer, Bart.," concerning his play, *The Sea-Captain*. On the other hand, "Epistles" was included in 1841 as part of the Yellowplush correspondence when it was retitled "Papers by Mr. Yellowplush, Sometime Footman in Many Genteel Families" for publication in *Comic Tales and Sketches*.

The question of the unity of Yellowplush's writings can be summed up: The second through ninth installments, although episodic and consisting of relatively self-contained units, are unified in form, banner title, and consecutive appearance. The first and last installments have a somewhat tenuous connection with the rest. Without contending either for the unity or discontinuity of the series as a whole, all the papers are printed here as they appeared in *Fraser's Magazine* with each installment dated. The preface Thackeray wrote for *Comic Tales*, which is appropriate for the contents of the two-volume collection, is printed here as an appendix.

Subsequent Editions

————◇————

The first republication of *The Yellowplush Correspondence* in book form occurred in Philadelphia in September, 1838. The enterprising firm of Carey and Hart printed one thousand copies of the series without authorization or permission.[1] It is Thackeray's first separately published book and is now both rare and expensive. It is, nevertheless, without authority. Its text varies from the original in over 1,030 places and omits "Mr. Yellowplush's Ajew" and, of course, the 1840 "Epistles to the Literati." The omission of "Ajew" resulted, no doubt, from the assumption by Carey and Hart that "The End of Mr. Deuceace's History" (the eighth paper) was also the end of Mr. Yellowplush's correspondence.

According to the "Preface" to *Comic Tales and Sketches*, supplied by Thackeray in 1841, the elegance of the style of the Yellowplush papers "made them excessively popular in America, where they were reprinted more than once" (67.8–9). The only reprinting I have found besides the Carey and Hart book is that of "Epistles to the Literati," the tenth installment, in *Corsair*, 7 March 1840. Thackery may have had this in mind, for he knew the *Corsair*, having had a short association with its editor, N. P. Willis, which had ended late in 1839 probably because the American was not paying. It is not likely, therefore, that the *Corsair* reprinting of "Epistles" was authorized. It departs from *Fraser's* text in 36 readings in purely routine ways. Although in addition it omits words and passages in nine places, creates a new paragraph, and erroneously changes a date, these are clearly unintentional and editorial alterations. On the other hand, the statement in the "Preface" to *Comic Tales* about American reprints may have been a mere bit of banter or promotional eloquence similar to some publishers' announcements of a 14th edition on a title page in an attempt to move old stock. The "Preface" goes on to say that "Major Gahagan" also appeared piratically in America, but no copy is known to exist. The Carey and Hart cost books (Historical Society of Pennsylvania) made no mention of it, though their publication of *Yellowplush* might

---

1. "Carey and Hart Cost Books, 1830–40" ms., Historical Society of Pennsylvania.

suggest that they had also published "Major Gahagan." This reference, too, could have been a mere puff or a joke about American piracies.

Yellowplush next appeared in volume one of *Comic Tales and Sketches, Edited and Illustrated by Mr. Michael Angelo Titmarsh*, 2 vols. (London: Hugh Cunningham, 1841). Its new title, "Papers by Mr. Yellowplush, Sometime Footman in Many Genteel Families," suggests the miscellaneous nature of its contents. Although we know—primarily from the "Preface"—that Thackeray had a hand in preparing *Comic Tales* for publication, there is no evidence to indicate which variations in the text were introduced by him. The authority of the *Comic Tales* version of the text might best be examined by comparing what Thackeray said about it with the variants it introduces and the common editorial practices of nineteenth-century publishers. Thackeray's "Preface," ostensibly written by Michael Angelo Titmarsh, opens with an explanation of the editorial procedures:

> A custom which the publishers have adopted of late cannot be too strongly praised, both by authors of high repute, and by writers of no repute at all—viz., the custom of causing the works of unknown literary characters to be "edited" by some person who is already a favourite with the public. The labour is not so difficult as at first may be supposed. A publisher writes—"My dear Sir,—Enclosed is a draft on Messrs. So-and-so: will you edit Mr. What-d'ye-call-'em's book?" The well-known author says—"My dear Sir,—I have to acknowledge the receipt of so much, and will edit the book with pleasure." And the book is published; and from that day until the end of the world the well-known author never hears of it again, except he has a mind to read it, when he orders it from the circulating library. [66.1–12]

Titmarsh is himself a fiction and his editorial method is a fiction, but it is not far from the truth. In the same preface he tells of a great dispute among the three fictional authors of the contents of *Comic Tales*, Major Gahagan, Yellowplush, and himself, over the editing which was finally settled by the toss of a coin in favor of Titmarsh; "and I shall be very glad, in a similar manner, to 'edit' any works; of any author, or any subject, or in any language whatever' (67.3–5). Then Titmarsh claims, "Mr. Yellowplush's Memoirs appeared in 'Fraser's Magazine,' and have been reprinted accurately from that publication" (67.6–7). Titmarsh's definition of "accurately," however, allows for omitting the first installment, "Fashnable Fax," and the opening letter to the second, "Miss Shum's Husband," altering chapter numbers, changing the overall title of the series, giving the third installment an additional title, omitting Yellowplush's signature at the end of installments, and nearly 700 other alterations, only a few of which can be regarded as undoubtedly authorial.

Nevertheless, given an understanding of the accepted practices of mid-nineteenth-century commercial printing establishments, the claim to accurate reprinting need not be considered false. The majority of the changes seem the reasonable result of the "cooperation" printers habitually offered their authors—correcting punctuation and typos, touching up the spelling, and inadvertently allowing a few new errors to creep in. Indeed, 62 of the emendations of the *Fraser's* text used in the present edition were first made in *Comic Tales*. As inoffensive, and in fact helpful, as the 700 changes introduced in the *Comic Tales* version of *Yellowplush* must have appeared to the printer or publisher, the total effect is remarkable. In *Comic Tales* Yellowplush's spelling is more consistent. In 137 cases *Comic Tales* corrects or partially corrects spelling according to standard rules. In 63 cases it substitutes one Yellowplushian spelling for another—at least 17 of these are clear attempts to make Yellowplush misspell consistently; the other 46 changes involve seldom used words. In only 32 cases does *Comic Tales* substitute possibly Yellowplushian spellings for correct spellings. Some of these appear to be printers' errors; the rest are formed by Yellowplush's "normal" spelling logic. Though all of these changes affect only a small percentage of the dialect spellings, they are noticeable enough to make a difference, and the effect is, I think, not necessarily desirable. After spelling, the most frequent changes are in punctuation—over 215, of which about 60 are of sufficient consequence to be placed in the list of selected variants. Most of the punctuation changes are arbitrary and merely make the pattern of punctuation slightly more consistent without altering the tone or texture perceptibly. Approximately fifty other changes involve wording or meaning in a substantive manner. These are listed and discussed in the apparatus. The rest of the changes are miscellaneous alterations in capitalization, division of compound words, or are obvious typographical errors. Whether the touching up of Yellowplush's punctuation and spelling originated with Thackeray when preparing copy for the printer of *Comic Tales* or when reading proof (if in fact he did either of those things) or whether the changes are wholly compositorial cannot be known, for the evidence—printer's copy and proof sheets—no longer exists.

The publication of *Comic Tales and Sketches* was a second joint commercial venture for Thackeray and Cunningham, the publisher. In July 1840 *The Paris Sketch Book* was published under the imprint of John Macrone, but by August, in a letter from Mrs. Thackeray to her mother-in-law, the publisher is identified as Cunningham, who had already, it appears, succeeded Macrone (*Letters*, I, 461). Records of the publisher are not known to survive, but it is clear from Thackeray's letters and from reviews that *The Paris Sketch Book* was at least a modest financial success. Whether this led to an overly optimistic initial print order for *Comic Tales* or whether that book was simply not as well received as *The Paris Sketch Book* is not known. However, in 1848, on the coattails of *Vanity Fair*, remaindered sheets of *Comic Tales* were re-issued with a new undated title page identifying Titmarsh as the author of, among other books, *Vanity Fair*.

Following the publication of *Comic Tales*, Yellowplush was immediately reprinted in Paris in the second volume of a work titled *Master Humphrey's*

Clock. By Charles Dickens, (Boz) To Which are added, Papers by Mr. Yellow-plush (Paris: Baudry's European Library, 1841). Although Thackeray was in and out of Paris several times in 1841 and spent some time working for *Galignani's Messenger*, there is no external evidence of any connection he might have had with the Baudry publication. Where *Comic Tales* departs from the text of *Fraser's Magazine*, the Baudry edition follows suit in all but thirty-four instances. The Paris edition introduces nearly four hundred and fifty variants of its own, most of which are minor punctuation and spelling changes, and the thirty-four restorations of Fraser's readings are all either corrections of typos in *Comic Tales*, fortuitous choices of normal alternatives, or easily editorialized changes. There is no suspicion of reference directly to the *Fraser's* text. There are, however, six new readings which warrant discussion as possibly authorial, though I conclude that five are editorial. At 32.5, where *Fraser's* has "Nex day his strattygam for becoming acquainted with Mr. Dawkins we exicuted...," Baudry has the more pleasing "was exicuted." "We" may be unlikely but is not impossible. The alteration may have pleased Thackeray, but there is no evidence that he made it or sanctioned it. It seems the work of an editor. At 74.1 Lady Griffin's response to Miss Kicksey's announcement of Deuceace's visit is given in *Fraser's* as "Mr. Deuceace here; and why, pray?" Baudry, forgetting, I think, that Lady Griffin has ice-water in her veins, substitutes an exclamation point for the semicolon. At 88.28 Yellowplush reports his own comments to Deuceace on his financial affairs. *Fraser's* has him say " 'Stuff, sir,' says I, forgetting my respeck...." Baudry, failing, I think, to recognize that the disrespect is in the word "stuff," intensifies it by omitting "sir." At 81.29–33 there is a sticky problem caused by Thackeray's characteristic though not too frequent use of quotation marks with indirect quotations. Normal convention calls for eliminating all the quotation marks, but having an opening mark seems to require a closing one. Where *Fraser's* closes the indirect quote along with the direct quote, Baudry closes it after "another" in this report of Lady Griffin's bantering of De l'Orge: " 'For her part, she wondered ... how any man could submit to such contemsheous behaviour from another; and then she told him how Deuceace was always snearing at him ... and how it was suttnly time to shew his sperrit.' " And finally, the rather cryptic "Here his letter." that introduces Smith's letter to Yellowplush at 130.17 in *Fraser's* is expanded, probably editorially, to "Here is his letter." in Baudry. None of these five changes is out of keeping with normal editorial intervention and cannot, it seems to me, support the notion that Thackeray marked the *Comic Tales* text for Baudry or read proof.

There is one more change, however, for which I have no explanation. It looks very much like an authorial change. But since it is the only one, it would be rash, I think, to surmise authorial revision. In *Fraser's* at 99.22, Miss Griffin retires in her interview with Lord Crabs "making play with the whites of her i's," but in Baudry she merely "turns up the whites of her i's." It is possible that Thackeray made the change, but the evidence seems to me inconclusive. One other noteworthy, but again editorial, change in the Baudry text is the addition of "Mr. Deuceace" as a running title for "Dimond Cut Dimond" and "Foring Parts." In the Table of Contents of *Comic Tales* an overall title, "Amours of Mr. Deuceace," was given to "Dimond Cut Dimond" and apparently was to extend through "The End of Mr. Deuceace's History." In the text itself, however, "Amours" appears to apply only to "Dimond," for it is not repeated in the titles of subsequent parts of Deuceace's story nor is it used as a running-title. In this arrangement "Skimmings," which has nothing to do with Deuceace, is the second number. The omission, or at least relocation, of "Skimmings" would be a logical act—but no edition in Thackeray's lifetime did that. The editor of Baudry's European Library went further than any other by adding the running-title to "Dimond Cut Dimond" and "Foring Parts," which relate to Deuceace's affairs but have nothing to do with his "amours," unless gaming and promenading are amours.

Except for the 1848 reissue of *Comic Tales,* Yellowplush was not published again until 1852. Charles Yellowplush did, to be sure, appear as a minor characater in "Reading a Poem" (*Britannia,* May 1 and 8, 1841) where his master, Loard Daudley, mentions that he writes and "has just had the impudence to republish his works" (i.e. in *Comic Tales*). Fitz-Jeames de la Pluche, whose writings appeared periodically in *Punch* from August, 1845, through February, 1846, has occasionally been said to be Yellowplush grown older and richer; but, though both Yellowplush and de la Pluche are cockney footmen, they are perceptibly different men with distinct biographies.

In 1852 *The Yellowplush Papers* appeared in a second unauthorized American edition, this time from the Appleton publishing house in New York. Evert A. Duyckinck, influential editor, critic, and publishers' advisor, was apparently at the root of the Appleton plan to publish a collection of Thackeray volumes in Appleton's Popular Library series. Five titles in six volumes had already appeared or were in production when Thackeray arrived in New York in November, 1852. Among these were *The Yellowplush Papers* reprinted from *Comic Tales.* When Thackeray saw that the Appleton *Yellowplush* included his satires of Bulwer Lytton from ten years earlier, "Yellowplush's Ajew" and "Epistles to the Literati," he incorporated an apology in the preface to the 1853 Appleton edition of *Mr. Brown's Letters to a Young Man About Town,* published in the same series. However, in 1853, Appleton reprinted *Yellowplush* from stereotyped plates in a form identical to the offending 1852 text (except that page 87 was for some reason reset with two inadvertent changes). The Appleton text departs from its source, *Comic Tales* in the ordinary ways though less often than any other reprint, introducing original though unauthorized readings only about 520 times. It is true that in 29 of these changes the Appleton version restores the *Fraser's* text reading altered by *Comic Tales,* but in almost every case this is the result of Appleton's tendency to regularize words which in *Comic Tales* take inconsistent Yellowplushian or erroneous forms. Most of the Appleton changes reflect a tendency to correct; so Yellowplush in Appleton's edition is somewhat less consistent in his misspellings than in *Comic Tales* and on the whole more often conventionally correct than in previous editions. The regularizing tendency is not, however, wholesale and could pass unnoticed. Although the Appleton edition was not authorized, it takes on considerable textual importance by the fact that it was used as the basis for the next authorial version in 1856.

The next edition of Yellowplush exists in two separate formats representing two separate but, so far as the text is concerned, invariant printings: *Miscellanies: Prose and Verse*, Vol. II (London: Bradbury and Evans, 1856), 1-151; and *The Memoirs of Mr. Charles J. Yellowplush and the Diary of C. Jeames de la Pluche, Esq.* (London: Bradbury and Evans, 1856), 1-151. Volume II of the *Miscellanies* was reprinted in 1857, 1860, and 1864; *The Memoirs of Mr. Charles J. Yellowplush* was reprinted in 1859. The only textual variations in the reprints are due to battered type. This edition is the last version of *Yellowplush* known to have authority, and again there is no evidence to indicate which variations in the text were introduced by Thackeray. Type for the 1856 version was set from Thackeray's own copy of the 1852 Appleton edition. Though Thackeray's specific instructions are no longer extant, he had partially marked the Appleton books for republication when he left on his second tour of America, leaving them with his amanuensis George Hodder. Apparently Hodder misunderstood his task, or he carried it out improperly, for in Thackeray's absence the volume with *Yellowplush* appeared in a form which displeased the author. His general comments to that effect are in an 1858 letter to John Blackwood (see Edgar F. Harden, "Thackeray's *Miscellanies*," *PBSA*, 71[4th Q, 1977], 497-508). The main objection was that Hodder had failed to suppress "Yellowplush's Ajew" and "Epistles to the Literati," for both of which Thackeray had already apologized to Bulwer, once in the preface to the Appleton edition of his contributions to *Punch*, and once directly by letter (*Letters*, III, 278). But there is no specific evidence to identify which of the variants actually incorporated in the *Miscellanies* version of *Yellowplush* derive from Thackeray's markings in the setting-copy or other direct instructions and which are the result of the amanuensis' inattention or over-eagerness. One category of non-authorial variants in the *Miscellanies* can, however, be identified—those introduced without authority in the Appleton reprint and retained in the *Miscellanies*. The significant instances of this Appleton influence on the text are recorded in the list of Variants in Authorial Editions and in the Variants in the Appleton Edition.

The last new edition in Thackeray's lifetime was in the authorized publication of *Miscellanies: Prose and Verse*, Vol. IV (Leipzig: Bernhard Tauchnitz, 1856), 1-198. Setting-copy was the 1856 London edition of *Miscellanies*—very likely a completely corrected copy of proofs or a copy of the volume itself. The Tauchnitz edition does restore 20 readings from the Appleton edition which, on the surface, might suggest that its setting-copy was uncorrected proofs of the London *Miscellanies* text retaining

Appleton readings later changed in the London proofs. But 13 of these restorations are corrections of typographical errors introduced by the *Miscellanies* and two others are the reintroduction of alternate spellings used earlier. Of the five remaining restorations of Appleton readings, four are substitutions of semicolons for colons which may reflect a Tauchnitz compositor's preference rather than proof corrections in the London *Miscellanies*. Only one variant, *Docter* (in *Fraser's, Comic Tales*, Appleton, and Tauchnitz) for *Doctor* (in *Miscellanies*; 129.18 in this edition) would suggest that the copy sent to Tauchnitz was uncorrected proofs of the *Miscellanies*. The London edition may have introduced the correct spelling after copy containing the incorrect but authoritative spelling was sent to Tauchnitz; but one telltale variant is not enough evidence to speculate on. There are 109 variations between the *Miscellanies* and the Tauchnitz edition (not counting variations in the spacing of dashes or the use of double leading which is meaninglessly chaotic in the Tauchnitz edition), but none of the noted variants bears the character of an authorial revision.

To sum up the textual history of *Yellowplush*, the 1837 Philadelphia edition, the 1841 Paris edition, and the 1856 Leipzig edition lack any authority. The *Comic Tales* version introduced about 720 new readings of which 61 seem to me the correction of inadvertent errors (accepted as emendations and listed in the apparatus). In addition, 47 seem to me undoubtedly to reflect Thackeray's wishes concerning the text in 1841 but not adopted for the present text (listed and marked with an asterisk in the Variants in Authorial Editions). About 198 other significant variants seem to me possible, but rather doubtful, authorial alterations (listed without asterisks in the variants table), and about 420 seem to me insignificant alterations most likely introduced by compositors or publishers' editors (not listed).

The Appleton edition introduced about 520 new readings, all unauthorized, of which 29 restored *Fraser's Magazine* readings; 4 others seem to me corrections of errors originating in *Fraser's* and left uncorrected in *Comic Tales* (accepted as emendations and listed in the apparatus). About 64 seem to me of sufficient importance to list (in Variants in the Appleton Edition) because, though without authority, they significantly alter the text presented in the 1856 *Miscellanies* edition. The rest seem to me of no significance even when they affect the *Miscellanies* text, and, therefore, are not listed. The Appleton text differs from the *Fraser's* text in about 1,200 readings.

The *Miscellanies* edition introduced about 630 new readings of which 96 restored *Fraser's* readings; 5 others seem to me to be corrections of errors in *Fraser's* left uncorrected in other editions (accepted as emendations and listed in the apparatus); 3 others seem to me undoubtedly to reflect authorial wishes for the 1856 text (listed and marked with a dagger in the Variants in Authorial Editions). About 114 other significant variants include what seem possible but rather doubtful authorial revisions (listed without a dagger in the variants table); and about 510 seem to me insignificant variants most likely introduced by compositors or publishers' editors (not listed). The *Miscellanies* text differs from *Fraser's* in about 1,730 readings.

The Illustrations
by Nicholas Pickwoad

———◇———

All the illustrations to *The Yellowplush Correspondence*, as it appeared in *Fraser's Magazine*, were etched by an assistant from designs by Thackeray. The year before, Thackeray had tried to prepare his own etchings for Harrison Ainsworth's novel, *Crichton*,[1] but, in addition to the problems which beset the publication of the book, found that he could not produce satisfactory designs in that medium. As he was still hoping to achieve recognition as a book illustrator, it was necessary for him to find a way round this difficulty, as etching was the medium most frequently used for book-illustration at the time. He must, therefore, have welcomed the chance that *The Yellowplush Correspondence* gave him to gain more experience without having the responsibility of another author's expectations hanging over him. We know that Thackeray used an assistant on these plates, because the drawing for the final one, "The Last Stroke of Fortune," has a note on it asking the assistant to leave out a female figure drawn on the front seat of the coach.[2] This was done, and the plate shows

---

1. William Harrison Ainsworth, *Crichton* (London, 1837). Thackeray was at work on illustrations for *Crichton* by July, 1836, (Ray, *Letters*, I, 297), at which time Ainsworth was still at work on the text. In the same month, Daniel Maclise was asked to supply illustrations, apparently in place of Thackeray, although the latter seems still to have been working on the book in October of that year, when he complained to his friend Edward Fitzgerald:

> I had a very handsome commission of £50 to make some etchings, but I have tried & made such miserable work that I must give them up I find. It is a sad disappointment, for I had hoped to have done much in that line. [Ray, *Letters*, I, 323]

In the event Maclise failed to produce any drawings, and in January, 1837, Thackeray agreed to try again in terms that suggest that Ainsworth had by then little hope of getting any illustrations at such short notice (Ray, *Letters*, I, 326). Again, however, Thackeray failed to produce satisfactory etchings ("I tried them on the Copper, but what I did was so bad, that I felt mortified at my failure," [Ray, *Letters*, I, 327]), and probably because of the delays that this must have caused, as well as the illness of the publisher Macrone and the transfer of the book to Richard Bentley, *Crichton* was published in February, 1837, without any illustrations at all. The book was eventually reissued with illustrations by Phiz.

2. The drawing is in the British Museum Print Room.

only Lord Crabs and his wife in the coach. For at least some of the publication of the story, Thackeray was in Paris, and this may have necessitated that he only send in drawings to London and have them transferred to plates there; but as his next series of etched plates, for Douglas Jerrold's *Men of Character*,[3] was also transferred by an assistant, although Thackeray was in London at the time, it can be assumed that he probably felt the need of some technical help.

The problem which always troubled Thackeray with his etched plates lay in the fact that a line drawn with a pen or pencil has a very different character from that of a line drawn on a metal plate with an etching needle. The former is extremely flexible, and can be varied at will by pressure exerted by the artist's hand, whereas the etching needle produces a line of a much more even quality, with the result that bold, sketchy drawing of the sort that Thackeray was accustomed to produce could not be copied line for line in an etching without a considerable loss of quality. When an experienced artist drew on the plate himself, this defect could be overcome by recreating the drawing to suit the new medium, using the original sketch as little more than a guide. Furthermore, drawing on the wax covered metal plate was not easy, but, by giving it up to another man, Thackeray effectively lost control of his illustrations the moment he finished his pencil drawings. Three[4] of these drawings have survived for *Yellowplush*, and a comparison with the printed plates shows exactly how conscientious the assistant was in copying them. For instance, the plate "Mr. Dawkins advises Mr. Blewett upon a difficult point at Ecarteé" reproduces almost every line, down to the fragmentary pattern on the carpet, and the same is true of the other examples. Where, however, the drawing is superior to the print is in the handling of the men's faces. Blewett, in particular, comes over very strongly in the drawing, his face full of malicious humor and advice, a man obviously duping his victim. In the transfer from drawing to plate, this extra quality is lost, and the vitality of the pencil line has tended to disappear. Thackeray's lack of familiarity with the medium led him to produce drawings that were basically unsuitable for this sort of transfer, for a line that is perfectly acceptable in light pencilling often looks coarse in dense black printing ink. This is particularly noticeable in the shading, where the closely laid parallel lines and cross-hatching have resulted in blank and monotonous areas of drawing,

---

3. Douglas Jerrold, *Men of Character*, 3 vols. (London, 1838). Following his failure with the *Crichton* illustrations, Thackeray did not attempt to transfer his designs for *Men of Character* onto the copper plates, but merely completed watercolors, which were then copied by an assistant onto the copper plates prior to etching them. It is possible that this assistant was one of Cruikshank's employees (see Blanchard Jerrold, *Life of George Cruikshank*, 2 vols., London, 1882, I.35). In this case, the assistant had the difficult task of converting rather impressionistic watercolors into line drawings on copper, and in doing so, some of the character of Thackeray's work was inevitably lost.

4. All three of these are in the British Museum Print Room. There is a fourth drawing, in the Princeton University Library, which is a study for Mary Shum in the first plate "Mr. Altamont's Evening Party."

which can be seen at their worst in the plate "The Calais Packet," where they are combined with poor perspective and figure drawing. The effect is to produce drab, uninteresting plates that belie Thackeray's real gift for summing up character and situation in his drawings.

It will be noticed in the last plate, "The Last Stroke of Fortune," that Deuceace's right hand is shown amputated, whereas the text states that it was his left. This was not the result, as has been suggested,[5] of Thackeray failing to appreciate that the engraver would reverse his drawing, for the original drawing also shows the right hand amputated. As the assistant in fact reversed all three of the surviving drawings onto the plates so that they would print the same way round, Thackeray must simply have forgotten which hand it was, rather than have assumed for this one plate that his assistant would not follow his normal practice.

Thackeray certainly had a modest view of the value of his plates in this case, for when he "struck for wages"[6] in March, 1838, he put a price of only two guineas on each plate, at a time when the newcomer John Leech was getting five and Cruikshank as much as twelve for etchings of a similar size.[7] It is clear from the letter in which he asked this price that he intended to have one plate for each number in which the story appeared; but, of the eight installments of Yellowplush's story, only five were in fact illustrated, which might be taken as suggesting that he was not altogether satisfied with the results. There is a drawing very similar in style to these for the scene "Mr. Yellowplush displaying his credentials,"[8] which appeared, completely redrawn, when the story was reprinted in the *Comic Tales and Sketches*. This may have been drawn for *Fraser's Magazine*, and then, for some reason, not included; or, alternatively, it may indicate that Thackeray at one time intended to use the same style of etching in the *Comic Tales and Sketches* plates and later changed his mind.

As *Comic Tales and Sketches* was made up from a number of different stories, Thackeray probably thought that new illustrations would serve not only to give a new appearance to the old material, but also, to give a greater sense of uniformity to the two volumes. Etching was chosen as the medium, but these illustrations represent a new departure for Thackeray in terms of technique and are far more sophisticated than anything he had attempted before. Instead of working on a plain copper plate, Thackeray drew his subjects onto a surface that had already been prepared by being scored over by closely spaced horizontal lines. By using an acid-resistant varnish, it was possible to etch areas of these lines to different depths, and thus vary their tonal value. Some of the plates were stopped out with the varnish five or six times, which gave, on account of the fineness of the lines, the semblance of genuine half-tone work. Certain areas of the plate which were to be highlighted could be stopped out

---

5. Joan Stevens, "A Thackeray Error," *Notes & Queries* (June, 1946), 209.

6. Ray, *Letters*, I, 351.

7. These figures are taken from John Harvey, *Victorian Novelists and Their Illustrators* (London, 1970), pp. 186–187.

8. In the Berg Collection, New York Public Library.

before the etching was started, and would appear as areas of white when printed; this, in effect, gave an extra color to the design.[9] The process of stopping out called for fine judgment and a great deal of experience, and it is clear that Thackeray must have had assistance. As he was in Paris whilst he was working on these plates, he chose a French engraver, Louis Marvy, to help him with them. Although Thackeray only refers to him as "filing my plates for me,"[10] the fact that he used the same etching technique again on the illustrations to *The History of Samuel Titmarsh and the Great Hoggarty Diamond* only when Marvy was once more working for him, appears to confirm that the French engraver was responsible for the special quality of these plates. Thus, in spite of the fact that Thackeray claimed that the plates were merely "touched up by some professional engravers,"[11] the etcher was as much responsible for their final appearance as the artist himself.

But whatever the extent of Marvy's contribution, his help was not entirely an advantage to Thackeray. It is an unfortunate fact that whenever he sought a more professional or up-to-date finish for his illustrations, the work of the assistant employed to carry out this work almost never sits easily with his own style. Here, the very sophistication of the etching technique demanded an equal sophistication from Thackeray, which he was not always able to give. His drawing is, however, considerably refined from that found in the first *Yellowplush* illustrations, and the surviving drawing for "Mr. Yellowplush displaying his credentials" shows exactly how. Compared with the print in the *Comic Tales and Sketches*, the most immediate difference lies in the size of the figures in relation to the area of the image. In the *Comic Tales and Sketches*, the figures are much smaller, and in consequence there is a larger area of background to fill. The smaller scale of the drawing has also resulted in finer, though not necessarily better, linework. In fact, without the new etching technique, Thackeray's drawing would appear weak and empty, but as it is, the careful stopping out has given the plates a more unified composition. A striking example of this is to be found in the plate, "Mrs. Shum's ejectment," where, by the careful use of light and dark shading, enough sense is given of the structure of the staircase and of the downward spiral movement to convey a sense of hurry and action. This illustration is also helped by some good figure drawing, but if the toning effect were removed, a much more concrete definition of the background would be needed. As it is, the plate gains in effect through its uncluttered appearance and the consequent concentration on the action. Much less successful is a plate

9. In Martin Hardie, *English Coloured Books* (London, 1906), p. 216, it is stated that these highlights were "systematically scraped out with a knife on the print itself." However, a close examination of the prints shows that much of the areas of white on the prints shows traces of the preliminary ruling, which means that nothing has been scraped off the paper.

10. Ray, *Letters*, II, 9–11.

11. W. M. Thackeray, *Works, Centenary Biographical Edition* (London, 1910), xxii, xxxi. Most of this letter is also given in Ray, *Letters*, II, 163, with a note saying that the end of the letter is cut away; thus *Letters* omits the remark about the professional engravers.

like "Mr. Deuceace's disinterested Declaration," where the background effects are comparatively unimportant, and where success is dependent on the drawing, which, in this case, is not very good. One likely reason for this lack of success is Thackeray's difficulty in handling figures, and especially groups, on such a small scale. This can be demonstrated by comparing the family group in *The Paris Sketch Book* plate "How to astonish the French" with the *Comic Tales and Sketches* plate "Mr. Perkins discovered in the Zoological Gardens," where the former carries a great deal more conviction than the latter.

The large areas of background certainly caused Thackeray some problems, because he was presented with a prepared surface of a fixed size. In the plate "Mr. Yellowplush displaying his credentials," there is an empty strip approximately half an inch wide on either side of the image in which can be seen the faint traces of two chairs. These were stopped out quite early in the etching process, presumably in an attempt to concentrate the viewer's attention on the group in the middle of the plate. On some of the other plates, Thackeray marked out areas on proof prints which he wanted burnished off, as he did on "Mr. Deuceace's disinterested Declaration." These annotated proofs, of which a complete set survives,[12] also show that the plates were etched in pairs on each copper plate, but with no connection by subject matter or volume. Thus "Mr. Deuceace's disinterested Declaration" is coupled with "The Major's interview with a celebrated character" from the second volume, which suggests that Thackeray had prepared all the illustrations before they were transferred to the plates. Another point of interest from these proofs is that the instructions on them are written in English, which means that they were not intended for Marvy. Possibly these proofs were sent to the English printers so that they could carry out these simple alterations after the plates had already been dispatched to London. The proofs are printed with black ink, but when they appeared in the published book, brown ink was used, possibly in an attempt to make them appear more attractive.

The overall impression gained from the plates is that Thackeray was unable to make the most of the technique that he was using. Some of the plates are successful, particularly "Mr. Dando declares his Name and Quality," and they are so because the vitality of Thackeray's drawing has survived into the print. It seems likely that the style was chosen in order to revitalize the stories and also to attract public attention by an unusual style of illustration. It took, however, a professional illustrator like H. K. Browne (Phiz) to realize the full dramatic potential of the technique, which he did in his illustrations to Charles Lever's *Roland Cashel* in 1849.

---

12. Dartmouth College Library, Hanover, New Hampshire.

Illustrations from
Comic Tales

Mrs Shum's ejectment.

Mr. Ducrow paying for his Papa's cigars.

Mr. Pickwick distinguishing his credentials.

The two celebrated literary characters at Sir John's

Editorial Procedures

◇

The purpose of the present edition is to give, as error free as possible, the text Thackeray produced as a series of papers in *Fraser's Magazine*, 1837–1840. In the absence of manuscript and proof materials, *Fraser's* is copy-text except in the instances noted below. Though all editions subsequent to *Fraser's* altered *Yellowplush* freely, the text provided here represents the earliest known version. The *Fraser's Magazine* version is chosen on the grounds that its inconsistencies are indicative of Yellowplush's character rather than being out of keeping with it. Yellowplush himself observes that "As for authografy, evry genlmn has his own: never mind spellin, I say, so long as the sence is right" (43.24–26). Yellowplush's writing habits tend to make most emendation not only superfluous but impossible. To impose consistency even of misspellings would be to impose on Yellowplush a characteristic which he does not possess.

Subsequent revisions by Thackeray are so inextricably mixed with changes imposed by publishers' editors and compositors that it is impossible to say whether later impositions of consistency are authorial or not. All attempts to recover Thackeray's intentions from the republications are subjective, and it is my opinion that the *Fraser's* version, except for its obvious errors, is a better representation of Yellowplush's writing than are the other versions, if for no other reason than that its inconsistencies convey more convincingly the spontaneity of Yellowplush's lapses in spelling and grammar. (This does not mean, by the way, that I think no one should attempt to distinguish between Thackeray's revisions and the tamperings of editors and compositors or to produce a text representing the author's intentions in 1841 or 1856. My own attempt to do so is recorded in the tables of the apparatus.) Another reason for choosing to represent the earliest text in this edition, however, is that the edition of Thackeray's works of which this volume is a part is on principle presenting the earliest completed version of each work in order that each text may represent more fully the writing characteristics Thackeray had developed at the time of first publication; thus, the edition as a whole will show Thackeray as he developed as a writer. To present final versions would in the case of some works be to obscure the Thackeray of the 1840's by an overlay of revisions imposed by the Thackeray of the late 1850's and 1860's. Though the revisions in *Yellowplush* are not extensive enough to reflect changes in the author, this work is prepared in the same manner as the other works in the edition. The revisions introduced by later editions can be studied in the Variants in Authorial Editions.

Copy-text for passages quoted from John Skelton's *My Book; or, the Anatomy of Conduct* in "Fashnable Fax and Polite Annygoats" is the first edition (London: Simpkin and Marshall, 1837). There are over 165 differences between Skelton's book and the passages quoted in *Fraser's*, but only four seem attributable to Thackeray's conscious efforts: the italicization of four phrases which he discussed or alluded to in the review itself. In addition one typographical error was corrected, two articles were added where they may have been left out accidentally in Skelton's book, *for* became *in* once, and *except* was rendered *excepting* in contexts where the difference is negligible. The foregoing changes are accepted in the present reading text and recorded as emendations in the copy-text; the first four on the grounds that the emphasis of the italics is clearly Thackeray's, and the other five on the grounds that they are conceivably Thackeray's. The remaining 160 or so changes involve punctuation of the sort *Fraser's* printers seem to have imposed on all quoted matter. The truth is that Skelton's syntax is held together primarily by dashes. The *Fraser's* version mitigates some of Skelton's eccentric, unorthodox pointing. In addition italics were used instead of quotation marks to indicate book titles, double quotes were changed to single quotes within the passages quoted, and three terminal dashes and semicolons became periods. These changes seem compositorial, revealing printers' habits, rather than authorial, revealing Thackeray's desire to clean up the text of an author whose book he otherwise ridiculed.

Copy-text for passages quoted from Lady Charlotte Bury's *Diary Illustrative of the Times of George IV.* in "Skimmings from 'The Dairy of George IV.'" is the first edition (London: Henry Colburn, 1838). There are nearly 120 differences between the original and the quoted version. Since the quoted passages in four instances run to more than fifty lines in *Fraser's*, it was easy to spot which sections within such passages were probably set from paste-ups from the original and which were set from a recopying; for, though there are changes throughout, the number is significantly less in those portions derived from full pages in the *Diary* than in the portions set from partial passages. It seems to me that copy for the original diary was rather rough, or that Henry Colburn's printers' tolerance for unconventional punctuation was greater than that of the *Fraser's* printers, for most of the changes are trivial alterations that bring the form of the original in line with *Fraser's* practice: foreign words are italicized, capital letters for titles of nobility are reduced to lower case except when accompanying a name, commas are added and deleted at will. Some of these changes were probably made by Thackeray when copying out the quotations, but the fact that he used paste-ups when it was convenient without imposing similar changes on those parts indicates, I believe, that his intention on the whole was to quote accurately. Most of the changes can be accounted for by scribal carelessness or the ingrained editorial propensity of printers to housestyle manuscripts. There are nine changes, however, which have substantive or near substantive effect on the text. Six of these I believe were intentional changes made by Thackeray and are recorded in the emendations. The other three are listed with the emendations with notes explaining why they are not adopted for this text.

Copy-text for the passages quoted from Edward Bulwer Lytton's *The Sea-Captain* in "Epistles to the Literati" is the fourth edition of the play (London: Saunders & Otley, 1839) which Yellowplush specifies in the review. There are over 40 differences between that edition and the quoted passages in *Fraser's* ranging from normal printers' alterations in punctuation to outright interpretive paraphrases given in quotation marks. The present text adopts from *Fraser's* quotations those alterations which affect the meaning even though a few of these may be unintentional. It is not always easy to know if the changes were made consciously. For example, at 124.15, the actress Miss Faucit had been induced "to take a part so inferior to her powers" in Bulwer's preface, but Yellowplush, perhaps deflating the delineation of that part in the play or perhaps simply through a memory lapse in copying, writes "to take a part so far inferior to her powers." On the other hand, in the series of extracts of Norman's speeches (at 126.5–127.14) the italicization of *stars* and *angels* is undoubtedly intentional because Yellowplush makes the point that "sea-captings should not be eternaly spowting and invoking gods, hevns, starrs, angels, and other silestial influences."

A basic assumption influencing the form of the textual apparatus is that the user is primarily interested in what the author may have done to the text as it appeared and reappeared. Although experience with Thackeray's proofs for other books does give one a sense of the kinds of changes Thackeray made (see particularly Edgar F. Harden, *The Emergence of Thackeray's Serial Fiction* [Athens, Ga.: University of Georgia Press, 1979]), attempts to distinguish authorial from non-authorial variation by applying this "sense" to the variants in *Yellowplush* is totally subjective. It does not seem to me desirable, as a means of avoiding subjectivity, to list all the variant readings found in *Comic Tales* and *Miscellanies* even though those editions have some authority. Nor does it seem a better alternative to list only changes in wording, omitting aspects of form such as spelling and punctuation variants. Such a list would be prepared on arbitrary grounds and include some word changes of no interest—being obvious mechanical slips—and omit some spelling and punctuation changes of actual importance to the meaning of the text.

The purpose of the textual apparatus is primarily to facilitate the study of the development of the text as it was changed by the author, but it also shows some ways in which it was influenced by editors in the printing and publishing trades. It is *not* the goal of the apparatus provided here to make possible the complete reconstruction of the various historical forms of the text in every particular. The full collation tables (in rough manuscript form) recording the variants between *Fraser's Magazine* and all other editions in Thackeray's lifetime are on deposit at the Mitchell Memorial Library, Mississippi State University. This material may be of use to future editors of *Yellowplush* wishing to follow alternative principles of emendation or to students of the history of punctuation or publishers' housestyles.

Silent Alterations

In *Fraser's Magazine*, letters and quotations of extracts from books were usually separated from the rest of the text by double spacing and were set in a smaller type-font but were not indented. These are elements of design or convention and were as much influenced by the dictates of the double column arrangement in *Fraser's Magazine* as by anything else. The design of block quotations is altered arbitrarily to the form used in this edition. Chapter headings and section headings were set in *Fraser's* in a variety of type-styles and sizes; they were arranged in one or more lines— all according to arbitrary decisions by the copy-editor or compositor. The chapter and section headings in this edition are equally arbitrary in line arrangement and typographic style. Likewise the initial letter and some following letters at the beginnings of chapters and numbers were in special sizes, small caps, etc. There is no evidence to indicate that any of these features in any way reflect authorial intention and are arbitrarily altered in the present edition. Mechanical failures such as turned letters and broken type are silently corrected. Certain printing conventions are silently made consistent: the separation of the parts of contractions (would n't, does n't), apparently already falling into disuse, judging from the irregularity of its appearance, is not maintained in this edition, and the use of double quotes at the beginning of each new line in letter headings and closings is altered when necessary to conform to the line arrangement in the present edition.

Emendations

———◇———

The list of emendations shows the changes I have made in the *Fraser's Magazine* text. I have not attempted to impose consistency on Yellowplush's highly inconsistent and—if one can believe his claims to self-improvement at the end of "Mr. Yellowplush's Ajew,"—developing style. Nor have I incorporated what might be judged to be later felicitous improvements in Thackeray's presentation of Yellowplush's writings in later editions. Insofar as these can be determined, they are presented in the list of Variants in Authorial Editions. Where *Fraser's Magazine* is copy-text, all but two of the emendations represent what I consider to be corrections of errors. They are (1) the suppression of the divisions and division titles imposed by installment publication in "Mr. Deuceace at Paris" that fulfills a wish expressed by Thackeray to James Fraser that the whole be printed in one issue of the magazine, and (2) the suppression of an editorial footnote in "Epistles to the Literati." Both are recorded as emendations and discussed in the notes.

Where the *Diary Illustrative of the Times of George IV* or Skelton's *My Book* or Bulwer's *Sea-Captain* is copy-text, the emendations represent only the changes I believe Thackeray made intentionally and which make a substantive difference in the text of the quoted passage. These emendations in quotations from other books are the only items in the emendations list representing Thackeray's own alterations. Readings that may represent Thackeray's preferences at the times of republication (i.e. *Comic Tales*, 1841, or *Miscellanies*, 1856) are recorded in the table of Variants in Authorial Editions. Readings introduced by the pirated Appleton edition have no authority, but four corrections of errors either slipped by unnoticed or were consciously accepted by Thackeray when he used the Appleton texts as the bases for the *Miscellanies* edition. The fact that these corrections are adopted as emendations and credited to the Appleton text does not suggest that they are authorial.

The first reading in each emendation entry is always that of the present edition. It is followed by symbols from the list below representing any editions which happen to use that reading. The second reading in each entry is that of the copy-text. For most of the work *Fraser's Magazine* is the copy-text. However, copy-text for quoted passages in those installments which are book reviews is the book being quoted. The symbol for the work which is copy-text for these passages is given after the second entry. Symbols for editions agreeing with the copy-text follow the second entry. Any further alternative reading is given next with the symbol identifying the edition using that reading.

Symbols Used in the Apparatus

 F = *Fraser's Magazine*
CT = *Comic Tales and Sketches* (London, 1841)
 A = Appleton edition of *The Yellowplush Papers* (New York, 1852)
 M = *Miscellanies* (London, 1856)
JS = John Skelton's *My Book* (London, 1837)
CB = Charlotte Bury's *Diary* (London, 1838)
LB = Lytton Bulwer's *The Sea-Captain* (London, 1839)

**Fashnable Fax and Polite
Annygoats**

[Note: John Skelton's *My Book*
is copy-text for Yellowplush's
quotations from it: 2.14–25;
2.39–3.23 and the footnote; 4.6–
15; 4.36–5.19; 7.5–8.6 and the
footnote; 8.22–27; 8.38–9.4.]

1.hd No. I.
◊ [no number] F
[Since the next installment
was labeled No. II., it can be
assumed that "Fashnable Fax"
was intended as No. I., though
when it was first printed the
plan for continuation was still
in doubt. This installment was
not reprinted in an authoritative
edition.]

2.15 *would emulate a polite carriage* F
◊ would emulate a polite carriage
JS

2.41 an anomaly F
◊ anomaly JS

3.fn.6 in F
◊ for JS

3.fn.7 *his mind's eye* F
◊ his mind's eye JS

3.fn.8 *suit ulterior ends* F
◊ suit ulterior ends JS

5.11 unfrequently F
◊ unfrequenly JS

5.16 the rose-water F
◊ rose-water JS

6.21 g'n'l'm'n);
◊ g'n'l'm'n) F
[Though Yellowplush's spelling
is eccentric, his punctuation
is quite conventional. This
lapse from convention seems,
therefore, an unintentional
error.]

7.10 excepting F
◊ except JS

8.fn.1 *turn away the man* F
◊ turn away the man JS

9.9–34 [The last four paragraphs
are presented in a single page-
wide column in *Fraser's Magazine*

to distinguish them from the
double-column format of
Yellowplush's writing. The italics
in this edition are added as a
comparable form of distinction.
It is not clear whether these
paragraphs, signed O.Y. (for
Oliver Yorke), are by Thackeray
or by William Maginn, the editor
of *Fraser's*.]

Miss Shum's Husband

10.9 about like
◊ about F

13.19 chaps' M
◊ chap's F CT

14.28 Buckmasters: CT M
◊ Buckmasters, F

16.10 was CT M
◊ was was F

16.12 gal, you! CT M
◊ gal! you, F

20.17 Mrs. CT M
◊ Mrs F

20.32 Eleven CT M
◊ twelve F
[There are twelve daughters, but
Mary is already there.]

21.36 feind CT M
◊ friend F
[*Friend* seems wrong because
the article is definite; CT's
"correction" seems authentic
because the spelling is
Yellowplushian; on the other
hand, "foul friend" may have
been an intended malapropism.
Cf. *29.36 fowl find.*]

23.22 stopped CT M
◊ stooped F

23.29 her, CT M
◊ her F

23.37 entered CT M
◊ ensered F

23.39 [¶] "My M
◊ "My F CT
[This is the only instance of
a change of speakers within
a paragraph. Although fairly
common in writings of all

periods, it appears erroneous in this work.]

25.16 *twice?"* CT M
◇ *twice?* F

Dimond Cut Dimond

27.18 mistake: CT
◇ mistake: F

30.28 tailors' M
◇ tailor's F CT

30.29 hossdealers' M
◇ hossdealer's F CT

33.2 Dawkins CT M
◇ Deuceace F

33.28 *Esq.,* CT M
◇ *Esq.* F

34.5 pitchfrock
[Not emended. Though possibly an error for *pitchforck*, the misspelling does not seem out ofkeeping for Yellowplush. All editions leave it as is.]

38.14 listning CT M
◇ istning F

Skimmings from "The Dairy of George IV."

[Note: Lady Charlotte Bury's *Diary* is copy-text for Yellowplush's quotations from it: 42.10–38; 43.29–44.43; 45.31–46.25; 47.23–48.37; 49.21–35; 49.40–50.24; 50.28–32.]

42.10 me, F CT M
◇ me; CB
[Required by the elided opening of the quotation.]

47.34 otherwise.— CB
[Not emended. *Fraser's* drops the dash and adds a question mark, but this alteration is as likely a printer's correction as an authorial one, and no point is made about it in the review.]

49.27 *that she was in love with Bernadotte* F CT M
◇ that she was *in love* with Bernadotte CB

49.28 *Madame de Stael was in love with Rocca* F CT M
◇ Madame de Stael was in love with Rocca CB
[The italicization of the passage here which parallels that in the previous entry makes it probable that the italics in both instances are authorial.]

50.2 the Sixteenth CB
[Not emended. The abbreviation *XVI.* in F CT M probably was made by Thackeray in copying the quotation, but like most abbreviations was probably done for convenience rather than a pointed desire for change.]

50.30 said CB
[Not emended. The alteration to *says* in F CT M is probably authorial, but is more likely a memory slip than a purposeful change.]

50.31 *This is very amiable in her* F CT M
◇ This is very amiable in her CB

50.32 and cannot fail to be F CT M
◇ and must be CB
[It might be argued that, like the *said/says* alteration above, this change resulted from memory lapse, but the added emphasis seems appropriate for the comments on the passage by the reviewer.]

50.37 gratitude CT M
◇ gratiude F
[There seems no reason to suppose this repetition of the word should be misspelled. It does not seem to me Yellowplushian.]

Foring Parts

51.11 Deuceace CT M
◇ Duceace F
[Though it is not inconceivable that Yellowplush would misspell *Deuceace*, this is the only instance of it in *Fraser's Magazine* and seems more likely a scribal error.]

56.2 *agrémens* CT M
◇ *agrêmens* F

[Deuceace's letter is in standard English; it does not follow that his French is flawless, but it does seem rather too subtle an effect to have him trip up on the only French word in the letter.]

57.15 Lend his CT M
◇ His F

58.37 concarning
[Not emended. Note: As a phonetic spelling this is impossible since the *c*, by rule, gives a *k* sound; but the *c* is "correct" and the *a* "wrong," so the spelling is possibly Yellowplushian.]

Mr. Deuceace at Paris I

61.17 leavings): a CT M
◇ leavings). A F
[The alteration avoids a sentence fragment.]

64.20 person CT M
◇ persone F

68.2 and—— CT M
◇ and —— F
[Although the copy-text is not consistent, it would seem that a spaced dash represents a word spoken but not printed. Interruptions in speech, as seems the case here, are represented by unspaced dashes.]

69.8 is in the CT M
◇ is the F

69.28 crownd) CT M
◇ crownd), F
[It seems more likely that the plan was to watch the king go to chapel than that, after seeing the king, Deuceace and party would go to chapel themselves.]

70.40 don't CT M
◇ dont F
[Yellowplush renders correctly the speech of characters using standard English. Speeches containing only one possibly dialectal spelling are probably in error.]

73.30 bedtime), CT M
◇ bedtime). F

[Though the change removes an inappropriate sentence fragment, the reading remains awkward.]

73.31 "who CT M
◇ who F

74.15 and—— CT M
◇ and —— F
[Dash indicates an interruption or a trailing off of speech.]

74.22 and——
◇ and/—— F
◇ and —— CT M
[The line break in the copy-text makes it impossible to say whether or not a space was intended. The dash is printed in this edition unspaced as an indication of a trailing off of speech.]

77.26 [omit] CT M
◇ C.Y. [new installment] MR. DEUCEACE AT PARIS. No. II. F
[See below, 89.29]

78.11 Billy CT M
◇ "Billy F
[This heading in Yellowplush's spelling is not quoted from his source. By analogy the numerals with succeeding letters are also not quoted. Hence the quotation marks are removed at 78.36 and 79.29.]

82.41 suxcaded
[Not emended. See above note for 58.37 *concarning*.]

85.14 secrit." CT M
◇ secrit. F

85.29 understand CT M
◇ undersand F
[Deuceace speaks standard English.]

86.8 waived CT M
◇ waved F
[Though *"Gallynanny's Messinger"* was probably not above this sort of error, it is the only error in the quoted material and seems inappropriate.]

87.7 are, CT M
◇ are

88.1 O*d*." M
◇ O*d*. F CT

88.21 affeckshn;" A M
◇ affeckshn; F CT

89.15 volé!"
◇ volé." F
◇ volé," CT M
[Yellowplush's writing
eccentricities do not seem to
extend to the punctuation. The
Bailiff's speech is marked by
repeated exclamations. The
copy-text period could well be
a broken exclamation point,
though there are no vestiges of
physical evidence for it. The
lower case letter following the
period suggests the change.]

89.29 [omit]
◇ [new installment] THE END OF
MR. DEUCEACE'S HISTORY. F CT
M
[The Installment for July 1837
began here. This title and
"MR. DEUCEACE AT PARIS. No.
II." (for the June installment)
were added when the story was
divided into three installments
against Thackeray's wishes
(see Introduction, p. 140). CT
omitted the less imaginative title
for the second part (77.26), but
not this one. It is inappropriate
as part of the title of the eighth
chapter, as CT M have it, for
there are ten chapters in all.]

100.6 think——" CT M
◇ think ——" F

100.20 pulls out CT M
◇ pulls it out F

103.10 into——
◇ into —— F CT M

103.23 sherts CT M
◇ sheets F

105.11 papers?" A M
◇ papers? F CT

106.14 à CT M
◇ *a* F
[Lord Crabs's language seems
otherwise always correct.]

107.8 protested CT M

◇ protected F
[Though *protected* may be what
Deuceace thought the bills
were, *protested* is a legal term
for dishonored bills. Lord Crabs
was not likely to confuse the
two. In Thackeray's handwriting
of a later period the difference
between an *s* and a *c* before a *t*
is minimal.]

107.33 but——" CT M
◇ but ——" F

109.5 forth CT M
◇ froth F

Mr. Yellowplush's Ajew

110.hd No. VII.
◇ [no number] F CT M
[Although this is the ninth
installment, treating the three-
installment Deuceace story
as a single unit, according to
Thackeray's wishes, makes this
the seventh unit.]

111.8 now CT M
◇ know F

112.10 fild CT M
◇ fid F

112.18 encyclopædias M
◇ enclycopædias F CT
[This is not a characteristic
of Bulwig's speech. Since
Yellowplush seems to be able
to represent the speech of others
accurately, this seems more likely
to be a scribal error than an
intentional representation of
Bulwig's pronunciation.]

112.35 pewiodicals? CT M
◇ pewiodicals? F

112.39 at——
◇ at —— F CT M

112.42 that——
◇ that —— F CT M

113.1 but——
◇ but —— F CT M

113.11 good CT M
◇ gool F

113.25 Correspondence.'" CT M
◇ Correspondence.' F

113.37 "the arthagraphy
◇ the arthagraphy F CT
◇ the "arthagraphy M

114.13 "and CT M
◇ and F

114.15 "who A M
◇ who F CT

114.20 'Sam Slick.' " CT M
◇ "Sam Slick." F

114.21 it's CT M
◇ its F
[Lord Bagwig makes no other
speaking errors.]

114.29 champagne CT M
◇ champaigne F

116.4 my mouth CT M
◇ mouth F

116.16 Dials. CT M
◇ Dials, F

117.4 to CT M
◇ to be F

117.13 'im, CT M
◇ 'im," F

117.18 Larner. CT M
◇ Larner, F

118.19 however——" CT M
◇ however ——" F

Epistles to the Literati
[Note: Bulwer's *The Sea-
Captain* is copy-text for 122.7–
37; 124.1–30; 126.5–127.14;
128.4–15; 129.6–10; 129.23;
129.25–26; 125.28–30; 133.31–
35; 133.40–134.5.]

119.hd No. VIII.
◇ Epistles to the Literati. No.
XIII. F
◇ [No number] CT M
[Though this installment
belongs to the "Epistles to the
Literati" series, of which it is
number XIII, its inclusion in
the *Yellowplush Papers* in 1841
suggests its appropriateness here
where it becomes, for the sake
of consistency, the eighth unit.
It was, in *Fraser's*, the tenth
installment. (See note above
110.hd and Introduction, p.
141).]

119.1–14 [Though not strictly speaking
an emendation, the first three
paragraphs, constituting the
"Notus," which in the copy-
text are distinguished from the
rest of the text by being printed
in a single page-wide column
rather than in double columns,
are presented in this edition in
italic type.]

120.11 stoary. CT M
◇ stoary.* [footnote:] *See the
last remarkable tale of Mr. Y—
—sh, in *Fraser's Magazine*. F
[Over a year had passed since
"Yellowplush's Ajew" had
appeared. This editorial footnote
seems superfluous for a collected
edition.]

124.15 so far F CT M
◇ so LB

126.6 Flora / Wooes F CT M
◇ Flora / Spreads all her blooms;
and from a lake-like sea / Wooes
LB

126.7 wind; F CT M
◇ wind! LB

126.17 [italics] F CT M
◇ angels LB
[This emendation is repeated at
126.33, and for *angel* at 127.6,
and for *stars* at 126.28, 126.36,
126.38, 127.2, 127.6, 127.14,
and for *starry* at 126.31, and for
star at 127.9.]

126.19 son! F CT M
◇ son— LB

127.5 home; / The F CT M
◇ home;— / The gale shall
chaunt our bridal melodies;—
/ The LB

127.10 born. F CT M
◇ born! LB

128.6 shelter. F CT M
◇ shelter! LB

128.7 up! F CT M
◇ up— LB

128.8 bride! Hast F CT M
◇ bride—hast LB

128.10 sweetness!" A M
◊ sweetness! F CT LB

128.12 "Oh CT M
◊ Oh F LB

129.27b my F CT M
◊ his LB

129.29–30 [small caps] F CT M
◊ The love ... shines LB

130.20 1839 CT M
◊ 1830 F
[The publication date, 1839 of
Bulwer's *Sea-Captain*, with a
preface to the fourth edition,
precedes "Smith's" letter, making
1830 impossible.]

132.6 out cunningly, F CT M
◊ [Not emended. Probably
Lord Ashdale did not go out
cunningly; rather he cunningly
put on Norman's cloak. A
comma after "out" or dropping
the comma after "cunningly"
would cause the text to reflect
this meaning more clearly.]

132.28 Ashdale's CT M
◊ Ashdale s F
[Smith's letter is in standard
English; the space in F suggests
the apostrophe merely did not
print.]

132.41 obstacle), CT M
◊ obstacle, F

[*Obstacle* is singular, but the
verbs *tantalize* and *retard* require
a plural subject. Thackeray's
manuscripts occasionally
provide only one of two
needed parenthesis marks; the
printer of *Fraser's Magazine*
may be responsible for the
erroneous placing of the closing
parenthesis.]

132.42 action; CT M
◊ action); F

132.44 curtain." M
◊ curtain. F CT

133.32 on the estate— F CT M
◊ on it; LB

133.33 lips)— F CT M
◊ *lips*); LB

133.33 can F CT M
◊ can always LB

133.33 [italics] F CT M
◊ to the little blackguards LB

133.34 at F CT M
◊ for LB

133.41 it! They F CT M
◊ it—they LB

133.42 ago. The F CT M
◊ ago!—the LB

134.5 beggars! F CT M
◊ beggars. LB

Variants in Authorial Editions

––––––––◇––––––––

Principles of Selection

The variants listed here include all the revisions which I believe Thackeray *may* have called for except for corrections of errors, which he may also have requested, found in the list of Emendations and not repeated here. If some of the changes omitted as insignificant are in fact Thackeray's, it is fruitless to speculate on which those changes are or on what might have been the author's intention in making such minor alterations. Without direct evidence, which in this case does not exist, any attempt to determine the authority of any of the readings I have listed as significant remains purely subjective. The temptation is to claim authority for the alterations one deems desirable. Extensive experience with Thackeray's surviving manuscripts and proof-sheets, or a careful reading of Edgar F. Harden's *The Emergence of Thackeray's Serial Fiction* (Univ. of Georgia Press, 1979), can lead to educated guesses as to which of the new readings were introduced by Thackeray.

The significance of the variants listed here does not lie in their source; that remains problematic. With the exception of certain spelling changes explained below, each variant is listed that makes a perceptible change in meaning or emphasis or gives the text some quality which it did not otherwise possess. I have listed the addition or deletion of words, the substitution of one word for another, the introduction of unique or uncommon Yellowplushian spellings, alterations in the spacing of dashes (which may convert a sign indicating an interruption or the trailing off of speech to one indicating the omission of a spoken but presumably unprintable word), and alterations in punctuation which perceptibly change the syntax of a sentence (as when a semicolon is changed to a question mark or an exclamation point is exchanged for a comma).

Alterations in punctuation which seem to be corrections of unorthodox pointing, rather than mere alternatives, are recorded either as accepted emendations or, in less decisive cases, as significant variations. Yellowplush's punctuation, unlike his spelling, is relatively orthodox. There is a good deal of latitude for inconsistency, but not more so than in Thackeray's writings employing standard English. It must be remembered that rhetorical pointing was as much a system as syntactical or grammatical pointing and that punctuation to mark rhetorical pauses might on occasion be used in the midst of syntactical units. Compositors' manuals of the day indicated the relative length of pauses represented by commas, semi-colons, colons, and periods. For the first three, it appears that the length of the intended rhetorical pause as well as the syntax determined the mark to be used.

Alterations in Yellowplush's spelling which seem to be corrections of inadvertently misspelled words are accepted as emendations to this edition and recorded in the list of Emendations. For example, at 23.37 *ensered* does not seem a possible Yellowplushian spelling for *entered*; so I emended it. On the other hand, though *concaming* (for *concerning*) is by standard orthographic rule impossible, I left it unchanged for the reason given in the Emendations (53.36; cf. also 82.41). Of the remaining spellings which are altered in subsequent authorial versions, I record the changes unless they introduce a standard English spelling or a common Yellowplushian spelling such as *wery*, *Pentonwil*, or *nothink*. In both cases, it seems to me more likely that a compositor gave way to his propensity to correct his copy, than that Thackeray actually cleaned up the spelling or imposed consistency of dialectic spelling. Likewise, most changes which reflect a simple but only partial impulse to normalize are not recorded as significant. For example, *excep* for *xcep*, or *bizziness* for *bizziniss* are listed only in the deposited Historical Collation. However, partial spelling corrections which may have required thought, such as *missiseses* to *missises*, are recorded, though their source is dubious. It is not expected that any two persons' judgment will coincide on all readings in this category chosen for inclusion. To be recorded, a reading had to have some claim to interest other than an ordinary normalizing impulse. To record all spelling changes would inflate the listing with repetitious entries and call undue attention to alterations which I think probably were made by a compositor or editor to suit his own conception of the work. These unlisted changes are significant, though, because in their overall effect they give a semblance of order to Yellowplush's "cacography."

The Text in 1841

An asterisk (*) marks each reading which I would include in a text representing what Thackeray wanted in 1841 when he prepared *Comic Tales*. In addition to the readings so marked, it might be assumed that it was Thackeray's intention that "Dimond Cut Dimond," "Foring Parts," and the three installments of Deuceace's adventures in Paris be grouped together under the single title, "The Amours of Mr. Deuceace." This would require moving "Skimmings from 'The Dairy of George IV.'" to a new position or omitting it altogether.

The Text in 1856

A dagger (†) marks those readings which in addition to those asterisked for the 1841 text I would include in a text representing what Thackeray wanted in 1856 when he prepared the *Miscellanies* edition. Moreover, though the *Miscellanies* edition itself does not reflect it, it is clear that Thackeray would have omitted "Yellowplush's Ajew" and "Epistles to the Literati" in 1856 had he had full control over the preparation and publication. At least his 1858 letter to Blackwood indicates that he wished those two installments had been suppressed (see Introduction).

The List

The first reading is that of the present edition which in all these cases is the same as that of *Fraser's Magazine*. Variant readings follow and are labeled with the symbols employed in the list of emendations (i.e. CT for the 1841 *Comic Tales*, A for the 1852 Appleton edition, and M for the 1856 *Miscellanies*). Most of the variants from the unauthorized Appleton edition are given in a separate table, for though they often caused the *Miscellanies* text to vary from *Fraser's* and *Comic Tales*, those readings are without authority (see Variants in the Appleton Edition). In the few instances where *Comic Tales* differs from *Fraser's* but *Miscellanies* does not follow suit because Appleton intervened, the Appleton symbol is added to prevent the appearance that such *Miscellanies* readings have authority. No other Appleton variants are recorded in this list.

Fashnable Fax and Polite Annygoats

[This installment was not reprinted in an Authorial version.]

Miss Shum's Husband

*10.hd No. II.
◇ I. CT M
[The altered installment number was caused by the omission of "Fashnable Fax."]

*10.1–12.7 [Introductory letter]
◇ [omitted] CT M

*12.9 Well then, *poor commonsy*, as they say: I
◇ I CT M

*12.11 old, and no mistake.
◇ old. CT M

†12.11 Edward CT
◇ James M

12.36 disreppytable CT
◇ disrepettable M

13.26 Tilbury
◇ Tilbry CT M

14.21 bullied
◇ bullyd CT M

*15.hd Chapter II.
◇ [omitted] CT M
[The three subsequent chapter headings were renumbered to suit this omission. No further record is made of these changes.]

15.31 gals
◇ girls M

16.1 girls
◇ gals CT M

16.14 a —"
◇ a—" CT M
[A space signals a word spoken but not printed; no space indicates a trailing off of speech or an interruption. Betsy had called her father a fool; Mary may or may not have repeated the word.]

16.25 her!
◇ her. M

16.25 Heaven!
◇ Heaven, CT
◇ Heaven A M

17.2 Philips
◇ Phillips CT M

*17.38 been
◇ bein CT M
[For *being*; *been* is potentially confusing in this context.]

*17.42 and, assuming
◇ assuming CT M

18.10 principle
◇ principal CT M
[This correction of a possibly confusing reading seems to me beyond Yellowplush's capability.]

18.12 umberelloes
◇ umbrellos CT M

*18.22 Cox's
◇ Coxy's CT M

18.23 waggin
◇ vaggin CT M

18.25 heard
◇ heerd CT M

18.32 Westminster A M
◇ Wesminster CT

18.36 while
◇ whil CT M

18.38 *of the*
◇ *of to the* CT M

18.39 Cartlitch's
◇ Cartlich's CT M

*18.43 hot
◇ 'ot CT M

19.28 a motion
◇ amotion M

*20.39 *women,"*
◇ *women!"* CT M

21.2 alderman,
◇ alderman. CT M

*21.19 dromestix
◇ deomestix CT M
[The original is likely an error, but not so egregious as to *require* emendation.]

21.36 kinds
◇ kind M

22.4   more;"
◇ more?" CT M

22.30 robin
◇ robing CT M

23.8   faintin
◇ faintain M

23.41 Ma'am
◇ Ma'm M

24.5   Saint
◇ St. CT M

24.19 missiseses
◇ missises CT M

24.22 nupshums
◇ nupshuls CT M

24.29 misses
◇ missis M

26.23 pound
◇ pounds M

26.28 SWEP
◇ SWEEP CT M

*26.31 C.Y.
◇ [omitted] CT M

Dimond Cut Dimond

*27.hd No. III.
◇ II. CT
◇ [omitted] A M
[See note for 10.hd, above.]

*27.title [*Comic Tales* adds a new title
above "Dimond Cut Dimond" in
larger type: THE AMOURS
OF MR. DEUCEACE. This
title was to apply to all the
Deuceace stories, but it was not
used in the runnintg titles, and
"Skimmings from 'The Dairy of
George IV.'" was left between
the first and second Deuceace
story.]

27.5   Court
◇ Cort M

27.9   Deuceace
◇ Deuceacre M

27.20 Holmax
◇ Holmax— CT M

27.21 suckles—
◇ suckles M

28.19 floor

◇ floar M

*29.2 is
◇ ise CT M

29.33 friend
◇ frend M

30.4   miserandum
◇ mimerandum CT M
[The original may be an error,
but *miser* seems a possible
appropriate malapropism.]

30.15 inkum
◇ incum M

30.15 hundred
◇ hunderd CT M
[Also at 30.16]

32.7   parshallities, wiz,—
◇ parshallities—wiz., CT M

32.14 Dawkinseses
◇ Dawkinses CT M

32.18 circkumstance
◇ cirkumstance M

32.42 grill
◇ gril M

32.44 which
◇ witch M

*33.1 antelope
◇ anvelope CT M
[*Envelope* is meant, so *antelope*
is not a cockney pronunciation,
but it does seem an attractively
possible malapropism.]

34.1   read
◇ red CT M

34.17 fack
◇ fac CT M

34.19 porpus
◇ porpos CT M

34.44 cool and slow as
◇ cool as M

35.5   hundred
◇ hunderd M

35.14 have half
◇ half CT

35.33 grows
◇ grous CT M

36.4   complyments
◇ complymints M

36.15 sir M
◇ Sir CT

36.29 me!"
◇ me." M

*36.43 [section division marked with
row of asterisks]
◇ [no division] CT M

38.14 sir?" M
◇ sir," CT

*39.9 C. Yellowplush.
◇ [omitted] CT M

**Skimmings from "The Dairy of
George IV."**

*40.hd No. IV.
◇ [No number given] CT M
◇ III.
[Reading recommended for an
1841 text. See note for 10.hd,
above.]

40.hd.fn [omit] These Memoirs were
originally published in *Frazer's
Magazine*, and it may be stated
for the benefit of the unlearned
in such matters, that "Oliver
Yorke" is the assumed name of
the editor of that periodical. M
[The misspelling of *Fraser's* and
the condescending tone in the
reference to Yorke point to
Thackeray's amanuensis, George
Hodder, as the source of this
footnote.]

41.8 injer
◇ injur CT M

41.13 before
◇ befor CT M

42.7 supearor
◇ superaor M

43.10 peculiary
◇ peculiarly M
[Probably a careless
compositorial "correction" since
pecuniary is the word Yellowplush
actually misspelled.]

43.15 xquizzit
◇ xqizzit M

44.7 to such
◇ for such CT M

45.22 *trumpery,*

◇ *trumpery!* M

†45.43 ear
◇ ears M

46.20 had
◇ has M

46.26 dishcord
◇ diskcord M

*46.27 'em, viz.
◇ 'em—viz., CT M

46.35 [No ¶] The old quean
◇ [¶] The old quean CT M
["The old quean" are the first
words of a new column. This
physical arrangement, more than
sense, suggests a new paragraph.]

47.2 carrickter
◇ carricter CT M

47.3 it's
◇ its M

47.14 Princiss
◇ Princis M

48.39 pictures
◇ picturs CT M

49.36 *to*
◇ [rom] M

50.27 extrack
◇ extrak M

50.34 princess!
◇ Princess! A
◇ Princess; M

50.40 a'nt
◇ an't M

50.41 bennyfactriss
◇ bennyfactris M

Foring Parts

*51.hd No. V.
◇ [No number given] CT M
◇ IV. [Reading recommended for
an 1841 text. See note for 39.hd
above.]

51.2 handsome
◇ andsome CT M

51.21 gingybread
◇ gingybred CT M

51.28 Heaven
◇ Heavin M

52.32 I now
◇ now I M

52.35 intence
◇ intense M
[The proper "correction" would
be 'intents.']

*52.40 Charles.
◇ Charles! CT M

52.41 "yes," "what's
◇ "yes, what's CT M

53.2 miserable
◇ misrable CT M

53.5 subjick
◇ subjik M

53.9 in such a
◇ in a M

53.18 swearing
◇ swaring CT M

53.23 Bayble
◇ Babyle M

53.29 avaridge)
◇ avaridg) M

53.29 milliuns
◇ milliums M

53.30 melumcolly
◇ mellumcolly M

53.36 sityouate
◇ sitouate M

54.11 to
◇ till M

54.12 opera-glasses
◇ opra-glasses CT M

54.38 fortun
◇ fortn M

55.3 you're
◇ you are M

55.4 nobillaty
◇ nobiliaty M

55.13 character at Paris
◇ character of Paris CT M
[Deuceace is trying out the
character of a man of fortune
at "Bolong" before he tries it at
Paris.]

†57.5 two thousand four hundred
◇ four thousand seven hundred
M

*57.6 be won.
◇ be sure. CT M

57.12 550
◇ 500 M
[Clearly an error.]

57.25 parrowgrafs
◇ parrografs CT M

57.26 knew M
◇ know CT

58.2 newspepper
◇ newspeper M

*58.16 why
◇ [ital.] CT M

58.24 Schwigschnaps
◇ Schwigshhnaps M

59.8 people!
◇ people. M

59.8 see the
◇ see of the M

*59.14 C. Y.
◇ [omitted] CT M

Mr. Deuceace at Paris I

*60.hd No. VI
◇ [No number given] CT M
◇ V. [Reading recommended for
an 1841 text.]

60.9 male
◇ mal CT M

60.20 was
◇ wos M

60.21 hansum
◇ ansum CT M

61.9 rittycule
◇ ryttycule CT
◇ rettycule M

61.12 Griffin
◇ Griffing CT M

61.16, 23, & 63.25 ladies'-maids
◇ ladies-maids CT M

*61.21 its
◇ his CT M

62.25 master
◇ muster M

62.29 Marobô
◇ Marobo CT M

62.32 of
◇ in M

62.34 complete a gentleman
◇ complete gentleman CT M
[Although Yellowplush feels far
superior to mere Frenchmen,
he does not see himself as
Deuceace's peer. Far from being
a gentleman, Yellowplush merely
contributes to the completeness
of Deuceace as gentleman.]

*62.42 "He
◇ He CT M
[Accepting this change requires
dropping the quote at 63.2 also.]

*63.2 inkum."
◇ inkum. M

63.18 maid
◇ made M

64.12 justas
◇ justass CT M

64.22 particklar
◇ partiklar M

64.67 possesst
◇ possest CT M

*65.1 and short
◇ and the short CT M

65.5 ways,—
◇ ways, CT M

66.20 Number
◇ chapter CT M
[*Chapter* is wrong even in the
CT version since section breaks
within "Deuceace at Paris" are
called chapters. The reference is
to "Foring Parts."]

66.42 segar
◇ seagar M

67.4 segars
◇ seagars M

67.24 morning
◇ morning? CT M

68.33 have
◇ has CT M
[The shift from third person
singular (Your Lordship) to
second person earlier in the
sentence makes either reading
possible in speech though *have* is

grammatically incorrect.]

68.39 smears
◇ snears CT
◇ sneers M
[Though quite possibly an error,
smears is not an inappropriate
pun and therefore may be an
intentional reading.]

69.2 from——
◇ from —— CT M
[Though the next word would
have been unprintable and
would have required a spaced
dash if spoken, the succeeding
sham politeness between
Deuceace and Crabs indicates
that Yellowplush's interruption
prevented the completion of the
sentence.]

69.22 hisself
◇ himself CT M

70.2 *comité* M
◇ *comitê* CT

70.14 affummatif
◇ affummatiff CT M

*70.27 mighty
◇ he was mighty CT M
[Though awkward, the elliptical
reading is not impossible.]

71.31 gentleman
◇ gentlemin M
[Cf. *coachmin*, line 30.]

*71.37 Earl
◇ the Earl CT M

72.17 addrasst
◇ addrast CT M

72.20 'un
◇ un CT M
[The apostrophe is probably an
error since it represents no left
out letter in the word "one," but
it may represent the omitted "w"
sound.]

*72.33 began, this gall,
◇ began this squall, CT M
[The copy-text reading is not
impossible; Miss Griffin is a gall
in that her singing is irritating
and in that her humped back

makes her a blot or sore to look
at. "This gall" can then be a
descriptive interruption. It is
possible, on the other hand,
that the compositor failed to
read Thackeray's handwriting.
He may have written "began
the squall" with the 's' closer to
"the" than to "q", giving "this
quall". It is fruitless to select the
"correct" form.]

73.24 we've
  ◇ wee've M

73.42 & 74.6 Kicksy
  ◇ Kicksey Ct M

74.4 staid
  ◇ stayed CT M

75.40 *Didn't*
  ◇ *Didnt* M

77.2 as I feel must
  ◇ as must CT M
  [Though quite clearly the result
  of compositorial eye skip, the
  alteration is more significant
  than most compositor errors.]

Deuceace at Paris II

77.27 Well;
  ◇ Well, CT M
  [Cf. the same usage, unaltered,
  in 'Epistles' at 123.39.]

77.30 rellatif
  ◇ relletif CT
  ◇ relletiff M

77.34 extravygans
  ◇ extravagans CT M

77.39 occoupied
  ◇ occupied CT M
  [Though the original seems an
  unlikely Yellowplushian spelling,
  it is not impossible.]

77.9 kept
  ◇ kep CT M

78.29 seldom
  ◇ seldum CT M

78.40 into
  ◇ in CT M

80.29 made
  ◇ make M

81.1 holding
  ◇ olding CT M

81.15 which
  ◇ wich CT M

81.39 room
  ◇ roam CT M

82.25 gracis
  ◇ graci's CT M
  [One might argue this is a
  dubious correction for though
  it makes the case clearer to the
  eye, it destroys the phonetic
  accuracy.]

82.27 bewtiflle
  ◇ bewtifle CT M

82.28 thiefs'
  ◇ thief's CT M

82.34 object
  ◇ objects CT M
  [The beloved object for each
  'roag' is himself, hence the
  appropriateness of the singular.
  The plural, too, is appropriate
  since the comment is collective.]

84.33 And
  ◇ and CT M

85.1 *lâche*
  ◇ *lâche* CT M

*85.12 Fitzclarence,
  ◇ Fitzclarence CT M
  [Though possibly an error, a
  slight rhetorical pause for effect
  may be indicated.]

85.34 Hôtel
  ◇ Hotel CT M

86.37 inflammayshn
  ◇ inflamayshn CT M

87.31 scoundrill
  ◇ scoundril CT
  ◇ scoundrel M

87.41 fust
  ◇ fuss CT M

88.2 [No ¶] The
  ◇ [¶] The CT M

88.7 misteak
  ◇ mistak M

88.17 gend'armes
  ◇ gendarmes CT M

88.17 *a-t'-il*
  ◊ *a-t-il* CT M

End of Deuceace

89.29 CHAP. VIII. LIMBO
  ◊ THE END OF MR. DEUCEACE'S
  HISTORY. / CHAP. VIII.—LIMBO
  F
  ◊ CHAPTER VIII. / THE END
  ...HISTORY. / LIMBO. CT M
  [Subordinating the section title
  under the chapter number is
  only a partial correction of
  Fraser's failure to print all 3 parts
  in one issue of the magazine.
  See historical introduction.]

89.39 Brittn
  ◊ Britttn A
  ◊ Brittin M

90.7 marrycle
  ◊ marycle CT M

90.23 stay;
  ◊ stay! M

90.25 disguise
  ◊ disgeise CT M

*90.24 is
  ◊ i's CT M

93.2 marriage
  ◊ marridge M

93.15 oppera
  ◊ oppra CT M

93.16 happier
  ◊ hapier CT M

93.25 before
  ◊ befor CT M

93.35 couple
  ◊ coople CT M

94.13 master's M
  ◊ masters CT

94.14 drove
  ◊ droav CT

94.29 *joué*
  ◊ *loué* CT M

95.26a prison?
  ◊ prison! CT M

95.28 betwigst
  ◊ betwixgst M

94.41 Crabs's

◊ Crab's CT M

95.44 home!
  ◊ home? CT M

97.15 *say so*
  ◊ [No ital.] CT M

99.23 britches
  ◊ britchis M

99.29 amaizd
  ◊ amazd M

100.10 prison
  ◊ prisn M

100.31 Honorable
  ◊ Honorabble CT M

101.32 Saint
  ◊ Sainte M

101.37 thousand
  ◊ thousnd CT M

101.41 carriage
  ◊ carridge M

102.2 *I*
  ◊ [rom] CT M

102.23 says
  ◊ said M

103.16 butns
  ◊ butins M

103.18 Vandôme
  ◊ Vandome M

*103.25 complete
  ◊ completed CT M

104.16 Crabs
  ◊ Crabbs M
  [Also 104.22]

*104.19 Prince of Talleyrand
  ◊ Prince Talleyrand CT M

*104.20 the Marshal
  ◊ Marshal the CT M
  [Cf. "Ajew" 195.a.23–4.]

*104.20 behalf H.
  ◊ behalf of H. CT M

104.29 Saint
  ◊ St. CT M

104.33 do
  ◊ du CT M

106.13 serious."
  ◊ serious?" CT M

106.29 can't. D—
  ◇ can't——D— CT M

107.11 *voulez-vous?*
  ◇ *voulez-vous!* CT M

107.42 ho,—
  ◇ ho!— CT M

109.28 saw
  ◇ see CT M
  [Yellowplush meant that when
  Deuceace turned around he
  saw his face, not that he can
  picture the face now at the time
  of writing.]

*109.33 CHARLES YELLOWPLUSH.
  ◇ [omitted] CT M

Mr. Yellowplush's Ajew

111.20 *Mista*wedwadLyttnBulwig
  ◇ Mistawedwad Lyttn Bulwig CT
  M

*111.29 both with a
  ◇ both, a M

112.6 Scott A M
  ◇ Scot CT

112.6 Doctor
  ◇ Docther CT M

113.19 *anēwithmon*
  ◇ *anëwithmon* CT M

113.25 pallitix
  ◇ paillitix M

113.28 twuth A M
  ◇ twth CT

*114.12 supported
  ◇ and supported CT M

114.24 Bullwig?
  ◇ Bullwig! CT M

115.3 Hwhat
  ◇ Hwat CT M

115.41 Brookes's
  ◇ Brooke's CT M

116.4 right;
  ◇ right? CT M

116.5 *yours?*
  ◇ *yours.* CT M

116.11 eye
  ◇ eyes M

116.28 Presence

116.28 Presence
  ◇ Pwesence CT M

116.29 sake!"—
  ◇ sake!—" CT M

116.33 looked
  ◇ looking M

116.38 nonsince
  ◇ nonsinse M

116.41 way.
  ◇ way: CT M

116.41 ye
  ◇ you M

116.43 for
  ◇ of M

117.17 barnet?
  ◇ barnet! M

117.22 faw!
  ◇ faw? M

117.22 litewatuwe
  ◇ litwatuwe M

117.34 revrint
  ◇ rivrint M

118.1 sprawlink
  ◇ spralink CT M

118.28 melancholy M
  ◇ melanchely CT

*118.34 CHARLES YELLOWPLUSH
  ◇ [omitted] CT M

Epistles to the Literati

119.hd No. XIII.
  ◇ [omitted] CT M
  ["Epistles" was the thirteenth
  in *Fraser's* series "Epistles to the
  Literati." See Historical Essay for
  further commentary.]

119.hd BART.
  ◇ BT. CT M

120.19 Barnet;
  ◇ Barnet! M

120.21 your A M
  ◇ yoor CT

121.29 else
  ◇ alse CT M

122.10 *acting*
  ◇ [No ital.] CT M

123.25 *Do*
  ◇ [No ital.] CT M

124.27 to the hope
  ◇ to hope M

124.39 languitch
  ◇ langwitch M

125.1 apinion
  ◇ apinian CT M

125.13 that those
  ◇ and those M

125.18 Raddicle
  ◇ Raddiccle CT M

125.26 see M
  ◇ se CT

125.30 *are*
  ◇ [No ital.] CT M

125.31 about your littery
  ◇ about littery M

125.36 acquentance
  ◇ aquentance M

125.39 *parrysample*
  ◇ *parrysampe* M

125.39 *is*
  ◇ [No ital.] CT M

126.7 Wooes
  ◇ Woos CT M

126.19 "Hark!
  ◇ "Hark? M

128.23 *Men*
  ◇ [No ital.] CT M

128.45 igspress
  ◇ ingspress CT M

129.9 treasure
  ◇ treasures M

130.5 while
  ◇ where M
  [Probably an error]

*132.16 am," and
  ◇ am." And CT M

132.16 in the
  ◇ in a CT M

132.18 Gaussen,
  ◇ Gaussen; CT M
  [Though a semicolon is correct
  according to syntactical
  punctuation, the comma lends
  a hurried pace which mocks the
  suspense of the plot summary.]

132.19 when
  ◇ when— CT M
  [Again syntax seems to demand
  punctuation, but its addition
  robs the text of its mock
  breathlessness.]

132.25 and
  ◇ and— CT M
  [Cf. previous entry for analogous
  situation.]

*132.26 rushes in—
  ◇ rushing in, CT M

133.38 "plovers!"
  ◇ plovers!" M

133.41 mice?
  ◇ mice! CT M
  [Cf. the repetition in line 43
  with a question mark.]

134.37 Mrs. M
  ◇ Mr. CT
  [This is the only reference to
  Mrs. Yellowplush, but there is no
  evidence to deny her existence.]

135.2 *I*
  ◇ [No ital.] CT M

Variants in the Appleton Edition

———◇———

The Appleton edition, set from *Comic Tales*, introduced about 520 new readings, all unauthorized since the edition was "pirated"—i.e., printed in America without the author's permission. Twenty-nine of these new readings restored *Fraser's Magazine* forms either by pure accident or by the correction of obvious errors introduced by *Comic Tales*. Four new readings seemed to me desirable corrections of errors in *Fraser's* repeated in *Comic Tales*; these are recorded as emendations.

The readings listed below seem to me of some importance; for, though they are without authority, they significantly alter the text which was presented in the *Miscellanies* edition. Since the *Miscellanies* text claims some authority, it might be assumed by the unwary that all its substantive readings should be accepted as Thackeray's. The following, introduced by Appleton, cannot have originated with Thackeray, and it cannot be assumed that Thackeray approved these readings just because they were retained in the *Miscellanies*. Below, the first reading is from *Fraser's* (unchanged in the present edition); the second reading is from Appleton (A). Unless otherwise noted, *Comic Tales* (CT) agrees with *Fraser's*, and *Miscellanies* (M) agrees with Appleton.

16.3 gave
  ◇ give

16.22 "O
  ◇ [¶] "O

20.24 arms.—
  ◇ arms—

21.33 my master's
  ◇ mymaster's CT
  ◇ mymayster's A
  ◇ my mayster's M

22.14 mother!"
  ◇ mother."

22.38 near the banks
  ◇ near banks

24.16 and don't
  ◇ and I don't

24.41 'em!)
  ◇ 'em)

25.27 missis
  ◇ misses

25.37 Queen
  ◇ Queene

26.26 ***[section division]
  ◇ [omitted]

27.6 it's
  ◇ its

29.6 hearty and as familiar as
  ◇ hearty as

30.38 I have mentioned
  ◇ I mentioned

30.43 Blewitt!
  ◇ Blewitt?

31.11 think?"
  ◇ think."

31.31 and then they
  ◇ and they

34.36 bust
  ◇ burst

35.14 shall have half
  ◇ shall half

35.33 it!
  ◇ it.

35.39 (and
  ◇ and

35.40 3)
  ◇ 3,

36.43 *** [section division]
  ◇ [double leading]

37.5 *** [section division]
  ◇ [double leading]

38.23 says my master
  ◇ says master

39.7 "I am
  ◇ "I'm

41.23 knows we
  ◇ knows that we

41.28 airs-/aparent
  ◇ airsaparent CT
  ◇ airsparent

44.29 never shall
  ◇ shall never

48.40 *in*
  ◇ in

52.36 salers a tramplink
  ◇ salers tramplink

54.29 dinner lasted till
  ◇ dinner till

54.35 *a*
  ◇ a

55.15 pound
  ◇ pounds

55.30 a thorough knowledge
  ◇ a knowledge

62.2 or a real
  ◇ or real

63.40 nor
  ◇ or

64.14 pound
  ◇ pounds

66.23 now was
  ◇ was now

66.42 do very well
  ◇ do well

68.5 his
  ◇ your

71.1 ask if you
  ◇ ask you if you

71.35 to coachmin
  ◇ to the coachmin

72.31 their very fust
  ◇ their fust

74.16 "And what
◇ "What

75.17 *tête-á-tête!*"
◇ *tête-á-tête.*"

86.18 *blow*
◇ blow

87.2 sea
◇ see

88.20 such
◇ that

91.13 child?
◇ child.

94.15 and up comes
◇ and comes

94.17 and the embassy-doar
◇ and embassy-doar

94.19 *Loi*"
◇ *loi!*"

98.1 and the purity
◇ and purity

102.30 commishnd
◇ comishnd

103.12 [¶] I
◇ I

106.33 he'd
◇ he had

108.17 Dawkins's
◇ Dawkins

108.20 of a will
◇ of the will

109.25 igstreme
◇ igstream

110.18 3d
◇ third

110.19 fust
◇ fust,

111.2 off
◇ of

111.11 Dioclesius
◇ Diolesius

111.12 LARNDER
◇ LARDNER

112.30 be the pwincipal
◇ be pwincipal

112.43 "Is it
◇ "It is

117.7 I'm a litherary
◇ I'm litherary

121.22 two
◇ too

121.22 and the cups
◇ and cups

121.33 you!
◇ you [plate damage] A
◇ you, M

122.14 with
◇ by

134.17 let us not
◇ let not

End-Line Hyphens

———◇———

Although little significance can be attached to hyphenation in Yellow-plush's writing, whenever an end-of-line hyphen in the copy-text divided a word that might be rendered either hyphenated or unhyphenated, a decision was required for this edition. Indicated in Table A is the form adopted in this edition for words ambiguously divided at the ends of lines in the copy-text.

Whenever the present edition hyphenates at the end of the line a word that might be written as one word or as a hyphenated compound, the correct form to be used in quotations or reprints is indicated in Table B.

Table A
Words Ambiguously Hyphenated in the Copy-text

Fashnable Fax

1.18	slap-up	2.11	schoolmaster
1.20	Whitechapel	2.34	Coachman
1.22	coachman	6.42	*second-hand*
2.4	old-fashioned	8.21	coal-heaver
		9.5	overpowerin

Miss Shum's Husband

14.6 sub-deputy
14.32 knock-kneed
14.32 shut-frill
16.6 vinmill
24.1 double-locked
24.48 sister-in-law

Dimond Cut Dimond

29.9 floot-playing
30.20 wine-marchant's
32.21 Strasbug-pie
34.39 long-winded
36.35 to-morrow

Skimmings from "The Dairy of George IV."

40.3 woodcox
41.28 airs-aparent
41.33 tator-tator
43.40 well-timed
45.3 scandle-mongers
47.25 harp-player
49.11 dairy-woman
49.13 backbitin
49.36 overthrow

Foring Parts

52.2 half-a-crownd
54.4 landlord
57.34 whist-player
58.22 cock-hat
59.5 jackasses

Mr. Deuceace at Paris

60.1 seventy-five
60.7 leftenant-general
61.10 well-bred
61.36 twenty-seven
61.37 cold-looking
66.12 tap-room

66.35 overhappy
67.34 a-year
68.21 steam-injian
68.29 spendthrift
68.38 half-asleep
70.31 *pot-fool*
72.15 fish-plate
74.9 hump-backed
77.16 *Mydear* [for *Medea*]
78.3 three-cornerd
79.16 lovesick
79.18 to-morrow
80.19 straitforard
83.7 pistle-shooting
89.19 dressing-gownd
90.25 a-year
90.31 stepmother
107.11 *voulez-vous*

Mr. Yellowplush's Ajew

110.14 Oystereasy
111.20 *Mistaw*edwadLyttnBulwig
111.23 drawing-room
113.3 milk-and-wathery
113.23 oatmale
116.23 fire-stealer

Epistles to the Literati

119.20 re-appearants
120.21 small-beear
122.1 *Sea—Capting*
123.14 blood-red
127.37 backopipe
130.31 sea-coast
131.11 overboard
131.16a sea-captain
132.32 honeymoon
133.9 outlines

Table B

End-line-hyphenated compound words in the present edition that were also broken in the copy-text are listed in Table A. Any new end-line hyphenated compound word in this text that should be quoted as a hyphenated word is listed here. End-line hyphens not found in either of these lists represent breaks in single, unhyphenated words.

2.3 liv'ry-coat	60.10 twenty-three
8.13 knife-boy	67.37 a-year
13.8 silk-stockins	73.11 a-year
14.12 tallow-chandlering	80.40 fire-eater
14.26 six-roomed	85.16 kea-hole
28.43 cut-away	92.9 mother-in-law
30.8 bill-files	93.39 gook-natured
32.33 soda-water	121.9 dressing-gownd
52.18 mask-head	

THE
TREMENDOUS ADVENTURES
OF
MAJOR GAHAGAN

Some Passages in the Life of Major Gahagan.

————◇————

"Truth is strange, stranger than fiction."

————◇————

I THINK it but right that in making my appearance before the public I should at once acquaint them with my titles and name. My card, as I leave it at the houses of the nobility, my friends, is as follows:—

MAJOR GOLIAH O'GRADY GAHAGAN, H.E.I.C.S.,

Commanding Battalion of

Irregular Horse,

AHMEDNUGGAR.

Seeing, I say, this simple visiting-ticket, the world will avoid any of those awkward mistakes as to my person, which have been so frequent of late. There has been no end to the blunders regarding this humble title of mine, and the confusion thereby created. When I published my volume of poems, for instance, "The Morning Post" newspaper remarked "that the Lyrics of the Heart by Miss Gahagan may be ranked among the sweetest flowerets of the present spring season." "The Quarterly Review," commenting upon my "Observations on the Pons Asinorum," (4to. London, 1836,) called me "Doctor Gahagan," and so on. It was time to put an end to these mistakes, and I have taken the above simple remedy.

I was urged to it by a very exalted personage. Dining in August last at the Palace of the T-l-r-es at Paris, the lovely young Duch-ss of Orl--ns (who, though she does not speak English, understands it as well as I do) said to me, in the softest Teutonic, *"Lieber Herr Major, haben sie den Ahmednuggarischen-jäger-battalion gelassen?"* *"Warum denn?"* said I, quite astonished at her R—l H——ss's question. The P——cess then spoke of some trifle from my pen, which was simply signed Goliah Gahagan.

There was unluckily a dead silence as H. R. H. put this question.

"*Comment donc?*" said H. M. Lo-is Ph-l-ppe, looking gravely at Count Molé, "*le cher Major a quitté l'armée! Nicolas donc sera maître de l'Inde!*" H. M—— and the Pr— M-n-ster pursued their conversation in a low tone, and left me, as may be imagined, in a dreadful state of confusion. I blushed, and stuttered, and murmured out a few incoherent words to explain—but it would not do—I could not recover my equanimity during the course of the dinner, and while endeavouring to help an English Duke, my neighbour, to *poulet à l'Austerlitz*, fairly sent seven mushrooms and three large greasy *croûtes* over his whiskers and shirt-frill. Another laugh at my expense. "Ah! M. *le Major,*" said the Q—— of the B-lg--ns, archly, "*vous n'aurez jamais votre brevet de Colonel.*" Her M——y's joke will be better understood when I state that his Grace is the brother of a minister.

I am not at liberty to violate the sanctity of private life by mentioning the names of the parties concerned in this little anecdote. I only wish to have it understood that I am a gentleman, and live at least in *decent* society. *Verbum sat.*

But to be serious. I am obliged always to write the name of Goliah in full, to distinguish me from my brother, Gregory Gahagan, who was also a Major (in the King's service), and whom I killed in a duel, as the public most likely knows. Poor Greg! a very trivial dispute was the cause of our quarrel, which never would have originated but for the similarity of our names. The circumstance was this:—I had been lucky enough to render the Nawaub of Lucknow some trifling service (in the notorious affair of Choprasjee Muckjee), and his Highness sent down a gold toothpick-case directed to Capt. G. Gahagan, which I of course thought was for me; my brother madly claimed it; we fought, and the consequence was, that in about three minutes he received a slash in the right side (cut 6) which effectually did his business;—he was a good swordsman enough—I was THE BEST in the universe. The most ridiculous part of the affair is, that the toothpick-case was his after all—he had left it on the Nawaub's table at tiffin. I can't conceive what madness prompted him to fight about such a paltry bauble; he had much better have yielded it at once, when he saw I was determined to have it. From this slight specimen of my adventures, the reader will perceive that my life has been one of no ordinary interest; and, in fact, I may say that I have led a more remarkable life than any man in the service—I have been at more pitched battles, led more forlorn hopes, had more success among the fair sex, drunk harder, read more, and been a handsomer man than any officer now serving her Majesty.

When I first went to India in 1802, I was a raw cornet of seventeen, with blazing red hair, six feet seven in height, athletic at all kinds of exercises, owing money to my tailor and everybody else who would trust me, possessing an Irish brogue, and my full-pay of 120*l.* a-year. I need not say that with all these advantages I did that which a number of clever fellows have done before me—I fell in love, and proposed to marry immediately.

But how to overcome the difficulty?—It is true that I loved Julia Jowler—loved her to madness; but her father intended her for a member of council at least, and not for a beggarly Irish ensign. It was, however, my fate to make the passage to India (on board of the Samuel Snob, East Indiaman, Captain Duffy) with this lovely creature, and my misfortune instantaneously to fall in love with her. We were not out of the Channel before I adored her, worshipped the deck which she trod upon, kissed a thousand times the cuddy-chair on which she used to sit. The same madness fell on every man in the ship. The two mates fought about her at the Cape—the surgeon, a sober, pious Scotchman, from disappointed affection, took so dreadfully to drinking as to threaten spontaneous combustion—and old Colonel Lilywhite, carrying his wife and seven daughters to Bengal, swore that he would have a divorce from Mrs. L., and made an attempt at suicide—the Captain himself told me, with tears in his eyes, that he hated his hitherto-adored Mrs. Duffy, although he had had nineteen children by her.

We used to call her the Witch—there was magic in her beauty and in her voice. I was spell-bound when I looked at her, and stark-staring mad when she looked at me! Oh, lustrous black eyes!—Oh, glossy night-black ringlets!—Oh, lips!—Oh, dainty frocks of white muslin!—Oh, tiny kid slippers!—though old and gouty, Gahagan sees you still! I recollect off Ascension, she looked at me in her particular way one day at dinner, just as I happened to be blowing on a piece of scalding hot green fat. I was stupified at once—I thrust the entire morsel (about half a pound) into my mouth. I made no attempt to swallow or to masticate it, but left it there for many minutes burning, burning. I had no skin to my palate for seven weeks after, and lived on rice-water during the rest of the voyage. The anecdote is trivial, but it shows the power of Julia Jowler over me.

The writers of marine novels have so exhausted the subject of storms, shipwrecks, mutinies, engagements, sea-sickness, and so forth—that, (although I have experienced each of these in many varieties,) I think it quite unnecessary to recount such trifling adventures: suffice it to say, that during our five months *trajet*, my mad passion for Julia daily increased; so did the Captain's and the Surgeon's; so did Colonel Lilywhite's; so did the Doctor's, the Mate's—that of most part of the passengers, and a considerable number of the crew. For myself, I swore—ensign as I was—I would win her for my wife; I vowed that I would make her glorious with my sword—that, as soon as I had made a favourable impression on my commanding officer, (which I did not doubt to create,) I would lay open to him the state of my affections, and demand his daughter's hand; with such sentimental outpourings did our voyage continue and conclude.

We landed at the Sunderbunds on a grilling hot day in December, 1802, and then for the moment Julia and I separated. She was carried off to her papa's arms, in a palankeen, surrounded by at least forty Hookah-badars; whilst the poor cornet, attended but by two dandies and a solitary beasty, (by which unnatural name these blackamoors are called,) made his way humbly to join the regiment at head-quarters.

The —th regiment of Bengal Cavalry, then under the command of Lieut. Colonel Julius Jowler, C.B., was known throughout Asia, and indeed Europe, by the proud title of the Bundelcund Invincibles—so great was its character for bravery, so remarkable were its services in that delightful district of India. Major Sir George Gutch was next in command, and Tom Thrupp, as kind a fellow as ever ran a Mahratta through the body, was Second Major. We were on the eve of that remarkable war, which was speedily to spread throughout the whole of India, to call forth the valour of a Wellesley, and the indomitable gallantry of a Gahagan; which was illustrated by our victories at Ahmednuggar (where I was the first over the barricade at the storming of the Pettah); at Argaum, where I slew with my own sword twenty-three matchlock-men, and cut a dromedary in two; and by that terrible day of Assye, where Wellesley would have been beaten but for me—me alone; I headed nineteen charges of cavalry, took (aided by only four men of my own troop) seventeen field-pieces, killing the scoundrelly French artillery-men; on that day I had eleven elephants shot under me, and carried away Scindia's nose-ring with a pistol-ball. Wellesley is a Duke and a Marshal, I but a simple Major of Irregulars; such is fortune and war! But my feelings carry me away from my narrative, which had better proceed with more order.

On arriving, I say, at our barracks at Dum Dum, I for the first time put on the beautiful uniform of the Invincibles; a light blue swallow-tailed jacket, with silver lace and wings, ornamented with about 3000 sugar-loaf buttons, rhubarb-coloured leather inexpressibles, (tights,) and red morocco boots with silver spurs and tassels, set off to admiration the handsome persons of the officers of our corps. We wore powder in those days, and a regulation pig-tail of seventeen inches, a brass helmet, surrounded by leopard-skin, with a bear-skin top, and a horse-tail feather, gave the head a fierce and chivalrous appearance, which is far more easily imagined than described.

Attired in this magnificent costume, I first presented myself before Colonel Jowler. He was habited in a manner precisely similar, but not being more than five feet in height, and weighing at least fifteen stone, the dress he wore did not become him quite so much as slimmer and taller men. Flanked by his tall Majors, Thrupp and Gutch, he looked like a stumpy skittle-ball, between two attenuated skittles. The plump little Colonel received me with vast cordiality, and I speedily became a prime favourite with himself and the other officers of the corps. Jowler was the most hospitable of men, and, gratifying my appetite and my love together, I continually partook of his dinners, and feasted on the sweet presence of Julia.

I can see now, what I would not and could not perceive in those early days, that this Miss Jowler, on whom I had lavished my first and warmest love, whom I had endowed with all perfection and purity, was no better than a little impudent flirt, who played with my feelings, because during the monotony of a sea voyage she had no other toy to play with; and who deserted others for me, and me for others, just as her whim or her interest might guide her. She had not been three weeks at head-quarters, when half the regiment was in love with her. Each and all of the candidates had some favour to boast of, or some encouraging hopes on which to build. It was the scene of the Samuel Snob over again, only heightened in interest by a number of duels. The following list will give the reader a notion of some of them:—

1. Cornet Gahagan.	Ensign Hicks of the Sappers and Miners. Hicks received a ball in his jaw, and was half choked by a quantity of carroty whisker, forced down his throat with the ball.
2. Captain Macgillicuddy, B.N.I.	Cornet Gahagan.—I was run through the body, but the sword passed between the ribs, and injured me very slightly.
3. Captain Macgillicuddy, B.N.I.	Mr. Mulligatawney, B.C.S., Deputy Assistant, Vice Sub-Controller of the Boggleywollah Indigo grounds, Ramgolly branch.

Macgillicuddy should have stuck to sword's play, and he might have come off in his second duel as well as in his first; as it was, the civilian placed a ball and a part of Mac's gold repeater in his stomach: a remarkable circumstance attended this shot, an account of which I sent home to the Philosophical Transactions: the Surgeon had extracted the ball, and was going off, thinking that all was well, when the gold repeater struck thirteen in poor Macgillicuddy's abdomen. I suppose that the works must have been disarranged in some way by the bullet, for the repeater was one of Barraud's, never known to fail before, and the circumstance occurred at *seven* o'clock.*

---

* So admirable are the performance of these watches, which will stand in any climate, that I repeatedly heard poor Macgillicuddy relate the following fact. The hours, as it is known, count in Italy from one to twenty-four: *the day Mac landed at Naples, his repeater rung the Italian hours from one to twenty-four;* as soon as he crossed the Alps it only sounded as usual.—G. O'G. G.

I could continue, almost *ad infinitum*, an account of the wars which this Helen occasioned, but the above three specimens will, I should think, satisfy the peaceful reader. I delight not in scenes of blood, Heaven knows, but I was compelled in the course of a few weeks, and for the sake of this one woman, to fight nine duels myself, and I know that four times as many more took place concerning her.

I forgot to say that Jowler's wife was a half-caste woman, who had been born and bred entirely in India, and whom the Colonel had married from the house of her mother, a native. There were some singular rumours abroad regarding this latter lady's history—it was reported that she was the daughter of a native Rajah, and had been carried off by a poor English subaltern in Lord Clive's time. The young man was killed very soon after, and left his child with its mother. The black Prince forgave his daughter and bequeathed to her a handsome sum of money. I suppose it was on this account that Jowler married Mrs. J., a creature who had not, I do believe, a Christian name, or a single Christian quality—she was a hideous, bloated, yellow creature, with a beard, black teeth, and red eyes. I do not believe that she had a single good quality: she was fat, lying, ugly, and stingy—she hated and was hated by all the world, and by her jolly husband as devoutly as by any other. She did not pass a month in the year with him, but spent most of her time, with her native friends. I wonder how she could have given birth to so lovely a creature as her daughter. This woman was of course with the Colonel, when Julia arrived, and the spice of the devil in her daughter's composition was most carefully nourished and fed by her. If Julia had been a flirt before, she was a downright jilt now; she set the whole cantonment by the ears, she made wives jealous and husbands miserable, she caused all those duels of which I have discoursed already, and yet such was the fascination of THE WITCH, that I still thought her an angel. I made court to the nasty mother, in order to be near the daughter, and I listened untiringly to Jowler's interminable dull stories, because I was occupied all the time in watching the graceful movements of Miss Julia.

But the trumpet of war was soon ringing in our ears; and on the battle-field Gahagan is a man! The Bundelcund Invincibles received orders to march, and Jowler, Hector-like, donned his helmet, and prepared to part from his Andromache. And now arose his perplexity: what must be done with his daughter, his Julia? He knew his wife's peculiarities of living, and did not much care to trust his daughter to her keeping—but in vain he tried to find her an asylum among the respectable ladies of his regiment. Lady Gutch offered to receive her, but would have nothing to do with Mrs. Jowler—the Surgeon's wife, Mrs. Sawbone, would have neither mother nor daughter;—there was no help for it—Julia and her mother must have a house together, and Jowler knew that his wife would fill it with her odious blackamoor friends.

I could not, however, go forth satisfied to the campaign, until I had learned from Julia my fate. I watched twenty opportunities to see her alone, and wandered about the Colonel's bungalow, as an informer does about a public-house, marking the incomings and outgoings of the family, and longing to seize the moment when Miss Jowler, unbiassed by her mother or her papa, might listen, perhaps, to my eloquence, and melt at the tale of my love.

But it would not do—old Jowler seemed to have taken all of a sudden to such a fit of domesticity, that there was no finding him out of doors, and his rhubarb-coloured wife (I believe that her skin gave the first idea of our regimental breeches), who before had been gadding ceaselessly abroad, and poking her broad nose into every *ménage* in the cantonment, stopped faithfully at home with her spouse. My only chance was to beard the old couple in their den, and ask them at once for their *cub*.

So I called one day at tiffin:—old Jowler was always happy to have my company at this meal; it amused him, he said, to see me drink Hodson's pale ale (I drank two hundred and thirty-four dozen the first year I was in Bengal)—and it was no small piece of fun, certainly, to see old Mrs. Jowler attack the currie-bhaut;—she was exactly the colour of it, as I have had already the honour to remark, and she swallowed the mixture with a gusto which was never equalled, except by my poor friend Dando, *à propos d'huîtres*. She consumed the first three platesful, with a fork and spoon, like a Christian; but as she warmed to her work, the old hag would throw away her silver implements, and, dragging the dishes towards her, go to work with her hands, flip the rice into her mouth with her fingers, and stow away a quantity of eatables sufficient for a sepoy company:—but why do I diverge from the main point of my story?

Julia, then, Jowler, and Mrs. J., were at luncheon: the dear girl was in the act to *sâbler* a glass of Hodson as I entered. "How you do, Mr. Gagin?" said the old hag, leeringly; "eat a bit o currie-bhaut"—and she thrust the dish towards me, securing a heap as it passed. "What, Gagy, my boy, how do, how do?" said the fat Colonel; "what, run through the body?—got well again—have some Hodson—run through your body too!"—and at this, I may say, coarse joke (alluding to the fact, that in these hot climates the ale oozes out as it were from the pores of the skin), old Jowler laughed: a host of swarthy chobdars, kitmatgars, sices, consomers, and bobbychies laughed too, as they provided me, unasked, with the grateful fluid. Swallowing six tumblers of it, I paused nervously for a moment, and then said—

"Bobbachy, consomah, ballybaloo hoga."

The black ruffians took the hint and retired.

"Colonel and Mrs. Jowler," said I solemnly, "we are alone; and you, Miss Jowler, you are alone too; that is—I mean—I take this opportunity to—(another glass of ale, if you please)—to express once for all, before departing on a dangerous campaign—(Julia turned pale)—before entering, I say, upon a war which may stretch in the dust my high-raised hopes and me, to express my hopes while life still remains to me, and to declare, in the face of heaven, earth, and Colonel Jowler, that I love you, Julia!" The Colonel, astonished, let fall a steel fork which stuck quivering for some minutes in the calf of my leg; but I heeded not the paltry interruption.—"Yes, by yon bright heaven," continued I, "I love you, Julia! I respect my commander, I esteem your excellent and beauteous mother; tell me, before I leave you, if I may hope for a return of my affection. Say that you love me, and I will do such deeds in this coming war as shall make you proud of the name of your Gahagan."

The old woman, as I delivered these touching words, stared, snapped, and ground her teeth like an enraged monkey. Julia was now red, now white; the Colonel stretched forward, took the fork out of the calf of my leg, wiped it, and then seized a bundle of letters, which I had remarked by his side.

"A cornet!" said he in a voice choking with emotion;—"a pitiful, beggarly, Irish cornet aspire to the hand of Julia Jowler! Gag—Gahagan, are you mad, or laughing at us? Look at these letters, young man, at these letters, I say—one hundred and twenty-four epistles from every part of India (not including one from the Governor-General, and six from his brother Colonel Wellesley)—one hundred and twenty-four proposals for the hand of Miss Jowler! Cornet Gahagan," he continued, "I wish to think well of you:—you are the bravest, the most modest, and, perhaps, the handsomest man in our corps, but you have not got a single rupee. You ask me for Julia, and you do not possess even an anna!—(Here the old rogue grinned, as if he had made a capital pun.)—No, no," said he, waxing good-natured; "Gagy, my boy, it is nonsense! Julia, love, retire with your mamma; this silly young gentleman will remain and smoke a pipe with me."

I took one; it was the bitterest chillum I ever smoked in my life.

*   *   *   *   *

I am not going to give here an account of my military services; they will appear in my great national autobiography, in forty volumes, which I am now preparing for the press. I was with my regiment in all Wellesley's brilliant campaigns; then, taking dawk, I travelled across the country north-eastward, and had the honour of fighting by the side of Lord Lake, at Laswaree, Deeg, Furruckabad, Futtyghur, and Bhurtpore; but I will not boast of my actions, the military man knows them, MY SOVEREIGN appreciates them; if asked who was the bravest man of the Indian army, there is not an officer belonging to it who would not cry at once GAHAGAN. The fact is, I was desperate; I cared not for life, deprived of Julia Jowler.

With Julia's stoney looks ever before my eyes, her father's stern refusal in my ears, I did not care, at the close of the campaign, again to seek her company, or to press my suit. We were eighteen months on service, marching and countermarching, and fighting almost every other day; to the world I did not seem altered; but the world only saw the face, and not the seared and blighted heart within me. My valour, always desperate, now reached to a pitch of cruelty; I tortured my grooms and grass-cutters for the most trifling offence or error—I never in action spared a man— I sheared off three hundred and nine heads in the course of that single campaign.

Some influence, equally melancholy, seemed to have fallen upon poor old Jowler. About six months after we had left Dum Dum, he received a parcel of letters from Benares (whither his wife had retired with her daughter), and so deeply did they seem to weigh upon his spirits, that he ordered eleven men of his regiment to be flogged within two days; but it was against the blacks that he chiefly turned his wrath: our fellows, in the heat and hurry of the campaign, were in the habit of dealing rather roughly with their prisoners, to extract treasure from them. They used to pull their nails out by the root, to boil them in kedgeree pots, to flog them and dress their wounds with cayenne pepper, and so on. Jowler, when he heard of these proceedings, which before had always justly exasperated him (he was a humane and kind little man), used now to smile fiercely, and say "D—— the black scoundrels! Serve them right, serve them right!"

One day, about a couple of miles in advance of the column, I had been on a foraging party with a few dragoons, and was returning peaceably to camp, when of a sudden a troop of Mahrattas burst on us from a neighbouring mango tope, in which they had been hidden: in an instant, three of my men's saddles were empty, and I was left with but seven more to make head against at least thirty of these vagabond black horsemen. I never saw, in my life, a nobler figure than the leader of the troop— mounted on a splendid black Arab: he was as tall, very nearly, as myself; he wore a steel cap, and a shirt of mail, and carried a beautiful French carbine, which had already done execution upon two of my men. I saw that our only chance of safety lay in the destruction of this man. I shouted to him in a voice of thunder (in the Hindostanee tongue of course), "Stop, dog, if you dare, and encounter a man!"

In reply his lance came whirling in the air over my head, and mortally transfixed poor Foggarty of ours, who was behind me. Grinding my teeth, and swearing horribly, I drew that scimitar which never yet failed in its blow,* and rushed at the Indian. He came down at full gallop, his own

---

* In my affair with Macgillicuddy, I was fool enough to go but with small swords:— miserable weapons, only fit for tailors.—G. O'G. G.

sword making ten thousand gleaming circles in the air, shrieking his cry of battle.

The contest did not last an instant. With my first blow I cut off his sword-arm at the wrist; my second I levelled at his head. I said that he wore a steel cap, with a gilt iron spike of six inches, and a hood of chain mail. I rose in my stirrups, and delivered "*St. George;*" my sword caught the spike exactly on the point, split it sheer in two, cut crashing through the steel cap and hood, and was only stopped by a ruby which he wore in his back plate. His head, cut clean in two between the eye-brows and nostrils, even between the two front teeth, fell, one side on each shoulder, and he gallopped on till his horse was stopped by my men, who were not a little amused at the feat.

As I had expected, the remaining ruffians fled on seeing their leader's fate. I took home his helmet by way of curiosity, and we made a single prisoner, who was instantly carried before old Jowler.

We asked the prisoner the name of the leader of the troop; he said it was Chowder Loll.

"CHOWDER LOLL!" shrieked Colonel Jowler. "Oh, fate! thy hand is here!" He rushed wildly into his tent—the next day applied for leave of absence.—Gutch took the command of the regiment—and I saw him no more for some time.

*   *   *   *   *

As I had distinguished myself not a little during the war, General Lake sent me up with dispatches to Calcutta, where Lord Wellesley received me with the greatest distinction. Fancy my surprise, on going to a ball at Government-house, to meet my old friend Jowler; my trembling, blushing, thrilling delight, when I saw Julia by his side!

Jowler seemed to blush too when he beheld me. I thought of my former passages with his daughter. "Gagy, my boy," said he, shaking hands, "glad to see you—old friend, Julia—come to tiffin—Hodson's pale—brave fellow, Gagy." Julia did not speak, but she turned ashy pale and fixed upon me with her awful eyes! I fainted almost, and uttered some incoherent words. Julia took my hand, gazed at me still, and said, "Come!" Need I say I went?

I will not go over the pale ale and curry bhaut again, but this I know, that in half an hour I was as much in love as I ever had been; and that in three weeks—I, yes I—was the accepted lover of Julia! I did not pause to ask, where were the one hundred and twenty-four offers? why I, refused before, should be accepted now? I only felt that I loved her, and was happy!

*   *   *   *   *

One night, one memorable night, I could not sleep, and, with a lover's pardonable passion, wandered solitary through the city of palaces until I came to the house which contained my Julia. I peeped into the compound—all was still;—I looked into the verandah—all was dark, except a light—yes, one light—and it was in Julia's chamber! My heart throbbed almost to stifling. I would—I *would* advance, if but to gaze upon her for a moment, and to bless her as she slept. I *did* look, I *did* advance; and, oh Heaven! I saw a lamp burning, Mrs. Jow., in a night-dress, with a very dark baby in her arms, and Julia, looking tenderly at an Ayah, who was nursing another.

"O, mamma," said Julia, "what would that fool Gahagan say, if he knew all?"

"*He does know all!*" shouted I, springing forward, and tearing down the tatties from the window. Mrs. Jow. ran shrieking out of the room, Julia fainted, the cursed black children squalled, and their d—d nurse fell on her knees, gabbling some infernal jargon of Hindostanee. Old Jowler at this juncture entered with a candle and a drawn sword.

"Liar! scoundrel! deceiver!" shouted I. "Turn, ruffian, and defend yourself!" But old Jowler, when he saw me, only whistled, looked at his lifeless daughter, and slowly left the room.

Why continue the tale? I need not now account for Jowler's gloom on receiving his letters from Benares—for his exclamation upon the death of the Indian chief—for his desire to marry his daughter: the woman I was wooing was no longer Miss Julia Jowler, she was Mrs. CHOWDER LOLL!!!

GOLIAH GAHAGAN, Major H.E.I.C.S.

Historical Recollections by Major Gahagan.

————◇————

I SIT down to write gravely and sadly, for (since the appearance of one of my adventures in this Magazine) unprincipled men have endeavoured to rob me of the only good I possess, to question the statements that I make, and themselves, without a spark of honour or good feeling, to steal from me that which is my sole wealth—my character as a teller of THE TRUTH.

The reader will understand that it is to the illiberal strictures of a profligate press I now allude; among the London journalists, none (luckily for themselves) have dared to question the veracity of my statements; they know me, and they know that I am *in London*. If I can use the pen, I can also wield a more manly and terrible weapon, and would answer their contradictions with my sword! No gold nor gems adorn the hilt of that war-worn scymitar, but there is blood upon the blade—the blood of the enemies of my country, and the maligners of my honest fame. There are others, however—the disgrace of a disgraceful trade—who, borrowing from distance a despicable courage, have ventured to assail me. The infamous editors of the "Kelso Champion," the "Bungay Beacon," the "Tipperary Argus," and the "Stoke Pogis Sentinel," and other dastardly organs of the provincial press, have, although differing in politics, agreed upon this one point, and, with a scoundrelly unanimity, vented a flood of abuse upon the revelations made by me in the last number of this Magazine.

They say that I have assailed private characters, and wilfully perverted history to blacken the reputation of public men. I ask, was any one of these men in Bengal in the year 1803? Was any single conductor of any one of these paltry prints ever in Bundelcund or the Rohilla country? Does this *exquisite* Tipperary scribe know the difference between Hurrygurrybang and Burrumtollah? Not he! and because, forsooth, in those strange and distant lands strange circumstances have taken place, it is insinuated that the relator is a liar, nay, that the very places themselves have no existence but in my imagination. Fools!—but I will not waste my anger upon them, and proceed to recount some other portions of my personal history.

It is, I presume, a fact which even *these* scribbling assassins will not venture to deny, that before the commencement of the campaign against Scindiah, the English General formed a camp at Kanouge on the Jumna, where he exercised that brilliant little army which was speedily to perform such wonders in the Dooab. It will be as well to give a slight account of the causes of a war which was speedily to rage through some of the fairest portions of the Indian continent.

Shah Allum, the son of Shah Lollum, the descendant by the female line of Nadir Shah (that celebrated Toorkomaun adventurer, who had well-nigh hurled Bajazet and Selim the Second from the throne of Bagdad); Shah Allum, I say, although nominally the Emperor of Delhi, was, in reality, the slave of the various warlike chieftains who lorded it by turns over the country and the sovereign, until conquered and slain by some more successful rebel. Chowder Loll Masolgee, Zubberdust Khan, Dowsunt Row Scindiah, and the celebrated Bobbachy Jung Bahawder had held for a time complete mastery in Delhi. The second of these, a ruthless Afghaun soldier, had abruptly entered the capital, nor was he ejected from it until he had seized upon the principal jewels, and likewise put out the eyes of the last of the unfortunate family of Afrasiâb. Scindiah came to the rescue of the sightless Shah Allum, and, though he destroyed his oppressor, only increased his slavery, holding him in as painful a bondage as he had suffered under the tyrannous Afghaun.

As long as these heroes were battling among themselves, or as long rather as it appeared that they had any strength to fight the battle, the British Government, ever anxious to see its enemies by the ears, by no means interfered in the contest. But the French Revolution broke out, and a host of starving sans-culottes appeared among the various Indian states, seeking for military service, and inflaming the minds of the various native Princes against the British East India Company. A number of these entered into Scindiah's ranks—one of them, Perron, was commander of his army; and though that chief was as yet quite engaged in his hereditary quarrel with Jeswunt Row Holkar, and never thought of an invasion of the British territory, the Company all of a sudden discovered that Shah Allum, his sovereign, was shamefully ill-used, and determined to re-establish the ancient splendour of his throne.

Of course it was sheer benevolence for poor Shah Allum that prompted our governors to take these kindly measures in his favour. I don't know how it happened that at the end of the war, the poor Shah was not a whit better off than at the beginning; and that though Holkar was beaten, and Scindiah annihilated, Shah Allum was much such a puppet as before. Somehow in the hurry and confusion of this struggle, the oyster remained with the British Government, who had so kindly offered to dress it for the Emperor, while his Majesty was obliged to be contented with the shell.

The force encamped at Kanouge bore the title of the Grand Army of the Ganges and the Jumna; it consisted of eleven regiments of cavalry and twelve battalions of infantry, and was commanded by the General in person.

Well, on the 1st of September we stormed Perron's camp at Allyghur, on the 4th we took that fortress by assault, and as my name was mentioned in General Orders, I may as well quote the Commander-in-Chief's words regarding me—they will spare me the trouble of composing my own eulogium.

*   *   *   *   *

"The Commander-in-Chief is proud thus publicly to declare his high sense of the gallantry of Lieutenant Gahagan, of the —— cavalry. In the storming of the fortress, although unprovided with a single ladder, and accompanied but by a few brave men, Lieutenant Gahagan succeeded in escalading the inner and fourteenth wall of the place. Fourteen ditches, lined with sword blades and poisoned chevaux-de-frise, fourteen walls bristling with innumerable artillery, and as smooth as looking-glasses, were in turns triumphantly passed by that enterprising officer. His course was to be traced by the heaps of slaughtered enemies lying thick upon the platforms; and, alas! by the corpses of most of the gallant men who followed him!—when at length he effected his lodgment, and the dastardly enemy, who dared not to confront him with arms, let loose upon him the tigers and lions of Scindiah's managerie:—this meritorious officer destroyed, with his own hand, four of the largest and most ferocious animals, and the rest, awed by the indomitable majesty of BRITISH VALOUR, shrunk back to their dens. Thomas Higgory, a private, and Runty Goss, Havildar, were the only two who remained out of the nine hundred who followed Lieutenant Gahagan. Honour to them! Honour and tears for the brave men who perished on that awful day!"

*   *   *   *   *

I have copied this word for word from the Bengal Hurkaru of September 24, 1803; and any body who has the slightest doubt as to the statement, may refer to the paper itself.

And here I must pause to give thanks to Fortune, which so marvellously preserved me, Serjeant-Major Higgory, and Runty Goss. Were I to say that any valour of ours had carried us unhurt through this tremendous combat, the reader would laugh me to scorn. No: though my narrative is extraordinary, it is nevertheless authentic; and never, never would I sacrifice truth for the mere sake of effect. The fact is this:—the citadel of Allyghur is situated upon a rock, about a thousand feet above the level of the sea, and is surrounded by fourteen walls, as his Excellency was good enough to remark in his dispatch. A man who would mount these without scaling-ladders, is an ass; he who would *say* he mounted them without such assistance, is a liar and a knave. We *had* scaling-ladders at the commencement of the assault, although it was quite impossible to carry them beyond the first line of batteries. Mounted on them, however, as our troops were falling thick about me, I saw that we must ignominiously retreat, unless some other help could be found for our brave fellows to escalade the next wall. It was about seventy-feet high—I instantly turned the guns of wall A. on wall B., and peppered the latter so as to make not a breach, but a scaling-place, the men mounting in the holes made by the shot. By this simple strategem, I managed to pass each successive barrier—for to ascend a wall, which the General was pleased to call "as smooth as glass," is an absurd impossibility. I seek to achieve none such:—

> "I dare do all that may become a man,
>
> Who dares do more, is neither more nor less."

Of course, had the enemy's guns been commonly well served, not one of us would ever have been alive out of the three; but whether it was owing to fright, or to the excessive smoke caused by so many pieces of artillery, arrive we did. On the platforms, too, our work was not quite so difficult as might be imagined—killing these fellows was sheer butchery. As soon as we appeared, they all turned and fled, helter-skelter, and the reader may judge of their courage by the fact that out of about seven hundred men killed by us, only forty had wounds in front, the rest being bayonetted as they ran.

And beyond all other pieces of good fortune was the very letting out of these tigers, which was the dernier resort of Bournonville, the second commandant of the fort. I had observed this man (conspicuous for a tri-coloured scarf which he wore,) upon every one of the walls as we stormed them, and running away the very first among the fugitives. He had all the keys of the gates; and in his tremor, as he opened the menagerie portal, left the whole bunch in the door, which I seized when the animals were overcome. Runty Goss then opened them one by one, our troops entered, and the victorious standard of my country floated on the walls of Allyghur!

When the General, accompanied by his staff, entered the last line of fortifications, the brave old man raised me from the dead rhinoceros on which I was seated, and pressed me to his breast. But the excitement which had borne me through the fatigues and perils of that fearful day failed all of a sudden, and I wept like a child upon his shoulder.

———————

Promotion, in our army, goes unluckily by seniority, nor is it in the power of the General-in-chief to advance a Cæsar if he finds him in the capacity of a subaltern:—*my* reward for the above exploit was, therefore, not very rich. His Excellency had a favourite horn snuff-box (for though exalted in station he was in his habits most simple):—of this, and about a quarter of an ounce of high-dried Welsh, which he always took, he made me a present, saying, in front of the line, "Accept this, Mr. Gahagan, as a token of respect from the first, to the bravest officer in this army."

Calculating the snuff to be worth a halfpenny, I should say that fourpence was about the value of this gift; but it has at least this good effect—it serves to convince any person who doubts of my story, that the facts of it are really true. I have left it at the office of this Magazine, along with the extract from the Bengal Hurkaru, and any body may examine both by applying in the counting-house of Mr. Colburn.* That once popular expression, or proverb, "Are you up to snuff?" arose out of the above circumstance; for the officers of my corps, none of whom, except myself, had ventured on the storming party, used to twit me about this modest reward for my labours. Never mind, when they want me to storm a fort *again*, I shall know better.

Well, immediately after the capture of this important fortress, Perron, who had been the life and soul of Scindiah's army, came in to us, with his family and treasure, and was passed over to the French settlements at Chandernagur. Bourquien took his command, and against him we now moved. The morning of the 11th of September found us upon the plains of Delhi.

It was a burning hot day, and we were all refreshing ourselves after the morning's march, when I, who was on the advanced piquet along with O'Gawler of the King's dragoons, was made aware of the enemy's neighbourhood in a very singular manner. O'Gawler and I were seated under a little canopy of horse-cloths, which we had formed to shelter us from the intolerable heat of the sun, and were discussing with great delight a few Manilla cheroots, and a stone-jar of the most exquisite, cool, weak, refreshing sangaree. We had been playing cards the night before, and Gawler had lost to me seven hundred rupees. I emptied the last of the sangaree into the two-pint tumblers out of which we were drinking, and holding mine up, said, "Here's better luck to you next time, O'Gawler!"

As I spoke the words—whish!—a cannon-ball cut the tumbler clean out of my hand, and plumped into poor O'Gawler's stomach. It settled him completely, and of course I never got my seven hundred rupees. Such are the uncertainties of war!

To strap on my sabre and my accoutrements—to mount my Arab charger—to drink off what O'Gawler had left of the sangaree—and to

---

* The Major certainly offered to leave an old snuff-box at our office; but it contained no extract from a newspaper, and does not *quite* prove that he killed a rhinoceros, and stormed fourteen entrenchments at the siege of Allyghur.

gallop to the General, was the work of a moment. I found him as comfortably at tiffin, as if he were at his own house in London.

"General," said I, as soon as I got into his paijamahs (or tent) "you must leave your lunch if you want to fight the enemy."

"The enemy—psha! Mr. Gahagan, the enemy is on the other side of the river."

"I can only tell your Excellency, that the enemy's guns will hardly carry five miles; and that Cornet O'Gawler was at this moment shot dead at my side with a cannon-ball."

"Ha! is it so?" said his Excellency, rising, and laying down the drumstick of a grilled chicken. "Gentlemen, remember that the eyes of Europe are upon us, and follow me!"

Each aide-de-camp started from table and seized his cocked-hat; each British heart beat high at thoughts of the coming *mêlée*. We mounted our horses, and galloped swiftly after the brave old General; I not the last in the train, upon my famous black charger.

It was perfectly true, the enemy were posted in force within three miles of our camp, and from a hillock in the advance to which we galloped, we were enabled with our telescopes to see the whole of his imposing line. Nothing can better describe it than this—

—A is the enemy, and the dots represent the hundred and twenty pieces of artillery which defended his line. He was moreover entrenched, and a wide morass in his front gave him additonal security.

His Excellency for a moment surveyed the line, and then said, turning round to one of his aides-de-camp:—"Order up Major-General Tinkler and the cavalry."

"*Here*, does your Excellency mean?" said the aide-de-camp surprised, for the enemy had perceived us, and the cannon-balls were flying about as thick as peas.

"*Here, Sir*," said the old General, stamping with his foot in a passion, and the A.D.C. shrugged his shoulders and galloped away. In five minutes we heard the trumpets in our camp, and in twenty more the greater part of the cavalry had joined us.

Up they came, five thousand men, their standards flapping in the air, their long line of polished jack-boots gleaming in the golden sunlight. "And now we are here," said Major-General Sir Theophilus Tinkler, "what next?" "O d—— it," said the Commander-in-Chief, "charge, charge—nothing like charging—galloping—guns—rascally black scoundrels—charge, charge!"—and then turning round to me, (perhaps he was glad to change the conversation,) he said—"Lieutenant Gahagan, you will stay with me."

And well for him I did, for I do not hesitate to say, that the battle *was gained by me*. I do not mean to insult the reader by pretending that any personal exertions of mine turned the day,—that I killed for instance a regiment of cavalry, or swallowed a battery of guns,—such absurd tales would disgrace both the hearer and the teller. I, as is well known, never say a single word which cannot be proved, and hate more than all other vices, the absurd sin of egotism; I simply mean that my *advice* to the General, at a quarter past two o'clock in the afternoon of that day, won this great triumph for the British army.

GOLIAH GAHAGAN, MAJOR, H.E.I.C.S.

Major Gahagan's Historical Reminiscences, 1804-1838.

———◇———

A PEEP INTO SPAIN—AN ACCOUNT OF THE ORIGIN AND SERVICES OF THE AHMEDNUGGAR IRREGULARS.

Head Quarters, Morella, Sept. 15, 1838.

I HAVE been here for some months, along with my young friend Cabrera; and, in the hurry and bustle of war—daily on guard and in the batteries for sixteen hours out of the twenty-four, with fourteen severe wounds, and seven musket-balls in my body—it may be imagined that I had little time to continue the publication of my memoirs, of which a couple of numbers have already appeared in this magazine. *Inter arma silent leges*—in the midst of fighting be hanged to writing! as the poet says; and I never would have bothered myself with a pen, had not common gratitude incited me to throw off a few pages. The publisher and editor of "The New Monthly Magazine" little know what service has been done to me by that miscellany.

Along with Oraa's troops, who have of late been beleaguering this place, there was a young Milesian gentleman, Mr. Toone O'Connor Emmett Fitzgerald Sheeny, by name, a law-student, and member of Gray's Inn, and what he called *Bay Ah* of Trinity College, Dublin. Mr. Sheeny was with the Queen's people not in a military capacity, but as representative of an English journal, to which, for a trifling weekly remuneration, he was in the habit of transmitting accounts of the movements of the belligerents, and his own opinion of the politics of Spain. Receiving, for the discharge of this duty, a couple of guineas a-week from the proprietors of the journal in question, he was enabled, as I need scarcely say, to make such a show in Oraa's camp as only a Christino general officer, or at the very least a colonel of a regiment, can afford to keep up.

In the famous sortie which we made upon the twenty-third, I was of course among the foremost in the *mêlée*, and found myself, after a good deal of slaughtering, (which it would be as disagreeable as useless to describe here,) in the court of a small inn or podesta, which had been made the head-quarters of several queenite officers during the siege. The pesatero or landlord of the inn had been despatched by my brave chapel-churies, with his fine family of children—the officers quartered in the podesta had of course bolted; but one man remained, and my fellows were on the point of cutting him into ten thousand pieces with their borachios, when I arrived in the room time enough to prevent the catastrophe. Seeing before me an individual in the costume of a civilian—a white hat, a light-blue satin cravat, embroidered with butterflies and other quadrupeds, a green coat and brass buttons, and a pair of blue-plaid trousers, I recognised at once a countryman, and interposed to save his life.

In an agonised brogue the unhappy young man was saying all that he could to induce the chapel-churies to give up their intentions of slaughtering him: but it is very little likely that his protestations would have had any effect upon them, had not I appeared in the room, and shouted to the ruffians to hold their hand.

Seeing a general officer before them (I have the honour to hold that rank in the service of his Catholic Majesty), and moreover one six feet four in height, and armed with that terrible *cabecilla* (a sword, so called, because it is five feet long) which is so well known among the Spanish armies—seeing, I say, this figure, the fellows retired, exclaiming, "*Adios, corpo di bacco, nosotros,*" and so on, clearly proving (by their words) that they would, if they dared, have immolated the victim whom I had thus rescued from their fury. "Villains!" shouted I, hearing them grumble, "away! quit the apartment!" Each man, sulkily sheathing his sombrero, obeyed, and quitted the camarilla.

It was then that Mr. Sheeny detailed to me the particulars to which I have briefly adverted; and, informing me at the same time that he had a family in England who would feel obliged to me for his release, and that his most intimate friend the English ambassador would move heaven and earth to revenge his fall, he directed my attention to a portmanteau passably well filled, which he hoped would satisfy the cupidity of my troops. I said, though with much regret, that I must subject his person to a search; and hence arose the circumstance which has called for what I fear you will consider a somewhat tedious explanation. I found upon Mr. Sheeny's person three sovereigns in English money (which I have to this day), and singularly enough a copy of "The New Monthly Magazine" for March, which contained my article. It was a toss-up whether I should let the poor young man be shot or no, but this little circumstance saved his life. The gratified vanity of authorship induced me to accept his portmanteau and valuables, and to allow the poor wretch to go free. I put the Magazine in my coat-pocket, and left him and the podesta.

The men, to my surprise, had quitted the building, and it was full time for me to follow, for I found our sallying-party, after committing dreadful ravages in Oraa's lines, were in full retreat upon the fort, hotly pressed by a superior force of the enemy. I am pretty well known and respected by the men of both parties in Spain (indeed I served for some months on the Queen's side before I came over to Don Carlos); and, as it is my maxim never to give quarter, I never expect to receive it when taken myself. On issuing from the podesta, with Sheeny's portmanteau and my sword in my hand, I was a little disgusted and annoyed to see our own men in a pretty good column, retreating at double-quick, and about four hundred yards beyond me up the hill leading to the fort, while on my left hand, and at only a hundred yards, a troop of the queenite lancers were clattering along the road.

I had got into the very middle of the road before I made this discovery, so that the fellows had a full sight of me, and, whizz! came a bullet by my left whisker before I could say Jack Robinson. I looked round—there were seventy of the accursed *malvados* at the least, and within, as I said, a hundred yards. Were I to say that I stopped to fight seventy men, you would write me down a fool or a liar: no, Sir, I did not fight, I ran away.

I am six feet four—my figure is as well known in the Spanish army as that of the Count de Luchana or my fierce little friend Cabrera himself. "GAHAGAN!" shouted out half-a-dozen scoundrelly voices, and fifty more shots came rattling after me. I was running, running as the brave stag before the hounds—running as I have done a great number of times before in my life, when there was no help for it but a race.

After I had run about five hundred yards, I saw that I had gained nearly three upon our column in front, and that likewise the Christino horsemen were left behind some hundred yards more, with the exception of three, who were fearfully near me. The first was an officer without a lance; he had fired both his pistols at me, and was twenty yards in advance of his comrades; there was a similar distance between the two lancers who rode behind him. I determined then to wait for No. 1, and as he came up delivered cut 3 at his horse's near leg—off it flew, and down, as I expected, went horse and man. I had hardly time to pass my sword through my prostrate enemy when No. 2 was upon me. If I could but get that fellow's horse, thought I, I am safe, and I executed at once the plan which I hoped was to effect my rescue.

I had, as I said, left the podesta with Sheeny's portmanteau, and, unwilling to part with some of the articles it contained—some shirts, a bottle of whiskey, a few cakes of Windsor soap, &c. &c.—I had carried it thus far on my shoulders, but now was compelled to sacrifice it *malgré moi*. As the lancer came up, I dropped my sword from my right hand, and hurled the portmanteau at his head with aim so true; that he fell back on his saddle like a sack, and thus, when the horse galloped up to me, I had no difficulty in dismounting the rider—the whiskey-bottle struck him over

his right eye, and he was completely stunned. To dash him from the saddle and spring myself into it was the work of a moment; indeed, the two
combats had taken place in about a fifth part of the time which it has
taken the reader to peruse the description. But in the rapidity of the last
encounter, and the mounting of my enemy's horse, I had committed a
very absurd oversight—I was scampering away *without my sword!* What
was I to do?—to scamper on, to be sure, and trust to the legs of my horse
for safety!

The lancer behind me gained on me every moment, and I could hear
his horrid laugh as he neared me. I leaned forward jockey-fashion in
my saddle, and kicked, and urged, and flogged with my hand, but all in
vain. Closer—closer—the point of his lance was within two feet of my
back. Ah! ah! he delivered the point, and fancy my agony when I felt
it enter——through exactly fifty-nine pages of the "New Monthly Magazine." Had it not been for "The New Monthly Magazine and Humorist,"
I should have been impaled without a shadow of a doubt. Am I wrong in
feeling gratitude? have I not cause to continue my contributions?

When I got safe into Morella, along with the tail of the sallying party,
I was for the first time made acquainted with the ridiculous result of the
lancer's thrust (as he delivered his lance, I must tell you that a ball came
whiz over my head from our fellows, and, entering at his nose, put a stop
to *his* lancing for the future). I hastened to Cabrera's quarter, and related
to him some of my adventures during the day.

"But, General," said he, "you are standing. I beg you '*chiudete l'uscio*'
(take a chair)."

I did so, and then for the first time was aware that there was some
foreign substance in the tail of my coat, which prevented my sitting at
ease. I drew out the Magazine which I had seized, and there, to my wonder, *discovered the Christino lance,* twisted up like a fish-hook, or a pastoral
crook.

"Ha! ha! ha!" said Cabrera (who is a notorious wag).

"Valdepeñas madrileños," growled out Tristany.

"By my cachucha di caballero" (upon my honour as a gentleman),
shrieked out Ros d'Eroles, convulsed with laughter, "I will send it to the
Bishop of Leon for a crozier."

"Gahagan has *consecrated* it," giggled out Ramon Cabrera; and so they
went on with their muchachas for an hour or more. But, when they
heard that the means of my salvation from the lance of the scoundrelly
Christino had been the Magazine containing my own history, their laugh
was changed into wonder. I read them (speaking Spanish more fluently
than English) every word of my story. "But how is this?" said Cabrera.
"You surely have other adventures to relate?"

"Excellent Sir," said I, "I have;" and that very evening, as we sat over our cups of tertullia (sangaree), I continued my narrative in nearly the following words:—

"I left off in the very middle of the battle of Delhi, which ended, as everybody knows, in the complete triumph of the British arms. But who gained the battle? Lord Lake is called Viscount Lake of Delhi and Laswaree, while Major Gaha——nonsense, never mind *him*—never mind the charge he executed when, sabre in hand, he leaped the six-foot wall, in the mouth of the roaring cannon, over the heads of the gleaming pikes, when, with one hand seizing the sacred peish-cush, or fish, which was the banner always borne before Scindiah, he, with his good sword, cut off the trunk of the famous white elephant, which, shrieking with agony, plunged madly into the Marhatta ranks, followed by his giant brethren, tossing, like chaff before the wind, the affrighted kitmatgars. HE, meanwhile, now plunging into the midst of a battalion of consumahs, now cleaving to the chine a screaming and ferocious bobbachee,* rushed on, like the simoom across the red Zaharan plain, killing, with his own hand, a hundred and forty thr—— but never mind—'*alone he did it*'—sufficient be it for him, however, that the victory was won; he cares not for the empty honours which were awarded to more fortunate men!

"We marched after the battle to Delhi, where poor blind old Shah Allum received us, and bestowed all kinds of honours and titles on our General. As each of the officers passed before him, the Shah did not fail to remark my person,† and was told my name.

"Lord Lake whispered to him my exploits, and the old man was so delighted with the account of my victory over the elephant (whose trunk I use to this day), that he said, 'Let him be called GUJPUTI,' or the lord of elephants, and Gujputi was the name by which I was afterwards familiarly known among the natives—the men, that is. The women had a softer appellation for me, and called me 'Mushook,' or charmer.

"Well, I shall not describe Delhi, which is doubtless well known to the reader; nor the siege of Agra, to which place we went from Delhi; nor the terrible day at Laswaree, which went nigh to finish the war. Suffice it to say that we were victorious, and that I was wounded, as I have invariably been in the two hundred and four occasions, when I have found myself in action. One point, however, became in the course of this campaign *quite* evident—*that something must be done for Gahagan.* The country cried shame, the king's troops grumbled, the seapoys openly murmured that their Gujputi was only a Lieutenant, when he had performed such

---

* The double-jointed camel of Bactria, which the classic reader may recollect is mentioned by Suidas (in his Commentary on the flight of Darius), is so called by the Marhattas.

† There is some trifling inconsistency on the Major's part. Shah Allum was notoriously blind: how, then, could he have seen Gahagan? The thing is manifestly impossible.

signal services. What was to be done? Lord Wellesley was in an evident quandary. 'Gahagan,' wrote he, 'to be a subaltern is evidently not your fate—*you were born for command;* but Lake and General Wellesley are good officers, they cannot be turned out—I must make a post for you. What say you, my dear fellow, to a corps of *irregular horse?'*

"It was thus that the famous corps of AHMEDNUGGAR IRREGULARS had its origin; a guerilla force, it is true, but one which will long be remembered in the annals of our Indian campaigns.

*　　*　　*　　*　　*

"As the commander of this regiment, I was allowed to settle the uniform of the corps, as well as to select recruits. These were not wanting as soon as my appointment was made known, but came flocking to my standard a great deal faster than to the regular corps in the company's service. I had European officers, of course, to command them, and a few of my countrymen as sergeants; the rest were all natives, whom I chose of the strongest and bravest men in India, chiefly Pitans, Afghans, Hurrumzadehs, and Calliawns, for these are well known to be the most warlike districts of our Indian territory.

"When on parade and in full uniform we made a singular and noble appearance. I was always fond of dress; and, in this instance, gave a *carte-blanche* to my taste, and invented the most splendid costume that ever perhaps decorated a soldier. I am, as I have stated already, six feet four inches in height, and of matchless symmetry and proportion. My hair and beard are of the most brilliant auburn, so bright as scarcely to be distinguished at a distance from scarlet. My eyes are bright blue, overshadowed by bushy eyebrows of the colour of my hair, and a terrific gash of the deepest purple, which goes over the forehead, the eyelid, and the cheek, and finishes at the ear, gives my face a more strictly military appearance than can be conceived. When I have been drinking (as is pretty often the case) this gash becomes ruby bright, and, as I have another which took off a piece of my underlip, and shows five of my front teeth, I leave you to imagine that 'seldom lighted on the earth,' (as the monster Burke remarked of one of his unhappy victims,) 'a more extraordinary vision.' I improved these natural advantages; and, while in cantonment during the hot winds at Chittybobbary, allowed my hair to grow very long, as did my beard, which reached to my waist. It took me two hours daily to curl my hair in ten thousand little corkscrew ringlets, which waved over my shoulders, and to get my mustachios well round to the corners of my eyelids. I dressed in loose scarlet trousers and red morocco boots, a scarlet jacket, and a shawl of the same colour round my waist; a scarlet turban three feet high, and decorated with a tuft of the scarlet feathers of the flamingo, formed my head-dress, and I did not allow myself a single ornament, except a small silver skull and cross-bones in front of my turban.

Two brace of pistols, a Malay creese, and a tulwar, sharp on both sides and very nearly six feet in length, completed this elegant costume. My two flags were each surmounted with a real skull and cross-bones, and ornamented one with a black, and the other with a red beard (of enormous length taken from men slain in battle by me). On one flag were of course the arms of John Company; on the other an image of myself bestriding a prostrate elephant, with the simple word 'GUJPUTI' written underneath in the Nagaree, Persian, and Sanscrit character. I rode my black horse, and looked, by the immortal gods, like Mars! To me might be applied the words which were written concerning handsome General Webb in Marlborough's time:—

> " 'To noble danger he conducts the way,
> His great example all his troop obey.
> Before the front the MAJOR sternly rides,
> With such an air as Mars to battle strides.
> Propitious heaven must sure a hero save
> Like Paris handsome, and like Hector brave!'

"My officers (Captains Biggs and Mackanulty, Lieutenants Glogger, Pappendick, Stuffle, &c. &c.) were dressed exactly in the same way, but in yellow, and the men were similarly equipped, but in black. I have seen many regiments since, and many ferocious-looking men, but the Ahmednuggar Irregulars were more dreadful to the view than any set of ruffians on which I ever set eyes. I would to heaven that the Czar of Muscovy had passed through Caubul and Lahore, and that I with my old Ahmednuggars stood on a fair field to meet him! Bless you, bless you, my swart companions in victory! through the mist of twenty years I hear the booming of your war-cry, and mark the glitter of your scimitars as ye rage in the thickest of the battle!*

"But away with melancholy reminiscences. You may fancy what a figure the Irregulars cut on a field-day—a line of five-hundred black-faced, black-dressed, black-horsed, black-bearded men—Biggs, Glogger, and the other officers in yellow, galloping about the field like flashes of lightning: myself enlightening them, red, solitary, and majestic, like yon glorious orb in heaven.

"There are very few men I presume who have not heard of Holkar's sudden and gallant incursion into the Dooâb in the year 1804, when we thought that the victory of Laswaree and the brilliant success at Deeg had completely finished him; taking ten thousand horse, he broke up his

---

* I do not wish to brag of my style of writing, or to pretend that my genius as a writer has not been equalled in former times; but if, in the works of Byron, Scott, Goethe, or Victor Hugo, the reader can find a more beautiful sentence than the above, I will be obliged to him, that is all—I simply say, *I will be obliged to him.*—G. O'G. G., M. H. E. I. C. S., C. I. H. A.

camp at Palimbang, and the first thing General Lake heard of him was, that he was at Putna, then at Rumpooge, then at Doncaradam—he was, in fact, in the very heart of our territory.

"The unfortunate part of the affair was this:—His excellency, despising the Marhatta chieftain, had allowed him to advance about two thousand miles in his front, and knew not in the slightest degree where to lay hold on him. Was he at Hazarubawg? was he at Bogly Gunge? nobody knew, and for a considerable period the movements of Lake's cavalry were quite ambiguous, uncertain, promiscuous, and undetermined.

"Such briefly was the state of affairs in October 1804. At the beginning of that month I had been wounded (a trifling scratch cutting off my left upper eyelid, a bit of my cheek, and my underlip), and I was obliged to leave Biggs in command of my Irregulars, whilst I retired for my wounds to an English station at Furruckabad, *alias* Futtyghur—it is, as every two-penny postman knows, at the apex of the Dooâb. We have there a can-tonment, and thither I went for the mere sake of the surgeon and the sticking-plaster.

"Furruckabad, then, is divided into two districts or towns; the lower, Cotwal, inhabited by the natives, and the upper (which is fortified slightly, and has all along been called Futtyghur, meaning in Hindostanee 'the-favourite-resort-of-the-white-faced-Feringhees-near-the-mangoe-tope-consecrated-to-Ram') occupied by Europeans. (It is astonishing, by the way, how comprehensive that language is, and how much can be con-veyed in one or two of the commonest phrases.)

"Biggs, then, and my men were playing all sorts of wondrous pranks with Lord Lake's army, whilst I was detained an unwilling prisoner of health at Futtyghur.

"An unwilling prisoner, however, I should not say. The cantonment at Futtyghur contained that which would have made *any* man a happy slave. Woman, lovely woman, was there in abundance and variety! The fact is, that, when the campaign commenced in 1803, the ladies of the army all congregated to this place, where they were left, as it was supposed, in safety. I might, like Homer, relate the names and qualities of all. I may at least mention *some* whose memory is still most dear to me. There was—

"Mrs. Major-General Bulcher, wife of Bulcher of the infantry.

"Miss Bulcher.

"Miss BELINDA BULCHER (whose name I beg the printer to place in large capitals).

"Mrs. Colonel Vandegobbleschroy.

"Mrs. Major Macan and the four Misses Macan.

"The Honourable Mrs. Burgoo, Mrs. Flix, Hicks, Wicks, and many more too numerous to mention. The flower of our camp was, however, collected there, and the last words of Lord Lake to me, as I left him, were,

'Gahagan, I commit those women to your charge. Guard them with your life, watch over them with your honour, defend them with the matchless power of your indomitable arm.'

"Futtyghur is, as I have said, an European station, and the pretty air of the bungalows, amid the clustering topes of mangoe-trees, has often ere this excited the admiration of the tourist and sketcher. On the brow of a hill, the Burrumpooter river rolls majestically at its base, and no spot, in a word, can be conceived more exquisitely arranged, both by art and nature, as a favourite residence of the British fair. Mrs. Bulcher, Mrs. Vandegobbleschroy, and the other married ladies above mentioned, had each of them delightful bungalows and gardens in the place, and between one cottage and another my time passed as delightfully as can the hours of any man who is away from his darling occupation of war.

"I was the commandant of the fort. It is a little insignificant pettah, defended simply by a couple of gabions, a very ordinary counterscarp, and a bomb-proof embrasure; on the top of this my flag was planted, and the small garrison of forty men only were comfortably barracked off in the casemates within. A surgeon and two chaplains (there were besides three reverend gentlemen, of amateur missions, who lived in the town) completed, as I may say, the garrison of our little fortalice, which I was left to defend and to command.

"On the night of the 1st of November in the year 1804, I had invited Mrs. Major General Bulcher and her daughters, Mrs. Vandegobbleschroy, and indeed all the ladies in the cantonment, to a little festival in honour of the recovery of my health, of the commencement of the shooting-season, and indeed as a farewell visit, for it was my intention to take dawk the very next morning and return to my regiment. The three amateur missionaries whom I have mentioned, and some ladies in the cantonment of very rigid religious principles, refused to appear at my little party. They had better never have been born than have done as they did, as you shall hear.

"We had been dancing merrily all night, and the supper (chiefly of the delicate condor, the luscious adjutant, and other birds of a similar kind, which I had shot in the course of the day) had been duly *fêted* by every lady and gentleman present; when I took an opportunity to retire on the ramparts, with the interesting and lovely Belinda Bulcher. I was occupied, as the French say, in *conter-*ing *fleurettes* to this sweet young creature, when, all of a sudden, a rocket was seen whizzing through the air, and a strong light was visible in the valley below the little fort.

" 'What, fire-works! Captain Gahagan,' said Belinda, 'this is too gallant.'

" 'Indeed, my dear Miss Bulcher,' said I, 'they are fire-works of which I have no idea: perhaps our friends the missionaries——'

" 'Look, look!' said Belinda, trembling, and clutching tightly hold of my arm; 'what do I see? yes—no—yes! it is—*our bungalow is in flames!*'

"It was true the spacious bungalow occupied by Mrs. Major General was at that moment seen a prey to the devouring element—another and another succeeded it—seven bungalows, before I could almost ejaculate the name of Jack Robinson, were seen blazing brightly in the black midnight air!

"I seized my night-glass, and, looking towards the spot where the conflagration raged, what was my astonishment to see thousands of black forms dancing round the fires; whilst by their lights I could observe columns after columns of Indian horse, arriving and taking up their ground in the very middle of the open square or tank, round which the bungalows were built!

"'Ho, warder!' shouted I (while the frightened and trembling Belinda clung closer to my side, and pressed the stalwart arm that encircled her waist), 'down with the drawbridge! see that your masolgees (small tumbrils which are used in place of larger artillery) be well loaded; you seapoys, hasten and man the ravelin! you choprasees, put out the lights in the embrasures! we shall have warm work of it to-night, or my name is not Goliah Gahagan.'

"The ladies, the guests (to the number of eighty-three), the seapoys, choprasees, masolgees, and so on, had all crowded on the platform at the sound of my shouting, and dreadful was the consternation, shrill the screaming, occasioned by my words. The men stood irresolute and mute with terror; the women trembling, knew scarcely whither to fly for refuge. 'Who are yonder ruffians?' said I; a hundred voices yelped in reply—some said the Pindarees, some the Marhattas, some vowed it was Scindiah, and others declared it was Holkar—no one knew.

"'Is there any one here,' said I, 'who will venture to reconnoitre yonder troops?'" There was a dead pause.

"'A thousand tomauns to the man who will bring me news of yonder army!' again I repeated. Still a dead silence. The fact was that Scindiah and Holkar both were so notorious for their cruelty, that no one dared venture to face the danger. 'Oh for fifty of my brave Ahmednuggarees!' thought I.

"'Gentlemen,' said I, 'I see it—you are cowards—none of you dare encounter the chance even of death. It is an encouraging prospect—know you not that the ruffian Holkar, if it be he, will with the morrow's dawn beleaguer our little fort, and throw thousands of men against our walls? know you not that, if we are taken, there is no quarter, no hope, death for us—and worse than death for these lovely ones assembled here?' Here the ladies shrieked and raised a howl as I have heard the jackalls on a summer's evening. Belinda, my dear Belinda! flung both her arms round me, and sobbed on my shoulder (or in my waistcoat-pocket rather, for the little witch could reach no higher).

" 'Captain Gahagan,' sobbed she, '*Go—Go—Goggle— iah!*'

" 'My soul's adored,' replied I.

" 'Swear to me one thing.'

" 'I swear.'

" 'That if—that if—the nasty, horrid, odious, black Mah-ra-a-a-attahs take the fort, you will put me out of their power.'

"I clasped the dear girl to my heart, and swore upon my sword that, rather than she should incur the risk of dishonour, she should perish by my own hand. This comforted her; and her mother, Mrs. Major General Bulcher, and her elder sister, who had not until now known a word of our attachment (indeed, but for these extraordinary circumstances, it is probable that we ourselves should never have discovered it), were under these painful circumstances made aware of my beloved Belinda's partiality for me. Having communicated thus her wish of self-destruction, I thought her example a touching and excellent one, and proposed to all the ladies that they should follow it, and that at the entry of the enemy into the fort, and at a signal given by me, they should one and all make away with themselves. Fancy my disgust when, after making this proposition, not one of the ladies chose to accede to it, and received it with the same chilling denial that my former proposal to the garrison had met with.

"In the midst of this hurry and confusion, as if purposely to add to it, a trumpet was heard at the gate of the fort, and one of the sentinels came running to me saying that a Marhatta soldier was before the gate with a flag of truce!

"I went down, rightly conjecturing, as it turned out, that the party, whoever they might be, had no artillery; and received at the point of my sword a scroll, of which the following is a translation:

" 'To Goliah Gahagan Gujputi.

" 'Lord of Elephants, Sir:—I have the honour to inform you that I arrived before this place at eight o'clock P. M. with ten thousand cavalry under my orders. I have burned since my arrival seventeen bungalows in Furruckabad and Futtyghur, and have likewise been under the painful necessity of putting to death three clergymen, (mollahs) and seven English officers whom I found in the village; the women have been transferred to safe keeping in the harems of my officers and myself.

" 'As I know your courage and talents, I shall be very happy if you will surrender the fortress, and take service as a Major General (Hookabadar) in my army. Should my proposal not meet with your assent, I beg leave to state that to-morrow I shall storm the fort, and on taking it shall put to death every male in the garrison, and every female above twenty years of age. For yourself I shall reserve a punishment, which, for novelty and exquisite torture, has, I flatter myself, hardly ever been exceeded. Awaiting the favour of a reply, I am Sir,

"'Your very obedient servant,
"'JASWUNT ROW HOLKAR.
"'Camp before Futtyghur, Sept. 1, 1804.
"'R. S. V. P.'"

"The officer who had brought this precious epistle (it is astonishing how Holkar had aped the forms of English correspondence), an enormous Pitan soldier, with a shirt of mail, and a steel cap and cape round which his turban wound, was leaning against the gate on his matchlock, and whistling a national melody. I read the letter and saw at once there was no time to be lost. That man, thought I, must never go back to Holkar. Were he to attack us now before we were prepared, the fort would be his in half an hour.

"Tying my white pocket-handkerchief to a stick, I flung open the gate and advanced to the officer; he was standing, I said, on the little bridge across the moat. I made him a low salaam, after the fashion of the country, and, as he bent forward to return the compliment, I am sorry to say I plunged forward, gave him a violent blow on the head which deprived him of all sensation, and then dragged him within the wall, raising the drawbridge after me.

"I bore the body into my own apartment, there; swift as thought, I stripped him of his turban, cummerbund, peijammahs, and papooshes, and, putting them on myself, determined to go forth and reconnoitre the enemy."

*　　　*　　　*　　　*　　　*

Here I was obliged to stop, for Cabrera, Res d'Eroles, and the rest of the staff, were sound asleep! What I did in my reconnaissance, and how I defended the fort of Futtyghur, I shall have the honour of telling on another occasion.

G. O.'G. G., M. H. E. I. C. S., C. I. H. A.

Major Gahagan's Historical Reminiscences.

———◇———

THE INDIAN CAMP.

Head Quarters, Morella, October 3, 1838.

It is a balmy night—I hear the merry jingle of the tambourine and the cheery voices of the girls and peasants, as they dance beneath my casement, under the shadow of the clustering vines—the laugh and song pass gaily round, and even at this distance I can distinguish the elegant form of Ramon Cabrera, as he whispers gay nothings in the ears of the Andalusian girls, or joins in the thrilling chorus of Riego's hymn, which is ever and anon vociferated by the enthusiastic soldiery of Carlos Quinto. I am alone, in the most inaccessible and most bomb-proof tower of our little fortalice; the large casements are open—the wind, as it enters, whispers in my ear its odorous recollections of the orange-grove and the myrtle bower. My torch (a branch of the fragrant cedar-tree) flares and flickers in the midnight breeze, and disperses its scent and burning splinters on my scroll, and the desk where I write—meet implements for a soldier's authorship!—it is *cartridge* paper over which my pen runs so glibly, and a yawning barrel of gunpowder forms my rough writing-table. Around me, below me, above me, all—all is peace! I think, as I sit here so lonely, on my country, England! and muse over the sweet and bitter recollections of my early days! Let me resume my narrative, at the point where (interrupted by the authoritative summons of war) I paused on the last occasion.

CHAP. I.

THE SORTIE FROM THE FORT.

I left off I think (for I am a thousand miles away from proof-sheets as I write—and, were I not writing the simple TRUTH, must contradict myself a thousand times in the course of my tale)—I think, I say, that I left off at that period of my story, when, Holkar being before Futtyghur, and I in command of that fortress, I had just been compelled to make away with his messenger; and, dressed in the fallen Indian's accoutrements, went forth to reconnoitre the force, and, if possible, to learn the intentions of the enemy. However much my figure might have resembled that of the Pitan, and disguised in his armour, might have deceived the lynx-eyed Mahrattas, into whose camp I was about to plunge, it was evident that a single glance at my fair face and auburn beard would have undeceived the dullest blockhead in Holkar's army. Seizing then a bottle of Burges's walnut catsup, I dyed my face and my hands, and, with the simple aid of a flask of Warren's jet, I made my hair and beard as black as ebony. The Indian's helmet and chain-hood covered likewise a great part of my face, and I hoped thus, with luck, impudence, and a complete command of all the Eastern dialects and languages, from Burmah to Afghanistan, to pass scot-free through this somewhat dangerous ordeal.

I had not the word of the night it is true—but I trusted to good fortune for that, and passed boldly out of the fortress, bearing the flag of truce as before; I had scarcely passed on a couple of hundred yards, when, lo! a party of Indian horsemen, armed like him I had just overcome, trotted towards me; one was leading a noble white charger, and no sooner did he see me than, dismounting from his own horse, and giving the rein to a companion, he advanced to meet me with the charger—a second fellow likewise dismounted and followed the first; one held the bridle of the horse, while the other (with a multitude of salams, aleikums, and other genuflexions) held the jewelled stirrup, and, kneeling, waited until I should mount.

I took the hint at once: the Indian who had come up to the fort was a great man—that was evident; I walked on with a majestic air, gathered up the velvet reins, and sprung into the magnificent, high-peaked saddle. "Buk, buk," said I, "it is good—in the name of the forty-nine Imaums, let us ride on;" and the whole party set off at a brisk trot, I keeping silence, and thinking with no little trepidation of what I was about to encounter.

As we rode along I heard two of the men commenting upon my unusual silence (for I suppose, I—that is, the Indian—was a talkative officer). "The lips of the Bahawder are closed," said one—"where are those birds of Paradise, his long-tailed words?—they are imprisoned between the golden bars of his teeth!"

"Kush," said his companion, "be quiet! Bobbachy Bahawder has seen the dreadful Feringhee, Gahagan Khan Gujputi, the elephant-lord, whose sword reaps the harvest of death: there is but one champion who can wear the papooshes of the elephant-slayer—it is Bobbachy Bahawder!"

"You speak truly, Puneeree Muckun—the Bahawder ruminates on the words of the unbeliever; he is an ostrich, and hatches the eggs of his thoughts."

"Bekhusm! on my nose be it! May the young birds, his actions, be strong, and swift in flight."

"May they *digest iron!*" said Puneeree Muckun, who was evidently a wag in his way.

O, ho! thought I—as suddenly the light flashed upon me. It was, then, the famous Bobbachy Bahawder, whom I overcame just now! and he is the man destined to stand in *my* slippers, is he? and I was at that very moment standing in his own! such are the chances and changes that fall to the lot of the soldier!

I suppose everybody—everybody who has been in India, at least—has heard the name of Bobbachy Bahawder; it is derived from the two Hindoostanee words, bobbachy—general, bahawder—artillery-man; he had entered into Holkar's service in the latter capacity, and had, by his merit and his undaunted bravery in action, attained the dignity of the peacock's feather, which is only granted to noblemen of the first class; he was married, moreover, to one of Holkar's innumerable daughters; a match, which according to the *Chronique Scandaleuse*, brought more of honour than of pleasure to the poor Bobbachy. Gallant as he was in the field, it was said that in the harem he was the veriest craven alive—completely subjugated by his ugly and odious wife. In all matters of importance the late Bahawder had been consulted by his Prince, who had, as it appears (knowing my character, and not caring to do anything rash in his attack upon so formidable an enemy), sent forward the unfortunate Pitan to reconnoitre the fort; he was to have done yet more, as I learned from the attendant, Puneeree Muckun, who was, I soon found out, an old favourite with the Bobbachy—doubtless on account of his honesty and love of repartee.

"The Bahawder's lips are closed," said he, at last, trotting up to me; "has he not a word for old Puneeree Muckun?"

"Bismillah, mashallah, barikillah," said I; which means, "my good friend, what I have seen is not worth the trouble of relation, and fills my bosom with the darkest forebodings."

"You could not then see the Gujputi alone, and stab him with your dagger?"

[Here was a pretty conspiracy!]—"No, I saw him, but not alone; his people were always with him."

"Hurrumzadeh! it is a pity; we waited but the sound of your jogree (whistle), and straightway would have galloped up, and seized upon every man, woman, and child in the fort: however, there are but a dozen men in the garrison, and they have not provision for two days—they must yield—and then, hurrah for the moon-faces! Mashallah! I am told the soldiers who first get in are to have their pick. How my old woman, Rotee Muckun, will be surprised, when I bring home a couple of Feringhee wives,—ha! ha!"

"Fool!" said I, "be still!—twelve men in the garrison! there are twelve hundred! Gahagan himself is as good as a thousand men; and as for food, I saw, with my own eyes, five hundred bullocks grazing in the court-yard, as I entered." This *was* a bouncer, I confess; but my object was to deceive Puneeree Muckun, and give him as high a notion as possible of the capabilities of defence which the besieged had.

"Pooch, pooch," murmured the men; "it is a wonder of a fortress, we shall never be able to take it until our guns come up."

There was hope then! they had no battering-train. Ere this arrived, I trusted that Lord Lake would hear of our plight, and march down to rescue us. Thus occupied in thought and conversation, we rode on until the advanced sentinel challenged us, when old Puneeree gave the word, and we passed on into the centre of Holkar's camp.

It was a strange—a stirring sight! The camp-fires were lighted; and round them—eating, reposing, talking, looking at the merry steps of the dancing girls, or listening to the stories of some Dhol Baut (or Indian improvisatore)—were thousands of dusky soldiery. The camels and horses were picketed under the banyan-trees, on which the ripe mangoe-fruit was growing, and offered them an excellent food. Towards the spot which the golden fish and royal purdahs, floating in the wind, designated as the tent of Holkar, led an immense avenue—of elephants! the finest street, indeed, I ever saw. Each of the monstrous animals had castles on their backs, armed with Mauritanian archers and the celebrated Persian matchlock-men: it was the feeding-time of these royal brutes, and the grooms were observed bringing immense toffungs or baskets, filled with pine-apples, plantains, bandannas, Indian corn, and cocoa-nuts, which grow luxuriantly at all seasons of the year. We passed down this extraordinary avenue (no less than three hundred and eighty-eight tails did I count on each side—each tail appertaining to an elephant twenty-five feet high—each elephant having a two-storied castle on its back—each castle containing sleeping and eating-rooms for the twelve men that formed its garrison, and were keeping watch on the roof—each roof bearing a flag-staff twenty feet long on its top, the crescent glistening with a thousand gems, and round it the imperial standard—each standard, of silk velvet and cloth of gold, bearing the well-known device of Holkar, argent an or gules; between a sinople of the first, a chevron truncated wavy. I took nine of these myself in the course of a very short time after, and shall be happy, when I come to England, to show them to any gentleman who has a curiosity that way). Through this gorgeous scene our little cavalcade passed, and at last we arrived at the quarters occupied by Holkar.

CHAP. II.

HOLKAR'S CAMP.

That celebrated chieftain's tents and followers were gathered round one of the British bungalows which had escaped the flames, and which he occupied during the siege. When I entered the large room where he sate, I found him in the midst of a council of war; his chief generals and viziers seated round him, each smoking his hookah, as is the common way with these black fellows, before, at, and after breakfast, dinner, supper, and bed-time. There was such a cloud raised by their smoke you could hardly see a yard before you—another piece of good luck for me—as it diminished the chances of my detection. When, with the ordinary ceremonies, the kitmutgars and consomahs had explained to the Prince that Bobbachy Bahawder, the right eye of the Sun of the universe (as the ignorant heathens called me), had arrived from his mission, Holkar immediately summoned me to the maidaun, or elevated platform, on which he was seated in a luxurious easy chair, and I, instantly taking off my slippers, falling on my knees, and beating my head against the ground ninety-nine times, proceeded, still on my knees, a hundred and twenty feet through the room, and then up the twenty steps which led to his maidaun—a silly, painful, and disgusting ceremony, which can only be considered as a relic of barbarian darkness, which tears the knees and shins to pieces, let alone the pantaloons. I recommend anybody who goes to India, with the prospect of entering the service of the native rajahs, to recollect my advice, and have them *well wadded*.

Well, the right eye of the sun of the universe scrambled as well as he could up the steps of the maidaun (on which, in rows, smoking as I have said, the musnuds or general officers were seated), and I arrived within speaking distance of Holkar, who instantly asked me news of the success of my mission: the impetuous old man thereon poured out a multitude of questions: "how many men are there in the fort?" said he:—"how many women? is it victualled? have they ammunition? did you see Gahagan Sahib, the commander? did you kill him?"—All these questions Jeswunt Row Holkar puffed out with so many whiffs of tobacco.

Taking a chillum myself, and raising about me such a cloud, that, upon my honour as a gentleman, no man at three yards' distance could perceive anything of me except the pillar of smoke in which I was encompassed, I told Holkar, in Oriental language, of course, the best tale I could with regard to the fort.

"Sir," said I, "to answer your last question first—that dreadful Gujputi I have seen—and he is alive; he is eight feet, nearly, in height; he can eat a bullock daily (of which he has seven hundred at present in the compound, and swears that during the siege he will content himself with only three a-week): he has lost, in battle, his left eye; and what is the consequence? O Ram Gunge, (O thou-with-the-eye-as-bright-as-morning-and-with-beard-as-black-as-night), Goliah Gujputi—NEVER SLEEPS!"

"Ah, you Ghorumsaug" (you thief of the world), said the Prince Vizier, Saadut Allee Beg Bimbukchee—"it's joking you are;"—and there was a universal buzz through the room at the announcement of this bouncer.

"By the hundred and eleven incarnations of Vishnou," said I, solemnly (an oath, which no Indian was ever known to break), "I swear that so it is; so at least he told me, and I have good cause to know his power. Gujputi is an enchanter, he is leagued with devils, he is invulnerable. Look," said I, unsheathing my dagger, and every eye turned instantly towards me— "thrice did I stab him with this steel—in the back, once—twice right through the heart; but he only laughed me to scorn, and bade me tell Holkar that the steel was not yet forged which was to inflict an injury upon him."

I never saw a man in such a rage as Holkar was when I gave him this somewhat imprudent message.

"Ah, lily-livered rogue!" shouted he out to me, "milk-blooded unbeliever! pale-faced miscreant! lives he after insulting thy master in thy presence? In the name of the Prophet, I spit on thee, defy thee, abhor thee, degrade thee! Take that, thou liar of the universe! and that—and that—and that!"

Such are the frightful excesses of barbaric minds! every time this old man said "Take that," he flung some article near him at the head of the undaunted Gahagan—his dagger, his sword, his carbine, his richly-ornamented pistols, his turban, covered with jewels, worth a hundred thousand crores of rupees—finally, his hookah, snake, mouthpiece, silver-bell, chillum and all—which went hissing over my head, and flattening into a jelly the nose of the grand vizier.

"Yock muzzee!" (my nose is off,) said the old man mildly; "will you have my life, O Holkar? it is thine likewise!" and no other word of complaint escaped his lips.

Of all these missiles, though a pistol and carbine had gone off as the ferocious Indian flung them at my head, and the naked scimitar, fiercely but unadroitly thrown, had lopped off the limbs of one or two of the musnuds as they sat trembling on their omrahs, yet, strange to say, not a single weapon had hurt me. When the hubbub ceased, and the unlucky wretches who had been the victims of this fit of rage had been removed, Holkar's good-humour somewhat returned, and he allowed me to continue my account of the fort; which I did, not taking the slightest notice of his burst of impatience, as indeed would have been the height of impoliteness to have done, for such accidents happened many times in the day.

"It is well that the Bobbachy has returned," snuffled out the poor Grand Vizier, after I had explained to the council the extraordinary means of defence possessed by the garrison. "Your star is bright, O Bahawder! for this very night we had resolved upon an escalade of the fort, and we had sworn to put every one of the infidel garrison to the edge of the sword."

"But you have no battering-train," said I.

"Bah! we have a couple of ninety-six pounders, quite sufficient to blow the gates open; and then, hey for a charge!" said Loll Mahommed, a general of cavalry, who was a rival of Bobbachy's, and contradicted therefore every word I said. "In the name of Juggernaut, why wait for the heavy artillery? Have we not swords? have we not hearts? Mashallah! Let cravens stay with Bobbachy, all true men will follow Loll Mahommed! Allah-humdillah, Bismillah, Barikallah!"* and drawing his scimitar he waved it over his head, and shouted out his cry of battle. It was repeated by many of the other omrahs; the sound of their cheers was carried into the camp, and caught up by the men; the camels began to cry, the horses to prance and neigh, the eight hundred elephants set up a scream, the trumpeters and drummers clanged away at their instruments. I never heard such a din before or after. How I trembled for my little garrison when I heard the enthusiastic cries of this innumerable host!

There was but one way for it. "Sir," said I, addressing Holkar, "go out to-night, and you go to certain death. Loll Mahommed has not seen the fort as I have. Pass the gate if you please, and for what? to fall before the fire of a hundred pieces of artillery; to storm another gate, and then another, and then to be blown up with Gahagan's garrison in the citadel. Who talks of courage? Were I not in your august presence, O star of the faithful, I would crop Loll Mahommed's nose from his face, and wear his ears as an ornament in my own pugree! Who is there here that knows not the difference between yonder yellow-skinned coward and Gahagan Khan Guj—I mean Bobbachy Bahawder? I am ready to fight one, two, three, or twenty of them, at broad-sword, small-sword, single-stick, with fists, if you please; by the holy piper, fighting is like mate and dthrink to Ga—to Bobbachy, I mane—whoop! come on you divvle, and I'll bate the skin off your ugly bones."

This speech had very nearly proved fatal to me, for, when I am agitated, I involuntarily adopt some of the phraseology peculiar to my own country; which is so uneastern, that, had there been any suspicion as to my real character, detection must indubitably have ensued. As it was, Holkar perceived nothing, but instantaneously stopped the dispute. Loll Mahommed, however, evidently suspected something, for, as Holkar, with a voice of thunder, shouted out, "Tomasha," silence, Loll sprung forward and gasped out—

"My Lord! my Lord! this is not Bob——"

But he could say no more. "Gag the slave!" screamed out Holkar, stamping with fury; and a turban was instantly twisted round the poor devil's jaws. "Ho, Furoshes! carry out Loll Mahommed Khan, give him a

---

* The Major has put the most approved language into the mouths of his Indian characters. Bismillah, Barikallah, and so on, according to the novelists, form the very essence of Eastern conversation.

hundred dozen on the soles of his feet, set him upon a white donkey, and carry him round the camp, with an inscription before him—'This is the way that Holkar rewards the talkative.'"

I breathed again; and ever as I heard each whack of the bamboo, falling on Loll Mahommed's feet, I felt peace returning to my mind, and thanked my stars that I was delivered of this danger.

"Vizier," said Holkar, who enjoyed Loll's roars amazingly, "I owe you a reparation for your nose: kiss the hand of your Prince, O Saadat Allee Beg Bimbukchee! be from this day forth Zoheir u Dowlut!"

The good old man's eyes filled with tears. "I can bear thy severity, O Prince," said he, "I cannot bear thy love. Was it not an honour that your highness did me just now, when you condescended to pass over the bridge of your slave's nose?"

The phrase was by all voices pronounced to be very poetical. The Vizier retired crowned with his new honours to bed. Holkar was in high good humour.

"Bobbachy," said he, "thou, too, must pardon me;—à-propos—I have news for thee. Your wife, the incomparable Puttee-Rooge, (white and red rose,) has arrived in camp."

"My wife, my Lord!" said I, aghast.

"Our daughter, the light of thine eyes! Go, my son; I see thou art wild with joy. The Princess's tents are set up close by mine, and I know thou longest to join her."

My wife! here was a complication truly!

Chap. IV.

THE ISSUE OF MY INTERVIEW WITH MY WIFE.

I found Puneeree Muckun, with the rest of my attendants, waiting at the gate, and they immediately conducted me to my own tents in the neighbourhood. I have been in many dangerous predicaments before that time and since, but I don't care to deny that I felt in the present instance such a throbbing of the heart as I never have experienced when leading a forlorn hope, or marching up to a battery.

As soon as I entered the tents a host of menials sprung forward, some to ease me of my armour, some to offer me refreshments, some with hookahs, attar of roses (in great quart bottles), and the thousand delicacies of Eastern life. I motioned them away. "I will wear my armour," said I; "I shall go forth to-night: carry my duty to the Princess, and say I grieve that to-night I have not the time to see her. Spread me a couch here, and bring me supper here; a jar of Persian wine well cooled, a lamb stuffed with pistachio-nuts, a pilaw of a couple of turkeys, a curried kid—anything. Begone! Give me a pipe; leave me alone, and tell me when the meal is ready."

I thought by these means to put off the fair Puttee Rooge, and hoped to be able to escape without subjecting myself to the examination of her curious eyes. After smoking for a while, an attendant came to tell me that my supper was prepared in the inner apartment of the tent (I suppose that the reader, if he be possessed of the commonest intelligence, knows that the tents of the Indian grandees are made of the finest Cashmere shawls, and contain a dozen rooms at least, with carpets, chimneys, and sash windows complete). I entered, I say, into an inner chamber, and there began with my fingers to devour my meal in oriental fashion, taking every now and then a pull from the wine-jar which was cooling deliciously in another jar of snow.

I was just in the act of despatching the last morsel of a most savoury stewed lamb and rice, which had formed my meal, when I heard a scuffle of feet, a shrill clatter of female voices, and, the curtain being flung open, in marched a lady accompanied by twelve slaves, with moon-faces and slim waists, lovely as the houris in Paradise.

The lady herself, to do her justice, was as great a contrast to her attendants as could possibly be; she was crooked, old, of the complexion of molasses, and rendered a thousand times more ugly by the tawdry dress and the blazing jewels with which she was covered. A line of yellow chalk drawn from her forehead to the tip of her nose (which was further ornamented by an immense glittering nose-ring), her eye-lids painted bright red, and a large dab of the same colour on her chin, showed she was not of the Mussulman, but the Brahmin faith—and of a very high caste; you could see that by her eyes. My mind was instantaneously made up as to my line of action.

The male attendants had of course quitted the apartment, as they heard the well-known sound of her voice. It would have been death to them to have remained and looked in her face. The females ranged themselves round their mistress, as she squatted down opposite to me.

"And is this," said she, "a welcome, O Khan! after six months' absence, for the most unfortunate and loving wife in all the world—is this lamb, O glutton! half so tender as thy spouse? Is this wine, O sot! half so sweet as her looks?"

I saw the storm was brewing—her slaves, to whom she turned, kept up a kind of chorus:—

"O the faithless one!" cried they; "O the rascal, the false one, who has no eye for beauty, and no heart for love, like the Khanum's!"

"A lamb is not so sweet as love," said I, gravely; "but a lamb has a good temper; a wine-cup is not so intoxicating as a woman—but a wine-cup has *no tongue*, O Khanum Gee!" and again I dipped my nose in the soul-refreshing jar.

The sweet Puttee Rooge was not, however, to be put off by my repartees; she and her maidens recommenenced their chorus, and chattered and stormed until I lost all patience.

"Retire, friends," said I, "and leave me in peace."

"Stir, on your peril!" cried the Khanum.

So, seeing there was no help for it but violence, I drew out my pistols, cocked them, and said:—"O houris! these pistols contain each two balls: the daughter of Holkar bears a sacred life for me—but for you!—by all the saints of Hindoostan, four of ye shall die if you stay a moment longer in my presence!" This was enough—the ladies gave a shriek, and skurried out of the apartment like a covey of partridges on the wing.

Now then was the time for action—my wife, or rather Bobbachy's wife, sate still, a little flurried by the unusual ferocity which her lord had displayed in her presence. I seized her hand, and, gripping it close, whispered in her ear, to which I put the other pistol—"O Khanum, listen and scream not; the moment you scream, you die!" She was completely beaten: she turned as pale as a woman could in her situation, and said, "Speak Bobbachy Bahawder, I am dumb."

"Woman," said I, taking off my helmet, and removing the chain cape which had covered almost the whole of my face—"*I am not thy husband*—I am the slayer of elephants—the world-renowned GAHAGAN!"

As I said this, and as the long ringlets of red hair fell over my shoulders (contrasting strangely with my dyed face and beard), I formed one of the finest pictures that can possibly be conceived, and I recommend it as a subject to Mr. Heath, for the next "Book of Beauty."

"Wretch!" said she; "what wouldst thou?"

"You black-faced fiend," said I, "raise but your voice, and you are dead!"

"And afterwards," said she, "do you suppose that *you* can escape?—the torments of hell are not so terrible as the tortures that Holkar will invent for thee."

"Tortures, Madam," answered I, coolly, "fiddlesticks! You will neither betray me, nor will I be put to the torture: on the contrary, you will give me your best jewels and facilitate my escape to the fort. Don't grind your teeth and swear at me. Listen, Madam; you know this dress and these arms, they are the arms of your husband, Bobbachy Bahawder—*my prisoner*: he now lies in yonder fort and, if I do not return before daylight, *at sunrise he dies*; and then, when they send his corpse back to Holkar, what will you, *his widow*, do?"

"O!" said she, shuddering, "spare me, spare me!"

"I'll tell you what you will do. You will have the pleasure of dying along with him—of *being roasted*, Madam—an agonising death, from which your father cannot save you, to which he will be the first man to condemn and conduct you. Ha! I see we understand each other, and you will give me over the cash-box and jewels." And so saying I threw my-self back with the calmest air imaginable, flinging the pistols over to her. "Light me a pipe, my love," said I, "and then go and hand me over the dollars; do you hear?" You see I had her in my power—up a tree, as the Americans say—and she very humbly lighted my pipe for me, and then departed for the goods I spoke about.

What a thing is luck! if Loll Mahommed had not been made to take that ride round the camp, I should infallibly have been lost.

My supper, my quarrel with the Princess, and my pipe afterwards, had occupied a couple of hours of my time. The Princess returned from her quest, and brought with her the box, containing valuables to the amount of about three millions sterling (I was cheated of them afterwards, but have the box still, a plain deal one). I was just about to take my departure, when a tremendous knocking, shouting, and screaming was heard at the entrance of the tent. It was Holkar himself, accompanied by that cursed Loll Mahommed, who, after his punishment, found his master restored to good humour, and had communicated to him his firm conviction that I was an impostor.

"Ho, Begum!" shouted he, in the ante-room (for he and his people could not enter the women's apartments), "speak, O my daughter! is your husband returned?"

"Speak, Madam," said I, "or *remember the roasting*."

"He is, Papa," said the Begum.

"Are you sure?—ho! ho! ho!" (the old ruffian was laughing outside)—"are you sure it is—ha! ha! ha!—*he-e-e!*"

"Indeed it is he, and no other. I pray you, father, to go, and to pass no more such shameless jests on your daughter. Have I ever seen the face of any other man?" And hereat she began to weep as if her heart would break—the deceitful minx!

Holkar's laugh was instantly turned to fury. "O, you liar and eter-nal thief!" said he, turning round (as I presume, for I could only hear) to Loll Mahommed, "to make your Prince eat such monstrous dirt as this! Furoshes, seize this man. I dismiss him from my service, I degrade him from his rank, I appropriate to myself all his property; and, hark ye, Furoshes, GIVE HIM A HUNDRED DOZEN MORE!"

Again I heard the whacks of the bamboos, and peace flowed into my soul.

*   *   *   *   *

Just as morn began to break two figures were seen to approach the little fortress of Futtyghur; one was a woman wrapped closely in a veil, the other a warrior, remarkable for the size and manly beauty of his form, who carried in his hand a deal box of considerable size. The warrior at the gate gave the word and was admitted; the woman returned slowly to the Indian camp. Her name was Puttee Rooge; his was—

G. O'G. G., M. H. E. I. C. S. C. I. H. A.

Major Gahagan's Historical Reminiscences.

———◇———

CHAP. IV.

FAMINE IN THE GARRISON.

THUS my dangers for the night being overcome, I hastened with my precious box into my own apartment, which communicated with another, where I had left my prisoner, with a guard to report if he should recover, and to prevent his escape. My servant, Ghorumsaug, was one of the guard. I called him and the fellow came, looking very much confused and frightened, as it seemed, at my appearance.

"Why Ghorumsaug," said I, "what makes thee look so pale, fellow?" (He was as white as a sheet.) "It is thy master, dost thou not remember him?" The man had seen me dress myself in the Pitan's clothes, but was not present when I had blacked my face and beard in the manner I have described.

"O Bramah, Vishnoo, and Mahomet!" cried the faithful fellow, "and do I see my dear master disguised in this way? For heaven's sake let me rid you of this odious black paint, for what will the ladies say in the ball-room, if the beautiful Feringhee should appear amongst them with his roses turned into coal?"

I am still one of the finest men in Europe, and at the time of which I write, when only two-and-twenty, I confess I *was* a little vain of my personal appearance, and not very willing to appear before my dear Belinda disguised like a blackamoor. I allowed Ghorumsaug to divest me of the heathenish armour and habiliments which I wore; and having, with a world of scrubbing and trouble, divested my face and beard of their black tinge, I put on my own becoming uniform, and hastened to wait on the ladies—hastened I say—although delayed would have been the better word, for the operation of bleaching lasted at least two hours.

"How is the prisoner? Ghorumsaug," said I, before leaving my apartment.

"He has recovered from the blow which the Lion dealt him: two men and myself watch over him: and Macgillicuddy Sahib (the second in command), has just been the rounds, and has seen that all was secure."

I bade Ghorumsaug help me to put away my chest of treasure (my exultation in taking it was so great, that I could not help informing him of its contents); and this done I despatched him to his post near the prisoner, while I prepared to sally forth and pay my respects to the fair creatures under my protection. What good after all have I done? thought I to myself, in this expedition which I had so rashly undertaken? I had seen the renowned Holkar, I had been in the heart of his camp; I knew the disposition of his troops; that there were eleven thousand of them, and that he only waited for his guns, to make a regular attack on the fort. I had seen Puttee Rooge; I had robbed her (I say *robbed* her, and I don't care what the reader, or any other man, may think of the act) of a deal box, containing jewels to the amount of three millions sterling, the property of herself and husband.

Three millions in money and jewels! And what the deuce were money and jewels to me or to my poor garrison? Could my adorable Miss Bulcher eat a fricassee of diamonds, or, Cleopatra-like, melt down pearls to her tea? Could I, careless as I am about food, with a stomach that would digest any thing—(once in Spain I ate the leg of a horse, during a famine, and was so eager to swallow this morsel that I bolted the shoe, as well as the hoof, and never felt the slightest inconvenience from either)—could I, I say, expect to live long and well upon a ragout of rupees, or a dish of stewed emeralds and rubies? With all the wealth of Crœsus before me I felt melancholy; and would have paid cheerfully, its weight in carats, for a good honest round of boiled beef. Wealth, wealth, what art thou? What is gold?—Soft metal. What are diamonds?—Shining tinsel. The great wealth-winners, the only fame-achievers, the sole objects worthy of a soldier's consideration, are beefsteaks, gunpowder, and cold iron.

The two latter means of competency we possessed; I had in my own apartments a small store of gunpowder (keeping it under my own bed, with a candle burning for fear of accidents); I had 12 pieces of artillery (4 long 48's and 4 carronades, 5 howitzers, and a long brass mortar, for grape, which I had taken myself at the battle of Assye), and muskets for ten times my force. My garrison, as I have told the reader in a previous number, consisted of 40 men, two chaplains and a surgeon: add to these my guests, 83 in number, of whom nine only were gentlemen (in tights, powder, pigtails, and silk stockings, who had come out merely for a dance, and found themselves in for a siege). Such were our numbers:

Troops and artillerymen	40
Ladies	74
Other noncombatants .	11
MAJOR G. O'G. GAHAGAN . .	<u>1000</u>
	1125

I count myself good for a thousand, for so I was regularly rated in the army: with this great benefit to it, that I only consumed as much as an ordinary mortal. We were then, as far as the victuals went, 126 mouths; as combatants we numbered 1040 gallant men, with 12 guns and a fort, against Holkar and his 12,000. No such alarming odds, if—

If!—ay, there was the rub—*if* we had *shot*, as well as powder, for our guns; *if* we had not only *men* but *meat*. Of the former commodity we had only three rounds for each piece. Of the latter, upon my sacred honour, to feed 126 souls, we had but

Two drumsticks of fowls, and a bone of ham.

Fourteen bottles of ginger-beer.

Of soda-water, four do. do.

Two bottles fine Spanish olives.

Raspberry cream—the remainder of two dishes.

Seven macaroons lying in the puddle of a demolished trifle.

Half a drum of best Turkey figs.

Some bits of broken bread; two Dutch cheeses (whole); the crust of an old Stilton; and about an ounce of almonds and raisins.

Three ham-sandwiches, and a pot of currant jelly, and 197 bottles of brandy, rum, madeira, pale ale (my private stock); a couple of hard eggs for a salad, and a flask of Florence oil.

This was the provision for the whole garrison!—The men after supper had seized upon the relics of the repast, as they were carried off from the table; and these were the miserable remnants I found and counted on my return: taking good care to lock the door of the supper-room, and treasure what little sustenance still remained in it.

When I appeared in the saloon—now lighted up by the morning sun, I not only caused a sensation myself, but felt one in my own bosom, which was of the most painful description. O my reader! may you never behold such a sight as that which presented itself:—eighty-three men and women in ball dresses: the former with their lank powdered locks streaming over their faces; the latter with faded flowers, uncurled wigs, smudged rouge, blear eyes, draggling feathers, rumpled satins—each more desperately melancholy and hideous than the other—each except my beloved Belinda Bulcher: whose raven ringlets never having been in curl, could of course never go *out* of curl; whose cheek, pale as the lily, could, as it may naturally be supposed, grow no paler; whose neck and beauteous arms dazzling as alabaster, needed no pearl-powder, and therefore, as I need not state, did not suffer because the pearl-powder had come off. Joy (deft link-boy!) lit his lamps in each of her eyes as I entered. As if I had been her sun, her spring, lo! blushing roses mantled in her cheek! Seventy-three ladies as I entered, opened their fire upon me, and stunned me with cross-questions, regarding my adventures in the camp—*she*, as she saw me, gave a faint scream (the sweetest, sure, that ever gurgled through the throat of a woman!)—then started up—then made as if she would sit down—then moved backwards—then tottered forwards—then tumbled into my—Psha! why recall,—why attempt to describe that delicious—that passionate greeting of two young hearts? What was the surrounding crowd to *us*? What cared we for the sneers of the men, the titters of the jealous women, the shrill "upon my word" of the elder Miss Bulcher, and the loud expostulations of Belinda's mamma?—the brave girl loved me, and wept in my arms: "Goliah! my Goliah!" said she, "my brave, my beautiful, *thou* art returned, and hope comes back with thee.—Oh, who can tell the anguish of my soul, during this dreadful, dreadful night!"—Other similar ejaculations of love and joy she uttered; and if I *had* perilled life in her service, if I *did* believe that hope of escape there was none, so exquisite was the moment of our meeting, that I forgot all else in this overwhelming joy!

*   *   *   *   *

[The major's description of this meeting, which lasted at the very most not ten seconds, occupies thirteen pages of writing. We have been compelled to dock off twelve-and-a-half; for the whole passage, though highly creditable to his feelings, might possibly be tedious to the reader.]

*   *   *   *   *

As I said, the ladies and gentlemen were inclined to sneer, and were giggling audibly. I led the dear girl to a chair, and, scowling round with a tremendous fierceness, which those who know me know I can sometimes put on, I shouted out, "Heark ye! men and women—I am this lady's truest knight—her husband I hope one day to be. I am commander, too, in this fort—the enemy is without it; another word of mockery—another glance of scorn—and, by Heaven, I will hurl every man and woman from the battlements, a prey to the ruffianly Holkar!" This quieted them. I am a man of my word, and none of them stirred or looked disrespectfully from that moment.

It was now *my* turn to make *them* look foolish. Mrs. Vandegobbleschroy (whose unfailing appetite is pretty well known to every person who has been in India) cried, "Well, Captain Gahagan, your ball has been so pleasant, and the supper was despatched so long ago, that myself and the ladies would be very glad of a little breakfast." And Mrs. Van giggled as if she had made a very witty and reasonable speech. "Oh! breakfast, breakfast by all means," said the rest; "we really are dying for a warm cup of tea."

"Is it bohay tay or souchong tay that you'd like, ladies?" says I.

"Nonsense, you silly man; any tea you like," said fat Mrs. Van.

"What do you say, then, to some prime GUNPOWDER?" Of course they said it was the very thing.

"And do you like hot rowls or cowld—muffins or crumpets—fresh butter or salt? And you, gentlemen, what do you say to some ilegant divvled-kidneys for yourselves, and just a trifle of grilled turkeys, and a couple of hundthred new-laid eggs for the ladies?"

"Pooh, pooh! be it as you will, my dear fellow," answered they all.

"But stop," says I. "O ladies, O ladies; O gentlemen, gentlemen, that you should ever have come to the quarters of Goliah Gahagan, and he been without—"

"What?" said they, in a breath.

"Alas! alas! I have not got a single stick of chocolate in the whole house."

"Well, well, we can do without it."

"Or a single pound of coffee."

"Never mind; let that pass too." (Mrs. Van and the rest were beginning to look alarmed.)

"And about the kidneys—now I remember, the black divvles outside the fort have seized upon all the sheep; and how are we to have kidneys without them?" (Here there was a slight o—o—o!)

"And, with regard to the milk and crame, it may be remarked that the cows are likewise in pawn, and not a single drop can be had for money or love: but we can beat up eggs, you know, in the tay, which will be just as good."

"Oh, just as good."

"Only the divvle's in the luck, there's not a fresh egg to be had—no, nor a fresh chicken," continued I, "nor a stale one either; nor a tayspoon-ful of souchong, nor a thimbleful of bohay; nor the laste taste in life of butter, salt or fresh; nor hot rowls or cowld!"

"In the name of Heaven!" said Mrs. Van, growing very pale, "what is there, then?"

"Ladies and gentlemen, I'll tell you what there is, now," shouted I. "There's

> Two drumsticks of fowls, and a bone of ham.
>
> Fourteen bottles of ginger-beer," &c. &c. &c.

And I went through the whole list of eatables as before, ending with the ham-sandwiches and the pot of jelly.

"Law! Mr. Gahagan," said Mrs. Colonel Vandegobbleschroy, "give me the ham-sandwiches—I must manage to breakfast off them."

And you should have heard the pretty to-do there was at this modest proposition! Of course I did not accede to it—why should I? I was the commander of the fort, and intended to keep these three very sandwiches for the use of myself and my dear Belinda. "Ladies," said I, "there are in this fort one hundred and twenty-six souls, and this is all the food which is to last us during the siege. Meat there is none—of drink there is a tolerable quantity; and, at one o'clock punctually, a glass of wine and one olive shall be served out to each woman: the men will receive two glasses, and an olive and a fig—and this must be your food during the seige. Lord Lake cannot be absent more than three days; and, if he be, why still there is a chance—why do I say a chance?—*a certainty* of escaping from the hands of these ruffians."

"Oh, name it, name it, dear Captain Gahagan!" screeched the whole covey at a breath.

"It lies," answered I, "in the *powder magazine*. I will blow this fort, and all it contains, to atoms, ere it becomes the prey of Holkar."

The women, at this, raised a squeel that might have been heard in Holkar's camp, and fainted in different directions; but my dear Belinda whispered in my ear, "Well done, thou noble knight! bravely said, my heart's Goliah!" I felt I was right: I could have blown her up twenty times for the luxury of that single moment! "And now, ladies," said I, "I must leave you. The two chaplains will remain with you to administer professional consolation—the other gentlemen will follow me up stairs to the ramparts, where I shall find plenty of work for them."

CHAP. V.

THE ESCAPE.

LOTH as they were, these gentlemen had nothing for it but to obey, and they accordingly followed me to the ramparts where I proceeded to review my men. The fort, in my absence, had been left in command of Lieutenant Macgillicuddy, a countryman of my own (with whom as may be seen in an early chapter of my memoirs, I had an affair of honour); and the prisoner Bobbachy Bahawder, whom I had only stunned, never wishing to kill him, had been left in charge of that officer. Three of the garrison (one of them a man of the Ahmednuggar Irregulars, my own body-servant, Ghorumsaug above named) were appointed to watch the captive by turns, and never leave him out of their sight. The lieutenant was instructed to look to them and to their prisoner, and as Bobbachy was severely injured by the blow which I had given him, and was moreover bound hand and foot, and gagged smartly with cords, I considered myself sure of his person.

Macgillicuddy did not make his appearance when I reviewed my little force, and the three havildars were likewise absent—this did not surprise me, as I had told them not to leave their prisoner; but, desirous to speak with the lieutenant, I despatched a messenger to him, and ordered him to appear immediately.

The messenger came back—he was looking ghastly pale: he whispered some information into my ear, which instantly caused me to hasten to the apartments, where I had caused Bobbachy Bahawder to be confined.

The men had fled!—Bobbachy had fled; and in his place, fancy my astonishment when I found—with a rope, cutting his naturally wide mouth almost into his ears—with a dreadful sabre-cut across his forehead—with his legs tied over his head, and his arms tied between his legs—my unhappy, my attached friend—Mortimer Macgillicuddy!

He had been in this position for about three hours—it was the very position in which I had caused Bobbachy Bahawder to be placed—an attitude uncomfortable it is true, but one which renders escape impossible, unless treason aid the prisoner.

I restored the lieutenant to his natural erect position: I poured half-a-bottle of whiskey down the immensely enlarged orifice of his mouth, and when he had been released, he informed me of the circumstances that had taken place.

Fool that I was! Idiot!—upon my return to the fort, to have been anxious about my personal appearance, and to have spent a couple of hours, in removing the artificial blackening from my beard and complexion, instead of going to examine my prisoner: when his escape would have been prevented—O foppery, foppery!—it was that cursed love of personal appearance, which had led me to forget my duty to my general, my country, my monarch, and my own honour!

Thus it was that the escape took place. My own fellow of the Irregulars, whom I had summoned to dress me, performed the operation to my satisfaction, invested me with the elegant uniform of my corps, and removed the Pitan's disguise which I had taken from the back of the prostrate Bobbachy Bahawder. What did the rogue do next?—Why, he carried back the dress to the Bobbachy—he put it, once more, on its right owner, he and his infernal black companions (who had been so won over by the Bobbachy, with promises of enormous reward), gagged Macgillicuddy who was going the rounds, and then marched with the Indian coolly up to the outer gate, and gave the word. The sentinel thinking it was myself, who had first come in, and was as likely to go out again (indeed, my rascally black valet said, that Gahagan Saib was about to go out with him and his two companions to reconnoitre)—opened the gates and off they went!

This accounted for the confusion of my valet when I entered!—and for the scoundrel's speech, that the lieutenant had *just been the rounds;*—he *had*, poor fellow, and had been seized and bound in this cruel way. The three men with their liberated prisoner, had just been on the point of escape, when my arrival disconcerted them: I had changed the guard at the gate (whom they had won over likewise); and yet, although they had overcome poor Mac, and although they were ready for the start, they had positively no means for effecting their escape, until I was ass enough to put means in their way. Fool! fool! thrice besotted fool that I was, to think of my own silly person when I should have been occupied solely with my public duty.

From Macgillicuddy's incoherent accounts, as he was gasping from the effects of the gag, and the whiskey he had taken to revive him, and from my own subsequent observations, I learned this sad story. A sudden and painful thought struck me—my precious box!—I rushed back, I found that box—I have it still—opening it, there where I had left ingots, sacks of bright tomauns, kopeks and rupees, strings of diamonds as big as ducks'-eggs, rubies as red as the lips of my Belinda, countless strings of pearls, amethysts, emeralds, piles upon piles of bank notes—I found—a piece of paper! with a few lines in the Sanscrit language, which are thus, word for word, translated:

EPIGRAM
(On disappointing a certain Major).
The conquering lion return'd with his prey,
And safe in his cavern he set it.
The sly little fox stole the booty away;
And, as he escaped, to the lion did say,
"Aha, don't you wish you may get it?"

Confusion! Oh, how my blood boiled as I read these cutting lines. I stamped,—I swore,—I don't know to what insane lengths my rage might have carried me, had not at this moment a soldier rushed in, screaming "The enemy, the enemy!"

CHAP. VI.

THE CAPTIVE.

IT was high time, indeed, that I should make my appearance. Waving my sword with one hand, and seizing my telescope with the other, I at once frightened and examined the enemy. Well they knew when they saw that flamingo-plume floating in the breeze—that awful figure standing in the breach—that waving war-sword sparkling in the sky—well, I say, they knew the name of the humble individual who owned the sword, the plume, and the figure. The infantry were mustered in front, the cavalry behind. The flags were flying, the drums, gongs, tambarines, violoncellos, and other instruments of eastern music, raised in the air a strange barbaric melody; the officers (yatabals), mounted on white dromedaries, were seen galloping to and fro, carrying to the advancing hosts the orders of Holkar.

You see that two sides of the fort of Futtyghur (rising as it does on a rock that is almost perpendicular), are defended by the Burrumpooter river, two hundred feet deep at this point, and a thousand yards wide, so that I had no fear about them attacking me in *that* quarter. My guns therefore (with their six and thirty miserable charges of shot), were dragged round to the point at which I conceived Holkar would be most likely to attack me. I was in a situation that I did not dare to fire, except at such times as I could kill a hundred men, by a single discharge of a cannon; so the attacking party marched and marched, very strongly, about a mile and a half off, the elephants marching without receiving the slightest damage from us, until they had come to within four hundred yards of our walls (the rogues knew all the secrets of our weakness, through the betrayal of the dastardly Ghorumsaug, or they never would have ventured so near). At that distance—it was about the spot where the Futtyghur hill began gradually to rise—the invading force stopped; the elephants drew up in a line, at right angles with our wall (the fools! they thought they should expose themselves too much by taking a position parallel to it!), the cavalry halted too, and—after the deuce's own flourish of trumpets, and banging of gongs to be sure—somebody, in a flame-coloured satin dress, with an immense jewel blazing in his pugree (that looked through my telescope like a small but very bright planet), got up from the back of one of the very biggest elephants, and began a speech.

The elephants were, as I said, in a line formed with admirable precision, about three hundred of them. The following little diagram will explain matters:

E is the line of elephants. F is the wall of the fort. G, a gun in the fort. *Now* the reader will see what I did.

The elephants were standing, their trunks waggling to and fro gracefully before them; and I, with superhuman skill and activity, brought the gun G (a devilish long brass gun) to bear upon them. I pointed it myself; bang it went, and what was the consequence? Why this:—

F is the fort as before. G is the gun as before. E the elephants as we have previously seen them. What then is x? x *is the line taken by the ball fired from G*, which took off *one hundred and thirty-four elephants'* trunks, and only spent itself in the tusk of a very old animal, that stood the hundred and thirty-fifth!

I say, that such a shot was never fired before or since—that a gun was never pointed in such a way. Suppose I had been a common man, and contented myself with firing bang at the head of the first animal? An ass would have done it, and prided himself had he hit his mark—and what would have been the consequence? Why, that the ball might have killed two elephants, and wounded a third; but here, probably, it would have stopped, and done no further mischief. The *trunk* was the place at which to aim; there are no bones there; and away, consequently, went the bullet, shearing, as I have said, through one hundred and thirty-five probosces. Heavens! what a howl there was, when the shot took effect! What a sudden stoppage of Holkar's speech! What a hideous snorting of elephants! What a rush backwards was made by the whole army, as if some demon was pursuing them!

Away they went. No sooner did I see them in full retreat, than, rushing forward myself, I shouted to my men, "My friends, yonder lies your dinner!" We flung open the gates—we tore down to the spot where the elephants had fallen; seven of them were killed; and of those that escaped to die of their hideous wounds elsewhere, most had left their tusks behind them. A great quantity of them we seized; and I myself, cutting up with my cimeter a couple of the fallen animals, as a butcher would a calf, motioned to the men to take the pieces back to the fort, where barbacued elephant was served round for dinner, instead of the miserable allowance of an olive and a glass of wine, which I had promised to my female friends, in my speech to them. The animal reserved for the ladies was a young white one—the fattest and tenderest I ever ate in my life: they are very fair eating, but the flesh has an India-rubber flavour, which, until one is accustomed to it, is unpalatable.

It was well that I had obtained the supply, for, during my absence on the works, Mrs. Vandegobbleschroy and one or two others, had forced their way into the supper-room, and devoured every morsel of the garrison-larder, with the exception of the cheeses, the olives, and the wine, which was locked up in my own apartment, before which stood a sentinel. Disgusting Mrs. Van! when I heard of her gluttony, I had almost a mind to eat *her*. However, we made a very comfortable dinner off the barbacued steaks, and when every body had done, had the comfort of knowing that there was enough for one meal more.

The next day, as I expected, the enemy attacked us in great force, attempting to escalade the fort; but by the help of my guns, and my good sword, by the distinguished bravery of Lieutenant Macgillicuddy and the rest of the garrison, we beat this attack off completely, the enemy sustaining a loss of seven hundred men. We were victorious; but when another attack was made, what were we to do? We had still a little powder left, but had fired off all the shot, stones, iron bars, &c. in the garrison! On this day, too, we devoured the last morsel of our food. I shall never forget Mrs. Vandegobbleschroy's despairing look, as I saw her sitting alone, attempting to make some impression on the little white elephant's roasted tail.

The third day the attack was repeated. The resources of genius are never at an end—yesterday, I had no ammunition; to-day I had discovered charges sufficient for two guns, and two swivels which were much longer, but had bores of about blunderbuss size.

This time, my friend Loll Mahommed, who had received, as the reader may remember, such a bastinadoing for my sake, headed the attack. The poor wretch could not walk, but he was carried in an open palanquin, and came on waving his sword and cursing horribly in his Hindoostan jargon. Behind him came troops of matchlock men, who picked off every one of our men who showed their noses above the ramparts, and a great host of blackamoors with scaling ladders, bundles to fill the ditch, fascines, gabions, culverins, demilunes, counterscarps, and all the other appurtenances of offensive war.

On they came—my guns and men were ready for them. You will ask how my pieces were loaded? I answer, that though my garrisons were without food, I knew my duty as an officer, and *had put the two Dutch cheeses into the two guns, and had crammed the contents of a bottle of olives into each swivel.*

They advanced—whish! went one of the Dutch cheeses—bang! went the other.—Alas! they did little execution. In their first contact with an opposing body, they certainly floored it; but they became at once like so much Welsh-rabbit, and did no execution beyond the man whom they struck down.

"Hogree, pogree, wongree-fum!" (praise to Allah, and the forty-nine imaums!) shouted out the ferocious Loll Mahommed, when he saw the failure of my shot. "Onward, sons of the Prophet! the infidel has no more ammunition—a hundred thousand lakhs of rupees to the man who brings me Gahagan's head!"

His men set up a shout, and rushed forward—he, to do him justice, was at the very head, urging on his own palanquin-bearers, and poking them with the tip of his cimeter. They came panting up the hill: I was black with rage, but it was the cold concentrated rage of despair. "Macgillicuddy," said I, calling that faithful officer, "you know where the barrels of powder are?"—He did. "You know the use to make of them?"—He did. He grasped my hand. "Goliah," said he, "farewell! I swear that the fort shall be in atoms, as soon as yonder unbelievers have carried it.—Oh, my poor mother!" added the gallant youth, as sighing, yet fearless, he retired to his post.

I gave one thought to my blessed, my beautiful Belinda, and then stepping into the front, took down one of the swivels;—a shower of matchlock-balls came whizzing round my head. I did not heed them.

I took the swivel, and aimed coolly. Loll Mahommed, his palanquin, and his men, were now not above two hundred yards from the fort. Loll was straight before me, gesticulating and shouting to his men. I fired—bang!!!

I aimed so true, that *one hundred and seventeen best Spanish olives were lodged in a lump in the face of the unhappy Loll Mahommed.* The wretch, uttering a yell the most hideous and unearthly I ever heard, fell back dead—the frightened bearers flung down the palanquin and ran—the whole host ran as one man—their screams might be heard for leagues, "Tomasha, tomasha," they cried, "it is enchantment!" Away they fled, and the victory a third time was ours. Soon as the fight was done, I flew back to my Belinda—we had eaten nothing for twenty-four hours, but I forgot hunger in the thought of once more beholding *her!*

The sweet soul turned towards me with a sickly smile as I entered, and almost fainted in my arms; but, alas! it was not love which caused in her bosom an emotion so strong—it was hunger! "Oh! my Goliah," whispered she, "for three days I have not tasted food—I could not eat that horrid elephant yesterday; but now—oh! heaven!" She could say no more, but sunk almost lifeless on my shoulder. I administered to her a trifling dram of rum, which revived her for a moment, and then rushed down stairs, determined that if it were a piece of my own leg, she should still have something to satisfy her hunger. Luckily, I remembered that three or four elephants were still lying in the field, having been killed by us in the first action, two days before. Necessity, thought I, has no law; my adorable girl must eat elephant, until she can get something better.

I rushed into the court where the men were, for the most part, assembled. "Men," said I, "our larder is empty; we must fill it as we did the day before yesterday; who will follow Gahagan on a foraging party?" I expected that, as on the former occasion, every man would offer to accompany me.

To my astonishment, not a soul moved—a murmur arose among the troops; and at last, one of the oldest and bravest came forward.

"Captain," he said, "it is of no use; we cannot feed upon elephants for ever; we have not a grain of powder left, and must give up the fort when the attack is made to-morrow. We may as well be prisoners now as then, and we won't go elephant-hunting any more."

"Ruffian!" I said, "he who first talks of surrender, dies!" and I cut him down. "Is there any one else who wishes to speak?"

No one stirred.

"Cowards! miserable cowards!" shouted I; "what, you dare not move for fear of death, at the hands of those wretches who even now fled before your arms—what, do I say *your* arms?—before *mine!*—alone I did it; and as alone I routed the foe, alone I will victual the fortress! Ho! open the gate!"

I rushed out, not a single man would follow. The bodies of the elephants that we had killed still lay on the ground, where they had fallen about four hundred yards from the fort. I descended calmly the hill, a very steep one, and coming to the spot, took my pick of the animals, choosing a tolerably small and plump one, of about thirteen feet high, which the vultures had respected. I threw this animal over my shoulders, and made for the fort.

As I marched up the acclivity, whizz—piff—whirr!! came the balls over my head; and pitter-patter, pitter-patter! they fell on the body of the elephant like drops of rain. The enemy were behind me; I knew it, and quickened my pace. I heard the gallop of their horse; they came nearer, nearer; I was within a hundred yards of the fort—seventy—fifty! I strained every nerve; I panted with the super-human exertion—I ran—could a man run very fast with such a tremendous weight on his shoulders?

Up came the enemy; fifty horsemen were shouting and screaming at my tail. Oh, heaven! five yards more—one moment—and I am saved!—It is done—I strain the last strain—I make the last step—I fling forward my precious burden into the gate opened wide to receive me and it, and—I fall! The gate thunders to, and I am left *on the outside!* Fifty knives are gleaming before my bloodshot eyes—fifty black hands are at my throat, when a voice exclaims, "Stop!—kill him not, it is Gujputi!" A film came over my eyes—exhausted nature would bear no more.

*   *   *   *   *

Chap. VII.

SURPRISE OF FUTTYGHUR.

WHEN I awoke from the trance into which I had fallen, I found myself in a bath, surrrounded by innumerable black faces; and a Hindoo pothukoor (whence our word apothecary), feeling my pulse, and looking at me with an air of sagacity.

"Where am I?" I exclaimed, looking round and examining the strange faces, and the strange apartment which met my view. "Bekhusm!" said the apothecary. "Silence! Gahagan Saib is in the hands of those who know his valour, and will save his life."

"Know my valour, slave? Of course you do," said I; "but the fort—the garrison—the elephant—Belinda, my love—my darling—Macgillicuddy—the scoundrelly mutineers—the deal bo—" * * *

I could say no more: the painful recollections pressed so heavily upon my poor shattered mind and frame, that both failed once more. I fainted again, and I know not how long I lay insensible.

Again, however, I came to my senses; the poothukoor applied restoratives, and after a slumber of some hours, I woke much refreshed. I had no wound; my repeated swoons had been brought on (as indeed well they might) by my gigantic efforts in carrying the elephant up a steep hill a quarter of a mile in length. Walking, the task is bad enough, but running, it is the deuce; and I would recommend any of my readers who may be disposed to try and carry a dead elephant, never, on any account, to go a pace of more than five miles an hour.

Scarcely was I awake, when I heard the clash of arms at my door (plainly indicating that sentinels were posted there), and a single old gentleman, richly habited, entered the room. Did my eyes deceive me? I had surely seen him before. No—yes—no—yes—it *was* he—the snowy white beard, the mild eyes, the nose flattened to a jelly, and level with the rest of the venerable face, proclaimed him at once to be—Saadut Allee Beg Bimbukchee, Holkar's prime vizier, whose nose, as the reader may recollect, his highness had flattened with his kaleawn, during my interview with him in the Pitan's disguise.—I now knew my fate but too well—I was in the hands of Holkar.

Saadut Allee Beg Bimbukchee slowly advanced towards me, and with a mild air of benevolence, which distinguished that excellent man (he was torn to pieces by wild horses the year after, on account of a difference with Holkar), he came to my bedside, and taking gently my hand, said, "Life and death, my son, are not ours. Strength is deceitful, valour is unavailing, fame is only wind—the nightingale sings of the rose all night—where is the rose in the morning? Booch, booch! it is withered by a frost. The rose makes remarks regarding the nightingale, and where is that delightful song-bird? Pena-bekhoda, he is netted, plucked, spitted, and roasted! Who knows how misfortune comes? It has come to Gahagan Gujputi!"

"It is well," said I, stoutly, and in the Malay language. "Gahagan Gujputi will bear it like a man."

"No doubt—like a wise man and a brave one; but there is no lane so long to which there is not a turning, no night so black to which there comes not a morning. Icy winter is followed by merry spring time—grief is often succeeded by joy."

"Interpret, oh riddler!" said I; "Gahagan Khan is no reader of puzzles—no prating Mollah. Gujputi loves not words, but swords."

"Listen then, oh, Gujputi; you are in Holkar's power."

"I know it."

"You will die by the most horrible tortures to-morrow morning."

"I dare say."

"They will tear your teeth from your jaws, your nails from your fingers, and your eyes from your head."

"Very possibly."

"They will flay you alive, and then burn you."

"Well; they can't do any more."

"They will seize upon every man and woman in yonder fort"—it was not then taken!—"and repeat upon them the same tortures."

"Ha! Belinda! Speak—how can all this be avoided?"

"Listen. Gahagan loves the moon-face, called Belinda."

"He does, Vizier, to distraction."

"Of what rank is he in the Koompani's army?"

"A captain."

"A miserable captain—oh, shame! Of what creed is he?"

"I am an Irishman, and a Catholic."

"But he has not been very particular about his religious duties?"

"Alas, no."

"He has not been to his mosque for these twelve years?"

" 'Tis too true."

"Hearken now, Gahagan Khan. His Highness Prince Holkar has sent me to thee. You shall have the moon-face for your wife—your second wife, that is;—the first shall be the incomparable Puttee Rooge, who loves you to madness;—with Puttee Rooge, who is the wife, you shall have the wealth and rank, of Bobbachy Bahawder, of whom his highness intends to get rid. You shall be second in command of his highness's forces. Look, here is his commission signed with the celestial seal, and attested by the sacred names of the forty-nine Imaums. You have but to renounce your religion, and your service, and all these rewards are yours."

He produced a parchment, signed as he said, and gave it to me (it was beautifully written in Indian ink—I had it for fourteen years, but a rascally valet, seeing it very dirty, *washed* it forsooth, and washed off every bit of the writing)—I took it calmly, and said, "This is a tempting offer; oh, Vizier, how long wilt thou give me to consider of it?"

After a long parley he allowed me six hours, when I promised to give him an answer. My mind, however, was made up—as soon as he was gone, I threw myself on the sofa and fell asleep.

*   *   *   *   *

At the end of the six hours the Vizier came back: two people were with him; one, by his martial appearance I knew to be Holkar, the other I did not recognise. It was about midnight.

"Have you considered?" said the Vizier, as he came to my couch.

"I have," said I, sitting up,—I could not stand, for my legs were tied, and my arms fixed in a neat pair of steel handcuffs. "I have," said I, "unbelieving dogs! I have. Do you think to pervert a christian gentleman from his faith and honour? Ruffian blackamoors! do your worst: heap tortures on this body, they cannot last long—tear me to pieces—after you have torn me into a certain number of pieces, I shall not feel it—and if I did, if each torture could last a life—if each limb were to feel the agonies of a whole body, what then? I would bear all—all—all—all—all—ALL!"—My breast heaved—my form dilated—my eye flashed as I spoke these words.

"Tyrants!" said I, "Dulce et decorum est pro patriâ mori." Having thus clinched the argument, I was silent.

The venerable Grand Vizier turned away, I saw a tear trickling down his cheeks.

"What a constancy," said he; "oh, that such beauty and such bravery should be doomed so soon to quit the earth!"

His tall companion only sneered and said, "*and Belinda*—"

"Ha!" said I; "ruffian, be still!—Heaven will protect her spotless innocence. Holkar, I know thee, and thou knowest *me*, too! Who with his single sword destroyed thy armies?—Who, with his pistol, cleft in twain thy nose-ring? Who slew thy generals? Who slew thy elephants? Three hundred mighty beasts went forth to battle: of these, *I* slew one hundred thirty-five!—Dog, coward, ruffian, tyrant, unbeliever! Gahagan hates thee, spurns thee, spits on thee!"

Holkar, as I made these uncomplimentary remarks, gave a scream of rage, and, drawing his cimeter, rushed on to despatch me at once (it was the very thing I wished for), when the third person sprang forward, and seizing his arm, cried—

"Papa! oh, save him!" It was Puttee Rooge! "Remember," continued she, "his misfortunes—remember, oh, remember my—love!"—and here she blushed, and putting one finger into her mouth and hanging down her head, looked the very picture of modest affection.

Holkar sulkily sheathed his cimeter, and muttered, " 'Tis better as it is; had I killed him now, I had spared him the torture. None of this shameless fooling, Puttee Rooge," continued the tyrant, dragging her away. "Captain Gahagan dies three hours from hence"—Puttee Rooge gave one scream and fainted—her father and the Vizier carried her off between them; nor was I loath to part with her, for, with all her love, she was as ugly as the deuce.

They were gone—my fate was decided. I had but three hours more of life: so I flung myself again on the sofa, and fell profoundly asleep. As it may happen to any of my readers to be in the same situation, and to be hanged themselves, let me earnestly entreat them to adopt this plan of going to sleep, which I for my part have repeatedly found to be successful.— It saves unnecessary annoyance, it passes away a great deal of unpleasant time, and it prepares one to meet like a man the coming catastrophe.

* * * * *

Three o'clock came; the sun was at this time making his appearance in the heavens, and with it came the guards, who were appointed to conduct me to the torture. I woke, rose, was carried out, and was set on the very white donkey on which Loll Mahommed was conducted through the camp, after he was bastinadoed. Bobbachy Bahawder rode behind me, restored to his rank and state; troops of cavalry hemmed us in on all sides;

my ass was conducted by the common executioner: a crier went forward, shouting out, "Make way for the destroyer of the faithful—he goes to bear the punishment of his crimes." We came to the fatal plain: it was the very spot whence I had borne away the elephant, and in full sight of the fort. I looked towards it. Thank Heaven! King George's banner waved on it still—a crowd were gathered on the walls—the men, the dastards who had deserted me—and women, too. Among the latter I thought I distinguished *one* who—Oh, gods! the thought turned me sick—I trembled and looked pale for the first time.

"He trembles! he turns pale," shouted out Bobbachy Bahawder, ferociously exulting over his conquered enemy.

"Dog!" shouted I—(I was sitting with my head to the donkey's tail, and so looked the Bobbachy full in the face)—"not so pale as you looked, when I felled you with this arm—not so pale as your women looked, when I entered your harem!" Completely chop-fallen, the Indian ruffian was silent: at any rate, I had done for *him*.

We arrived at the place of execution—a stake, a couple of feet thick and eight high, was driven in the grass; round the stake, about seven feet from the ground, was an iron ring, to which were attached two fetters; in these my wrists were placed—two or three executioners stood near with strange-looking instruments: others were blowing at a fire, over which was a caldron, and in the embers were stuck other prongs and instruments of iron.

The crier came forward and read my sentence. It was the same in effect as that which had been hinted to me the day previous by the Grand Vizier. I confess I was too agitated exactly to catch every word that was spoken.

Holkar himself, on a tall dromedary, was at a little distance. The Grand Vizier came up to me—it was his duty to stand by, and see the punishment performed. "It is yet time," said he.

I nodded my head, but did not answer.

The Vizier cast up to heaven a look of inexpressible anguish, and with a voice choking with emotion, said, "*Executioner—do—your—duty!*"

The horrid man advanced—he whispered sulkily in the ears of the Grand Vizier, "*Guggly ka ghee, hum khedgeree,*" said he, "*the oil does not boil yet*—wait one minute." The assistants blew, the fire blazed, the oil was heated. The Vizier drew a few feet aside, taking a large ladle full of the boiling liquid, he advanced, and—

*　　　*　　　*　　　*　　　*

*　　　*　　　*　　　*　　　*

Whish! bang, bang! pop! the executioner was dead at my feet, shot through the head; the ladle of scalding oil had been dashed in the face of the unhappy Grand Vizier, who lay on the plain howling. "Whish! bang! pop! Hurrah!—charge!—forwards!—cut them down!—no quarter!" I saw—yes, no, yes, no, yes!—I saw regiment upon regiment of galloping British horsemen, riding over the ranks of the flying natives! First of the host, I recognised, oh, Heaven! my AHMEDNUGGAR IRREGULARS! On came the gallant line of black steeds and horsemen; swift, swift before them rode my officers in yellow—Glogger, Pappendick, and Stuffle; their sabres gleamed in the sun, their voices rung in the air. "D— them!" they cried, "give it them, boys!" A strength supernatural thrilled through my veins at that delicious music; by one tremendous effort, I wrenched the post from its foundation, five feet in the ground. I could not release my hands from the fetters, it is true; but, grasping the beam tightly, I sprung forward—with one blow, I levelled the five executioners in the midst of the fire, their fall upsetting the scalding oil-can; with the next, I swept the bearers of Bobbachy's palanquin off their legs; with the third, I caught that chief himself in the small of the back, and sent him flying into the sabres of my advancing soldiers!

The next minute, Glogger and Stuffle were in my arms, Pappendick leading on the Irregulars. Friend and foe in that wild chase, had swept far away. We were alone, I was freed from my immense bar; and ten minutes afterwards, when Lord Lake trotted up with his staff, he found me sitting on it.

"Look at Gahagan," said his lordship. "Gentlemen, did I not tell you we should be sure to find him *at his post?*"

The gallant old nobleman rode on: and this was the famous BATTLE OF FURRUCKABAD, or SURPRISE OF FUTTYGHUR fought on the 17th of November, 1804.

*　　*　　*　　*　　*

About a month afterwards, the following announcement appeared in *Boggleywollah Hurkaru,* and other Indian papers: "Married, on the 25th of December, at Futtyghur, by the Rev. Dr. Snorter, Captain Goliah O'Grady Gahagan, Commanding Irregular Horse Ahmednuggar to Belinda, second daughter of Major-general Bulcher, C. B. His Excellency, the Commander-in-chief, gave away the bride; and after a splendid *déjeuné,* the happy pair set off to pass the Mango season at Hurrygurrybaug. Venus must recollect, however, that Mars must not *always* be at her side. The Irregulars are nothing without their leader."

Such was the paragraph—such the event—the happiest in the existence of

G.O'G.G.M.H.E.I.C.S.C.I.H.A.

Editorial Apparatus
for
The Tremendous Adventures of Major Gahagan

Appendix A

Addition to Installment Two in Comic Tales

(This portion follows immediately as an uninterrupted part of the install-ment, p. 18. Gahagan's signature was omitted in Comic Tales.*)*

Gleig, Mill, and Thorn have all told the tale of this war, though some-how they have omitted all mention of the hero of it. General Lake, for the victory of that day, became Lord Lake, of Laswaree. Laswaree! and who forsooth was the real conqueror of Laswaree? I can lay my hand upon my heart, and say that *I* was. If any proof is wanting of the fact, let me give it at once, and from the highest military testimony in the world, I mean that of the EMPEROR NAPOLEON.

In the month of March, 1817, I was passenger on board the Prince Regent, Captain Harris, which touched at St. Helena on its passage from Calcutta to England. In company with the other officers on board the ship, I paid my respects to the illustrious exile of Longwood, who received us in his garden, where he was walking about in a nankeen dress and a large broad-brimmed straw-hat, with General Montholon, Count Las Cases, and his son Emanuel, then a little boy, who I dare say does not recollect me, but who nevertheless played with my sword-knot and the tassels of my Hessian boots during the whole of our interview with his Imperial Majesty.

Our names were read out (in a pretty accent, by the way!) by General Montholon, and the Emperor, as each was pronounced, made a bow to the owner of it, but did not vouchsafe a word. At last Montholon came to mine. The Emperor looked me at once in the face, took his hands out of his pockets, put them behind his back, and coming up to me smiling, pronounced the following words:—

"*Assye, Delhi, Deeg, Futtyghur.*"

I blushed, and taking off my hat with a bow, said—"*Sire, c'est moi.*"

"*Parbleu! je le savais bien,*" said the Emperor, holding out his snuff-box. "*En usez vous, Major?*" I took a large pinch (which, with the honour of speaking to so great a man, brought the tears into my eyes), and he continued as nearly as possible in the following words:—

"Sir, you are known; you come of an heroic nation. Your third brother, the Chef de Bataillon, Count Godfrey Gahagan, was in my Irish brigade."

Gahagan.—"Sire, it is true. He and my countrymen in your Majesty's service stood under the green flag in the breach of Burgos, and beat Wellington back. It was the only time, as your Majesty knows, that Irishmen and Englishmen were beaten in that war."

Napoleon (looking as if he would say "D— your candour, Major Gahagan.")—"Well, well; it was so. Your brother was a Count, and died a General in my service."

Gahagan.—"He was found lying upon the bodies of nine-and-twenty Cossacks at Borodino. They were all dead, and bore the Gahagan mark."

Napoleon (to Montholon).—"*C'est vrai, Montholon, je vous donne ma parole d'honneur la plus sacrée, que c'est vrai. Ils ne font pas d'autres, ces terribles Ga'gans.* You must know that Monsieur gained the battle of Delhi as certainly as I did that of Austerlitz. In this way:—*Ce belître de Lor Lake,* after calling up his cavalry, and placing them in front of Holkar's batteries, *qui balayaient la plaine,* was for charging the enemy's batteries with his horse, who would have been *écrasés, mitraillés, foudroyés* to a man, but for the cunning of *ce grand rouge que vous voyez.*"

Montholon.—"*Coquin de Major, va!*"

Napoleon.—"Montholon! tais-toi. When Lord Lake, with his great bull-headed English obstinacy, saw the *fâcheuse* position into which he had brought his troops, he was for dying on the spot, and would infallibly have done so—and the loss of his army would have been the ruin of the East India Company—and the ruin of the English East India Company would have established my empire (bah! it was a republic then!) in the East; but that the man before us, Lieutenant Goliah Gahagan, was riding at the side of General Lake."

Montholon (with an accent of despair and fury).—"*Gredin! cent mille tonnerres de Dieu!*"

Napoleon (benignantly).—"*Calme-toi, mon fidèle ami.* What will you? It was fate. Gahagan, at the critical period of the battle, or rather slaughter, (for the English had not slain a man of the enemy,) advised a retreat."

Montholon.—"*Le lâche! Un Français meurt, mais il ne recule jamais.*"

Napoleon.—"*Stupide!* Don't you see *why* the retreat was ordered? — don't you know that it was a feint on the part of Gahagan to draw Holkar from his impregnable retrenchments? Don't you know that the ignorant Indian fell into the snare, and issuing from behind the cover of his guns, came down with his cavalry on the plain in pursuit of Lake and his dragoons? Then it was that the Englishmen turned upon him; the hardy children of the north swept down his feeble horsemen, bore them back to their guns, which were useless, entered Holkar's entrenchments along with his troops, sabred the artillerymen at their pieces, and won the battle of Delhi!"

As the Emperor spoke, his pale cheek glowed red, his eye flashed fire, his deep clear voice rung as of old, when he pointed out the enemy from beneath the shadow of the Pyramids, or rallied his regiments to the charge upon the death-strewn plain of Wagram. I have had many a proud moment in my life, but never such a proud one as this; and I would readily pardon the word "coward," as applied to me by Montholon, in consideration of the testimony which his master bore in my favour.

"Major," said the Emperor to me in conclusion, "why had I not such a man as you in my service? I would have made you a Prince and a Marshal!" and here he fell into a reverie, of which I knew and respected the purport. He was thinking, doubtless, that I might have retrieved his fortunes, and indeed I have very little doubt that I might.

Very soon after, coffee was brought by Monsieur Marchand, Napoleon's valet-de-chambre, and after partaking of that beverage, and talking upon the politics of the day, the Emperor withdrew, leaving me deeply impressed by the condescension he had shewn in this remarkable interview.

Appendix B

Preface by Michael Angelo Titmarsh for Comic Tales

PREFACE.

A CUSTOM which the publishers have adopted of late cannot be too strongly praised, both by authors of high repute, and by writers of no repute at all—viz., the custom of causing the works of unknown literary characters to be "edited" by some person who is already a favourite with the public. The labour is not so difficult as at first may be supposed. A publisher writes—"My dear Sir,—Enclosed is a draft on Messrs. So-and-so: will you edit Mr. What-d'ye-call-'em's book?" The well-known author says—"My dear Sir,—I have to acknowledge the receipt of so much, and will edit the book with pleasure." And the book is published; and from that day until the end of the world the well-known author never hears of it again, except he has a mind to read it, when he orders it from the circulating library.

This little editorial fiction is one which can do harm to nobody in the world, and only good to the young author so introduced; for who would notice him, in such a great, crowded, bustling world, unless he came provided with a decent letter of recommendation? Thus Captain Peter Simple brought forward the ingenious writer of "Rattlin, the Reefer;" thus Mr. William Harrison Rookwood took Dr. Bird by the hand; thus the famous Mr. Theodore Eye lately patronized the facetious Peter Priggins, whose elegant tales of Oxford life must have charmed many thousand more persons than ever will read this "Preface." Take one more instance:—"The History of Needlework in all Ages:" a book of remarkable interest, and exciting to a delirious pitch. Many people now would have passed over the book altogether, who, when they saw that it was "edited" by a Countess, instantly looked out her ladyship's name in the Peerage, and ordered the work from Ebers's.

When there came to be a question of republishing the tales in these volumes, the three authors, Major Gahagan, Mr. Fitzroy Yellowplush, and myself, had a violent dispute upon the matter of editing; and at one time we talked of editing each other all round. The toss of a half-penny, however, decided the question in my favour; and I shall be very glad, in a similar manner, to "edit" any works, of any author, on any subject, or in any language whatever.

Mr. Yellowplush's Memoirs appeared in "Fraser's Magazine," and have been reprinted accurately from that publication. The elegance of their style made them excessively popular in America, where they were reprinted more than once. Major Gahagan's Reminiscences, from the "New Monthly Magazine," were received by our American brethren with similar piratical honours; and the Editor has had the pleasure of perusing them likewise in the French tongue. To translate Yellowplush was more difficult; but Doctor Strumpff, the celebrated Sanskrit Professor in the University of Bonn, has already deciphered the ten first pages, has compiled a copious vocabulary and notes, has separated the mythic from the historical part of the volume, and discovered that it is, like Homer, the work of many ages and persons. He declares the work to be written in the Cockniac dialect; but, for this and other conjectures, the reader is referred to his Essay.

"The Bedford-row Conspiracy," also, appeared in the "New Monthly Magazine;" and the reader of French novels will find that one of the tales of the ingenious M. Charles de Bernard is very similar to it in plot. As M. de Bernard's tale appeared before the Conspiracy, it is very probable, that envious persons will be disposed to say, that the English author borrowed from the French one; a matter which the public is quite at liberty to settle as it chooses.

The history of "The Fatal Boots" formed part of "The Comic Almanack" three years since; and if the author has not ventured to make designs for it, as for the other tales in the volumes, the reason is, that the "Boots" have been already illustrated by Mr. George Cruikshank, a gentleman with whom Mr. Titmarsh does not quite wish to provoke comparisons.

In the title-page, the reader is presented with three accurate portraits of the authors of these volumes. They are supposed to be marching hand-in-hand, and are just on the very brink of immortality.

M. A. T.

Paris, 1 April, 1841.

Appendix C

Illustrations from *Comic Tales* for
The Tremendous Adventures of Major Gahagan

GAHAGAN.

From the great portrait by Titmarsh in the Gallery of H.H. the Nawaub of Budge Budge.

The Major discovering the infidelity of Mrs Thomas a Kell.

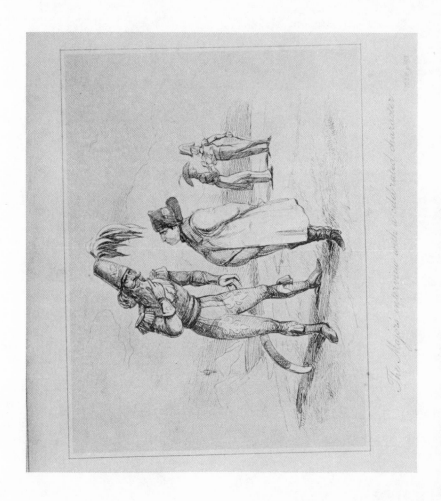

The pilgrims on the road to Stamford Bridge

Composition and Publication

While in the full swing of writing *Yellowplush*, Thackeray augmented his income with other contributions to *Fraser's* and several reviews for *The Times*. In February, 1838, the same month that saw the conclusion of Yellowplush's account of Deuceace's story, he published in *The New Monthly Magazine* a fictitious autobiographical story by Major Goliah O'Grady Gahagan titled "Some Passages in the Life of Major Gahagan." The story could stand alone, though in the light of subsequent history we may assume that from the beginning Thackeray foresaw the possibility of using *Gahagan* serially. Whatever the case, he submitted a shorter additional sketch by Gahagan the next month in which he refers to the previous month's story. This time the sketch was titled "Historical Recollections by Major Gahagan"—a second stand-alone sketch. During the next seven months *Gahagan* dropped from sight. Thackeray concluded six more numbers of *Yellowplush*, and then apparently turned to *Stubbs's Calendar; or The Fatal Boots*, an almanac done in collaboration with George Cruikshank, for publication at the end of the year. There is no record of a publication by Thackeray during September when his letters indicate he was working on *The Fatal Boots* and when his second daughter, Jane, began a decline that ended in her death, age eight months, in March of the next year. There is some doubt as to whether Thackeray wrote "Passages in the Life of Dolly Duster" which appeared in *The New Monthly* in October and November. If he did, his August and September writing schedule was full indeed, for the next installment of Major Gahagan's story also appeared in November. This time he referred to the two earlier sketches and promised continuations, which appeared in *The New Monthly* in December, 1838, and February, 1839. These three installments are titled "Major Gahagan's Historical Reminiscences." Concluding *Gahagan*, Thackeray began his first real novel, *Catherine*.

The February 1838 appearance of *Gahagan* was not the Major's literary debut. He had authored "The Professor," a story of the petty intrigues of "Professor" Dondolo, an adventurer who tries to seduce an oystermonger's daughter. Gahagan as narrator has no presence in the story as character. In fact the Gahagan of "The Professor" is more like the narrator of *Vanity Fair* than he is like the veteran of Indian and Spanish wars who narrates the Major's historical reminiscences.

The five installments of "historical" war fiction which Gahagan contributed to *New Monthly* actually hang together as a unit more effectively than do Yellowplush's contributions to *Fraser's*. Though in both cases the presence and personality of the narrator is the primary unifying element, Gahagan's story is more or less coherent and continuous—the history of his loves and battles uninterrupted by the extraneous book reviews and digressions characteristic of *Yellowplush*. None of the *Gahagan* manuscript is known to survive.

Although the first verifiable republication of *Gahagan* in book form occurred in London in 1841 in the collection *Comic Tales and Sketches*, there remains some evidence that an American edition and a French translation preceded it. In the preface to *Comic Tales*, Thackeray writes, "Major Gahagan's Reminiscences from the 'New Monthly Magazine,' were received by our American brethren with ... piratical honours; and the Editor has had the pleasure of perusing them likewise in the French tongue" (above, p. 67). In addition, Frederick S. Dickson in his bibliography (appended to James Grant Wilson's *Thackeray in the United States* [London, 1903], pp. 229-230) notes, "On August 24, 1839, Thackeray's first letter appeared in the 'Corsair' and the editor [N. P. Willis] refers to the writer as the 'author of "The Yellowplush Correspondence," the "Memoirs of Major Gahagan," &c. &c.'" Dickson argues that on the basis of Thackeray's preface to *Comic Tales* and the *Corsair* editor's comment, "it is conceivable that some editor of these papers might have published the whole series under the title of 'The Memoirs of Major Gahagan,' using the various titles from the magazine as chapter headings, but it is hardly likely that the editor of the 'Corsair,' desiring to advertise the ability of his correspondent, should have made use of a title that had never been in existence."

A search of contemporary reviews of Thackeray's works provides no evidence to indicate that there was an American edition of *Gahagan* in 1839, for all known reviews cite *New Monthly*. That periodical had, apparently, a sufficient American circulation to justify Willis's remark in *The Corsair*. Even Thackeray's comments in *Comic Tales* are ambiguous; so, until a copy of an 1839 American edition of *Gahagan*, or some record of the publication of such an edition, comes to light, one must assume that the first republication of *Gahagan* in book form is in the second volume of *Comic Tales and Sketches*, 2 vols. (London: Hugh Cunningham, 1841).

Though Thackeray participated to some extent in the publication of *Comic Tales* (see Introduction to *Yellowplush*), there is no evidence to indicate which variations in the text were introduced by him. *Comic Tales* purports to be "edited" by the fictitious Mr. Michael Angelo Titmarsh (see the Preface in Appendix B). The *Comic Tales* edition of *Gahagan* adds roughly five pages of text to what was the second installment in *New Monthly*. (The five-page addition made for *Comic Tales* is found in Appendix A.) In addition, *Comic Tales* provides a chapter title, "Allyghur and Laswaree," for the second installment of the *New Monthly* issue. The third installment, complete with its title, becomes chapter 3. The fourth magazine installment originally contained a titled introduction and three titled chapters: 1, 2 and misnumbered 4; in *Comic Tales* the introduction and chapters 1 and 2 become the single chapter 4, and the magazine's misnumbered chapter 4 becomes the book's chapter 5. In addition, for the first time a title is provided for the entire series, *The Tremendous Adventures of Major Gahagan*, and Gahagan's signature in its various permutations is removed from the end of all but the fourth installment. There are, furthermore, nearly 600 textual alterations, of which 30 seem to me corrections of inadvertent errors in *New Monthly* (accepted as emendations and listed in the apparatus), 23 others appear to me undoubtedly to reflect Thackeray's wishes concerning the text in 1841 (these are not adopted for the present text but are listed and marked with an asterisk in the Selected Variants), 55 others seem to me possible, but rather doubtful, authorial alterations (listed without asterisks in the Selected Variants), and just under 500 seem to me insignificant alterations probably introduced by compositors or publisher's editors; these are not listed. They include more than 50 changes of spelling (most either correct the spelling or substitute one commonly used spelling for another), and roughly 325 punctuation changes (most of which are arbitrary and merely make the pattern of punctuation slightly more consistent without altering the tone or texture perceptibly). And, of course, there are miscellaneous alterations in capitalization and the division of compound words and a few obvious typographical errors.

With the exception of the 1848 reissue of *Comic Tales*, *Gahagan* was not published again until 1852. In that year, it appeared in an unauthorized edition titled *The Confessions of Fitzboodle; and Some Passages in the Life of Major Gahagan*, published in New York by the Appleton publishing house. Five titles in six volumes, including *Gahagan*, had already appeared or were in production when Thackeray arrived in New York in 1852. (See the Introduction to *Yellowplush* for further details of the Appleton Series.) Since the Appleton text is unauthorized and non-authoritative, the fact that it varies from its source, *Comic Tales*, in approximately 180 readings would appear to have no interest—except, perhaps, for seven corrections of errors originating in *New Monthly* and left uncorrected in *Comic Tales* (accepted as emendations and listed in the apparatus). But the Appleton text takes on considerable textual importance by the fact that Thackeray used it as the basis for the next authorial edition in 1855. Thirty readings introduced by Appleton and retained by *Miscellanies* seem to me of sufficient importance to list (in Selected Variants in the Appleton Edition) for, though without authority, they significantly alter the text as it was preserved in the authorized 1856 *Miscellanies* edition. The remaining 150 or so changes not only lack authority but significance, even when they affect the *Miscellanies* text; these are not listed.

The 1855 edition of *Gahagan* exists in two separate formats representing two separate but, so far as the rest of the text is concerned, identical printings: in hard cover as part of *Miscellanies: Prose and Verse*, Vol. 1 (London: Bradbury and Evans, 1855) and in paper wrappers as *The Tremendous Adventures of Major Gahagan* with the same imprint. Type for the 1855 edition was set from Thackeray's own copy of the unauthorized 1852 Appleton edition. Though Thackeray had partially marked the Appleton books for republication before he left on his second tour of America, there is no specific evidence to identify which of the variants actually incorporated in the *Miscellanies* edition of *Gahagan* derive from his markings in the setting copy or other direct instructions and which are the result of the inattention or over-eagerness of the amanuensis with whom he left the marked copy. (See Introduction to *Yellowplush*, p. 148.) The *Miscellanies* edition effected about 245 additional changes of which 41 restored, probably by coincidence, *New Monthly* readings; four other readings seem to be corrections of errors in *New Monthly* left uncorrected in all earlier editions (accepted as emendations and listed in the apparatus). Eight other readings seem to reflect authorial wishes for the 1856 text (listed and marked with a dagger in the Selected Variants). Twenty-eight other significant variants seem possible but rather doubtful authorial revisions (listed without a dagger in the Selected Variants). The other 165 or so variants seem insignificant and were probably introduced by compositors or publisher's editors; these are not listed.

Gahagan appeared one more time during Thackeray's lifetime in an authorized edition—*Miscellanies: Prose and Verse*, Vol. III (Leipzig: Bernard Tauchnitz, 1856). Setting copy was the 1855 London edition of *Miscellanies* in either a completely corrected copy of proofs or a copy of the volume itself. The Tauchnitz edition made 20 changes producing readings corresponding to Appleton edition readings—which, on the surface, might suggest that its setting copy was uncorrected proofs of the London *Miscellanies* text retaining the Appleton readings later changed in the London proofs. However, all of these restorations of spelling and punctuation might easily have resulted from coincidence. There are 49 variations between the *Miscellanies* and the Tauchnitz editions, but only four are of any interest. At 26.21 (in this text), the Tauchnitz edition, like the Appleton and preceding texts, reads *mangoe*. *Miscellanies* had changed it to *mango*—a common spelling which Tauchnitz had no compelling reason to change. This is the reading most suggestive of the possibility that the Tauchnitz edition was set from early proofs of the *Miscellanies*. At 60.24, in installment five, the Tauchnitz edition changed *post?* to *post!* in a question that was meant to record surprise. There is a small chance that it could represent an authorial change requested for, but not effected by, *Miscellanies*; but it is probably merely a compositorial change. The substitution of *three* for *these*, at 40.7, in reference to the pistols Gahagan draws is probably a misreading or typographical error. And the deletion, at 41.26, of one *Ha!* from Chowder Loll's father-in-law's remarks over his daughter's bedroom wall results from the miscorrection of a typo in *Miscellanies* where *Ha! ha! ha!* [NM, CT, A] is rendered *Ha! a ha!* in *Miscellanies*. I conclude that, though authorized, the Tauchnitz edition is purely derivative, representing no fresh authority.

It would be foolish to say that the unlisted variants have no effect on the text. Though individually the changes seem insignificant, taken together they do make palpable changes. For example, the paragraph beginning *When I appeared*, on page 45 (*New Monthly*), appears in *Comic Tales* with seven of the 16 dashes deleted. In one sense the appearance is tidier—in another, the links between the succession of thoughts are reduced. Thackeray's practice in proofreading and revising other works suggests that these are not his changes. I do not think, therefore, that these changes merit publication. They would tend to clog even more the record of changes for which some claim can be made that the author either made them or desired that they be made. No editor can claim to know what Thackeray wanted, but the text presented here and the alternative readings recorded in the apparatus will give most readers an adequate basis for exercising their own judgment to determine from available evidence what the text should have been. The full record of variants is available from the Mitchell Memorial Library, Mississippi State University, for the cost of reproduction and postage.

Editorial Procedures

As with *Yellowplush* and all other works in the Tennessee Edition, the reading text prepared for this edition represents the earliest known complete version. In the absence of any prepublication forms, *The New Monthly Magazine* is copy-text. This text has been emended only when evidence indicates it to be in error. For the most part, emendations correct routine matters not worth bringing to the reader's attention— providing missing quotation marks and apostrophes and correcting the spelling of names and words where the misspelling could not be justified as possibly intentional but seemed rather to be a normal typographical error. The restoration of apparently omitted words is more obviously important. All corrections, however, are listed as emendations.

The text still contains inconsistencies and seeming errors which are worth further commentary here. Readers will no doubt notice that when Gahagan uses a foreign word, be it authentic or an invention, he occasionally provides a translation—sometimes accurate, sometimes not. These translations appear variously within parentheses, either inside or outside quotation marks, or simply between commas following the quoted word or phrase. Speculating from analogy with Thackeray's works for which manuscript still exists, I would guess that the *Gahagan* manuscript had few or no quotation marks, parentheses or commas to indicate translations— Thackeray relying either on the internal structure of the sentences or the good services of a compositor to render the text readable. Though inconsistencies in form may be startling or irritating, I contend that the text is readable in all but one instance (36.24), where I have emended. Imposing further consistency would not necessarily render the text more Thackerayan.

Unlike Yellowplush, Gahagan is a conventional speller. The occasional misspellings of English and French words are, in every case, the sorts of errors one is accustomed to find in proofs and, of course, in printed books where the proofs were incompletely corrected. For the most part, these spelling errors have been corrected. Alternative acceptable spellings, however, have been allowed to stand. For example, the "or" "our" or the "ise" "ize" endings are not regularized. Both forms can be found in Thackeray's manuscripts elsewhere and both forms were current in England and America, though one form has since prevailed over the other in each country.

The Spanish and Indian words pose a slightly different problem; for, while Gahagan uses words in these languages with seeming ease, he occasionally invents as he goes. The word "bobbachy" is given two separate, wildly different translations. Thackeray seems to call attention in this way to Gahagan's lack of knowledge of the language and to his inventiveness. Hence, one hestitates to "correct" those parts of the text which may be intentionally "erroneous." One might note, both as a mitigation of this criticism of Gahagan and as an explanation of the editorial difficulty here, that many of the terms Gahagan uses can be found in dictionaries giving two or three spellings. Most notable of these is the word "scimitar," which is spelled in three different ways (scimitar, scymitar, cimeter), all accepted by the *Oxford English Dictionary*. Each installment spells the word consistently, however; so we may be dealing with the spellings of compositors rather than that of the author or the narrator. A similar situation exists with the Indian word *barikillah*, at 33.25 in the present edition, also spelled *barikallah*, at 37.7. *Miscellanies* is the only text that imposes consistency. Both are kept for the present edition because it is an Indian word that had not been absorbed into the English language and thereby given a standard English spelling. Gahagan's own spelling, therefore, may be as conventional as any other.

Two other temptations to emend might be noted, since my failure to emend them may seem inadvertent. In a footnote (p. 5) discussing the reputation of Barraud's repeater watches we find the following apparent disagreement in number between subject and verb: "So admirable are the performance of these watches...." The watches perform, apparently, with a single standard of excellence but, the implication (borne out by the footnote's anecdote) is that the watches are capable of many performances according to the demands of place and circumstance. Correcting the grammar by making the verb singular would eliminate the latter meaning, while making a plural of *performance* would undermine the implication that the watches maintain a single standard of performance regardless of circumstances. Though the reading is doubtful, any correction would be no less doubtful; therefore, no change is made. Similarly, in installment four, describing a magnificent avenue of war elephants, Gahagan writes, "Each of the monstrous animals had castles on their backs, armed with Mauritanian archers and the celebrated Persian matchlockmen ..." (34.18–20). Though it may be more likely that each of the animals had "a castle on its back," as we find in the Appleton text, it is tempting to believe that Gahagan's feeling for grandeur and excitement is incompatible with petty accuracy of detail.

No attempt has been made to incorporate what might be judged to be later felicitous improvements in Thackeray's presentation of Gahagan's writings in later editions. Such improvements, as far as they can be determined, are included in the list of Selected Variants in Authorial Editions. The same list contains alterations dictated by the change in format from magazine serial to book. All of the emendations made in the text for the present edition, then, are corrections of errors.

Readings introduced by the Appleton edition have no authority, but when they correct errors in the text, they are adopted as emendations of the copy-text. Of course, many of the unauthorized readings were retained—whether by oversight or design no one knows—when *Miscellanies* was printed from the Appleton text. The significant alterations thus introduced are recorded in the table of Selected Variants in the Appleton Edition. Tauchnitz edition readings, likewise, have no authority (see discussion above in Composition and Publication).

Silent Alterations

Textual matters which are governed by format have been altered silently according to publishers' specifications. Letters within Gahagan's narrative are separated in *The New Monthly Magazine* from the rest of the text by double-spacing and placed in quotation marks. Block quotations, likewise, are separated by double-spacing, are set in a smaller type font, and are indented. Tables are not separated from the text by spacing, but are indented or centered. Charts are merely centered and double-spaced. Chapter and section headings are set in the type styles and sizes normally employed by the copyeditors or compositors of the magazine; initial letters and some following letters at the beginnings of chapters and numbers are in special sizes, small caps, etc. All of these typographical features are elements of design arbitrarily determined by the editors and printers of *New Monthly*; there is no evidence to indicate that these features reflect authorial intention. Therefore, no specific record is made when typographical elements are altered in the present edition. Mechanical failures such as turned letters and broken type are also silently corrected.

Emendations

The first reading in each emendation entry is always that of the present edition. It is followed by symbols from the list below representing editions which also use that reading. The second entry is the copy-text reading, followed by its symbol and symbols for editions which also use that reading. Any further alternative readings follow in like pattern. Appleton and Tauchnitz readings, which have no independent authority, are cited only when they introduced the emendation.

The New Monthly Magazine is the copy-text; however, in the 1841 *Comic Tales* text Thackeray added several pages to Installment 2. This addition is given in the Appendix as it first appeared, along with the Preface to *Comic Tales*.

List of Symbols:

NM = 1838-39, *The New Monthly Magazine*

CT = 1841, *Comic Tales and Sketches* (London)

A = 1852, Appleton edition, *The Confessions of Fitz-Boodle; and Some Passages in the Life of Major Gahagan* (New York)

M = 1856, *Miscellanies: Prose and Verse* (London)

T = 1856, Tauchnitz edition, *Miscellanies* (Leipzig)

Title. *The Tremendous Adventures of*
    Major Gahagan CT M
    ◊ [installment titles only] NM
    Major Gahagan, Installment 1

1.19 T-l-r-es CT M
    ◊ T-ll-r-es NM

2.4 Pr— M-n-ster CT
    ◊ Pr— M-n-st-er NM
    ◊ Pr. M-n-ster M

3.6 Snob, M
    ◊ Snob NM CT

3.35 *trajet* T
    ◊ *trajét* NM CT M

3.37 passengers, A M
    ◊ passengers', NM CT

7.22 *d'huîtres* CT M
    ◊ *d'huitres* NM

    Major Gahagan, Installment 2

15.16 enemy's CT M
    ◊ enemies' NM

15.32 them one by one M
    ◊ them by one NM CT

17.14 *mêlée* CT M
    ◊ *mélée* NM

17.21 [No ¶]—A M
    ◊ [¶]—A NM CT

17.38 galloping— CT M
    ◊ galloping NM

    Major Gahagan, Appendix
    [Note: See the Appendix for several
    pages of text added to the 1841
    Comic Tales edition.]

64.28 Lake." A M
    ◊ Lake. CT

    Major Gahagan, Installment 3

19.26 *mêlée* CT M
    ◊ *mélée* NM

22.6 What CT M
    ◊ Which NM

24.31 underlip T
    ◊ under lip NM CT
    ◊ under-/lip M
    [Cf. 26.12 in the text.]

25.37 Deeg CT M
    ◊ Dug NM
    [Cf. 8.39 in the text.]

27.23 daughters, A M
    ◊ daughters; NM CT

27.33 *fêted* CT
    ◊ *fêtéd* NM

    ◊ *fêted* A M

28.21 shrill CT M
    ◊ shrill, NM

28.37 beleaguer CT M
    ◊ beleague NM

30.10 Pitan CT M
    ◊ Pitau NM

    Major Gahagan, Installment 4

32.31 closed," A M
    ◊ closed, NM CT

32.31 —"where A M
    ◊ —where NM CT

35.41 Ghorumsaug CT M
    ◊ Ghorumsang NM
    [See 43.4, 43.7, 43.20, 43.26,
    44.1.]

36.24 muzzee!" (my nose is off),
    ◊ muzzee!" "my nose is off," NM
    CT
    ◊ muzzee! my nose is off," M

41.24c ho!" (the CT M
    ◊ ho! (the NM

41.25 —"are CT M
    ◊ —are NM

    Major Gahagan, Installment 5

43.7 Ghorumsaug," CT M
    ◊ Ghorumsaug, NM

43.7 "what CT M
    ◊ what NM

43.7 fellow?" CT M
    ◊ fellow? NM

43.8 "It CT M
    ◊ It NM

43.9 him?" CT M
    ◊ him? NM

48.10 Holkar's CT M
    ◊ Holka's NM

49.26 Macgillicuddy CT M
    ◊ Magillicuddy NM

50.4 ducks'-eggs
    ◊ duck's-eggs NM
    ◊ ducks' eggs CT M

52.17 men CT M
    ◊ man NM

52.41 Vandegobbleschroy's CT M
    ◊ Macgillicuddy's NM

53.19 cheeses—
   ◇ chesses— NM
   ◇ cheeses,—CT M

54.27 on the former occasion
   ◇ on former occasion NM
   ◇ on former occasions CT M

54.35 dies!" CT M
   ◇ dies! NM

54.36 "Is CT M
   ◇ Is NM

55.31 "Silence! CT M
   ◇ "Silence!" NM

56.36 morning." M
   ◇ morning?" NM CT

58.3 Grand A M
   ◇ grand NM CT

59.25 Grand CT M
   ◇ grand NM

60.26 FURRUCKABAD CT M
   ◇ FURRUCKABAO NM

60.34 déjeuné CT
   ◇ déjeûné NM M

60.40 G.O'G.G.M.H.E.I.C.S.C.I.H.A.
   ◇ G.O'G.M.H.E.I.C.S.C.I.H.A.
   NM CT
   ◇ G. O'G. M. H. E. I. C. S. C. I.
   H. A. A
   ◇ G. O'G. G., M. H. E. I. C. S.
   C. I. H. A. M
   [The emendation restores the
   initial for Gahagan's last name
   but does not regularize the
   signature.]

Variants in Authorial Editions

Principles of Selection

The variants listed here include all the revisions which I believe Thackeray *may* have called for except for corrections of errors, which he may also have requested, found in the list of emendations and not repeated here. If some of the changes omitted as insignificant are in fact Thackeray's, it is fruitless to speculate on which those changes are or on what might have been the author's intention in making such minor alterations. Without direct evidence, which in this case does not exist, any attempt to determine the authority of any of the readings I have listed remains purely subjective.

The significance of the variants listed here does not lie in their source; that remains problematic. With the exception of certain spelling changes explained below, each variant is listed that makes a perceptible change in meaning or emphasis or gives the text some quality which it did not otherwise possess. I have listed the addition or deletion of words, the substitution of one word for another, and alterations in punctuation which perceptibly change the syntax of a sentence (as when a semicolon is changed to a question mark or an exclamation point is exchanged for a comma).

Alterations in punctuation which seem to be corrections of unorthodox pointing, rather than mere alternatives, are recorded either as accepted emendations or, in less decisive cases, as significant variations. Gahagan's punctuation and spelling are relatively orthodox and consistent, except in instances already cited (see Editorial Procedure) involving the spelling of foreign words or alternate, equally acceptable, spellings of English words. In addition, it must be remembered that rhetorical pointing was as much a system as syntactical or grammatical pointing and that punctuation to mark rhetorical pauses might on occasion be used in the midst of syntactical units. Compositors' manuals of the day indicated the relative length of pauses represented by commas, semicolons, colons, and periods. For the first three, it appears that the length of the intended rhetorical pause as well as the syntax determined the mark to be used.

The Text in 1841

An asterisk (*) marks each reading which I would include in a text representing what Thackeray wanted in 1841 when he prepared *Comic Tales*. In addition to the readings so marked, the concluding passages for chapter 2, given in Appendix A, were added in 1841.

The Text in 1856

A dagger (†) marks those readings which *in addition to those asterisked for the 1841 text* I would include in a text representing what Thackeray wanted in 1856 when he prepared the *Miscellanies* edition.

The List

The first reading is that of the present edition which in all these cases is the same as that of *New Monthly*. Variant readings follow and are labeled with the symbols employed in the list of emendations. The variants from the unauthorized Appleton edition are given in a separate table, for though they often caused the *Miscellanies* text to vary from *New Monthly* and *Comic Tales*, those readings are without authority (see Selected Variants in the Appleton Edition). The *Miscellanies* readings in this table are affected in this way by the Appleton edition in only one instance (52.40).

Installment 1

1.14 flowerets NM CT
   ◇ flowrets M

3.19 Witch NM
   ◇ witch CT M

*3.28b burning. NM
   ◇ burning! CT M

3.43 hand; with NM
   ◇ hand. With CT M

*4.8 Asia, and indeed Europe, NM
   ◇ Asia and Europe CT M

5.32 stomach: a NM
   ◇ stomach. A CT M

5.fn1 performance NM

◇ performances CT M

*6.17 eyes. I do not believe that she had a single good quality: she NM
   ◇ eyes: she CT M

7.16 Hodson's NM
   ◇ Hodgson's CT M
   [See also 179.29, 179.33, and 182.7]

*7.26 company:—but NM
   ◇ company. But CT M

7.29 "How you NM
   ◇ "How do you CT M

7.30 o NM
   ◇ o' CT M

7.32b do?" NM CT
◇ do," M

*8.40 actions, NM
◇ actions—CT M

8.41 them; if NM
◇ them. If CT M

9.40 failed in its NM CT
◇ failed its M

9.fn1 go but NM
◇ go out CT M

10.18 CHOWDER LOLL NM CT
◇ Chowder Loll M

10.30 you— NM
◇ you, CT M

11.11 mamma NM CT
◇ mama M

11.24 CHOWDER LOLL!!! NM
◇ CHOWDER LOLL! CT
◇ Chowder Loll! M

*11.25 GOLIAH GAHAGAN, Major
H.E.I.C.S. NM
◇ [omitted] CT M

Installment 2

*12.1 one NM
◇ some CT M

*12.2 in this Magazine) NM
◇ in a monthly magazine) CT M

12.12 nor NM
◇ or CT M

*12.21 me in the last number of this
Magazine. NM
◇ me. CT M

*14.3 by the General NM
◇ by General Lake CT M

*16.9 of this Magazine NM
◇ of my publisher CT M

*16.11 Mr. Colburn NM
◇ Mr. Cunningham CT M

*16.fn1 at our NM
◇ at Mr. Cunningham's CT M

*16.fn3 Allyghur. NM M
◇ Allyghur. M. A. T. CT

17.1 the work NM M
◇ a work CT

17.8 was at this NM
◇ was this CT M

17.14 at thoughts NM
◇ at the thoughts CT M

17.23 him additional NM
◇ him an additional CT M

*18.12 GOLIAH GAHAGAN, MAJOR,
H.E.I.C.S. NM
◇ [omitted] CT M
[Note: The rest of installment
two appeared for the first time in
CT; see Appendix.]

63.10 EMPEROR NAPOLEON CT
◇ Emperor Napoleon M

63.17 Cases CT
◇ Casas M

63.27 Futtyghur. CT
◇ Futtyghur? M

64.21 rouge CT
◇ rogue M

64.39 retrenchments CT
◇ intrenchments M

Installment 3

*19.5 I had NM
◇ I have had CT M

*19.6 to continue NM
◇ to think about CT M

*19.6 memoirs, of which a couple of
numbers have already appeared
in this
◇ magazine. NM
◇ memoirs. CT M

†19.10 pages. The publisher and
editor of "The New Monthly
Magazine" little know what
service has been done to me
by that miscellany. ¶Along NM
CT
◇ pages. ¶Along M

†20.36 Magazine" for March, which
contained my article. It NM
CT
◇ Magazine," containing a portion
of my adventures. It M

22.14 enter—— NM CT
◇ enter— M

†22.15 "The New Monthly Magazine
and Humorist," NM
◇ "The New Monthly Magazine

and Humourist," CT
◊ that Magazine, M

†22.16 Am I NM CT
◊ Was I M

†22.17 have I NM
◊ Have I CT
◊ Had I M

†22.17 contributions? NM CT
◊ contributions to that periodical?
M

22.33 cachucha NM
◊ cachuca CT M

22.37 muchachas NM
◊ muchacas CT M

23.14 HE NM
◊ He CT M

25.9 Mars! NM CT
◊ Mars. M

25.14 MAJOR NM CT
◊ Major M

25.38 him; taking NM
◊ him. Taking CT M

27.4 an European NM CT
◊ a European M

28.23 terror; NM CT
◊ terror! M

28.25 some the NM
◊ some said the CT M

29.2 adored,' NM
◊ adored!' CT M

30.23 apartment, there; NM
◊ apartment; there, CT M

*30.32 G. O.'G. G., M. H. E. I. C. S.,
C. I. H. A. NM
◊ [omitted] CT M

Installment 4

*31.hd THE INDIAN CAMP [letter]
CHAP. I. THE SORTIE FROM THE
FORT NM
◊ CHAPTER IV. THE INDIAN
CAMP—THE SORTIE FROM THE
FORT [letter] CT M

31.2 night—I NM
◊ night. I CT M

31.4 vines—the NM
◊ vines. The CT M

32.5 Burges's NM
◊ Burgess's CT M

32.16 me; one NM
◊ me. One CT M

33.4 such NM
◊ Such CT M

33.7 words, bobbachy—general,
bahawder—artillery-man; he
NM
◊ words—bobbachy, general;
bahawder, artilleryman. He CT
M

33.28 dagger?" NM CT
◊ dagger." M

33.29 conspiracy!]— NM
◊ conspiracy!] CT M

35.24 mission: the NM
◊ mission. The CT M

*40.9 if you stay NM
◊ if ye stay CT M

40.12 action—my NM
◊ action. My CT M

40.29 escape?—the NM
◊ escape? The CT M

40.36 *prisoner:* he NM
◊ *prisoner.* He CT M

41.7 if NM
◊ If CT M

41.12 sterling NM
◊ sterling. CT M

41.13 one). NM
◊ one.) CT M

41.24 sure?—ho! NM
◊ sure? Ho! CT M

41.25 is—ha! ha! ha!— NM
◊ is?—Ha! ha! ha! ha!— CT
◊ is?—Ha! a ha!— M

Installment 5

43.27 prisoner? NM
◊ prisoner, CT M

44.30 12 NM
◊ 14 CT M
[Although the actual count is
probably 14, the "error" is left
here and at 45.2, where all
editions say 12, on the grounds

that Gahagan's account is full
◇ of invention and inaccuracy.]

†44.41 MAJOR G. O'G. GAHAGAN NM
◇ MAJOR G. O'G. GAHAGAN
CT
◇ MAJOR-GEN. O'G. GAHAGAN
M

45.10 do. do. NM CT
◇ ditto ditto. M

45.11 bottles fine NM CT
◇ bottles of fine M

*46.8 Oh, NM
◇ Oh! CT M

50.12 it. NM
◇ it, CT M

*50.28 The infantry were NM
◇ The ruffians were CT M

51.8 line, at right NM M
◇ line, right CT

51.8 fools! NM CT
◇ fools; M

51.32 it, and prided NM
◇ it, prided CT M

52.40 food. NM
◇ food, CT
◇ food; A M

53.2 end—yesterday, NM
◇ end. Yesterday, CT
◇ end. Yesterday M

53.15 garrisons NM
◇ garrison CT M

54.6 ran NM M
◇ run CT

54.7 leagues, NM
◇ leagues. CT M

55.20 "Stop!— NM CT
◇ "Stop;— M

58.19 "Papa! NM
◇ "Papa; CT M

59.26 agitated exactly to NM CT
◇ agitated to M

59.29 "It is yet time," NM CT
◇ "Is it yet time?" M
[It seems illogical for the Vizier
to ask Gahagan if the time of
execution had arrived. Rather,
he is informing Gahagan that
there is still time to accept
Holkar's commission; or perhaps
he means "yet" in the obsolete
sense of "now", informing
Gahagan that his time of
exection had arrived.]

59.37 advanced, and— NM CT
◇ advanced, M

60.4 natives! NM CT
◇ natives. M

†60.11 wrenched NM CT
◇ wrested M

60.17 into NM
◇ on to CT M

60.35 Hurrygurrybaug NM
◇ Hurrygurrybang CT M

Variants in the Appleton Edition

The following readings, introduced without authority by the Appleton edition, significantly affect the authorized *Miscellanies* text. About 160 other changes which appeared in the same way affect the *Miscellanies* text insignificantly. Six other Appleton readings have been adopted as emendations.

Installment 1

6.14 suppose it NM CT
   ◇ suppose that it A M

7.1 I had learned NM CT
   ◇ I learned A M

7.4 and outgoings NM CT
   ◇ and the outgoings A M

7.22 platesful NM CT
   ◇ platefuls A M

8.24 Jowler! NM CT
   ◇ Jowler. A M

10.20 absence.— NM CT
   ◇ absence. A M

10.29 said NM CT
   ◇ says A M

Installment 2

12.1 SIT NM CT
   ◇ SAT A M

13.24 fight the NM CT
   ◇ fight a A M

14.10 [asterisks] NM CT
   ◇ [omitted] A M

15.13 impossibility. NM CT
   ◇ impossibility A
   ◇ impossibility, M

16.5 in this NM CT
   ◇ in the A M

16.8 doubts of my NM CT
   ◇ doubts my A M

16.31 Gawler NM CT
   ◇ O'Gawler A M
   [Though this is the only instance
   of the omission of the O' in this
   name, it seems possible that
   Gahagan's familiarity with the
   old man is revealed by it. In
   any case the "correction" was
   introduced without authority.]

Appendix

64.41 plain CT
   ◇ plains A M

Installment 3

20.12 intentions NM CT
   ◇ intention A M

28.15 larger NM CT
   ◇ large A M

Installment 4

34.18 had castles on their backs NM
CT
◊ had a castle on its back A M

34.29 glistening NM CT
◊ glittering A M

35.23 me news of the success NM
CT
◊ me the success A M

36.35 indeed would NM CT
◊ indeed it would A M

39.9 in oriental NM CT
◊ in the oriental A
◊ in the Oriental M

Installment 5

43.27 Ghorumsaug," NM CT
◊ Ghorumsaug?" A M

47.21 Oh, NM CT
◊ Oh! A M

47.25 butter, NM CT

◊ butther, A M

48.41 fled!— NM CT
◊ fled;— A M

49.29 rascally black valet NM CT
◊ rascally valet A M

52.28 was NM CT
◊ were A M
[There is some question as
to what was in the supper
room and what was locked in
Gahagan's apartment—see 45.18
where he identifies somewhat
ambiguously what belonged
in his "private stock." The
Appleton alteration may be a
correction.]

53.24 wongree-fum!" NM CT
◊ wongree-fum;" A M

55.40 woke NM
◊ woke, CT
◊ awoke, A M

End-Line Hyphens

Table A
Words Ambiguously Hyphenated in the Copy-text
The following compound and hyphenated words were divided ambiguously at the end of a line in the copy-text. They are listed here in the form which they take in the present edition or in which they should be quoted if they are also ambiguously hyphenated at the end of a line in the present edition.

4.28	swallow-tailed	28.42	waistcoat-pocket
8.3	high-raised	31.11	orange-grove
9.30	horsemen	31.12	cedar-tree
16.7	fourpence	32.11	somewhat
17.35	sunlight	32.15	overcome
20.1	chapel-churies	32.25	high-peaked
20.8	blue-plaid	32.35	elephant-lord
21.6	portmanteau	33.18	anything
21.43	whiskey-bottle	36.21	mouthpiece
24.37	corkscrew	37.23	yellow-skinned
25.30	black-faced	39.15	moon-faces
27.25	shooting-season	49.1	forehead
28.4	midnight	49.8	half-a-bottle
28.17	to-night	55.11	super-human

Table B

End-line-hyphenated compound words in the present editon that were also broken in the copy-text are listed in Table A. Any new end-line hyphenated compound word in this text that should be quoted as a hyphenated word is listed here. End-line hyphens not found in either of these lists represent breaks in single, unhyphenated words.

6.33 battle-field	38.37 to-night
15.27 tri-coloured	39.40 winé-cup
24.20 *carte-blanche*	43.14 ball-room
26.14 two-penny	45.39 Seventy-three
34.14 mangoe-fruit	46.42 divvled-kidneys
34.25 twenty-five	50.4 ducks'-eggs
36.19 richly-ornamented	52.26 garrison-larder
36.21 silver-bell